Praise for Elmer Kelton

"[A] masterful Western author."
—*Lubbock Avalanche-Journal*

"Elmer Kelton is truly a Texas legend."
—former governor of Texas Rick Perry

"Elmer Kelton is to Texas what Mark Twain was
to the Mississippi River."
—Jory Sherman,
author of *The Barons of Texas*

"One thing is certain: as long as there are writers
as skillful as Elmer Kelton, Western
literature will never die."
—*True West* magazine

"San Angelo novelist Kelton knows intimately
the work and ways of the West. That's why
real cowboys love his writing."
—*Southern Living*

"Kelton, like fine wine, just keeps getting better and better."
—*Tulsa World*

"Elmer Kelton has surely established himself as one of
the grand masters of Western literature."
—*El Paso Scene*

Forge Books by Elmer Kelton

BUFFALO WAGONS

{ and }

CLOUDY
IN THE WEST

Elmer Kelton

FORGE®

A TOM DOHERTY ASSOCIATES BOOK | NEW YORK

This is a work of fiction. All of the characters, organizations, and events portrayed in these novels are either products of the author's imagination or are used fictitiously.

BUFFALO WAGONS AND CLOUDY IN THE WEST

Buffalo Wagons copyright © 1956, 1984 by the Estate of Elmer Kelton
Cloudy in the West copyright © 1997 by the Estate of Elmer Kelton

A Forge Book
Published by Tom Doherty Associates, LLC
175 Fifth Avenue
New York, NY 10010

www.tor-forge.com

Forge® is a registered trademark of Tom Doherty Associates, LLC.

ISBN 978-0-7653-8148-4

Forge books may be purchased for educational, business, or promotional use. For information on bulk purchases, please contact the Macmillan Corporate and Premium Sales Department at 1-800-221-7945, extension 5442, or write to specialmarkets@macmillan.com.

First Edition: July 2015

Printed in the United States of America

0 9 8 7 6 5 4 3 2 1

{ Contents }

BUFFALO WAGONS

{ ONE }

The buffalo were gone.

Gage Jameson turned in his saddle atop a hill where the grass cured and curled an autumn brown. Squinting his blue eyes in the glare of the prairie sun, he frowned at the company hide train lumbering along far behind him, the six-yoke ox teams hardly straining at the double wagons.

Three months out, supplies about gone, and not enough hides to build a Sioux lodge.

Grimness touched Jameson's bearded, sun-darkened face as he stepped down from the big bay hunting horse and felt the drying grass crunch beneath his heavy boots. He was a man in his mid-thirties whose gray-touched hair and long growth of wiry black beard made him look far older. His wide-brimmed, grease-stained hat was pulled low to shade his eyes.

Last year, down in that valley yonder, his Sharps Big Fifty rifle had felled sixty-two buffalo in one stand, so many that the Miles and Posey skinners had had to return the second day to finish taking the hides.

Now, with the first autumn weeks of 1873 slipping by,

it had been ten days since he had sighted that last shaggy old bull. He had lifted his rifle for the kill, then had lowered it and ridden away, leaving the aged beast to graze alone on the short buffalo grass where once they had grazed in numbers so large that no man could count them.

What was one hide? One hide, when long stinking ricks of them piled up at Dodge City, awaiting shipment on the Santa Fe. No man could guess at the number. But this Jameson knew: the great Arkansas River herd was gone, like the Republican herd before it. Next spring the melting snows would bare carcasses by the hundreds of thousands scattered all over these Kansas plains.

A graveyard, it would be. A vast graveyard of gleaming white bones.

A blur of movement on another hill caused Jameson to jerk around, his hide-tough hand tightening instinctively on the sixteen-pound Sharps he carried.

He eased then, recognizing the sorrel horse Nathan Messick rode. Messick was his chief skinner and hide handler, and now and again he helped Jameson search out the buffalo. Rail-thin and gangling, Messick stood like a telegraph pole in his stirrups, waving his hat in long grand sweeps.

He's found buffalo, Jameson thought, a stir of excitement in him. There had been a time when it took a big herd to excite him. Of late, it was a great satisfaction to find fifteen or twenty head. He remounted and crossed the open, brushless valley in a long trot, the brown grass rustling underfoot. In places it reached to the bay horse's knees.

Climbing the hill, he found Messick still sitting there gravely waiting for him, his narrow shoulders slumped. An emptiness settled in Jameson as he read Messick's solemn eyes. "I thought you'd found buffalo."

Messick grunted. "Not exactly. I just wanted you to come look."

Messick reined his horse around and moved off the slope, his long shanks raised a little to heel the sorrel's ribs. Jameson trailed him, content in his weariness to move at a casual pace. Still young enough as years went, he no longer possessed the drive he used to have. Youth was slipping away from him, he knew. The frontier took it out of a man. The frontier and the war.

"There it is," Messick said somberly.

Scattered over several hundred yards of ground lay the bloated carcasses of some twenty skinned buffalo, now so rank that Jameson's horse snorted and shied away. Someone had shot them from running horses like a bunch of sport-crazy excursionists, instead of picking them off slow and easy from a quiet stand the way any sensible hide hunter would do.

"Tenderfeet," Jameson said harshly. "Even ruined half the hides, getting them off."

It had always bothered him, the awesome waste that attended the work of even the best hide hunters. Now he was galled at this senseless destruction which came at a time when the buffalo were getting to be so precious few.

"Hunters like that," Messick said slowly, "there ought to be a law against them. Spoil it for them that *does* know how."

Jameson shook his head. "Blame the money panic. They're hungry back East—no jobs, no food. And the railroad letting its construction crews go. They're swarming out here like flies. Anybody who can get his hands on a gun and a horse wants to hunt buffalo."

He saw something move, out by the most distant carcasses. His eyes cut questioningly to Messick's, and Messick said, "Buffalo cow. They shot her but let her get away."

"Why didn't you put her out of her misery?"

"I'll help you find them, and I'll skin them afterwards. But I ain't shootin' no buffalo."

Jameson rode to her. The gaunt cow moved painfully, dragging a shattered hind leg. Her bag was swollen and fevered with spoiled milk. One of those big bloated calves must have been hers. She was slowly dying on her feet, waiting for the gray wolves to come and drag her down.

Jameson stepped from the saddle and lifted the Big Fifty. Its octagonal barrel was thick and heavy and hard to hold true, but at this range it couldn't miss. The deep roar rolled back to him in the chill air. He ejected the hot cartridge case, let it lie on the ground a moment to cool, then shoved it back into his coat pocket to reload later. His nose pinched at the sharp smell of gunpowder.

"Tenderfeet," he said again, angrily.

He well remembered the awe which had held him spellbound years ago, when he had sighted his first herd of buffalo. He had been only a kid then, before the war. The buffalo had been one rippling blanket of black and brown, moving slowly across the land before him, the front of the herd lost in the dust of the northern horizon, the end of it still far out of sight to the south. The rumble of their tread, the rattle of dewclaws, had gone on and on for more than a day.

And he remembered how old Shad Blankenship had snorted at him in '68, when Jameson had asked how long it might take to kill out the buffalo.

"By Judas Priest, young'un, there'll always be buffalo. Ten thousand hunters and the U.S. Cavalry couldn't get more than the natural increase, one year to the next. Kill all the buffalo? Boy, you're talkin' out of your head."

Now here it was—one old bull, one crippled cow, for ten days' ride. And these bloated, wasted carcasses.

Suddenly Jameson was weary of it, weary of the endless, hopeless hunt, weary of stench and sweat and caked dirt and disappointment, weary of scratching at the lice it seemed a man could never get rid of while he hunted the buffalo.

He drew the straight-edged ripping knife from his belt and knelt beside the cow, starting to slit the hide up the belly while fat ticks crawled for cover in the thick dirty hair.

"We'll salvage this one, at least," he said, his voice brittle. "Then we're going. I've had me a bellyful."

"Where to, Gage?"

"Back to Dodge City. The Arkansas herd is finished."

Dodge City, said the sign at the new frame depot. But everybody here just called it Dodge, for it was hard to use the word "city" and not smile doing it.

Dodge wasn't much to look at, a raw-looking, raw-smelling town of lumber shacks and dugouts and soddies and dirty tents, and a row of one-story frame business houses fronting each side of the shiny new railroad tracks. On down the way yonder extended sod corrals and a long row of hide stacks that you could smell almost as far as you could see, when the weather was a little warm and the wind from the wrong direction.

Something else was growing now: great piles of white buffalo bones, waiting to be shipped East for fertilizer and bone china and Lord knew what else.

Last year the railroad construction gangs had found

Dodge already a bustling little village, huddled up on the north bank of the Arkansas River, halfway between Missouri and Santa Fe. It had started out as a whisky camp for the soldiers at Fort Dodge, five miles to the east. Then the buffalo hunters had located there, and for a while they called it Buffalo City. By the time the railroad came, there were by actual count one general store, three dance halls and six saloons.

But to a buffalo hunter coming in after three months out on the prairie, the town was as pretty as a new bride. Didn't matter whether the lumber was painted or not, long as the ladies were. Nobody complained if dirt trickled down from sod roofs and got matted in a man's hair or fell into his collar and went gritty there. At least there *were* roofs.

Who was going to be bothered if the bar was nothing more than a raw buffalo hide stretched across a framework of poles? Who would holler if the whisky was maybe pure alcohol with a little coffee coloring, or even that tobacco-and-pepper-treated contraband stuff that some of the guttier ones slipped off and traded to the Indians? It tasted as good as French wine if you'd been out on the buffalo range for months. And by the time you started getting critical, you ought to be dragging it back to the prairie anyhow.

Two miles out, Jameson's crew came upon an old man in tattered clothes and dry-split leather shoes pitching buffalo bones into a wire-patched wagon that threatened to fall down and die right there. A layer of white dust clung to him from these chalky bones that still had a peculiar stench of death even after the months of bleaching in the sun.

This, the bone picking, was the last grim harvest.

Some of the wagon crew hadn't smiled, hadn't spoken a civil word in three weeks, for they were being paid by the hide, and the hides were mighty few. Now, as Dodge finally showed up ahead of them, a yell burst from dry throats. A fair sight she was.

Jameson grinned, though it came near to cracking his wind-dried lips. He wasn't a hard-drinking man, but like the others he found pleasure in the thought of bellying up to one of those flint-hide bars. The change, if nothing else.

Nathan Messick rode up beside him and pointed. Worry was in his eyes. It always was.

"Ever see so many outfits camped? Scattered to kingdom come, all over the edge of town and up and down the river."

"Poor hunting, Nathan. Out of supplies, sick of hunting and not finding anything. Maybe getting a little worried about the Indians."

"They could be out picking bones. There's a million of them."

Jameson shrugged. "Pride, I reckon. *I* wouldn't want to do it. Would you?"

"Nope, I reckon not."

Rough-looking men lounged in scattered camps, hunkering over fires for lack of anything better to occupy their time. They had gathered here in town, waiting, not knowing what they were waiting for, not knowing what else to do. As the Miles and Posey wagons drew close, the men would walk out and gaze curiously at the hides Jameson was bringing in.

Ahead of him Gage saw a familiar figure standing in a camp, and he smiled broadly. The old man's back was turned to him, but he would recognize Shad Blankenship if he found his hide in a tanyard.

Shad was an old-time mountain man. He had drifted up the Missouri and dodged Sioux and Blackfeet way back in the days of the beaver trade. And although white men often skinned him, no Indian had ever laid a hand on Shad's thick growth of rust-red hair.

"Nathan," Jameson said, "take them on to the Miles and Posey yards. I'll be along directly, after I chew the fat with Shad a little."

Shirt sleeves rolled up halfway to the elbow and sweat soaking his old hickory shirt, the old hunter had put a wagon jack under the axle of one of his three hide wagons and was taking the wheel off to tar the hub. At the call of his name he turned quickly, his blackened hand raised in greeting, his red-bearded old face broken with a grin.

"Hya-a-a there, young'un." As far as Shad was concerned, Gage Jameson was a young'un and always would be. Shad had picked him up as a half-starved runaway kid back there twenty years ago, nursemaided him along, wiped his nose for him, and made a frontiersman out of him.

Shad's big shaggy black dog came trotting out, growling deep in its throat, Blackfoot-mean, until it caught Jameson's scent. The growl stopped. It wagged its tail in recognition.

Jameson stepped down out of the saddle and patted the dog's head. "Hi there, Ripper. You catching enough rabbits to keep that old musk hog fed?"

Blankenship walked out, grinning. "I don't need no dog to feed me, young'un. I'm still a better hunter than you'll ever be, and don't you forget it."

He shoved his big hand forward, then drew it back quickly.

"Forgot about that tar. Wouldn't want to muss up a hide skinner's clean hands." There was a shade of irony in the way he said that. He wiped the hands on his trousers, already so black that a little extra wouldn't be noticed.

"Them your wagons going yonder?" he asked, then nodded his own answer. His grin was gone. Jameson could see that Shad hadn't done much grinning lately, either.

"You done as well as any of them, I reckon. A heap sight better than *I* done."

Looking closer now, Jameson could see worry clouded deep in the pale blue eyes. It was the same discouragement he'd seen in all the faces that had come out to watch his wagons pass.

Shad Blankenship motioned apologetically to the wagon he was working on. "Them wheels don't really need any tar. It's oozing out all over. But hell, what else is there for a man to do? He'd go crazy sittin' here waitin' for the buffalo to come back."

Jameson frowned. "You really think they'll come back, Shad?"

The old man shrugged gloomily and turned back to the wagon. He started to lift the wheel into place again. Jameson got hold of it with him and fitted it onto the hub. Shad faced him then, and his eyes held a hopelessness.

"They ain't, Gage, they ain't. They're gone, and we'll never see things again the way they was. Wish sometimes I'd died back yonder while things was the way they used to be. Wish I'd never seen the way the country's been ruined."

Jameson put his hand gently on the hunter's thin shoulder. "Come on into town directly and I'll buy you a drink. We'll talk about old times."

Shad's eyes were bleak and pinched in the corners.

"Ain't the town she used to be, Gage. New bunch has taken over. There's every kind of riffraff in there now, just waitin' to see if you got any money on you. There's some will cut your guts out with a dull knife or strangle you with a leather cord. And if the cutthroats don't get it, them crooked gamblers will."

Jameson thought he knew what the trouble was. No matter how many months old Shad had worked for it, or what he'd had to go through, when he got his big chapped hands on a roll of money he was drawn to the poker tables like a fly to a freshly skinned buffalo. Likely as not they'd taken him the first night he hit town. Lucky he hadn't lost his wagons, to boot.

Shad shook a crooked finger at Jameson. It had been broken in some trading-post brawl long since forgotten.

"You tell them men of yours they better watch out for theirselves. Quick as they get paid off, there'll be a dozen wolves around to pick their bones."

"I'll tell them."

He had long wondered why an old frontiersman like Shad, wily and sure as a fox out on the prairie, should forever be so improvident when he came to town. He had made a couple or three fortunes in his time, and they had all gone the same way. He would never accumulate anything of value and hang onto it if he lived to be a hundred and six.

Shad frowned darkly. "I been thinkin,' Gage. Thinkin' about going East to Missouri and taking up farming."

Jameson blinked in surprise. Shad added quickly, "I growed up on a farm in Tennessee, don't you know that? Had me a right smart reputation. Wasn't no young'un there could plow a straighter furrow or get more work out of a pair of mules. But the place just naturally got a little too small for me and my Paw both. So when I decided I couldn't whup him, I took my old squirrel gun and lit out."

Jameson smiled and shook his head. "You'll never do

it, Shad. Maybe there was a time you could've gone back, but you'll never do it now."

"You don't think so?" Old Shad narrowed his eyes and poked his finger at Gage. "I get the chance, young'un, I'll show you. You just wait."

Jameson caught up to his hide wagons just before they reached the Miles and Posey yards. The partners leased from the Santa Fe a long stretch of ground adjacent to the tracks, where the hides could be loaded directly onto the cars with a minimum of extra handling.

The hide stacks Jameson had seen here the last time were greatly diminished, but the smell of them was about as strong as ever. He watched some of the yard crew toss hides onto a press and squeeze them down into a tight bale to be shipped. Down at the lower end a huge rick of buffalo bones was steadily growing. Miles and Posey was branching out.

C. T. Posey stood in front of the unpainted frame office, chewing a dead cigar and frowning thoughtfully at a short load of hides in a sagging old wagon.

Jameson reined up and waited, grinning. That was Posey, all right. He handled them by the tens of thousands, but he could still enjoy haggling with a hunter over fifty or sixty common cowhides.

Trying not to be obvious about it, the man on the wagon was showing Posey the hides with the hair side up. And seeing right through him, Posey was turning them over to the flesh side, one by one, so he could tell how many bullet holes, peg holes and knife slashes were in them.

Posey saw Jameson and nodded a greeting, then went back to his trade. He studied a moment, wrote a figure on a piece of paper, then showed it to the hunter. The man shook his head determinedly. Posey shrugged and started toward the office. The hunter ruefully called him back. Posey nodded and did some figures on the paper. Then he wrote out a check and handed it to the hunter. The hunter, grinning now, climbed on his wagon, flipped the reins and headed for the end of the hide stack where some of the yard crew would unload him.

It was an old stunt of Posey's to beat the price down as far as it would go, then give the seller a few extra dollars on the check to bring it up to some nice round figure. Always left the man smiling, outtraded or not. He'd be back someday with another load.

Posey strode up and shook Jameson's hand, a genuine gladness in what could be the deadest poker face in town when necessary.

"Mighty pleased to see you, Gage."

"You may not be when you look at my wagons."

Posey stood back and surveyed Jameson's incoming hide train, his hands shoved deep in his pockets. He chewed heavily on the unlighted cigar, a nervous twitch pinching one side of his face. He was dressed in tailor-made clothes of good fabric but was undisturbed about the drying mud caked on his shoes and his trouser cuffs. He was a slight, balding Yankee trader, a pleasant man to work for as long as you played it straight. Cheat him and you'd better never come back.

Posey shifted the cigar to the other side of his mouth. "Can't complain, the way some of the others have come in. Stump Johnson hardly had a wagonload."

"How about the hide prices?"

"A little better. Should get better yet. Prospect of a scarcity."

Jameson looked at the men sitting on the wagons, men bearded and dirty, with a trail-weariness in their eyes.

"As long as prices are up, could you give the boys a little bonus? They haven't made much this trip."

Posey came about as near smiling as he ever would. "Maybe I can see my way clear." As the wagons pulled up and halted he spoke loudly, "You boys pile off of there and go over to the Dutchman's. Tell him I said give you a good feed. The yard crew can take care of the wagons."

The men jumped down laughing, exulting at the feel of Dodge's half-muddy ground beneath their feet.

"How about you, Gage?" Posey asked.

Jameson shrugged. "Not hungry. I'll go later."

Ever since he had arrived he had noticed a tall, well-dressed man of about his own age standing at the door of the shack, watching him, watching the wagons. Now Posey motioned to the man. "Come here, Ransom. Want you to meet somebody."

The man stepped forward, a smile lifting the ends of his trimmed mustache. "You don't have to tell me. He's Gage Jameson. I've heard plenty already. My name's King, Jameson. Ransom King."

He stood an inch or two taller than Jameson. He wore black trousers and a white shirt with a string tie. His flat-brimmed hat with its rounded crown was as clean as a man could expect to find in a place like Dodge. Jameson wouldn't exactly call him a dandy, like Hickok or Cody, but he was well above the average cut. More than that, he looked like he might be man enough to wear the clothes and get away with it.

"Glad to know you, King. Seems to me I've heard the name around. Hide hunter, aren't you?"

King smiled. "That's right. Been hoping for a good while that we'd cross trails somewhere."

He turned then to Posey. "I can see you're going to be busy a while, C. T., so I'll work on up the street and come back later. You sure you're not ready to meet my price on those hides?"

"Not yet," Posey answered with good humor. "You're just trying to make a killing on one deal so you can retire."

"Now, C. T.," King responded with a laugh, "that's not fair. You know I'm a man of simple tastes and a small ambition. All I want is to get rich."

He started to move away, a spark of laughter still dancing in his eyes. "See you later, C. T., and you'd just as well make up your mind to pay me my price. You're going to do it sooner or later anyway, so why not now?"

He reached for Jameson's hand again. "Glad to've met you, Jameson. Perhaps we can get better acquainted over a bottle of good whisky, if you come down to Wash's saloon."

"Maybe later," Jameson said. As King walked away, Jameson looked to Posey with a question in his eyes. Posey answered it.

"Good hunter, that King. He's had luck right along, even with the buffalo playing out. And when it comes to selling, he's as independent as a hog on ice. I'll spar around with him a little, but in the end I'll have to give him what he's asking. I know it, and so does he."

Jameson tested the name on his tongue. "Ransom King. Sounds like something out of a book."

Posey shrugged. "May be where he got it. Lots of people around here aren't using the names their mothers gave them." He turned and walked into his little frame office, Jameson following him. "That King," Posey said, shaking his head. "They lost the pattern after they made him."

He dug into a desk and brought out a record book. Blowing the dust off it, he asked, "Want to watch the yard crew count off the hides?"

"Won't be necessary." Jameson pulled a tally book out of his pocket. "Got the figures here for every wagon."

Posey picked it up and riffled the pages. "And they'll be correct, too, right down to the last kip." Humor was in his eyes.

While Posey pulled open a drawer at the bottom of his heavy rolltop desk and brought out a bottle and two glasses, Jameson looked around the office. It was strictly a working man's setup, not meant for entertaining royalty. Papers were piled high and seemingly without care on top of the desk and the heavy iron safe in the corner. But Jameson would bet his Big Fifty, reloading outfit and all, that Posey knew where to find anything he needed. Not a single picture on the bare wall, but there was a solitary little calendar, notes scribbled in careful hand around many of the dates. Three Indian-tanned buffalo robes lay rolled up along one wall.

There was a faint aroma of tobacco and whisky, but it was overpowered by the strong smell of heavy grease and buffalo hides.

Once Jameson had asked Posey if the stink ever bothered him.

"Sometimes," came the bland comment, "when the prices start dropping."

Posey poured two shot glasses full. Jameson took his down in one long, appreciative swallow, his face squinching up at the burn of the whisky. It was good bourbon. Posey had it shipped to him all the way from Kentucky.

He eased out a long breath and nodded in approval. "First one I've had in months."

"Didn't you take some along for medicinal purposes?"

"We turned that wagon over the third week out. Broke every bottle but one. We *did* have to save that one for medicinal purposes."

He turned serious. "How does it look, C. T.?"

Posey shook his head. "Not good, Gage, not good. She's cutting mighty thin. You saw how many hunters are camped around town here. They've scoured the whole Arkansas. By spring there won't be enough hides left to sweat a pair of mules. Indians are restless, too. Cheyennes killed one of Stump Johnson's men.

"Trouble is, there's nowhere to go from here. The army's turning hunters back from the northern territory because of the Medicine Lodge treaty. And south—well, you know what's to the south."

Jameson squeezed the whisky glass. "The Cimarron. And below that, the Canadian. And buffalo, C. T. . . . there's bound to be a world of buffalo down there."

"And a world of Comanches."

Jameson looked directly into Posey's eyes. "Comanches or not, I want to go."

Posey straightened, taken aback. "Knowing you, I shouldn't be surprised. But I can't afford to send any Miles and Posey wagons down there. Not till I know we've got a better than even chance of bringing the men back alive and the wagons full of hides. Right now, I don't think we have that chance."

Jameson stood up and looked out the open door toward the hide wagons with their light load. "We haven't got much choice, have we? It's go south or pick bones. And C. T., I'm no bone picker."

Posey shrugged. "You're right, Gage. We both know it. But the question is, when? The time's not right, not yet."

"And when will the time be right? When somebody goes down there and proves it can be done. What's going to happen when somebody comes back from Texas with a string of wagons piled high with hides? I'll tell you. It won't matter if the whole outfit has arrows sticking out of it like the quills on a porcupine—men'll run all over each other trying to get down there. Price of wagons and teams will shoot up. You'll be offering two dollars a day—maybe three—trying to get skinners and teamsters.

"I want to be that first man."

Posey only stared at him. "I'd like to do it, Gage. I'd like to let you go. But Jason Miles is half of this partnership, and he'd hit the ceiling. Me, I'm the flighty type. I'll shoot the works on a scheme that looks halfway good. Jason is so hidebound he wouldn't invest a nickel if he couldn't see a dime lying in front of him. So we balance each other off. I keep Jason prodded along, and he keeps my feet on the ground. Right now, no amount of persuasion would move Jason Miles."

Jameson's eyes grew keen. He pointed his chin toward the big safe in the corner. "That money the company's been holding for me—got it at hand? Got it where I could get it if I wanted it right quick?"

Posey's face tightened in worry. "Yes, but what's going on in that Indian mind of yours?"

"Just this, C. T.: if Miles and Posey doesn't want to send me, I'll go on my own. There's buffalo down there in Texas. I'm going to get them!"

{ TWO }

Jameson stood at the door, watching the yard crew take up reins and holler at the heavy-muscled ox teams as they moved the hide wagons down to unload them at the end of the stacks. He noted that the crew was no longer so large as it used to be.

"The frontier's fading fast," he said. "So's the hide game. Man's got to make himself a stake now—get into something that'll last—or pretty soon there won't be much chance left. I'm thirty-five already. Forty's looking at me from around the corner. How many more years have I got to make myself a start, C. T.? I've got to do it soon or I'll be going around in circles like old Shad Blankenship.

"Shad doesn't know anything but the frontier. He can see it getting away from him, and he's scared. What's going to be left for him when it's gone? He's been out here since they dug the Arkansas River, and what's he got to show for it? What's he ever *going* to have? Nothing."

He squatted down in the doorway, in the manner of a man in camp, and leaned against the doorjamb. "I've saved money since I've been working for Miles and Posey, but it won't be enough. And I can't add much to it hanging around up here where the buffalo are all gone.

"So I'll take what money I've got and buy wagons with it, and supplies. I'll hire me a tough crew and go down where the buffalo are. Sure, I know it's risky. But what that ever amounted to anything wasn't a gamble?"

Posey studied him long and hard. He leaned down and filled Jameson's glass again, then his own.

"You're right, Gage. You generally are. But what kind of outfit could you put together with the money you've got, and still buy supplies? Five or six wagons at the outside. How many men could you hire, even if you found some willing to go? Not enough to put up much defense. The Comanches could swallow up a little outfit in five minutes. You need a big one."

Posey had a way of looking at a man and into him.

"There's more to it than just the money, Gage. What else is it?"

Fingering the glass, staring out at the sweating yard crew, Jameson was a minute in answering.

"You didn't see this country before the hide hunters got thick, C. T. But I did. I came out here with a freighting outfit when I was just a kid. There was nothing but a few army posts along the immigrant trails. Stray off a few miles and you were in land only a handful of white men had ever seen. Every kind of wild game you could imagine. And the plains themselves, reaching on and on as far as a man could see, just the way it must have been when God finished it.

"It wasn't all littered up with buffalo bones, or houses, or railroads, or busted-down wagons. It wasn't spotted with rotting corpses.

"And the buffalo . . . I've seen them in herds so big that in the rutting season you could hear the bulls fighting from miles away. I've seen a big herd on winter mornings with the steam hanging low over them like a cloud of smoke.

Once a man sees those things, they're never really out of his mind again. He never forgets. He doesn't know what they mean to him till they're gone. Then he keeps looking, hoping maybe he'll find it somewhere else.

"Maybe that's a big part of it, C. T. Maybe down there I'll find it again the way it used to be. And even if I don't, I won't be satisfied till I've gone and looked."

Posey had chewed his cigar down to half size. "And what if you *do* find it? It'll be spoiled again in a little while. You'll help spoil it yourself."

Jameson said ruefully, "Funny, isn't it? We thought it would stay like that forever. Seemed like the country was so big that nothing we did would matter. But we spoiled it. Now I'm ready to go along and watch it happen all over, just to get to see it once again the way it used to be."

Posey sat a while, frowning, that nervous twitch in his face as he studied his hands and chewed his cigar. He was deep in thought. Finally he spoke. "Look, Gage, I've got money of my own, money Jason Miles hasn't got any claim on. You go on and buy whatever you need. Make it big enough so you can defend yourself. I'll back you just as far as you need to go."

Jameson stood there like someone had clubbed him.

"C. T., I . . . I don't hardly know what to say."

"You don't have to say anything. Just come back."

Jameson rubbed his smooth-shaven chin and looked at himself in the barber's cracked mirror. He had to grin at the whiteness of his face where whiskers had shielded his skin from sun and wind since he had taken the wagons out months ago. On the rough floor at his feet lay a thick mat of hair that the barber had whacked off. The short hair felt unnatural now, freshly washed out with strong soap.

The barber said, "Better watch yourself a day or two till you get used to it, or you'll catch cold. You're like a fresh-sheared sheep."

Behind a partition stood a big wooden washtub, more than half full of cold water. Two buckets bubbled and steamed atop a big cast-iron heater. The barber slowly poured their contents into the tub, then stirred until the water was evenly warm.

Over the back of a wooden chair Jameson draped a suit of clean new clothes he had bought down the street. Undressing, he threw the dirty clothes into a corner, far from the clean ones. He settled into the warm water for a long, comfortable soak, lighting a black cigar and leaning back relaxed, wondering if a man could ever get all the buffalo smell off.

A barber sees about as many people as anybody in town except maybe a bartender. Jameson called to him beyond the partition.

"Heard anybody quote prices on wagons and teams lately?"

The barber was sweeping the hair into a dusty pile to throw it out the back door. "If you got any to sell, you're hubbin' it, mister. There's plenty for sale and mighty few buyers."

"I was thinking I might buy a few wagons and a good string of mules if the price was right."

The barber stopped sweeping and looked around the partition. "Better not say that too loud. They'll run over you."

Jameson picked up the rough brown bar of soap and began to rub it briskly over his wet arms and shoulders.

"You might spread the word that I'm in the market. Name's Gage Jameson. With Miles and Posey."

Bath finished, he strode far down to the edge of town, where an aging Negro woman lived in a rude shack close to the riverbank. She did washing and ironing while her husband helped hustle teams at the Miles and Posey yards. Under his arm Jameson carried a sackful of dirty clothes, on his shoulder his bedroll.

He found Callie out back of the shack, shoving firewood into the flames under a huge smoke-blackened pot full of boiling water, a big red neckerchief tied over her hair.

Seeing him, she dropped the wood and began to shake excitedly, grinning broadly as if he had come back from the dead. "Mister Gage, Mister Gage. I declare I thought them Injuns had got you."

"Callie, I was so dirty they were afraid to touch me."

He dropped the sack on the ground, along with the bedroll. "Brought some clothes and some bedding. Wish you'd give every bit of it a good slow boiling, right down to the last pair of socks."

She shook her head. "I'll do it, but boilin' is almighty hard on clothes. These buffalo hunters do beat all, the way they want their stuff boiled."

He grinned. "Callie, I've seen men bet a hundred dollars on which one could reach in his pocket and come up with a louse first. That's why we boil our clothes."

He looked at the poor frame shack she lived in, and pity moved him. Once he had asked the old woman about it, and she had told him of the good cabin she and Rufe had shared in Georgia, before freedom. Then she had added with a fierce pride, "I wouldn't trade back, Mister Gage. This one, it ain't much. But it's all ours."

He dug into his new coat and brought up a paper-wrapped package. "Got something here for you. Traded it off of old Limping Wolf's Sioux when we came across them a while back."

Excitedly she tore the paper off and found a pair of fancy leather moccasins with a fine job of beadwork. Her eyes widened, and her white teeth gleamed proudly. Then she sobered.

"Mister Gage, you shouldn't of. With all the pretty girls there is in town, you could've found you a good one to give them to."

Gage said evenly, "There are pretty ones, but there aren't many good ones. That's why I got the moccasins for you."

Later he walked through the open door of a frame dance hall, pausing to let his eyes accustom themselves to the dimmer light indoors. A chubby barman gave him a crooked-toothed grin and lifted a big hand in greeting.

"Jameson. Gage Jameson!" He held a bottle high, beckoning with his chin. "It's on me, Gage."

Shaking hands, Jameson looked out over the room. Not much business yet. Some of his own crew sat at a big table, drinking and playing cards. They nodded at him.

"How's business, Wash?" Jameson asked while the man poured each of them a drink.

Wash had been a buffalo hunter too, but he had early decided there must be some easier way to make a living. And he hadn't been able to think of anything with so steady and sure a trade as the whisky business. Once he had tried to talk Jameson into going in partnership with him. But Jameson hadn't been able to picture himself as a saloon keeper. Sure, he was looking for something that would beat buffalo hunting. But this wasn't it.

"Business is getting slow, Gage," Wash complained. "Hide trade is falling off fast. Should've set up in Wichita or Ellsworth, I reckon. Cattle drives from Texas really pour the silver into those towns. They tell me a cowboy ain't got no bottom to him when it comes to putting away drinking liquor. But I don't suppose Dodge City will ever get any of that cattle trade. We come too late."

Jameson finished his friendly drink with Wash, then angled across the room to where the lanky skinner Messick sat at a corner table, laboriously scrawling a letter. Jameson pulled out a chair and sat down facing him.

Painfully Messick said, "Writin' to my sister. Got to tell her about George Hobart."

Jameson nodded. "That's what I figured."

The memory of it brought an angry twist to his face— the sight of three men lying dead in the remains of a hide camp, wagons and stock gone, their bodies ripped by gunfire, slashed by knives.

"How much are you going to tell her?"

"Just that her husband is dead, and we found him there. What else can I say? I can't tell her what they did to him— the way they scalped him and . . ."

Messick broke off, long face purpling.

"Worst job of butchery I ever saw," Jameson said. "No old warrior would've taken any pride in it. Young bucks, maybe. Likely got ahold of some firewater."

Messick's eyes narrowed with rekindled anger. "And maybe it wasn't Indians at all. Maybe it was hide thieves, coverin' up. Wagons was gone, you know."

Jameson shrugged. Messick had spent a lot of time among Indians, and he liked them. "It was probably Indians, all right. They're stirred up over the buffalo killing. But we'll never know."

He stood up again, digging into his pocket. He brought

out forty dollars and looked at it a moment. He'd spend it here anyway. Might as well see it go where it was needed.

He pitched the money onto the table. "Put this in with the letter. Tell her we found it in his pocket."

Jameson started to walk back to where the rest of the Miles and Posey crew sat. Just then a man shoved through the door, slammed it shut behind him and hollered in high good humor. "Whisky for everybody, Wash!"

It was Ransom King. He stood there chewing on a black cigar that must have been a foot long. His teeth gleamed happily beneath his trimmed mustache. "Sold my hides," he announced loudly for everyone to hear. "Got my own price, and it was a honey. Go on up, boys, don't be bashful. And don't let Wash give you the cheap stuff."

King moved to the bar, leaned over it, and reached way down, bringing up a bottle. He had known just where it would be. He looked at it quizzically, seeing that half of it was gone.

"Hey, Jameson," he called, "come on over and have one with me. Told you I'd get my price out of Posey."

Jameson grinned. It had been a long time since he'd met anyone like Ransom King. King caught his elbow and gave him a gentle shove toward a chair. "Sit down, my friend, and let's drink a toast to salesmanship."

Seated, Jameson noted that the bottle in King's hand held good whisky, if the label didn't lie. It wasn't the stuff Wash commonly served over the bar. It struck Jameson that King was the kind who would know what was the best and make sure he got it.

King poured them each a drink and lifted his glass. "Here's to the buffalo."

Jameson downed his with care, for another free drink

or two would leave him walking on air, unused to it as he was. King took his with one swallow, cleared his throat and poured a second one. Jameson put his hand over his own glass, declining another.

King walked to a set of wooden stairs that started in a back corner and disappeared into the high ceiling.

"Hey, Rose," he shouted, "come on down here."

He came back without yelling again. Jameson smiled. "Sure she heard you?"

"She heard me," King replied confidently. "She listens for me."

He scratched a match across the seat of his good pants and held the flame to the end of the twisted cigar until the tobacco began to glow. He puffed big clouds of strong smoke, getting the cigar going, squinting his eyes against the smoke's bite.

"Yes sir," he said, "with those hide stacks dwindling down, old C. T. isn't in any position to haggle over a good batch of hides. He's got to pay for them. You ought to have heard him holler."

The thought of it struck King funny. He threw his head back and laughed. At first Jameson thought he might have emptied a bottle or two before he had ever come in here. Then he decided this was just the way King acted when he was feeling good.

He wondered how King might act if he felt bad. Even with the laughter there was a steel-keen look to King's square face. No doubt those sparkling eyes could as easily turn to flint.

A woman came down the stairs, trying to be graceful but lacking the ability. Dark-haired, young, she wore a golden gown cut low in front with two thin straps up over her wide, soft shoulders. The dress fit tightly against her ample upper body and down over her trim hips.

"See there?" King winked. "Told you she heard me."

He pushed to his feet and strode across to take her by the arm. "Come on over, Rose, and meet a real buffalo hunter. Rose Tremaine, this is Gage Jameson. They say he's even better than me."

Rose smiled at Jameson. He nodded and spoke to her. He remembered having seen her here before. And not with King.

"Sold those hides, sweetie," King said, pinching her chin so hard that it was white a moment, then red. "We'll celebrate a little tonight, you and me."

King walked over to the scuffed piano. The cigar sticking up at a jaunty angle, he picked out a rowdy dance hall tune with one finger. "Give us a little music, Rose," he said.

By this time everybody was watching Rose, and Jameson could see in her brown eyes how she gloried in this admiration. She seated herself at the piano and began to play and sing the tune King had started. King stood a while with his elbow on the piano, watching her like a hungry cat watching a mouse. Finally he walked back to the table where Jameson sat.

"Quite a gal, that one," King said.

Jameson nodded. She did look mighty good to a man who had been three months out on the buffalo range.

"You ought to get acquainted with her, Jameson," King said.

"Looks to me like you've already got the deed."

King shrugged. "Women are all right for a while, for a little diversion. Can't seem to get along without them. But you get tired of one after so long. I've been hoping someone would come along and take Rose off my hands. Man needs a change in diet occasionally."

Jameson smiled, thinking he might be tempted if he didn't have so much of more importance on his mind.

King poured himself a third drink. As quickly as it had come, the laughter went out of his face and he turned serious.

"Barber told me you're in the market for wagons and teams."

"That's right."

"I've done some thinking about it. The way I see it, you must be planning to go south."

Jameson looked at him in surprise. King explained, "You're a man of considerable reputation as a hunter, Jameson. You wouldn't waste money on wagons to hunt in this country. The army's not letting anybody up into that northern territory. So you *must* be going south."

Jameson studied King's changeable face, wondering what the man was aiming at.

"There's buffalo down there, Jameson," King said with enthusiasm. "Big herds that can load a man's wagons with flint hides in a hurry. I've seen a few of them, just enough to set my blood to racing and the seat of my pants to itching. I took four wagons south of the Arkansas last spring. But you could fairly smell Indian in the air. Half my men panicked and deserted me. I had to turn back before we had skinned out a wagonload.

"A man could make himself a small fortune down there, Jameson, a first-rate hunter with plenty of guts and more than common judgment. They tell me you're that kind of man."

Jameson took the compliment without reply, knowing King was working up to something.

"Main thing," King said, "would be to take enough men and wagons that an outfit could defend itself. The Comanches aren't foolish. They fight when they think they can win. When they don't think they can, they don't try."

He drank half the whisky out of his glass and pointed his finger at Jameson. "Now it happens I know a man who has a string of wagons and all the teams you'll need. He'll sell them cheap. Tell you what, you make the rounds and price the wagons and mules that you find. Whatever kind of deal you're offered, my man'll do better, I guarantee you."

Jameson eyed him levelly. "Where's your profit, King? You're not doing this for nothing."

King broke into a high, loud laugh. "They were right about you, Jameson, you're a perceptive man. All right, I have a motive of my own. I wanted to get on your warm side so you'd let me take my own wagons with you into Texas. I wasn't going to make that proposition until I'd built you up for it. But there it is."

Jameson rubbed his chin thoughtfully, then slowly shook his head. "This is going to be my own expedition, King. I don't want to have to consult anybody or worry what anybody else thinks. I'm my own boss. You can't be that way when there's another outfit with you. I've seen too many hunters go off together, then fall out. No real leader, everybody a free agent. A little friction starts and you're done for."

"There won't be any conflict. You'll be the wagon master. What you say goes, any time."

Jameson shook his head. "I'm sorry, King."

Ransom King studied Jameson, his eyes unreadable. Presently he shrugged. "No harm done, and no hard feelings. What I said about those wagons still stands. Come around to my camp when you've priced the others. My man'll make you a better deal."

Jameson smiled a little. "No motive this time?"

King laughed. "He owes me money, and I want to get paid." He looked at Rose, and he looked at the stairs. "See you tomorrow, Jameson?"

Jameson nodded, beginning to like this tall, brash man. "Tomorrow."

Old Shad Blankenship was pacing impatiently about his camp when Jameson rode up into the firelight.

"About decided you wasn't comin' after all," he said half peevishly, raking the fire restlessly with a stick. "Been dark an hour. Thought you'd found you some redheaded filly and plumb forgot about that bottle you were going to bring me."

"Now, Shad," Jameson grinned, "do you think a filly could make me forget the man who taught me how to shoot a buffalo gun and talk sign language and cure out a green hide?"

A flicker of humor showed behind Shad's deep scowl as he grabbed the bottle from Jameson's hand and began to worry the cork out of it.

"If she couldn't, you're a sight older than I think you are. When I was a few years younger a filly could make me forget my own name. Way it is, the whisky's all that's left for me. That and the cards."

There wasn't a great deal of the whisky left, either, by the time Shad finally laid the bottle aside, wiping his hand on his ancient, deep-stained old buckskin jacket from which most of the fringe was long since gone. Shad frowned at Jameson as the glow began to work upward in him.

"Now what's this foolishness I hear about you wantin' to buy wagons and mules?"

"Where did you hear it?"

"Man, it spread over town like the cholera through an Injun camp. Been a dozen men here to ask me about you. Have you plumb lost your head?"

"I hope not."

"What good is wagons when the buffalo is gone?"

"There's buffalo to the south, Shad."

Blankenship snorted and uncorked the bottle again. "Jason Miles would jump ten feet and fall over dead."

"He's not in on it. Just C. T. Posey and me."

Shad stared hard at Jameson until he was sure the younger man wasn't joshing him. "Then you *have* lost your head."

"Shad, sooner or later somebody's going to go down there. It had just as well be me."

Blankenship narrowed his eyes, and he slowly shook his head. "Come spring, your scalp'll be dried and hanging from some heathen Comanche's lodgepole, that's for sure. But don't listen to me. Go on down there and get yourself knocked over."

He held the bottle out to arm's length, trying to read the label. "Just let me get my paws on some of your money first. You want to buy wagons? All right, I'll sell you mine."

Jameson looked sharply at him. "Sell me yours? What would you ever do, Shad? You've been a hide man so long you'd starve to death trying to make an honest living."

"The hide business is goin' to the devil, and I ain't makin' the trip with it. I'm heading back to the settlements and take up farming, like I told you."

"It wouldn't last a month. You'd be back out here skinning buffalo if you had to walk the whole way barefooted."

Shad Blankenship flared, the whisky beginning to get him. "A man crazy enough to do what you're figuring on ain't in no shape to be givin' advice. Just buy my wagons. Three of them, and the teams—the whole works, tools, camp gear, lock, stock and barrel—for a thousand dollars. And cheap at the price."

Studying the old man, Jameson wished Shad hadn't said it. The outfit was worth far more than he was asking for it.

"Shad, that's the whisky talking. Let's let it wait till morning."

"If you don't buy it, I'll sell it to somebody else."

Jameson finally shrugged. "All right, if that's the way it's got to be, you've just sold out. What say I give you a hundred of it here and send the rest on ahead?"

Blankenship shook his head, angering. The hint was plain enough—he couldn't take care of the money.

"I'll take it all right now, right here, thankee."

"Shad, you won't get out of town with a dime of it."

Blankenship arose quickly, his fists knotting. "By Judas Priest, you listen to me, young'un! I was a grown man trapping beaver and dodging the Blackfeet before your Maw and Paw ever even thought of you. Don't you think I got sense enough to know what I'm about? You just pay me, that's all you got to do."

Unwillingly Jameson said, "All right, Shad, however you want it."

He knew what would happen as soon as Shad got his hands on the cash. He had seen it too many times.

"Look, Shad, keep your wagons. Come with me to Texas. We'll split the take according to what each man puts in."

It was exactly the deal he had turned down for Ransom King. But he knew Shad Blankenship. Shad would be worth three of most men, if he ever got out of Dodge.

But Shad's feelings were hurt. "I ain't gonna take orders from you, young'un, just because you got the most
wagons. No, sir, you just take me to town and pay me off,
right now. I'm goin' to Missouri."

Jameson spent most of the next day riding through the
camps scattered up and down the river, looking at wagons
and mules. He found many men eager to sell. The prices
they quoted him were low compared to what they had been
last spring.

He could have gotten oxen even cheaper, but winter was
coming on. Mules would be better for the long haul where
feed had to be carried. And mules were faster in a pinch.
Trouble with mules, the Indians liked them too. Nothing ap-
pealed to an Indian's horse-stealing tendencies more than
the thought of a fat mule's hind leg smoking over an open fire.

Late in the day, before angling toward Ransom King's
camp, Jameson stopped to see Shad Blankenship. One
look at Shad's pain-twisted face, his sick and stricken eyes,
told him the whole story.

"I been a first-class fool, Gage," the old man lamented,
running his gnarled fingers miserably through his rusty
mat of long hair. "You had me pegged right enough. I got
drunk and fell into a poker game. Them highbinders melted
my roll like a snowbank in August. I ain't goin' to Missouri. I ain't even got the cash to get out of Dodge."

There was no use saying I told you so, even if Jameson
had been of a mind to. He laid a hand on Shad's shoulder
and sat down beside him on the dirty old buffalo robe the
hunter had spread out inside his grimy tent. He looked at
Shad with sorrow in his eyes, and a disturbing thought took
hold of him:

A few more years the way I'm going and I'll be just like him.

That was why he *had* to go down and find that Texas herd, had to make him a stake now while there was still time.

"How about going south with me, Shad?"

"I'd be in your way. I ain't got sense enough to get in out of the rain."

"Shad, you're still the best hide man in the business, barring none. I'll be needing your advice down there."

"You're just feeling sorry for me. You got no call to."

"That's not it. I need those sharp eyes of yours. There's few hunters can bring down as many buffalo as you can and smoke up as few cartridges doing it. You didn't lose your rifle in that poker game, did you?"

"No."

"Then oil it up. You'll be using it."

{ THREE }

R ansom King shifted to one side in the saddle. "Yonder's his camp," he said. "Looks like a hog sty, but he's got the goods to sell."

The wagons were scattered around in no particular order, some of the harness done up on the wheels, some of it thrown carelessly out on the ground. Cooking utensils lay about, unwashed, some of them caked up with dried-out food. The whole place had an unpleasant odor to it that wrinkled Jameson's nose.

Jameson counted the wagons to himself, raising and dropping his hand. Six doubles and a single. They were of several kinds and of various sizes, as if they had been picked up a few at a time. Most were good Studebaker wagons or their equals. A few wouldn't do for a bone hauler.

A bulky man walked out slowly, carrying himself with a deliberate ease that tried to say he wasn't afraid of anybody in the world.

But Jameson's keen eye told him this bearded man was only a weak imitation, a bluff, hollow inside.

"Gage Jameson, Adam Budge," King said by way of introduction.

Budge shook hands but stared belligerently with black eyes, as if this transaction wasn't going to be to his liking. His hands were grimy, his black beard dirty and greasy. Half the buttons were gone from his salt-crusted shirt.

The man stood awkwardly a minute before he broke his silence. "King says you want to buy wagons. I got them to sell."

Jameson nodded. "Tell you right now, I've had some cheap prices quoted to me today."

Budge glanced questioningly at King. King said, "Whatever they are, Budge'll beat them. You want to look over the outfit?"

Jameson walked among the wagons, carefully checking under them and over them. Finally he said, "Three would have to come out. I'll take the others, if the price is right. Now how about the mules?"

"Down on the riverbank," Budge said. "Got a man herding them."

An unkempt stock tender sat on the ground, holding an old horse that stood hip-shot. He had the mules bunched loosely on the grass not far from water.

Jameson rode slowly into them, looking for harness sores, making the mules move around so he could tell if any of them limped. He found a cripple or two that way and eased them out of the bunch. He cut back a couple of old and unthrifty mules that might have a hard time getting through the winter, and on a long haul at that. He looked for well-built animals with long legs placed solidly under their bodies like the legs under a table. He looked for flat backs, good head, good ear, good foot and bone. He cut back two or three narrow-bodied mules with legs too close together that indicated a lack of stamina. He always remembered what Shad had told him once about picking mules.

"You see one that's got forelegs comin' out of the same hole like a rabbit's, you leave him alone. One knee says to the other, 'You let me by this time and I'll let you by the next.'"

A wild-eyed mule wheeled as Jameson came to him. He lashed out with a hind foot and narrowly missed Jameson's leg. Quickly Jameson cut him out, too. He didn't want any fractious mule getting a whole team in a jackpot and tearing up a pair of wagons, especially wagons loaded with flint hides that might fetch two dollars or more apiece.

Back in camp, Ransom King sought out cups from a wooden box in a wagon bed and poured coffee. Jameson looked dubiously at his cup, which had a thin scum of grease on it. His eyes caught King's and he knew King had the same thought. But Jameson had been around hide camps so much that it took a lot to make him sick. For courtesy's sake he sipped the bitter black coffee without comment.

Budge scowled over his own coffee. "All right," he said sharply, "what'll you give?"

Jameson leaned forward, setting the cup down. "Well, I've had good wagons offered to me as cheap as three hundred dollars a pair, and mules at fifty a head. I know that's mighty little, but some of these boys are desperate."

Jameson felt a pleasant tremor of excitement, the tingle that always came to him when he was trying to make a close trade. He was that much like Posey. This was cheaper than he had ever hoped for. Used to be that a good new wagon and a well-matched team could run a man an easy thousand dollars.

Budge chewed his whiskered lip, showing a set of yellow teeth streaked brown from tobacco. "Last spring they was worth a sight more."

Jameson shrugged, keeping his face bland. "I can buy them from somebody else."

King said, "Budge will sell them to you."

Budge nodded his shaggy head, the reluctant words dragging from him like pulled teeth. "Yeah, yeah, I reckon so."

Jameson said, "Four thousand even for the ten wagons and that string of mules, minus the ones I cut out. All right?"

Budge sloshed his coffee around, trying to get the sugar up off the bottom of the cup. He drank, then wiped a filthy sleeve across his mouth. "Yeah, I reckon that'll have to do."

Jameson relaxed slowly, letting out a long breath. For weeks on the prairie he'd thought about taking his own expedition south if Miles and Posey didn't go for the idea. He hadn't let himself hope for anywhere near this many wagons.

"When do you want to be paid?" Jameson asked. Budge said, "I want to square up a few accounts"—he flicked a half-resentful glance at King—"and catch the first train East. I'd be obliged if you paid me tonight."

"How about coming to the Miles and Posey office with me?"

Budge shook his head. "Can't. I got to go see a man who'll take them cut-back mules and extra wagons off my hands. He'll rob me, but leastways I can get the money tonight and catch that train."

He scratched his black chin. "You know where the Queen of the Arkansas Saloon is?"

Jameson nodded. It was a rat hole of a place, a half dug-out on the wrong side of the tracks. Cheap whisky, low-stakes poker.

Budge said, "The man I got to see owns the place. Why don't you meet me there?"

Jameson wasn't sure it suited him, carrying four thousand dollars in cash. It would be well dark before he got back. But he had seen hide buyers moving around freely all over Dodge in the past, their pockets stuffed with greenbacks. If anybody ever molested them, he hadn't heard about it.

"All right," he said, dismissing the thought. He looked at King. "Ready to go?"

Riding away, King smiled. "You got you a great buy back there."

"I know it. Just one thing worries me. Budge isn't the type. A skinner or a teamster, maybe, but not a man to own and boss a string of wagons."

King shrugged. "Maybe he's found that out. That's why he's selling."

"What kind of a squeeze have you got on him, King?"

"I just told him I was tired of waiting, and if he didn't pay me I'd peel the hide off of him, an inch at a time. He looks rough, Jameson, but he's as scary as a squawking old hen."

Jameson caught C. T. Posey just as he was closing his office, and got the four thousand dollars in cash out of the big safe. He shoved it into the deep pocket of his coat. Then he strapped his six-shooter on over the coat, just in case.

It wasn't far to the saloon, so he unsaddled his horse and turned him loose in the company yard. Then he walked over the tracks and down on the other side.

None of Dodge City looked very polished or respectable,

but here was the seamiest part of it, raw frame saloons and dance halls, others built of nothing more than sod, a few even dug into the ground, only the top half reaching above ground level. He heard fiddle music and rough laughter. Yonder he saw a woman standing watching him, the yellow flicker of lamplight behind her outlining her in a doorway. She spoke to him, but he didn't catch the words and didn't want to.

A lantern hung on either side of the door at the Queen of the Arkansas, yellow flame licking at the wick. The nearly flat sod roof was only waist-high to Jameson, most of the building being dug into the ground. He thought idly what would happen to this place if a sudden cloudburst should send water cascading down the street. It would fill up like a jug.

A match suddenly flared, and a man's face glowed as he touched the flame to a cigarette. "You Jameson?"

"Yes."

"Then go on inside. Budge is waitin' for you."

Vaguely disturbed, Jameson hesitated a moment, looking through the ground-level windows and seeing light inside. Carefully then, he moved down the warped wooden steps to the sunken doorway.

The wall-trapped reek of smoke and whisky and unwashed bodies slapped him in the face. It reminded him of a wolf den he had crawled into once. This was like it, more den than house.

The light was dim, for the owner was stingy with his lanterns. But Jameson easily spotted Adam Budge's bulk. He sat at a table with another man, his broad back turned to the door. His shirt was soaked with sweat. The man at the table looked up at Jameson. He was a cheap gambler, Jameson remembered, who went by the name of Frenchy.

Dirty, unkempt, he was not in the class with the gamblers who stayed around the bigger places.

Budge licked his lips, and his voice had a high pitch to it. "Jameson, c-c-come on over."

Jameson hesitated, with a sudden quickening of alarm. *Budge is scared half to death,* he thought. His hand moved down toward the six-shooter.

"Hold it, friend!" The words were short-clipped. Jameson glanced quickly at the bar. The tender held a shotgun, aimed straight at him.

"Go shut the door, Mick," said Frenchy. The man behind Jameson shoved the door shut and took the bartender's shotgun. "Now come on over," Frenchy said to Jameson. Jameson slowly stepped forward, looking into the muzzle of Frenchy's derringer, knowing the shotgun was at his back. He felt his six-shooter being jerked from the holster.

Budge's chin was trembling. So were his hands, placed judiciously on the table where all could see them.

"Now," said Frenchy, rising to his feet, "where is it?"

"Where is what?" Jameson bluffed, knowing it was a waste of time.

"The money. You got it. Budge has told us all about it."

Budge's voice shrilled desperately, "Jameson, they're fixin' to kill us!"

Jameson said, "Somebody's steered you wrong. There isn't any money."

In the back of his mind was a wild hope that when they reached for him to search him, he might grab a gun.

So suddenly he didn't see it, a leather whip or something lashed at his face. A cry swelled in his throat, and he bent over, his hands clawing at the fire which seared his cheeks.

"Don't stall me around," Frenchy gritted. "Where's that money?"

Jameson made no reply, clenching his teeth against the burn. The lash struck again, across the back of his neck.

"Search him."

Rough hands jerked him around. Through pain-reddened eyes Jameson saw that the man behind him had set the shotgun down, just out of his reach. Hands dug into his coat pockets.

"Here it is, Frenchy. Holy smoke, look at them greenbacks!"

For a second then, while they feverishly eyed the money, Jameson thought he might have a chance. He reached for the shotgun. But someone was ready. A gun barrel slanted across his skull, sent him sprawling on the packed dirt floor amid cigarette butts and dried tobacco juice. He lay half conscious, brain hammering with pain.

"Supposed to be four thousand there," someone said. "Count it."

They ran through it and satisfied themselves.

The bartender said, "What're we gonna do with them two? Can't have them runnin' loose. Give me the word, Frenchy, and I'll shoot them both."

"No," replied Frenchy, more concerned over the money than over the men. "Too much noise. Knife's just as good and a heap quieter."

A cry of terror from Adam Budge helped bring Jameson groping back to consciousness. "Don't do it," Budge quaked. "I won't tell nobody, Frenchy, I swear it. You can keep the money, only don't do it."

Budge arose shaking, letting his chair fall back across Jameson's legs. He began to dodge away from the man with the knife. He kept crying, "No, Frenchy, no!" He pushed the table out, trying to keep it between them.

Without moving, Jameson sought the shotgun with his

eyes. It still stood where it had been, propped against the sod wall. A slim chance, but the only one he had.

The door burst open. Two men stood there, guns in their hands. In the split second before the guns roared, Jameson recognized Ransom King and saw a wild fever in the man's eyes that was like a look into hell. Jameson grabbed for the shotgun, got it, and rolled over onto his back.

He saw the bartender drop the knife and spin away from the force of the first two bullets, then fall, limp as a sack of grain. Frenchy whirled toward the door, bringing up the derringer. Jameson swung the shotgun around and squeezed the trigger, the roar of it swelling like a dynamite blast in the tiny room. The impact slammed Frenchy against the wall. He fell forward then and lay crumpled, his fingers convulsively digging into the packed earth.

The third man cowered back, raising his hands.

Beside King stood a heavy-bodied man with ragged beard, wolf-gray eyes shining in savage pleasure. He turned his six-gun to the third man and shot him where he stood, triggering two more bullets into his body after he fell.

"That's enough, Trencher." King spoke sharply.

"I reckon it is," the man called Trencher replied calmly. "He's dead." His eyes glittered, his wide mouth lifting a little at the corners. Standing there in the heavy, circling cloud of gun smoke, he flexed his gun hand nervously, eyes flicking back and forth among the fallen men, as if hoping one of them might move a little.

But they never would again.

Jameson pushed up weakly, leaning against the dirt wall and rubbing the back of his head where the gun barrel had struck him.

Budge was on his knees along the same wall, his face

chalk-white, his body shaking so Jameson could actually hear his teeth clicking. Budge tried to talk, but all that would come from his throat was a hollow squeak.

Ransom King stepped behind the bar and picked up a bottle. He blew dust from a glass and poured it half full. He handed it across to Jameson. "Here. You need this."

Jameson downed most of it and braced himself against its fiery jolt.

King lifted the bottle to his lips and took a long pull. Face suddenly flushed and twisted, he spat it out across the bar. "Wow!" he exclaimed. "Man who'd sell stuff like that doesn't deserve to live anyhow."

He walked out from behind the bar and handed the bottle to the trembling Budge.

"Buck up, Budge, and drink this. We got some money to count."

The whole thing had happened in the span of a few seconds. Now that it was over, reaction set in. Jameson's hands began to quiver, a little like Budge's. He pulled up a chair and sat down to let the spell pass, drinking a little more of the poor whisky in an effort to settle himself. He grinned sheepishly. "Some time to get scared, now that it's over."

King shrugged. "Man who doesn't get scared once in a while is the rankest kind of a fool."

"You were just in time," Jameson said. "How did you know?"

King grinned then, the tension gone. "I didn't. It was just luck. Budge there isn't exactly a paragon of virtue. I got to thinking how easy it would be for him to take the money, quick as you paid him, and skip out on our little debt. The more I thought about it, the more worried I got. So I came over here to keep him honest. Just happened to peep in that window yonder first, and saw what the deal was."

Jameson sat there, letting the strength come back to him as he watched the big man Trencher filling his deep coat pockets with bottles from behind the bar.

Finally he said, "King, after this, if there's ever anything you want, just let me know."

King smiled. "Well now, as a matter of fact, there is. I still want to take my wagons to Texas with you."

Jameson looked down at the dead men sprawled out on the dirt floor.

"After this, how could I say no?"

{ FOUR }

Sharp cold clung to the early-morning air. Gage Jameson looked at the stars and shivered. He fastened the top button of his woolen coat, wondering why it always took so long to shake the chill when a man was fresh out of bed.

He ate breakfast at the Dutchman's. He had arranged for the Dutchman to feed his men so they could get started without the delay that came from cooking and washing all the camp utensils. Besides, it was likely to be the last town meal they would get for a long time.

"My bunch all been in?" he asked, sipping his hot coffee and chewing on a thick slice of sugar-cured buffalo ham.

The stout old cook shrugged. "*Ach*, and more. You say please to feed fifteen men. It is already more than thirty that have come. I think you got a bunch of bums say they with you and they not."

Jameson frowned, until the humor of it touched him. He ought to have known the word would get around. Finishing up, he gave the old man twenty dollars.

"That cover it?"

The cook nodded vigorously, rubbing his stubby fingers over the paper money as if it had been silk. "*Ja, ja,* and you come again soon *wieder.*"

Soberly Jameson said, "I hope so."

He walked briskly on down to the yards, the coffee and the hot meal making him warmer now. He could hear the restless stir of men and mules, the rattle of trace chains and the popping of leather as teams were pulled into place and hitched to the wagons. Men laughed and cursed and hollered one to another. Mules balked. Mules squealed and kicked. He heard the quick gust of breath from one as another's hind feet slammed into its stomach. A man yelled, and leather slapped hard across a mule's rump.

Jameson caught his horse and threw his heavy saddle across its back. He rubbed his hand over the saddle, liking the feel of it. It was one he had just bought, one somebody had picked up from a Texas trail hand in a cow town down the tracks. High cantle, high horn to tie a rope to. It was sturdily built, and Jameson thought it would be like riding a rocking chair after the light saddles he had been used to.

He looked up into the sky and picked out the Dipper, then the North Star. It wasn't easy to find now, for daylight was rapidly washing it out. He turned his back on the star and looked ahead in the direction to which the wagon tongues were pointed.

South. South across the deadline. South toward Texas.

Nervousness began to ripple in him now that the time was upon him. It always did when he set off for someplace he'd never been. He began itching to be on the move.

He would be glad to get away from Dodge again, away from its evil-smelling saloons, its gambling dens, the shady men who hung around them—not hunters, not men who toiled with leather-tough hands, but leeches who stole from other men what they had earned with their sweat, and sometimes with their blood.

Yet he could remember the eagerness with which he had gone into Dodge, an eagerness that seemed to grow a little more each trip. A taste for the whisky, a desire to play a little poker, an urge to look at the girls.

It wasn't what he really wanted, yet it was here, unbidden, and it was growing, a general aimlessness that eventually would put him in the same shape as old Shad Blankenship. There was no hope for Shad. He was too old to change.

Jameson wondered if soon there might no longer be hope for himself. Dodge was a reminder to him that time was going on, that he didn't have long left to find something permanent, something he could anchor to and hold solid.

He swung into the saddle and walked his bay horse down the line of wagons, seeing that the mules were harnessed up. He checked the trail wagons in each pair, making sure their short tongues were firmly bolted to the coupling poles of the lead wagons. His horse stepped gingerly, the bite of nippy air bringing out a touch of bronc that still slept within him.

Up at the head of the line he came to the chuck wagon, its hoops standing like barren ribs, the cover rolled up in the bed of the wagon with the heavy load of cooking gear and supplies, flour and sugar, baking powder, dried apples—and most of all, plenty of coffee.

Shad Blankenship stood leaning relaxed against his own saddled horse and eyeing Jameson quizzically. He trimmed a thick shaving off a plug of Lorillard tobacco and shoved

it into his mouth. His breath already had a sweetish tobacco smell, and a trickle of brown worked into the rusty
beard.

"What do you think of the layout, Shad?"

Shad never had been one to mince words. "I think that
if a marshal was to come snooping around, about two-
thirds of this crew you hired would drown theirselves tryin' to get across that river. What jailhouse door did you
prize open?"

"I wanted them tough. They won't stampede back to
town the first time we run into an Indian with the paint on."

Shad shrugged, still not liking it.

"Well, there's one of them ain't goin'. He got in a little
argument last night and didn't have a sharp enough knife.
Other feller just naturally gutted him. Shows what kind of
an outfit *we* got."

Jameson swore under his breath. One man lost and they
hadn't even started yet.

Shad said, "We'll have to watch them like hawks or first
thing you know some of them are liable to run off with our
stock."

Jameson was still troubled about the man they were
short. "I figured you and me are strong enough to handle
them."

Put that way, there wasn't much Shad could do except
sourly nod assent. "I reckon."

Despite the early hour, despite the chill which still penetrated the men's light coats, a good-sized crowd of on-
lookers gathered. This expedition had aroused a lot of
comment. Most people agreed it was foolhardy. Jameson
would be so busy fighting Indians he couldn't hunt buffalo.

He'd had poor luck finding men who would hire on. He

didn't try to get any of the Miles and Posey men, for he felt that would be unfair to the company. Besides, C. T. Posey wanted to send them out for one last attempt up against the edge of the northern treaty territory. Jameson had managed to get three men who had worked for Miles and Posey a little in the past. They weren't what he wanted, but they were all he could get.

Then Ransom King came to his rescue and rounded up a crew for him.

"These are good men that'll take you down there and bring you back," King had said. Then he had reflected a moment and added, "Maybe 'good' isn't just the right word. 'Tough' is more like it."

Now Jameson pointed his chin toward the crowd of on-lookers who stood around and watched. "They'll do a lot of thinking, Shad, sitting around here doing nothing. Then they'll get the fever. There'll be other outfits down there by winter, unless I miss my guess."

Shad observed, "It'll be a good thing we was the first."

Jameson gave him a dig in the ribs. "That's what I've been trying to tell you all along."

C. T. Posey came striding up, chewing rapidly on his cigar. If anything, he was more nervous than Jameson.

"Look at me," he said, holding out his hand. "Quivering like a whipped pup and not even going."

He rubbed the palms of his hands on his trousers. "Everything looks good, Gage. You won't have to worry about the military. Won't be a patrol across your route in two days."

Jameson glanced at Shad Blankenship, grinning. It never ceased to amaze him how Posey could know what was going on at Fort Dodge. The army was supposed to keep hunters from working south of the Arkansas. But it was a careless hunter who couldn't slip past the soldiers. It was as if a tacit agreement existed between the hide outfits and the officers at the fort.

He remembered what Colonel Dodge had said when J. Wright Mooar asked him about heading south. "Boys, if I were hunting buffalo, I would go where the buffalo are."

It was almost universally agreed among the plains army officers that destruction of the buffalo was the quickest way to peace. The reservation looked good to a hungry Indian.

Ransom King rode up to them mounted on a fine big sorrel with three stocking feet. Jameson hadn't seen the horse before and stopped to admire its good lines, the deep heart girth, the strong legs that could carry a man all day and not give out.

King nodded at Jameson, then said to C. T. Posey, "What did you think of those hides, C. T.?"

Posey replied, "I thought they were plenty expensive."

King threw back his head and laughed. Presently he said to Jameson, "My wagons are ready, any time yours are." His gaze swept down Jameson's line of wagons and to the extra horses and mules bunched at the lower end.

Jameson said, "We're about ready, I think. I've already lost a man, and the wagons haven't turned a wheel."

King nodded. "Heard about it from some of my crew. Fool got in a fight over a poker game. Just a five-dollar bet, that's all it was."

Jameson started walking down the line of wagons, leading his horse and making a last check of each wagon as he passed it. The wagons contained primers and gunpowder and lead, corn and salt and everything else it would take for a long hunt on the prairie. Jameson reasoned that as the hides stacked up, the supplies would diminish and make room for them.

"Mighty little to die for, five dollars," he mused to King, who rode slowly beside him.

"Lots of people die over money," King replied lightly. "What else *is* worth dying for, when you boil it down? But if I ever do it, it won't be over any measly five dollars."

Jameson frowned. That was a mighty narrow way of looking at life, the way he saw it. Or death, either.

A woman pushed through the crowd and stopped in front of it, holding her long gray coat tight at the throat, not caring that her slender ankles showed amid a swirl of petticoats.

"There's Rose," Jameson said, "wanting to tell you good-bye."

King nodded, resignation in his face. "I'm glad I'm getting to do it. I'm bored to death with her."

Jameson smiled. "If I had to die, that's the way I'd want to do it, bored to death by someone as good-looking as that."

King shrugged. "Well, I gave you the chance. You didn't take her."

He started to pull away, toward Rose. He turned back to say, "I've thrown my extra animals in with yours, and my wagons will drop in behind when yours lead out. See you later, down the trail."

He moved his horse out and swung down beside Rose.

Jameson rode back to the head of the line. A lean, long-legged man strode toward him in the dawn, wearing faded old army clothes, carrying a rifle in his hand and a heavy roll of bedding over his shoulder. It was the skinner, Messick. Dropping the roll in the street, Messick leaned the rifle against it and raised his hand in greeting.

"Mornin', Gage."

"Morning, Nathan."

Messick glanced over Jameson's wagons, where everything seemed to be ready to travel. "I want to go with you."

Jameson said, "I didn't aim to steal anybody from Miles and Posey."

"You ain't stealin' me. I just quit. I've worked with you so long, Gage, there ain't anybody else I can get along with."

Jameson smiled, glad to have him. Messick never was one to add any cheer, but with a man like him in charge of the hides there wouldn't be any spoiled goods. "Hop up on a wagon, then. We're fixing to roll."

Messick pitched his bedding up onto the chuck wagon, shoved his rifle under the seat, and climbed up beside the little cook. The cook nodded at him, clenching the whipstock in one hand, the lines and the coils of his rawhide whip in the other. Two thin men, one short, one uncommonly tall.

Shad Blankenship rode up to Jameson, rocked back in the saddle and spat a stream of tobacco juice at a lanky gray dog which nosed around a wagon wheel. Then Shad's big black dog charged up and put the intruder to flight, trotting back with a grand air of self-importance.

Shad waved his hand at the line of wagons. "All set, Gage."

C. T. Posey was there, too. He held out his hand, and Jameson bent down to take it.

"I envy you in a way, Gage," the hide buyer said. "I never saw this country the way it used to be. I'd like to see it, just once in my lifetime. But I'm smart enough to know my limitations, and you have none. Best of luck to you."

"Thanks, C. T."

Then Jameson pulled away and looked back at his long string of wagons, the stamping mules, the impatient men.

"All right, Shad. Let's take them to Texas."

{ FIVE }

Angling southwestward, he didn't try to push the wagons hard the first day. With untried mules, untried wagons and untried men, it was better to take it easy and watch. By the time he reached Crooked Creek late in the afternoon, he had seen half a dozen mules and at least a couple of men he probably should have left in Dodge.

Too late now to do much about it. He had other mules he could put into the teams. But he was stuck with the men.

Shad Blankenship rode up to him and pointed to the creek. "Pretty good camping spot over here. Want to pull up the wagons?"

"Not till we get across. I get nervous on the wrong side of a creek or river. Spent too many days watching them flood and wishing I'd gotten across them when I could have."

Shad argued, "This one ain't fixin' to get out of banks. Ain't a cloud in sight."

"Call it a policy. We're crossing it anyhow."

Normally it was an easy crossing. It would have been this time, except for the nigh leader on the chuck wagon. He had been kicking and fighting all day. When the cold water splashed around his legs, he came in two.

The pots and pans, buckled on the chuck box, set up a clatter as the wagon began to jerk. The cook cracked a whip over the mule's ears and swore in language such as Jameson had seldom heard before, a careless mixture of the most profane of both English and Spanish. Jameson grinned, wondering how a man so small could have so powerful a voice.

The mule kept pitching and kicking, getting his forelegs over the neck of the animal beside him and stirring the whole team into a frenzy. They whipped the wagon back and forth at the water's edge until it began to rock.

The thin, bewhiskered cook began looking for a way to get off, but it was too risky. The moment he jumped, the well-loaded wagon might tip over on him.

Jameson spurred back across the stream. Plunging in next to the mules, he grabbed the reins up close and wrapped them around his saddle horn, pulling the nigh leader's head hard against his leg. He half dragged the reluctant animal across the stream. By the time he got him out on dry ground the mule had stopped fighting. But it was rolling its eyes and dancing about in the traces.

Breathing hard, Jameson said, "He needs to be worked till his belly drags—work the foolishness out of him."

The cook was still talking to himself. "Needs a good dose of hickory limb right between the ears, that's what he needs. I thought for sure I was fixin' to get me a bath in that cold water."

Jameson began to see humor in it then. He couldn't help but think that a bath wouldn't have hurt the young cook much. But he had found that some of the best hide-camp cooks never washed anything but their hands. That much Jameson demanded.

He had tried this cook's handiwork in Dodge before he hired him. Now, in the first night camp, he knew he hadn't made a mistake. The cook was a short, thin Texan named Pruitt—"Reb" Pruitt they called him, because he had been in the army of the Confederacy. He was thirty or thereabouts, with a deep browned skin and an irresponsible growth of whiskers that made him look much older. He had come up the trail to Abilene with a couple of thousand Longhorn steers and a salty bunch of Texas cowhands. The way Jameson heard it, he had been in some sort of scrape down there and couldn't afford to return to Texas—not the settled parts, anyway. So he'd been cooking for the hide outfits.

Homesick, he had seized upon the chance to see his native state again, even though it would be only the buffalo plains, a couple of hundred miles from any settlement—or any law.

After Jameson had dropped his tin plate and cup into a washtub with the rest, he called the men together. Old Shad Blankenship stood beside him as he counted them. Ransom King and his small crew stood in the background, listening.

The little Texas cook rattled the tinware as he washed it in the tub, and he grumbled constantly to himself. But he was listening, too.

"I've called you together in a bunch," Jameson said, "because there's a thing or two that needs saying. I want them said right at the start, so no man can claim he didn't hear them.

"There aren't any tenderfeet in this outfit. I chose you on purpose because you all knew something about the hide business. There's not a man among you who hasn't fought

Indians, so I don't think the sight of a feather or the smell of gunpowder is going to run you off. But if you think it might, I want you to say so right now.

"It's one thing to loaf around Dodge and talk brave. It's another to belly down in the grass a thousand miles from home and try to get some Indian before he puts an arrow through you. Anybody who wants to turn back can do it right now, and no hard feelings. But after today, there won't be any turning back. Not for me and not for you. We're going down into Comanche country, and we're not coming back till every wagon is loaded with hides.

"Now then, is there anybody that wants to leave?"

The cook had stopped rattling the tinware. Jameson stared hard at the silent faces, one by one. Not a man moved. He hadn't thought they would.

The utensils began to clatter again.

"The next thing," Jameson went on, "is the Indians. Now we're not going down there to fight. We're going down there after buffalo hides, and that's all. We'll go a long way to get out of a fight if we have to. A battle is too costly, even when you win it. You always lose men and you always lose stock. Wagons aren't any good to us without the men to load and handle them or the stock to pull them.

"We're bound to run into Indians. But there won't be any shooting unless it has to be done. If they act friendly, we'll treat them accordingly. If they're hostile, we'll try to keep out of their way. We'll fight only as a last resort.

"So I don't want any itchy trigger fingers around here. If any man gets us in trouble needlessly . . . I'll shoot him."

He paused a moment, studying the faces as that soaked in. He wasn't sure exactly why, but he cast a glance at King's man Trencher.

"The last thing," Jameson said, "is about the hides.

They're mine. I'm paying you well for skinning and stretching and for handling the mules. But every so often somebody gets a notion he can make more by stealing hides and stashing them away for himself.

"Well, it won't work here. I know that most of you aren't wearing any halo. But I don't care what you've done in the past as long as you shoot straight with me.

"In the first place, there'll be no way for a thief to come back and get the hides. In the second place, I'll be keeping a good tally of the buffalo killed and the hides we stack up. If I ever catch any man trying to steal from me, he'll wish the Comanches had him."

The cook had stopped washing the utensils and sat staring at Jameson, the wash water dripping from his fingers. Only when Jameson turned away did he go back to his job. And he had stopped grumbling to himself.

Jameson walked out to where his bed lay on the ground, still rolled up. He sat down wearily.

A heavy silence hung over the camp a while, an uneasy silence as the men weighed what he had said. He could feel the resentment from some of them. It had been strong talk. But it had needed saying.

Finally he heard the riffle of cards and someone saying, "Who's game for a little poker?"

Jameson leaned back against his bedroll. He had brought a few tents, but they wouldn't be used while the weather was still good. He enjoyed sitting in the open, watching the stars brighten against the darkening sky.

Shad Blankenship stuffed his stinking old pipe with tobacco and lighted it with a burning stick from the Texan's dying cook fire. He flopped down beside Jameson and puffed silently on the pipe. Shad chewed tobacco all day, but at supper he always spat out his quid. He customarily lighted up a pipeful of tobacco and smoked it out before crawling into his blankets.

Shad took an awl from his pocket. With it he carefully began to worry a diagonal hole through the end of a big lead rifle bullet. Jameson watched him with curiosity as the old man finished one and blew the lead shavings out of it, wiping it slick on the leg of his trousers. Shad put that one in his pocket and started on another.

"What's that for?" Jameson asked him finally.

Shad held the second one up and eyed it critically. "That there is a squaller."

"Squaller? Never heard of it."

"Man told me about them last spring. Says they work pretty good."

"What're they for?"

"Maybe I'll show you sometime, before we get off of this trip."

Jameson knew there was no use prodding him. Shad would tell him in his own good time, if he wanted to. Or he might not do it at all, for he could be as contrary as an old bear.

Shad fixed up four or five bullets with the holes in them, then put away the awl. Presently he glanced at Jameson, puffing the pipe.

"Some of them Sunday-school boys didn't much like it, you puttin' it to them so blunt. But I reckon you'd just as well square off with them right at the first. You ain't exactly got a camp meeting here, and they ain't no deacons."

"It's a hard life, Shad, and it takes hard men. Think I can handle them?"

Blankenship drew deeply on his pipe. "You *got* to."

* * *

They had breakfast over with and the mules all hitched to the wagons by daybreak. All of them, that is, except the nigh leader on the chuck wagon, the same knot-head that had come so near to turning the wagon over in the creek. With a lightning-quick flick of his hind foot he dealt the cook a glancing blow to the left leg that sent him spinning.

So angry he couldn't even cuss, the cook tried to get up, fell, tried to reach the mule with a whip, couldn't, and finally grabbed up a handy rock and heaved it at him. It missed.

Jameson ran to the man. He knelt down and carefully felt of the leg.

"Doesn't seem to be broken. Need somebody to drive for you?"

Pruitt got his voice back and exercised it well, showing a wide range of vocabulary. Then he said, "All I need is the loan of your buffalo gun and one cartridge."

Jameson wanted to smile, but he didn't. Seldom had he seen such magnificent anger.

"I'll take that mule out of the traces and throw him back with the loose bunch," Jameson offered.

The cook considered that, then slowly shook his head. "No, leave him where he's at. I'll get a right smart of pleasure popping his rump with a whip every time he wiggles an ear."

Two teamsters finished harnessing the cook's team for him while Jameson helped him up into the wagon seat. Pruitt rubbed his leg tenderly.

"Come noon," he said, "it'll be blacker than the ace of spades."

He picked up his heavy rawhide whip with a certain fondness and fixed a baleful eye on the mule. "Ready, any-time."

They moved out without further incident, and things went well enough until past noon. About two o'clock Shad Blankenship motioned Jameson up to the lead and pointed toward a rise in the prairie. Jameson squinted. It was a long way off, and at first he thought it was a couple of antelope, watching the wagons in their great curiosity.

But Shad Blankenship had the eagle-keen eye of a man who'd been dodging Indians for forty years.

"Cheyenne," Shad said. "They been watching us quite a spell."

"Hunting party?"

The old man grunted and shrugged his shoulders. "More than likely. But then an Injun will hunt for a good many things besides game, you give him half a chance."

Jameson looked back at the wagons, not liking the way they were straggling out. He didn't think anybody else had seen the Indians yet. He reached down for the reassuring feel of the saddle gun under his leg. He had left the heavy Fifty in one of the wagons.

"I'll ride out and have a look," he said. "You better get those wagons pulled up close together. Have them ready to circle in a hurry."

Shad moved to comply, then pulled up short and pointed back to the rise. "You don't need to ride out. They're comin' to us."

Suddenly the two Indians had multiplied to twenty-five or thirty, moving down toward the wagons. Not fast—just an easy walk—easy and determined the way only an Indian could be.

"Powwow, looks like," Jameson said. "But pull those wagons into a circle, just the same."

By now others had seen the Indians, and the word passed back down the line like fire crackling through the cured dry grass. Gun barrels glinted as the men on the wagons prepared themselves. The stock tender quickly shoved the spare horses and mules in close. At Shad's signal the wagons began pulling into a circle, the stock inside.

King spurred his horse into a lope. Flanked by his hulking man Trencher, he pulled to a stop beside Jameson.

"War party?" he asked. Jameson saw no excitement about the man, nor a trace of fear. King was as cold as the waters of the Arkansas in January.

"Hunting party, I imagine. But it could turn into a war party if they like the odds. We can't let them come into camp."

He noticed the way Trencher deliberately drew his saddle gun from its sweat-caked scabbard. No need to check the load. It would always be loaded. Trencher's eyes were hard, eyes that enjoyed looking down the barrel of a rifle at an Indian. Or maybe at anybody.

Jameson said, "Go easy on that rifle."

A sudden defiance flashed into Trencher's gray eyes, as if to say: I'm King's man, not yours.

Jameson spoke evenly. "What I said last night goes for you, too."

King reached across and touched Trencher's arm. "He's the wagon master. Listen to him."

Trencher nodded resentfully. He wasn't a man who liked to be ordered around. Jameson had an idea he would as soon tell King where to head in as he would anybody else. And King more than likely would knock him flat on his back.

The Indians stopped a couple of hundred yards from the wagons. The leader made some show of handing his weapons over to the braves beside him so the white men would know he was coming in unarmed.

He was Cheyenne, all right, a warrior of some years, obviously a leader of standing. He rode in slowly, proud, arrogant, dark eyes touching each man briefly, then somehow picking Jameson as the leader. He was looking at Jameson as he reined up twenty feet short and swung his arm in an arc, pointing northward. He did it twice, and there was no mistaking what he meant by it.

You're over the line, he was saying in effect. You're on forbidden ground. Go north, to your own treaty lands.

Jameson shook his head negatively and pointed south. He swept his hand toward the wagons and again pointed south.

Even at the distance, he could see anger flare in the old warrior's black eyes. The Cheyenne pointed at his own chest, then northward, and said something.

Jameson looked at Shad, puzzled. "He's trying to talk English."

The Indian tried it again. *"So-ja. So-ja."*

Shad spoke. "He said 'soldier.' He's trying to say he's fixin' to fetch the soldiers."

Trencher lifted his rifle. "He ain't bringing no soldiers."

Jameson's pistol leaped into his hand.

"Trencher!" He let the man hear the deadly click of the hammer.

Trencher lowered the rifle. His eyes seared Jameson, and there was murder in them. Then he roughly jerked his horse around and spurred back toward the King wagons.

King said, "Trencher's got a head like a rock."

Without patience, Jameson replied, "You remember the agreement. Either he takes orders from me or he leaves the outfit."

"I'll talk to him, and he'll take orders. I'll need him, later on."

The Indian had sat solemnly watching it all. His eyes had widened when Trencher brought up the rifle, and his hands had lifted on the rawhide reins tied to the lower lip of his paint horse. But he had made no move to run.

To Shad Blankenship, Jameson said, "You speak Cheyenne, and I'm poor at it. Tell him we want to treat with him. Tell him there's no need for the soldiers."

It took Shad four times as many words to get it into Cheyenne, and he made much use of his hands, Indian style. The Indian replied, talking for at least a minute. It took Shad only seconds to put it into English.

"He says we're south of the treaty line in Cheyenne hunting grounds. Says the buffalo is scarce enough without us makin' an extra swath through them. Says get, and get fast."

"Tell him we've got gifts for him. Tell him we're passing through his land without killing any buffalo. Tell him we're going across the Cimarron to the Staked Plains, into the Comanche country."

Shad translated that, and Jameson thought he could almost see a smile on the old Indian's face. The Cheyenne talked for two minutes.

Jameson eased a little. "I thought he might be happier if we promised him gifts."

A spark of laughter came into Shad's pale eyes. "It ain't the gifts made him grin. It's that we're goin' into the Comanche country. Says this is one bunch of buffalo hunters he won't have to worry about again."

Jameson winced. The man who said Indians had no sense of humor didn't know much about Indians. But occasionally their jokes got a little too close to where a man lived.

King guffawed. His sense of humor was as bad as an Indian's, Jameson thought sourly.

"Go get him some tobacco, Shad," Jameson said, "and a little sugar."

Blankenship brought these things and handed them to the Cheyenne. The old warrior received them with dignity. He began talking again. In a moment Shad turned back to Jameson.

"Says this ain't much. Says the white men killed most of the buffalo, and his braves' bellies are empty. Says ain't we got somethin' for his men?"

Impatience stirred in Jameson. They hadn't killed any buffalo yet. How could they furnish meat for all these Indians?

He heard a stamping of hoofs and the squeal of fighting mules. He looked back toward the wagons, straightening as an idea hit him.

"Tell him yes, we've got something for him. Just wait a little."

Quickly Jameson rode to the chuck wagon.

"Pruitt, hand me a piece of rope." He signaled a couple of men to come to him. "Help me unharness this mule, then go get another one out of the loose bunch to take his place."

Reb Pruitt came close to smiling as Jameson put a loop around the cantankerous nigh leader's neck and pulled the harness off.

Jameson led the mule back and handed the rope to the chief. The old Indian made no effort to hide his delight at this tasty gift. His smile didn't even break when the mule stretched its neck, teeth gleaming, and tried to bite a chunk out of the paint horse.

The Cheyenne wished them a good trip over the Cimarron, then led his unwilling prize away.

Jameson signaled the wagons to move out again. And as the chuck wagon came by, a new mule in harness, the little Texas cook said:

"Jameson, I reckon you're a fair to middlin' kind of a Yankee after all."

The Cimarron!

For years Jameson had heard of it. Now he was seeing it for the first time as it quartered its way slowly down across the plains.

It wasn't much to look at here, the banks sandy, almost flat. Dried salt glistened on the ground far beyond the present bounds of the river, showing where it overflowed during its occasional sudden floods. The river itself was two hundred yards wide, maybe closer to three.

"Looks shallow enough to wade," he said as Shad Blankenship pulled his horse up beside him and looked down at the reddish water which moved sluggishly through the sand.

"Don't fool yourself," Shad said. "There's a heap sight more to this river than meets the eye. She's quicksand, all the way."

Jameson knew. He'd heard a lot about this river. Its deep bed was filled with sand. Through it moved a treacherous undercurrent which dragged down the unwary. He had seen other quicksand streams filled with the rotting corpses of buffalo which had been bogged down and had died there, helpless. Men said this one was the worst of all.

"We'd better hunt us a crossing," Jameson said.

While the wagons waited, he and Shad moved up the

river. A few hundred yards away they found an old, well-beaten buffalo trail leading into the water. He looked up at Shad.

"You seldom go wrong, following the buffalo trails."

"Maybe," Shad said. "But there ain't no crossing safe forever. The sand moves around."

Jameson spurred into the water. Within fifteen feet of the bank he could feel the drag of the quicksand on his horse's feet. The bay felt it, too. He moved quickly, nervously, not letting his feet stay in one place long enough to get caught. Jameson rode him all the way across, Shad following.

Gaining the far bank, Jameson reined up to let his horse breathe.

"Not too bad," he said. "We need to pack it some."

On the other side again, they signaled the wagons up to the crossing. Then they went for the extra mules and horses.

"We'll put them back and forth across, six or eight times," Jameson said. "Pack the bottom down so the wagons can get over easier."

By the time the horses and mules had splashed across the muddy river for the last time, the bottom was as solid as Jameson could ever hope for it to be. They unhitched the doubled wagons and took them across one at a time. The chuck wagon was the first to go.

Reb Pruitt popped his whip at the team. The mules hit the water, splashing mud over the Texan as he cursed them on. Only once did the wagon slow down. The whip popped and sang, Pruitt standing up in the bed of the wagon, his lusty voice reaching clearly across the river. In moments the wagon had gained the far bank and pulled up, the dirty water trailing back to the river in deep ruts the iron rims had left. Pruitt pulled up far out of the way and proceeded to make camp.

The next wagon rolled in, and the next, and the next. When half of them were over, the mules were brought back and hitched to the trail wagons.

When all had finished the crossing, Jameson sat his horse on the bank and looked back at the angry boil of red mud which bled slowly down the river from the line where the wagons had gone over.

Shad Blankenship swung down beside him and stretched his weary legs. "Life's full of river crossings of one kind and another, seems like. We've put a tough one behind us, Gage."

Jameson nodded and faced back around. He looked south across the great reach of open, rolling plains. From here on, they would have little to go by. There were no maps, no descriptions other than the vaguest kinds.

Ahead of them now lay the Llano Estacado, the Staked Plains, the great unknown land. Anglos had probed at the edges of this great mystery, but few had penetrated deeply into it. None were known ever to have gone completely across.

Far, far to the south lay the settlements of Texas. To the east strung the great dusty cattle trails over which millions of Longhorns were being trekked northward to the shining new ribbons of steel. To the west huddled the ancient adobe villages of New Mexico.

Yet here in the center was this vast tableland of buffalo grass, stretching on and on, dreaded because it was unknown. Unknown because none had yet had the heart it took to try it. Even the army had left it alone. Most of the maps still left it blank.

A few went so far as to say why. A few said the word that really explained: *Comanche!*

Gage Jameson looked southward into the edge of this great land and felt a chilling awe come over him. He knew he was going where few white men had ever gone. He might see land no white man's eyes had ever seen.

Never before in his life had he felt so alone, had he felt this tingle that moved up his spine as he looked southward into the forbidden land. He had crossed the Cimarron. Somehow he knew that something had changed. Nothing would ever be quite the same again.

{ SIX }

South of the Cimarron, then across the narrow neutral strip. And one day Jameson knew they must be in Texas.

Already he had begun to see a difference. Here the grass did not grow tall and rank as it had in Kansas. He had heard tell of this great turf of short grass stretching down across the Texas plains like a huge rolling carpet. Hardly more than boot-top high, the dry leaves curling like thin wood shavings—buffalo and mesquite grass, with a strength unmatched by the taller feed to the north. And it had a little longer to go before winter too, because this was farther south.

He stepped out of the saddle and poked with the toe of his heavy boot at the cured brown grass. He kneeled and felt of it and looked up keenly at Shad Blankenship.

"Been a good while since it rained, you can tell that. And the summer has been plenty hot down here, I'd bet my boots. But look how much green this stuff still carries at the base."

Shad nodded. "Sure, she's a real buffalo country, Gage. That's why they like to drift south come fall. Grass down here stays strong through the winter—don't dry up and go weak like broomstraw. You mark me, young'un, there's gonna be buffalo enough down here for everybody."

So they moved on south, the iron wheel rims leaving the dry grass broken and crushed to the ground, the trails stretching out behind like endless ribbons. Gage Jameson rode far out in the lead, topping every rise, his eyes searching eagerly for the distant black dots that meant buffalo grazing out across the plains.

But he didn't see them. Always there were buffalo chips, some not long dry. In places great concentrations of the shaggy beasts had grazed the grass down almost to the ground. Everywhere there were the deep corduroy buffalo trails, often dozens of them running parallel, only feet apart.

But now the buffalo had gone.

Three days the wagons lumbered slowly along, the crews breaking camp late and setting up again early in the afternoons, while Gage Jameson, Shad Blankenship and Ransom King scattered out to scour the prairie, to search up and down every creek and header they could find. Each evening the riders followed the wheel tracks into camp and dismounted stiffly from tired horses, their faces telling the other men without need for words. There weren't any buffalo.

Firewood was scarce on these long stretches of grass, even up and down some of the little creeks. Reb Pruitt began using wood only to kindle his fires, then kept them going with dried buffalo chips.

"Some deal," the Texan laughed, raking the fire and adding the fuel that was a staple of the plains. "We come after buffalo hides and all we find is buffalo chips."

But if it was a joke to Pruitt, some weren't taking it that way.

Jameson could feel the restlessness among the crew even before the complaints began. The first he heard was from a man named Tully, one of the three old Miles and Posey men he had been able to hire. It wasn't meant for his ears, but he heard it anyway, from the off side of a wagon.

"The boys was beginnin' to say he was jinxed that last trip out. Maybe they was right. He never found much buffalo then. He ain't findin' any now. There's plenty of sign—we've all seen it. But where's the buffalo?"

Jameson made no reply—didn't even let the men know he had heard. Out in camp this way, they always tended to gripe when things weren't running to suit them. A man had to expect it.

But the fact that they were talking began to rowel him. He rode harder, looked a little farther each time he went out.

Then one day, along with the buffalo sign, he found something else. Horse sign, and a lot fresher. Unshod horses, a couple of them with ragged hoofs badly in need of a trimming. He followed them a way, coming at length to a creek lined with hackberries. There the men had dismounted to drink and water their mounts. The footprints remained plain in the mud. No heels. No straight-edged leather soles. These had been flat-bottomed moccasins, the toes tending inward.

Comanches.

In camp he told Shad Blankenship. Shad just nodded his rusty head.

"Seen it yesterday. Found an antelope they'd put an arrow in and took the guts and a hindquarter from."

"Why didn't you tell me?"

"No use getting the camp all stirred up. Anyhow, you

knowed there was gonna be Injuns before you ever started."
A flicker of humor showed in Shad Blankenship's sharp
old eyes. "I thought we was huntin' buffalo."

Impatience prodded Jameson. Shad's idea of a joke
would be a scalp-hungry Indian catching a bald man.

"I want to know about the Indians, anyway, in case they
decide to start hunting us," Jameson retorted.

It was a hunter's paradise, if the hunter had anything besides buffalo on his mind. Every day Jameson spotted antelope grazing in scattered bunches. At sight of him their
heads would bob up, and off they would go in a flash of
broad white tails. They would run a while, then stop upon
a rise and look back at him, standing in single file like a
string of Indians, poised to run again if he angled their way.

Then there were the lobo wolves, bigger than most dogs,
ranging far out from water, preying on jackrabbits and
prairie hens and anything else that didn't get out of their
way, watching all the while for buffalo or other large animals that might be lamed or mired or somehow at a
disadvantage. Their slashing fangs could bring down a full-
grown buffalo, with their superb teamwork and just a little
luck.

Along the creeks Jameson saw quail, mink, skunk and
raccoon, and on one timbered stream, beaver.

It seemed to him that he had never in his life seen anything quite like it. Here in the brown weeks before the on-
set of winter, these high Texas plains seemed to be reaching
their peak. The grass was cured. The game was fat and
sleek, putting on hair for the cold times not far distant.
The prairie and its teeming life drowsed under an autumn
sun that had lost the sullen scorch of summer but still
possessed a gentle and loving warmth.

A wonderful country, Jameson thought.

But where were the buffalo?

Taking care of the livestock was the biggest problem he had, for here on the Llano Estacado lived the best natural horse thieves ever born. With so many horses and mules, hobbling and sidelining every one of them at night would be a monumental task. Instead, he circled the wagons, putting the horses and mules inside the circle for protection against the rare skill of the Comanche.

A sudden low growl almost at his ear snapped Gage Jameson out of a sound sleep in the middle of the night. He sat up straight, shoving back his blankets and grabbing at the six-shooter under his pillow. A gentle hand touched his shoulder.

"Quiet," Shad Blankenship whispered. "The old dog says there's somethin' out yonder that don't belong."

Blankenship's shaggy black mongrel, almost invisible in the pale moonlight, growled in deep-grained hatred.

Jameson held his breath, listening.

All he could hear was the gentle night breeze with its autumn chill, searching restlessly among the wagons. That, and the dry rumble deep in the throat of the big black dog.

Shad Blankenship sat rigid, listening, too. But Jameson knew Shad couldn't hear anything. Age had sharpened his eyes, but his hearing wasn't what it used to be.

The dog suddenly stiffened, hackles rising. Jameson sank to the ground, looking in the same direction, trying to see some movement against the sky. He waited a long moment, hardly breathing. Then he caught it—the form of a man crouched low, stepping slowly, carefully, almost straight at the wagon under which Jameson lay. He saw the slant of a feather.

Indian. Jameson wondered how many more there were.

The dog's growl went louder. The Indian stopped suddenly, hearing it.

There was not enough light for good aim. Jameson drew back the hammer, aimed by instinct, and squeezed the trigger.

With the sudden crash of the gun, mules and horses jumped, hoofs clumping excitedly on the thick turf of grass. Men burst out of their blankets, yelling. Other guns sounded, the racket echoing off into the night as men fired at shadows and at the wind whispering through the grass.

After a time all went silent again. Men settled down to watchful waiting. Some few even crawled back into blankets and went to sleep again. But most were awake for good, talking nervously in low voices if they talked at all.

Shad Blankenship was as calm as a stock pond on a still day. He stretched out on his blanket, unworried. "I reckon they got as big a scare as we did. They won't be nosing around any more tonight."

"Wonder how many there were?" Jameson mused. "I only saw the one."

"Ain't any tellin'. Maybe just a lone buck wantin' to steal him a horse and make a good showing back in camp. Or maybe a whole passel of them hoping to catch us asleep and leave us afoot. What difference does it make now?"

"Lucky thing that dog of yours smelled them coming."

Blankenship snorted. "Luck, is it? You didn't think I kept that shaggy old monster around for his looks, did you? Wasn't for him, they'd have laid me out in the grass a long time ago."

Jameson grinned, the tension leaving him. "Well, from now on I don't care if he looks like Lucifer, just so he keeps on hating Indians."

Best they could make out next morning was that four,

maybe five Indians had attempted the raid on the stock. Spots of red in the dry grass proved that Jameson had at least winged a would-be horse thief.

Ransom King came out to look over the sign.

"From now on," Jameson told him, "we'll keep two men on guard at all times, in one-hour shifts. With the stock inside the circle, and that black dog around, we shouldn't have any trouble."

King frowned. "Maybe all the trouble won't be from the Indians."

Jameson looked sharply at him. "What's that supposed to mean?"

"There's a lot of loose talk drifting around the camp. They're saying, some of them, that you're not ever going to find any buffalo. They're saying they don't mind Indian risk when they're skinning hides and making money. But they're not getting any hides."

With a nettle of anger Jameson said, "What do *you* think, King?"

King smiled quickly. "If I didn't believe in you, I wouldn't have joined you with my wagons."

Sometime that night someone shook Jameson's shoulder. He sat up quickly, reaching for the pistol, thinking the Indians were back. But it was a hide handler named Ludlow, a silent, morose, black-bearded man who never mixed with the others, always stayed to himself.

"I think some of the boys has shucked the harness, Jameson," he said. "Tully is gone. I don't know how many of the others."

Jameson stood up angrily, throwing aside the blankets.

"Tully had guard duty just before me," Ludlow said. "He was supposed to wake me up when it come time to relieve him. He never did."

"There was another man on guard. Where is he?"

"One of Tully's buddies. He's gone, too."

Jameson stomped out into the wagon circle. "Everybody up!"

As the men gathered in the darkness he mentally counted them off. Three gone. Tully and the other two old Miles and Posey hands.

It was too dark to check the livestock, but Jameson knew within reason that they had taken a horse apiece. Saddles too, and he had few of those. He saw his own bay hunting horse standing nearby and felt relief that they hadn't gotten him.

The rest of the men knew now what had happened. He could not tell by their faces whether they were considering trying the same.

Shad Blankenship watched Jameson closely as the anger played in his face. "Nothin' you can do about it now, Gage. They're gone.

Jameson said in a brittle voice, "We're *going* to do something. If we don't, some of the rest may pull the same stunt."

He crawled back between his blankets, but he didn't sleep any more. At the first paling of the night sky he was up and punched Shad awake.

"Roll out, Shad. I may need those eyes of yours."

The cook got up, too. Yawning and scratching and talking incessantly, Pruitt soon had coffee boiling for them, and a bait of antelope meat was ready by the time the two saddled their horses. Jameson impatiently wolfed his down, swung into the saddle and spurred out.

Shad, a slow eater, caught up to him after a while. Jameson was moving into a long-reaching trot, sometimes in a lope, his grim eyes following horse tracks in the grass. The thick turf kept the hoofs from cutting into the ground much, but the brittle grass, broken underfoot, made a trail a man could read.

All morning they rode, slowing down to save the horses when it became clear that they weren't going to make a fast catch. Sometime past noon Jameson began to regret his haste in eating breakfast. Hunger commenced to tug at him. The long ride over the unchanging prairie had drained the anger from him, leaving only a stolid determination. He would catch those men if he had to ride all the way back to the Cimarron.

Presently Shad reached back into his saddlebags and brought out a little bundle done up in oilskin. "Cold biscuits and meat," he said. "Good thing I come. You'd have starved flat to death."

Jameson grinned then, relaxing from the grimness that had held him.

They stopped at a little stream and watered and rested the horses. Impatience prickled Jameson, but judgment told him to wait. Though he could push himself till he dropped, he couldn't ever afford to overpush the horses. He sat and drummed his nervous fingers on his boots, while Shad Blankenship lay so relaxed that Jameson couldn't tell whether he was napping or not.

Presently they were on the go again, pushing as hard as they dared. Along late in the afternoon, Jameson reined up and squinted at something far ahead.

"What does that look like to you, Shad?"

Shad stared, his eyes narrowed against the sun, the reddish brows knitted up close. "It's them. They're restin' by that creek yonder."

Jameson waited a moment before he moved out, looking for a way to ride in close without being seen. He reined the bay around, riding back the way they had come until he passed down under a rise and well out of sight. Then he angled westward, crossing the creek and coming up in cover of underbrush.

Near the quarry, the two men reined in to study the situation closer.

"Asleep, I think," Shad whispered. "All three of them. Must've rode half the night and all day. Horses about give out, I reckon, and the men, too. If we was Comanches we could get us three juicy new scalps."

"Not looking for scalps, Shad. I just aim to get them horses back."

Dismounting, they tied their own horses. Saddle guns in hand, they eased forward. The creek was shallow, the water not reaching quite to the tops of Jameson's black boots as they waded across. The leather was so heavily greased that little of it would seep through.

The two were within twenty yards of the sleeping men when one of the horses suddenly raised its head and whinnied. Tully jerked erect, blinking and feeling desperately for the rifle that lay beside him.

"Don't touch it," Jameson said evenly. "Just stand up there and leave it alone. The rest of you the same."

The other two were awake now. One glared at the other. "Thought you was gonna keep watch."

"Shut up," Tully barked impatiently at them. Then to Jameson he said sullenly, "All right, so you caught up with us. Now I guess you're taking us back."

"No," Jameson said, "I don't want you back. I don't want to have to watch you all the time we're out."

"Then what did you trail us for?"

"Those horses. They're mine."

The runaways stiffened. Tully licked his dry lips. His

voice lifted. "Look, Jameson, this is the middle of Comanche country. You wouldn't set a man afoot out here, would you?"

"You'll have your guns. And you're halfway to the Cimarron already. Walk all night and hide all day. You can be in Dodge in a couple of weeks if you get high behind."

Tully's eyes were frightened. He looked down at his rifle on the ground, then up at Jameson, but he didn't dare make the try.

"Pick up their guns, Shad," Jameson said. "We'll carry them with us a ways, then drop them off."

The men looked around them at these endless plains which reached on into infinity. They were awesome enough to a man on horseback, but they were terrifying to a man afoot. Jameson could see dread settle over the runaways like a black shroud.

A hollowness was in Tully's voice. His eyes pleaded. "Jameson, this is the worst thing you could do to a man."

"Not quite," Jameson replied flatly, without pity. "Hanging's rougher. That's what horse thieves generally get."

He waited until Shad brought up their horses. Mounting, he started to push the three runaways' mounts southward again. Then he stopped just long enough to untie canteens and sacks of supplies from behind two saddles and let them drop to the ground. He gave them this gesture of mercy, and this one only.

After they had ridden a while, pushing the three horses in front of them, Jameson dropped the guns to the ground and looked back. The three men trailed them at a walk, a far piece behind. They wouldn't get to the rifles in time to use them.

Shad Blankenship grinned. "I been worried all day

what you was gonna do when you caught up to them. I was afraid this morning you was fixin' to shoot all three."

"This morning," Jameson said flatly, "I was mad enough to."

It was well past midnight by the stars when Jameson's instinct led him to the camp, and he saw the red glow of campfire coals, kept barely alive by the succession of guards. They turned the horses loose. Then, before he did anything else, Jameson walked around the camp, grimly counting the men rolled up in their blankets.

Ransom King sat at the remains of the campfire, drinking black coffee which Pruitt kept on the coals all night for the guards. He didn't get up as Jameson and Shad approached wearily. He sat there, watching.

Jameson poured himself a cup of coffee, and Shad followed suit. Jameson sat on his heels, his eyes touching Ransom King. King silently studied him a while before he brought out the question. The way he said it, it wasn't really a question at all.

"You fetched back the horses but no men."

"They won't be coming back."

King's eyebrows arched, and in the firelight his gaze dropped to Jameson's gun.

Jameson said, "I didn't shoot them. But by the time they walk all the way back to Dodge, they may wish I had."

King poured the dregs of coffee out into the grass, pushed to his feet and stood there, some dark humor seeming to stir him.

"You've got a soft streak in you, Jameson. *I'd* have shot them."

He walked off into the darkness, toward his wagon.

Shad Blankenship watched him disappear, then commented, "He would have, too. He's got it in his eyes."

Jameson nodded. He remembered the fury in King's eyes that night the man had rescued him in the Dodge saloon. He knew King could catch afire as easily as he could break into wild laughter.

Jameson finished his coffee, letting it drive out the chill the night air had settled upon him. Then he crawled into his own blankets. But he didn't sleep. He lay awake, listening, watching.

Sometime up in the morning Shad Blankenship's snoring broke off. He lay quiet a little, then raised up on one elbow.

"You ain't ever been asleep, have you?" he said, frowning.

Jameson shook his head. Weariness was stone-heavy on him, but worry was heavier.

There was a little admiration in the old man's voice, and admiration didn't come lightly to Shad Blankenship. "Then sleep. Nobody is fixin' to slip away this far up in the mornin'. Anyhow, I'll watch. It don't take much sleep for an old man."

Jameson hadn't expected the men to like the way he had set the runaways afoot. He wasn't much surprised, then, when at breakfast he felt the hostile eyes of some of the crew upon him. They didn't say anything. They didn't have to. But he could smell revolt in the air, just as he could smell a faint hint of winter in the dawn wind.

He ate in silence, counting those men he felt might side with him, and the count didn't come to much. Only two men were left with whom he had ever worked—Shad Blankenship and Messick.

Looking at Reb Pruitt, he mentally gave him a question mark. This small, thin man was a good cook, and Jameson had an idea he was a scrapper from way back yonder in spite of his flapping jaw. But Jameson was a Yankee, and so was the rest of the crew. He didn't think Pruitt was going to get worked up much over any kind of a fight between Yankees. More likely he would sit on his hands and grin as he watched it.

He glanced at the hide handler Ludlow, that brooding, heavy-bearded man who sat to himself now as he ate. He made friends with no man, and he never spoke except when it was necessary to the work.

Jameson shook his head. No, he didn't think Ludlow would help him, either. There would be no one except Shad Blankenship and Messick. And maybe Ransom King. Maybe. . . .

One thing was certain, Jameson couldn't afford to get out of sight of the camp. It was his conviction that most of the crew—maybe all of it—would appropriate horses and mules and head north the minute he was gone over the hill.

"Shad," he said, "I've been trying to keep north, so we wouldn't have so far to go if we were forced to run for it. But now I'm pointing them south, across the Canadian. We'll find buffalo if we have to drive all the way to the Rio Grande."

Jameson allowed himself to ride as far ahead as he could without letting the wagons drop back out of his sight. They crossed over the sandy Canadian, fighting its treacherous undercurrent much as they had done at the Cimarron. Then they pushed on south, angling a little westward.

Long days came and went, and long nights in which Jameson slept little or not at all, trusting hardly anyone any more. Bone-weariness and the lack of sleep sank his eyes back deep beneath his brows, put an aching slump in his shoulders. But he kept on riding, kept on watching the men, kept on looking for buffalo.

In camp at evening the men gathered silently around a poker game that started as soon as supper was over and lasted far into the night. Almost invariably the winner was the man who promoted the game, a short, fat little skinner named Blair Farley, a man with a loud, quarrelsome voice and thick, stubby fingers which were amazingly efficient with a deck of cards. His greedy eyes seemed able to read a man's thoughts. Already his pocket was stuffed with IOUs against half the wages the men might expect to earn on this expedition—if they found buffalo.

This too was making the crew surly, knowing that much of their pay already was gone. It added to the charge of tension that slowly built up in the camp.

Sometimes even Shad Blankenship's eyes turned longingly to that poker game.

Then one day about noon Jameson heard a shout and blinked quickly at a movement atop a promontory half a mile southward. Shad Blankenship had ridden out on a scout. Now he came spurring his dun horse, the dust rising behind him.

One thought raced to Jameson's mind. Comanches. He reached down for his saddle gun and at the same time yelled to the men on the wagons.

"Look sharp. It may be trouble."

But it wasn't trouble. Shad eased up on the speed as he loped in. He drew rein and stopped the heaving horse just in front of Jameson. A wide grin cut across his dusty, red-bearded face.

"We've found them, Gage," he said excitedly, loudly enough for the men to hear him. "They're over that hill yonder and down the valley, a million of them. We've found the buffalo!"

{ SEVEN }

The weariness seemed to lift from Jameson's wide shoulders and the burning tiredness from his blue eyes as he stepped stiffly off his horse atop the hill. He gazed down the creek with its scattering of big cottonwoods, its banks lined with smaller timber. His look moved on out across the level prairie where not a mesquite or sagebrush blocked the view. His pulse quickened.

There they were, the buffalo, scattered in small grazing bunches as uncountable as the stars in a crisp night sky, fly-specks out yonder as far as a man could see. They brought up bittersweet memories of old days on the Republican and the Arkansas, times that had vanished with the high-plains wind.

There were bunches of cows, many of them trailed by big stocky, glossy calves, blackish brown now after shedding the reddish hair of their first months. Some calves grazed alone, already weaned. In among the cows he could see young spike bulls, not old enough yet to challenge the big bulls for mastery, not ready to take their place as sires. The older bulls grazed separately now, in little groups of three or four to as many as twenty. Breeding season was over.

Far out yonder amid the specks of black, Jameson saw a band of antelope, and a big gray timber wolf sneaking along looking for the crippled or sick, the buffalo warily eyeing him, an occasional bull tossing his head threateningly.

Jameson watched a pair of old bulls in a buffalo wallow, rolling in the dust, digging in with their horns and throwing dirt high over their backs with their massive heads, trying to drive away the buffalo gnats.

Presently the wagons came. Men walked to the top of the hill to gaze out upon the sight. The threat of rebellion had disappeared like a wisp of smoke.

No one shouted. No one jumped up and down. Men stared silently or swore softly to themselves. They stood there a long time as if they couldn't see enough of it, as if they had never seen buffalo before. Even the somber Ludlow, who had never shown any emotion except an everlasting contempt for his fellow man, softened and smiled a little, squatting on the grass and unconsciously whetting a skinning knife against the black leather tops of his high boots.

"You men just stay here and look a while," Jameson said. "Shad and I are going to hunt a good place to make camp."

The creek flowed in a northerly direction, emptying into the Canadian somewhere above. The two men rode southward toward the head of it. Bands of buffalo grunted and scattered away from water. The animals would run off a way, then stop and turn to look back with their tiny weak eyes, water dripping from the long stringy beards that sometimes almost dragged the ground.

"Ain't got much fear for a man on horseback, have they?" Shad commented. "Ain't been choused much— maybe none at all."

Jameson nodded in satisfaction. "That's a hopeful sign. Means the Indians haven't been hunting around here."

Jameson picked a flat spot high up enough from the creek bed so that a sudden rise of floodwater wasn't likely to wash away the camp, yet close enough so that water-carrying would not become burdensome. A few big cottonwoods there would spread shade over the men working in camp during the heat of the autumn afternoons. Smaller timber would provide fuel for the fires and poles for the rough, semipermanent corrals that would take the place of the wagon circle in protecting the stock at night.

Jameson saw more buffalo grazing upwind along the creek.

"Shad," he said, "you go bring the wagons, I'll try to get us some fresh meat."

He slipped the saddle gun out of the scabbard, circled around downwind of the buffalo and came up behind them. When he was close enough, he let them see him. They started down the creek toward the camp site, shuffling along in a trot. He picked out a nice fat cow which either hadn't had a calf this year or had already weaned it so she could store up flesh to carry the next calf already conceived within her. He let her pass on through the camp site so there wouldn't be any lingering smell from the butchering.

When she was about right, he spurred in and fired at her from the saddle, aiming at her lungs. The second shot slowed her, and the third brought her to the ground. He stepped down from the horse, dropped the reins and moved up. Taking care that she didn't thrash her head and catch him on those sharp curved horns, he stepped in with his thick-bladed ripping knife and cut her throat to bleed her and lessen the risk of spoiling the meat.

Soon the wagons arrived. The crew began setting up

camp, unloading gear, emptying several wagons which would be used to haul fresh green hides back to camp as the kill got under way.

Messick and another skinner set to work on the cow Jameson had killed. They slit through the jawbone first and took out the tongue. They ripped the hide up the belly and skinned out the legs past the knee. With their curved skinning knives they began to lay the hide back away from the flesh, working from the belly downward toward the back bone on one side, then straining together as they turned the heavy carcass over to skin out the other. Normally they would hitch a pair of mules to peel the hide off once they got it started. But this kill was for meat, and the hide under the carcass would help to keep it clean.

Jameson put the other men to work chopping posts and poles for corrals and digging holes to set the posts in.

With a purpose before him now, something there that he could see, he no longer felt his weariness. Having something to work for gave him new wind and new will. He walked back and forth through camp a hundred times, making plans, directing work, pitching in where it wasn't going fast enough. When it looked as if the corral job was moving along satisfactorily, he walked out to the flat area downwind of camp, the hide-drying and stretching ground. It had to be cleared of tree limbs, dead stumps and other obstructions.

By dark the fence posts were up. The poles hadn't been laid between them, and there wasn't time now before night. But long ropes tied to the posts made a handy enough substitute for one night. Maybe tomorrow. . . .

He flopped down across his bedroll, savoring the good dry smell of burning wood and thinking he would rest a while before supper.

When he awoke the sun was coming up red on the cloudless eastern horizon. Someone, Shad of course, had spread blankets over him to protect him from the night chill. He pushed them back and grinned sheepishly at the old man who sat cross-legged, studying him with amusement in the glow of dawn light.

"Thanks, Shad."

Shad made a "forget it" motion with his big old freckled hand. "You look a heap sight better this mornin'. Got them black satchels out from under your eyes for a change. Think you're ready to shoot some buffalo?"

"That's what we came for."

The hump steak from the fat buffalo cow, he thought, was the finest he'd ever sunk a tooth in.

Ransom King walked over and sat down beside him as he finished breakfast. King was already shaved. He wore clean clothes, although they were rumpled from the trip.

"I'm ready to do some shooting this morning, Jameson, if you are."

Jameson nodded. "We'd better pick our hunting grounds so we won't be shooting at each other. Shad and I will go south this morning. Why don't you work north, down the creek?" He looked at King's rifle and saw that it was a Sharps like his own.

"We'd better learn the sound of each other's guns," Jameson said. "Maybe it'll be important someday, if we hear guns that don't belong to us."

King said, "Good idea. I'll do my own shooting, as far as I can. If my skinners get to catching up with me too fast Trencher can help me bring down a few."

They waited around camp, helping finish preparations until Jameson's big pocket watch showed it to be nine o'clock. There was plenty to do.

"Let's get started, Shad," Jameson said finally. "They ought to have grazed by now."

With bellies full of the strong grass and the morning sun getting warm, the buffalo would settle down, stop moving around. Listless then, they were less likely to scare away at the roar of the big guns.

Jameson slipped on his coat with the deep pockets that held extra shells. He fastened the cartridge belt around his waist, every one of the thirty-two loops holding a loaded cartridge. Shad Blankenship did the same.

"Never have taken a good look at that gun of yours, Shad," Jameson said. Shad handed it to him. It was a Sharps Forty-five, a fourteen-pounder with a thick octagonal barrel that could stand the heat of a lot of firing. Jameson rubbed his hands over its smooth finish and read the two words imprinted deeply on the left-hand side of the breech, *Patented 1869*.

"Used to carry a Fifty, didn't you?"

Shad grunted. "Used to be young, too. But for a man of my age, this fourteen pounds turns to forty soon enough. I just got to get a mite closer sometimes, that's all."

The wagons followed them, drawn by four mules apiece. Two mules could do it, but a man never could tell what might be over that next hill in strange country. Four mules in a run could pull a heap faster than two.

In half an hour the two horsemen rode partway up an eminence, far enough so that they could easily see over it. A couple of hundred buffalo were scattered under the brow of the hill, some still grazing a little, most of them full and resting, already chewing cuds, lying with noses to the wind.

"Fair chance of a good stand down there for both of us," Jameson said, and the old man nodded.

Jameson didn't need to wet his finger and stick it up to get the drift of the breeze. It was out of the northwest and had been all morning. They rode back down from the point and eased a little farther south, so the breeze blew from the buffalo to them.

The skinners crawled out of the wagons and squatted in the grass, patiently sharpening their ripping and skinning knives on the steel that each man carried on his belt. One man drank water from a five-gallon keg that was wrapped in a piece of old woolen blanket, wet to keep it cool. Here the men would wait, out of the way, until the shooting was done.

Blair Farley was already shuffling his cards, trying to promote a time-passing game.

There was nothing to tie the horses to, but nothing was needed. They had been trained to stand where the reins were dropped. Jameson and Shad left them and walked directly up the side of the little hill. Pausing a moment at the top to look the situation over, they started down again on the other side, walking carefully, directly at the buffalo.

It was a peculiarity of the buffalo that he paid little attention to a man afoot, especially if the man walked straight at him. Jameson thought it was probably because the buffalo could detect little motion that way, his eyes being weak and sometimes half grown over with thick hair. Many times Jameson had walked up within rock-throwing distance of buffalo before they began to shy away. On horseback he could never have approached so close.

Two hundred yards from the buffalo, Shad said quietly, "About far enough. Too close the first time and they're sure liable to scatter."

Carefully, making as little motion as possible, Jameson sat down, taking off his cartridge belt and laying it on the dry grass before him where he could easily reach it. He removed the coat and laid it out where he could get to the extra cartridges in the pockets and keep the belt loops full. He laid down his canteen, which he might have to use to cool the barrel.

He looked at Shad, seated six feet from him so they wouldn't be in each other's way. His eyes asked, "Ready?" and Shad nodded.

There was usually a leader in any bunch. If this leader moved away, the others would follow him. Without him, the buffalo generally stood around in confusion. There never was any sure way to know which one the leader was. For that, a man had to depend on instinct.

A big cow was looking around suspiciously, her nose in the air, testing the breeze. Jameson eased down to a prone position, setting up the rest stick over which to lay the heavy barrel of the Big Fifty. He studied the breeze, thought he knew how much to allow for it. He shoved the cartridge into the breech, took long, deliberate aim, held his breath and squeezed the trigger.

The deep roar was enough to set a man's ears to ringing. The cow jerked violently and began backing up, slinging her head. He had missed the target, he knew. He had shattered her jaw. A few more seconds of this, throwing the blood around that way, and she would stampede the whole bunch.

At the heavy boom of the gun, the other buffalo shied. Those which had been lying down jumped up. But they didn't run. They stood in confusion, not knowing what was happening, not seeing any enemy.

Jameson aimed and fired again, correcting his windage. The puff of dust just behind the cow's shoulder was right where he had tried to hit her. She squatted back, hind legs going limp. She swung her head from side to side, then lay over heavily, kicked a time or two and sank slowly into death, her little black eyes staring into nothingness.

Shad Blankenship squeezed off a shot. Another buffalo staggered a step, then fell.

Jameson looked up and saw the white smoke of the gunpowder rising, drifting off into the gentle wind. On a still day a man could nearly suffocate himself in smoke with a Sharps. And no joke about it, he could deafen himself eventually, exposing his ears to the roar of the big guns year in and year out.

They settled down to shooting them, taking their time to keep from overheating the guns, yet wasting no time, either. Nearly every shot bagged a buffalo, although sometimes it took an extra bullet or two to dispatch one. Instead of running, the other buffalo would look on in bewilderment. After the first few shots, they stopped shying from the roar of the guns. A few even lay back down, losing interest in the strange noise and going back to chewing their cuds.

"Good thing we got a little breeze," Shad said quietly. "Keeps them from gettin' the blood smell."

At length an old cow began to move away, and it looked for a moment as if the rest of the bunch would follow, breaking up the stand. Jameson drew a bead, allowing more windage for the long shot because she was at least four hundred yards away. The first shot stopped her momentarily, sent her squatting. But she got up again and began to move once more, dragging a little.

Jameson thought the stand was lost. Then she stopped and turned sideways, looking back as if to find her hidden assailant. Shad's rifle roared at the broad target. The dust puff from the brown hair was just where it should have been. She went down and stayed down.

Jameson looked at the old man in admiration. "Did you ever miss a shot in your life?"

"Once. Didn't eat for four days, either."

After a while, lying still in the sun, Jameson could feel sweat work from under his hat and trickle slowly down his dusty face. It burned his eyes. When he rubbed them he got gunpowder in them from his hands, and that made it worse. His shoulder ached from the recoil from the big rifle.

He could feel the intense heat from his heavy gun barrel and knew it needed to cool anyway. Opening the breechblock, he picked up the canteen and poured water down the muzzle, jerking his hand away from the scalding steam. When the barrel had cooled some, he pushed the corner of a greased patch into the eyelet of his wiping stick. He ran it into the barrel and worked it up and down to break loose the accumulation of burned powder.

He laid the rifle down to let it cool off. Already he could count some thirty buffalo lying dead or dying on the ground. Shad Blankenship was still shooting, waiting as long as two minutes sometimes between shots. He wasted precious little powder.

It had always been a puzzle to Jameson why the buffalo would stand and take this murderous fire instead of stampeding away. They nosed curiously at the fallen, and now and then a cow hooked at one of the dead. Each time one acted as if it had begun to get the scent of blood, Shad or Jameson brought it down.

For two hours the stand held up, the band of buffalo slowly diminishing. At last the surviving animals commenced to get the blood scent, and then they broke into a run.

"Want to follow them up, Gage?" Shad asked. "They'll settle down in a little while."

Jameson shook his head. "I reckon we've done enough killing for now."

He stood up and walked out among the fallen buffalo. He flinched at the sight of the dead, glassy eyes, the bloody mouths and noses that resulted from the lung shots. Here and there a buffalo still breathed, still kicked. Those Shad and Jameson saw, they finished with their pistols.

Flies already were buzzing around the dead, especially those shot earliest, where the blood had crusted and turned black.

Shad Blankenship shook his head. "A bloody business, Gage. Man has to get himself a hard stomach to stay in it, and there's few that really enjoy it."

"I never have, Shad. In a way, it doesn't hardly seem right. God put them here, and I expect He had a good reason. Now we're killing them off as fast as we can skin them."

Shad shrugged. "It's a business. About the only one left any more. A man didn't do this, he'd just about starve to death. If we don't shoot them, somebody else will. It's gonna be done, regardless."

Jameson nodded. "It's *got* to be done. It's a bloody job, but I don't reckon it's any worse than killing cattle in a slaughterhouse, except for the waste. And there's not much we can do about the waste. It's too far to market for the meat.

"And as long as there's buffalo, there'll never be any settlement. They feed the Indian and keep him fighting. There's no room for the farmer where the buffalo graze. There's no room for the cowman, either. It's a question of which we're going to have, the buffalo or the settler. When you look at it that way, it's not much of a question, is it?"

They signaled the skinners, who brought up the wagons. Each skinner moved along, testing the sharp blade of his knife across the rump of a fallen cow. If she quivered in reflex, she wasn't quite dead and he moved on to another. If there was no movement, he set right in to skinning.

Shad and Jameson climbed to the top of the hill and sat down there to watch the operation, and to keep an eye out for Indians that might have been drawn by the gunfire.

Shad bit himself a fresh chew of tobacco.

"Funny thing, ain't it? We talk all the time about civilization, and how do we get it? By killin', that's how. I first come out here, it was the beaver. We trapped beaver so the high-toned boys back East could sport them a beaver hat.

"Of course we weren't lookin' ahead. All we bothered about was makin' money. But what was really happening, we was gettin' to know the country. We was opening it up for them that was to come later. When the beaver trade folded, some of us started scouting for immigrant trains and surveyors and one thing and another, and we was shootin' game to feed them. Then the hide trade started, and we commenced to killin' the buffalo.

"And all the time we was killin' the Injuns, too. Killin' so we could have civilization. Some way to get it. Like a marshal I seen once, come to settle down a wild town. Slams his pistol down on the bar and he says, 'We're gonna have peace around here if I have to kill every one of you to get it.'"

Shad shook his rusty head. "And what happens to us old hands then, when civilization does come? We don't fit in. We brung it, but they got no place for us. We wind up in jail, or beggin', or livin' off the county. I seen many of them old mountain men thataway, just drunk theirselves

to death. They'd destroyed the only kind of life they could
fit in."

Jameson put his hand on Shad's patched knee. "There'll
always be a place for you, Shad, as long as I'm around."

Shad looked him straight in the eyes and said, "How do
you know there'll even be a place for *you*, Gage?"

{ EIGHT }

The autumn weeks drifted by, the skies of an evening taking on that deep horizon-line purple that meant winter was nearly here. The hair on the buffalo became thicker now. Before long there would be good robe hides that fetched an extra price.

The hunting was all a man could want. Always the drying area was covered with a patchwork of hides, sometimes stretching two hundred yards along the creek. Each day the wagons came in off the hunting grounds loaded with fresh hides green and heavy, sticky with blood and undried flesh. The handlers pitched them down and spread them out upon the ground, dusting them with poison to keep the bugs away. Then they would stretch them on the grass with the hair side down, securing them by pounding pegs down through tiny holes slit in the edge. Here the hides would stay for three or four days, sometimes five or six now that the autumn's daytime heat had largely waned. When well dried, they would be turned over, hair side up. Finally cured, these flint hides would be loaded upon one of the wagons and lashed down, their space on the drying ground given up to fresh hides just coming in.

"Doing mighty well," Jameson said to Shad Blankenship

late one afternoon, watching the handlers peg out forty green hides from that day's shooting. "Never saw hunting grounds stand up any better."

"Me, neither," Shad agreed. "Only moved camp twice, and then just a little ways up the creek so we wouldn't have so far to hunt and pack hides. Wouldn't be surprised if we're in Dodge before Christmas."

"You getting ready to go back, Shad?"

Shad pondered a moment, then darkly shook his head. "No, to tell the truth, I ain't. You know what always happens to me when I get to town. This is where I belong at. Even if it *is* a messy job, and a man gits sick of the killin', sometimes I wish I never had to go back. Wish all this would never change."

He turned to Jameson, melancholy in his pale eyes. "What is it gets into a man, Gage? Even with all the blood and sweat and dirt, this is a heap sight better than being in town, drinkin' that swill they sell for whisky, chokin' to death on tobacco smoke while you're losing everything you own in a crooked poker game. What is it gets into a man and sends him runnin' back to town like an ox to the slaughter, ready to take his whippin' again? Why is it a man don't ever have no better sense?"

Jameson shrugged. He didn't have an answer to that. He needed one himself.

Every time he left town, he fully intended to stay out until it was absolutely necessary that he return, and then to stay only long enough to pick up new supplies. But good intentions weren't enough. Now, already, he was beginning to get that restless itch, to start picturing Dodge in glowing colors. He didn't want it to be that way. He wished he could change it. But there it was.

If only he had him something to tie to. . . .

Shad nudged him. "Yonder comes Ransom King and his wagon."

Jameson watched, nodding. "A good hunter, Shad. He's a crack shot. He can put a bullet in a buffalo about as handy as anybody I ever saw."

"Yeah, and seems to enjoy it, too. Ever watch him when he's got a stand? Shoots for all he's worth. Somethin' takes hold of him, and he loses that nice smile. Worries me sometimes he'll burn up his gun barrel. And when the buffalo run, he jumps on his horse and takes out after them. Strings them out sometimes for a mile or two. Like a kid on a picnic."

Jameson commented, "Gets a lot of buffalo."

"And makes the rest of them so wild you can't get in a mile of them on horseback."

King rode in beside his skinners' wagon and dismounted, a little stiff from the ride. He watched distastefully as they pitched the day's green hides onto the ground. A big drop of half-congealed blood splashed off onto the leg of his trousers.

"Dammit," he shouted in sudden anger, "watch what you're doing."

Quickly he slapped at the blood with his hands, trying to get it off. Then he rubbed his hands together, scowling darkly at the smear of drying blood on them.

Shad said quietly, "Some of the polish is comin' off now, and the brass is beginning to show."

Even in camp Ransom King managed to stand a head taller than anyone else in appearance. He was the only man who shaved every day without fail. Even Jameson didn't try to do that. Often Jameson and Shad threw in when the work was heavy, skinning hides or moving them around. But King always found someone else to handle the dirtier details, avoiding the stain that stamped other men with the brand of their trade.

Seeing Jameson and Blankenship, he moved toward them, leading his horse. He had his laughing days and his black days. This was a black one. There was no dash or fun about him. He still scowled. He wiped the dust and sweat from his face with a clean handkerchief.

"Damn this business anyway."

In a light voice, trying to ease King's dark mood, Jameson remarked, "I always thought you liked the hide business. The excitement and shooting . . . selling your hides and counting your money."

King shoved the handkerchief back into his pocket. His mouth twisted as he watched his men spreading out the hides. "The shooting, sure. I like the feel of a gun in my hand. Always did. Like the feel of power it gives you. But the rest of it . . ."

His eyes narrowed, and he cursed under his breath. "My stomach turns over every time I get the grease and blood of them on me. And the smell, Jameson, it sticks to a man like death. Get so I hate the sight of the lousy monsters. I'll be glad when the last one is dead and rotted."

Jameson looked at him questioningly. "For a man who hates the business, you've done mighty well at it."

"The money, Jameson, the money. You'd be surprised what-all I can stand if there's enough money in it."

There hadn't been any trouble during these weeks, nothing a man could rightly call trouble. Once a handful of Indians had tried to work up to the corral in the dead of night and get off with some horses and mules. But Shad's old black dog stopped that, just as he had done before.

The only other trouble was King's man, Trencher.

He had been busy enough at first so that he wasn't much

bother to anyone. But later, as camp routine got old, he started getting restless. He began sitting in on Blair Farley's poker games and losing steadily. His IOUs to Farley were mounting up. Trencher sulked around, his eyes narrowed and mean, looking for a chance to stumble over someone's feet.

One night Shad Blankenship was busy tarring a wagon hub and spat a stream of tobacco juice without much attention to where it went. Part of it splashed on Trencher's boots, already thoroughly stained by mud and blood and buffalo grease. Roughly Trencher grabbed the old man's thin shoulder and spun him around. He wrapped his fingers in Shad's short beard and jerked Shad's face up close to his own, so hard that tears came to Shad's eyes.

Jameson saw it from afar and came running. But he didn't need to. Shad raised his boot and stomped down hard on Trencher's instep. Then his knee came up sharply, and Trencher doubled over in agony. Shad slapped him across the face with the tarbrush, leaving a heavy black smear. He planted the sole of his boot firmly on Trencher's hip pocket and roughly sent him sprawling under the feet of a mule.

Startled, the mule began to jump and kick. Trencher scrambled away on hands and knees, haste making him look ridiculous.

Shad's black dog piled in on him to make it worse, his long teeth seeking blood. Shad called him off.

Men who had seen it started to laugh. But when Trencher stood up, scowling and dusting himself, his furious eyes stabbing at them through the smear of tar, they shut up. He turned back to Shad, crouching a little.

But Shad stood his ground, his big fist clenched around a wrench. The dog was growling, black hair standing stiff.

"By Judas Priest," Shad said angrily, "I was gougin' eyes and bitin' ears before you was ever weaned. Next time you come at me, bucko, you better have you a doctor handy."

For a moment they glared at each other. Shad didn't give an inch. Presently Trencher turned and stalked away. From then on, he never came at Shad again. He often eyed him from a distance, a goading hatred in his heavy face. But he always gave Shad plenty of air.

"I reckon I handled that." Shad's words were clipped in lingering anger.

"I reckon you did," Jameson agreed worriedly. "But you better watch your back from now on. Trencher looks like he'd have the memory of a bull elephant."

Blair Farley had been watching, hands tucked into the waistband beneath his heavy paunch. Jameson motioned him aside and said sharply, "You caused this, you and those poker games of yours. Cause me any more trouble like this and I'll let you walk back to Dodge!"

"It ain't my fault if Trencher's got his dander up," Farley replied in a whiny voice that grated against a man's nerves.

"No? Well, I'll tell you something else that had better set you to thinking. You haven't got a friend left in camp, Farley. Most of them hate you because you've been winning their money. We're a long way from town. We ever get in a scrap with Indians, what's to keep somebody from potting you during the excitement? Then nobody would owe anything."

He saw fear strike in Farley's eyes. "You don't think somebody would?"

Jameson shrugged. "You know these men. What do you think?"

Farley walked away, visibly shaken by a thought that never had come to him before. Jameson heard someone ask him about a poker game, and Farley turned it down.

Later Jameson spoke to Ransom King about Trencher. King listened, frowning in thought. "I'll let him shoot a few buffalo," he said. "That's all he needs. Let him kill something and it drains that meanness out of him for a while."

Jameson shook his head wonderingly. "I guess you know him. But you've got a mighty peculiar taste in helpers."

"I don't pretend to like him, Jameson. He's crude and he's mean. But I can handle him, and he's a good man for the job he does. As long as I make money, I can tolerate anything or anybody."

Came a time when the buffalo were thinning. The bunches were so small now that Jameson and Shad never got to hunt together any more. They separated, each taking a wagon and his own skinners, trying only to keep within the sound of each other's guns. There had been some Indian sign lately, and Jameson's eyes constantly searched the skyline.

Shad said, "Been the time of year the Comanches like to go south and raid the settlements. That's maybe why we ain't seen much of them. But they'll be back here for the winter."

One day after Jameson had killed enough buffalo for his skinners to have an afternoon's work, he sought out Shad Blankenship and found him already through, sitting on a rise watching his men.

"Let's go hunt a new camp site, Shad, one where there'll be more buffalo."

They set out up the creek. There were buffalo, all right, but badly scattered. They rode ten miles, maybe twelve, and finally reached the rocky head of the creek, where a strong stream of cold, clear water burst forth from a fissure in the rocks to form a year-round spring.

Up here were more buffalo. Jameson liked the idea of camping by the spring. It was a good place, with lots of hackberry, stunted elm, and most of all the big cottonwoods. In places the buffalo had rubbed the trunks almost slick getting rid of the spring-shed hair, with its itchy lice and ticks. Even after all these months, a tuft of shed hair still stuck, here and there.

Shad Blankenship was worried.

"Look at them buffalo," he said, "turn tail and run quick as they see us. They ain't been so wild back down the creek. These buffalo has been hunted, Gage. Hunted on horseback."

"Indians, you think?"

"What else? Maybe we better have us a look around."

They skirted the spring and eased southward. Presently Jameson pulled up short, tilting his head to listen. "Shad, did you hear something?"

Shad shook his head. "Gettin' so deaf I can't hear thunder."

Gage listened a little, finally stepping down and dropping the reins, standing free of the horse so not even the squeak of the saddle would keep him from hearing. The sound grew. It was like thunder. But it rolled steadily, without a break, gradually swelling louder. Soon Gage could feel the ground begin to tremble a little beneath his feet.

"Stampede," he said sharply. "Buffalo stampede!"

His heart quickened. He stepped back into the stirrup and swung up, automatically looking about him for a place of escape and seeing little but the rolling prairie, the stream, the spring—nothing that would stop a crushing tide of buffalo.

"We've got to make a run for it, Shad," he said. "Let's get over that rise yonder so we can see how they're heading. Maybe we can get out of the way before they get here."

They spurred up over the rise. Even before they reached the top Jameson could see the cloud of dust that rose into the plains sky. Then he saw the buffalo coming fast, directly toward them.

"Lord," Shad breathed, "must be ten thousand head."

They were fanned out over a half-mile front. Jameson's bay horse was fidgeting nervously, wanting to run. Jameson felt his own pulse pounding.

"That way, Shad," Jameson shouted, pointing.

"Maybe we can get past the edge of the herd before they run us down."

He spurred then, spurred hard, and the bay horse answered with speed. His long legs reached out. Jameson knew this was the payoff for his having bought a horse of strong body and strong lungs. Behind him he could almost feel the breath of the buffalo on the back of his neck. It was the movement of air set in motion by the surging body of the stampeding herd. Beside him Shad was leaning over in the saddle, talking to his dun horse, urging him to more speed.

Jameson looked back once at this thundering black sea of buffalo that would pound horse and man to powder if ever they made a misstep, if ever they fell in the path of this living avalanche. He saw the bobbing black heads, the black eyes, the little streams of saliva that trailed from the mouths of the running animals. He could feel the fear that swept the buffalo, that kept them surging forward, and it became his own fear, swelling in his chest, choking off his breath.

Little by little the spurring riders worked toward the edge of the herd. Some of the leaders were even with them now, running along beside them. Jameson looked back often, gauging how much farther they had to go, already feeling the power begin to play out in the big bay horse beneath him. He kept urging the horse on.

And finally . . .

"We're clear, Shad!"

They pulled up then to let the herd roar past them. A rush of wind and dust whipped their faces. The horses danced fearfully, still strung high from the long, hard run.

In a little while the herd had gone on past. Down there somewhere the buffalo would run themselves out, and they would settle down to graze again, as peaceful as if nothing had happened.

"Reckon what tetched them off?" Shad asked, trying to rub the dust from his watering eyes.

"I've got a sneaking idea," Jameson replied. They trotted their horses a little, easing them down to a walk, cooling them gradually.

The sound of the stampede faded away and there was nothing left to show for it but a wide swath of trampled grass and a lingering of stifling dust that slowly drifted out on the easy breeze.

Now Jameson began to hear something else.

"Shooting, Shad. And I thought I heard somebody yell."

Shad's eyes narrowed. Presently he heard it, too.

"Coming from somewhere across that hill yonder," Jameson said.

Dismounting and leading their horses, the two men cautiously worked up the hillside. They dropped the horses' reins and crouched as they neared the top, keeping low to present as little silhouette as possible. Shad Blankenship dropped to his belly.

"Look yonder, Gage. Ever see such a sight in your life?"

Down there a large group of Comanche warriors, stripped to breechclouts and all mounted on good horses, had driven a group of buffalo into a mass. Now they circled them, the dozens of hoofs churning up a billowing cloud of dust to drift away with the wind. Most of the Indians loosed arrows into the herd as rapidly as they could restring their bows. Now and again, as a buffalo made a rush to get out of the surround, a warrior charged after him with a lance. Those few Indians who had rifles were using them principally on the animals which broke into a run.

Jameson was glad he had brought the binoculars out of his saddlebags. He raised them to his eyes and watched a lancer lope up behind a running buffalo, holding the lance across his body, the off end the highest, his knees tucked under a rope wound around the horse's body. When he had gained the position he wanted, he thrust downward with the lance, shoving it hard, then pulling it out again as the buffalo faltered. The lancer pierced the animal a second time, pushing in and holding the lance until the buffalo went down.

He saw a bowman ride in close and loose an arrow at a running bull. As the missile drove home, the buffalo turned sharply, heading into the horse, sending it rolling. The Indian scrambled to his feet, grabbing his fallen bow and what spilled arrows he could snatch off the ground. In desperation he sent arrow after arrow into the charging animal, so rapidly Jameson lost count. The buffalo went to its knees, still hooking at the Indian. The warrior walked back to his horse, carefully looked him over for injuries, then remounted and returned to the slaughter.

Not a single animal escaped the Comanches.

Now the fun was over and the work part began. Other Indians materialized out of a brushy draw to start the skinning, the butchering of the meat. Jameson watched, fascinated, the skilled hands of the red men.

These were the Comanches, savage, brutal. Yet truly they were children of the land, nomads, akin to nature and the creatures in a way the white man could never be, following the rains, following the grass, following the buffalo.

Shad nudged Jameson. "This ain't the girly show at no fancy dance hall, young'un. They find out we're up here, we're liable to put on a little show ourselves."

"I wonder where their camp is," Jameson mused, still watching through the binoculars.

"It don't matter to me. I ain't been invited and don't aim to go."

Jameson grinned at him. Shad wasn't scared. But he had the deep-grained caution that had kept his hair on through forty years of dodging Indians.

Jameson said, "I've got a notion to trail them, at least far enough to locate their camp. I'd rather find it now than stumble on it some day by accident."

The wrinkles deepened in Shad's ruddy face as he narrowed his eyes, looking down upon the Comanches. "Whatever you say. You're the wagon master. We better step soft, though. Me, I'm an old man, and I've lived out a full life. But you're still owin' the house."

The Indians brought up pack horses. Rolling the meat in the fresh hides, they loaded it onto the horses and headed out, leaving little but scattered patches of blackened blood to show where the slaughter had taken place.

"Don't waste much, do they, Shad?" Unlike the white man, Jameson thought.

Shad shook his head. "Winter coming on, they can't afford to."

It wasn't hard to follow the Indians. It wasn't as if the Comanches were trying to hide their trail. Up here, in the middle of their stronghold, they probably had no thought of any need to do so. Riding slowly, his eyes squinted, nervously searching out the skyline and every patch of brush as they rode along, Jameson could feel the flesh crawl up the back of his neck. His mouth was dry, and he constantly licked his lips. But he kept riding, and he kept watching.

"They ever see us," Shad Blankenship said softly, "she's gonna be the biggest horse race you ever saw."

Jameson nodded, his hand tight and sweaty on the reins, his knee pulling in for the welcome feel of the saddle gun under his leg. He had left the Fifty with the skinners, so he wouldn't have to handle its heavy bulk on the ride. Now he wished he had it.

"Most of those horses looked like good ones," he commented. "Mighty good for Indians."

Shad Blankenship reined up, intently studying something ahead, then nodding as he satisfied himself that it was nothing to be alarmed about. "Comanches are good horsemen. Besides, they probably stole most of these from the Texans. Every fall, before winter sets in, they raid the settlements. Generally strike in the full of the moon. Comanche moon, they call it down there.

"Steal horses, women, children, anything else that ain't nailed down. What they don't steal, they kill or burn up.

Then they hit it off back up to this country and winter on these plains. Ain't nobody ever reached them up here. The only ones know the trail are the Comanchero traders out of New Mexico. They're strictly contraband. They come out and trade for the stock the Indians have stole. That's where the Comanches get the guns and powder and other white-man stuff you see them with nowadays."

Sticking with the brush, they followed the trail six or seven miles along the edge of a draw that led eventually to another creek, much like the one on which the hide hunters had been camping.

They caught the drift of wood smoke before they saw the village.

"Yonder it is," Shad whispered finally, "on that flat aside the creek."

Jameson slipped out of the saddle and lifted the binoculars from the saddlebag again. He could feel his hair stiffen as he looked down on the tall buffalo-hide lodges, forty or fifty of them, strung out up and down the creek. It seemed to be a new camp, for the grass was not trampled out yet. Smoke curled upward from the smoke flaps, which were opened downwind. Indians hurried up and down through camp like so many ants, cutting the fresh buffalo meat into strips for drying, spitting huge chunks of it to be roasted immediately. It was mostly a woman's job from here on. The warriors who had done the killing now lolled around in camp, some of them washing themselves in the cold water of the creek.

Dogs fought up and down the camp site, struggling over fallen scraps of meat. Some of the children threw rocks at them. One pair of scrapping dogs felled a squaw, causing her to drop a huge chunk of red meat in the sand. Grabbing a stick, she chased the tail-tucking dogs all the way down to the creek while loafing men made fun of her.

Elsewhere, other women were working on the fresh hides, pegging them out, scraping them religiously clean so they could be tanned later with a mixture of liver and brains. Watching, Jameson lost much of the tension that had drawn taut within him.

Suddenly he saw something that didn't belong, something that made him draw his breath in sharply and lower the binoculars, lifting them again as if he didn't believe it.

Then he handed them to Shad. "Take a look," he said, his voice unsteady. "See if that's really a white woman there, scraping a hide."

Shad took the glasses, searching among the lodges. Then he stopped. His red-bearded jaw dropped. "By George, I do believe it is. There, I see a squaw kickin' at her. She's a captive, right enough."

His binoculars back, Jameson studied the woman. He couldn't tell much about her. She wore deerskin clothing, old and greasy, evidently the castoffs from some squaw. He couldn't make out her face or guess her age. He could tell only that she was slender, even thin, that her light-colored hair reached far down below her shoulders.

He saw a brave come up behind her, look around quickly, then grab her long hair. He jerked her head back and with his other hand made the sign of scalping her. Then he gave her a rough shove forward.

A curse came up under Jameson's breath. His hands gripped the glasses so hard that they hurt. He saw another Indian walk up angrily and berate the brave. This man, Jameson thought, was probably the chief of the band—at least a leader of higher rank than the warrior. Even so, the warrior paid him scant attention. He turned insolently and strode off, leaving the leader staring after him.

For a moment then, the leader studied the white woman, who had gone back to scraping the green hide. She didn't look at him. The chief turned and walked away in a dejected attitude.

Jameson lowered the glasses. "Shad, I don't know how we're going to do it. But we're going to get her out of there!"

{ NINE }

—⟐—

"Y ou're crazy, Jameson. It's not worth the risk."

Ransom King paced angrily back and forth before the campfire, his eyes jabbing at Jameson. "Do you really think you could get that woman out of there?"

Jameson stood motionless, his questioning gaze drifting from King to the other men standing around in the edge of firelight. He was still half stunned with surprise. He had never expected this opposition from King. Now he wondered how many more felt as King did.

"We've got to try."

"You think the Comanches will just hand her over to you? Have you any idea how it could be done?"

"I've got a notion how we might do it."

"*Might* do it!" King's voice was heavy with sarcasm. "*Might*. Even by the tone of your voice you admit how slim the chance is. You're crazy, Jameson, you're about to jeopardize everything we've come down here for. Use a little judgment, man."

A stir of anger worked at Gage Jameson. It colored his voice. "King, I thought you'd be the first one to say 'Let's go.' Now I don't know what to think. I know it's not cow-ardice."

"Of course it's not cowardice. It's common horse-sense. I've got an investment here, a big investment, and a chance of a big return. So have you. Do you think I want to throw it away, and maybe die too, on a ten-to-one chance of res-cuing some woman you saw through a pair of field glasses? How do we know who she is, or what she is? She may have been there so long she doesn't even *want* out. Ever think about that? For all we know, she might be some dance-hall floozie like Rose."

"Even if she was," Jameson said, "I'd do it."

"Then you're an even bigger fool."

Stiffly they faced each other over the campfire. The men watched them silently, staying back in the edge of dark-ness. Jameson couldn't tell how the sentiment went.

"Listen, Jameson," King argued, "Blankenship says they probably took her on a raid in the Texas settlements. A Texan. They were almighty independent a few years ago. If those Rebels want her back, I say let them come up here and take her themselves. I spent four years fighting them. I wouldn't risk what I've got here for a freight-car load of them."

"She's a white woman, King. You can talk all night, but you can't alter that."

King rocked back and forth on his heels, chewing his lip, his eyebrows drawn down half over his eyes.

"A woman. Just because it's a woman we're supposed to give up everything and go. It always did make me tired, listening to high-flown talk about the sanctity of woman-hood. They put women up on a pedestal like some brass god, when all the time that's all they are—just brass. I've known a lot of them, Jameson. Even married one once.

They're just animals like the rest of us. No better and perhaps a lot worse."

Jameson attempted no answer to that. Even in his anger
he could understand King. Only two things meant much to
this brash hide hunter—excitement and money. Money
most of all.

King made one last attempt. His voice was level now,
persuasive instead of bludgeoning. "Look at the percent-
ages, Jameson. Chances are heavy you won't even come
out alive. But *if* you do, stop and consider. We've had good
hunting here. There are still plenty of buffalo. Indians
haven't bothered us to speak of. This new camp probably
doesn't even know about us. We can move twenty or thirty
miles and they never will know.

"But what happens if you raid that camp? Then we've
got to move, fast and far. We may have to go so far to get
out of their reach that we'll run out of buffalo. Those wagons are half empty yet. It would mean ruination, Jameson. Ruination."

But to Jameson there was no choice. There hadn't been
one since the moment he had seen the woman in that
Comanche camp.

He turned away from King, turned to the other men.

"I'm not telling any man he's got to go. There's no use
lying to you, it's going to be dangerous. But I'm asking for
volunteers."

The camp was silent and still, except for the cold night
breeze moving through, flickering the campfire. Jameson
searched the faces, red in its glow. Shad Blankenship
stepped up beside him.

Reb Pruitt solemnly took off his sack apron, laid it on
the chuck-box lid and walked to Jameson's side.

Then came the lanky skinner Messick. But there it

stopped. Vainly Jameson looked to the men for more help. They stood there, staring at the fire or at the ground or off into darkness, not meeting his eyes. And then he realized.

It was King. King had hired them for him. Even yet their allegiance was to King, not to Jameson. Disappointment settled within him.

Four against the Comanche camp.

A shadow raised up from out in the darkness some- where. Ludlow, his beard black as the night, walked up, folding a knife blade against his leg. He shoved the knife into his pocket and tossed a whittling stick into the blaze. He gave the other men a lingering look of contempt and stood beside Reb Pruitt.

Five now. And five was all it was going to be.

Knowing that, Jameson said to them, "I won't hold you to it. You know five is mighty slim."

They didn't move.

Reb Pruitt said, "She's a Texas woman, Jameson. I'll go if I have to go by myself."

Jameson didn't say it, but the thought ran through his mind: No wonder it took us four years.

Then King restlessly dug his toe into the ground. "Oh, the devil," he said, "no use being so dramatic about it. We'll all go."

Looking around quickly in surprise, Jameson saw him nod.

"It's still a crazy fool idea," King said grudgingly, "and it'll probably get us all killed. But I knew all the time we'd have to go, if we couldn't discourage you. We can't afford to lose you, Jameson. This expedition would sink like a rock in the river."

Jameson smiled and shook King's hand. "Thanks, King. I knew you weren't afraid."

"Afraid? The only thing I'm afraid of is that someday I may get as stupid as you are. Call me when you're ready. I'm going to catch me some sleep."

For Jameson there was no rest. He put the men to breaking camp, loading the wagons. When they got back—*if* they got back—these wagons had to be ready to roll.

At last he lay down in his blankets, but sleep wasn't in him. He turned restlessly a while before he gave it up. He looked wonderingly at Shad Blankenship, rolled up and snoring. Shad could sleep through a cannonade.

Jameson got to his feet and walked to the chuck wagon. He dipped water from a bucket and into the coffeepot. He poured a little fresh coffee among the old grounds and set it all on the coals, punching them up for extra heat.

He heard Reb Pruitt's voice behind him. "That's my job."

He turned and tried to smile. That wasn't in him, either. "Guess neither one of us can sleep."

They sat there watching the pot, wondering if it ever would come to a boil. He felt a deep need for talk, for something to take his mind off whatever was coming.

"What part of Texas are you from, Reb?"

"South Texas. The brush country."

"Fought in the war, did you?"

Pruitt nodded. "If you could call it fightin'. I got there late. Seemed like mostly all we could do was retreat and listen to the officers tell us we was just backin' up for a fresh run at the Yanks. We was always out of powder or lead or something to eat. Seemed like all we had left was guts, and they ain't worth much when your stomach's empty."

"It wasn't much fun for us either, Reb."

Pruitt poked restlessly at the fire. "I reckon not."

Sitting there watching Pruitt, Jameson felt a strong liking growing in him for this lean, hungry-looking little cowboy cook. There was more to the man than had earlier met his eye.

"It's none of my business," Jameson said, "and you can say so if you want to. But they tell me you got in trouble down there and can't go back. Something serious?"

Pruitt shrugged. "I shot a yellow-leg cavalry lieutenant with a sawed-off shotgun."

"Kill him?"

"No, I wasn't tryin' to. But where I hit him, it put him in the infantry for a good spell."

Only a pale rind of moon lighted their way as they moved along. But Jameson knew the direction. He kept his horse unerringly on it, moving at a jog trot across the silver tableland. Ransom King rode silently beside him, keeping his thoughts to himself.

Behind them came the men, all except a few they had left to guard the wagons and have them ready to move. Poker-playing Blair Farley had elected to stay, perhaps taking to heart what Jameson had said about someone shooting him during the thick of action to keep from having to pay a gambling debt.

There hadn't been enough saddles to go around, or horses, either. Several rode mules bareback. As they strung out of camp, Jameson counted fourteen men.

Angling across the flat prairie, they finally struck the other creek. Jameson reined up, studying it in the darkness. He looked at the Dipper, judging the amount of time he still had before daylight. The early-morning chill had him stiff, his back aching a little from the cramped way the cold had made him ride.

"Pass the word back," he whispered. "It's not far now. Nobody talks. Nobody smokes. One wrong move and there'll never be another."

He touched spurs lightly to the horse, easing him down into the bitter-cold creek and across. His heart quickened as he heard the other mounts splashing over behind him. Crisp air like this could carry sound a long way.

Up the other side, he kept riding, getting off some distance from the water. He remembered the line of timber and brush that had lain behind the village, indicating a draw that fed water into the creek in time of rain. This draw, he figured, would give them cover. He looked back again and saw the men bunched up close behind him, guns in their hands, ready.

Stars in the east had begun to pale when they moved their horses and mules up into the brush behind the village. Jameson caught the grease-smoke smell that always betrayed an Indian camp. The wind had stilled now in this pre-dawn darkness, but the chill was sharp enough to set a man to trembling.

He dismounted to let his horse blow, and the others followed his example. They walked the horses, leading them to cool them down gradually.

As the sky lightened, he could pick out the lodges one by one, their conical shapes rising up against the horizon, the poles above the smokeflaps showing clearer in approaching dawn. He was looking at the village from the opposite side now, and he no longer could be sure exactly where he had seen the white woman. He waited, and studied, and finally he thought he knew which lodge it would be. The question was, did she sleep there, or was it merely one where they made her work?

He could see no movement in the camp as yet. Part of it, at least, would be because of the buffalo the Indians had taken yesterday. They would have gorged themselves last night, eaten all they could stuff in, and then they would have fallen into a drugged sleep.

Scattered throughout the length of the village he saw horses hobbled or staked, twenty-five or thirty head. But most of the horses—a couple of hundred—were in a loosely held herd down past the lower end of camp, scattered over several acres of flat, grassy ground along the creek. Way out to one edge he saw an Indian horse herder sitting sleepily on the ground, holding the leather rein of a mount that stood droop-headed over him.

Jameson had had little experience with Comanches, but he knew within reason that an Indian on the war trail would never be far from his horse. Even sleeping, he would have the mount staked or tied close at hand. Stealing horses from a war party was well-nigh an impossibility, unless you were another Indian.

But now the Comanches were on their own ground, seemingly inviolate here on their impregnable Llano Estacado, easing down to the long monotony of winter life. And like white soldiers when they thought they were safe, they had let down their guard.

"We've got to have that horse herd," Jameson whispered to Shad.

Shad chewed heavily on his tobacco, frowning, his pale eyes leisurely working from one end of the camp to the other, not missing a horse track or a buffalo bone.

"Then let's just take it," he said casually.

He pointed his red-bearded chin. "That second lodge from the end yonder—ain't it the one where we seen her?"

"Yep." Jameson felt more secure in his judgment now, for he had picked the same one.

"Reckon she's still there?" Shad asked.

Jameson shook his head. "I hope so. It's the best bet we've got."

"The minute they see what we're after, they'll kill her."

Jameson's hand was tight on the saddle gun. "I know it. So we've got to get her before they see what we're really up to."

He lifted his chin, studying the sky. Light enough now, he thought.

"Shad, I want you to take King and most of the men and run off that horse herd. Make a lot of noise. Push it straight across the creek, and be in a hurry. The Comanches will be boiling after you like a swarm of hornets."

Shad smiled a little at the anticipation of action. "And how do you figure on amusing yourself in the meantime?"

"I'll take Pruitt and Ludlow and Messick. While you draw the warriors off on that end, we'll get busy down here. Later on we'll meet you somewhere across the creek, on the way back to camp."

He paused, then added, "If we're lucky."

Shad and the other riders moved away slowly, keeping under cover of the brush. Jameson held his breath until his lungs ached, listening for a giveaway noise like a horse stumbling or snorting in this knife-sharp morning air. It seemed to him that the strike of hoofs was gunshot-loud, but he knew that was imagination. Any minute he expected the camp dogs to sound the alarm.

He worried most about those men riding bareback. An

Indian could give you a whale of a fight bareback, but these were white men used to saddles. Some weren't used to riding at all. They would have a hard time just staying on, if the going got rough. Their guns wouldn't be much help.

For a time then, Shad's men were out of sight as the brush swallowed them up. There was not even the muffled sound of hoofs. Jameson turned to the remaining three men. "Better check your guns again. One miss-lick now and we're dead."

A dog began to bark, somewhere down toward the horse herd. Another dog picked it up, and another and another. In a few seconds the alarm had racketed back into camp, every dog there adding to it his own excited yelp. Holding his breath again, Jameson peered through the brush and saw the horse guard straighten, looking around.

He thought desperately, now's the time, Shad, if you're ever going to do it!

And Shad did it. A sudden rattle of guns exploded toward the horse herd. Snapping unexpectedly out of sleep, the horses jumped one way and the other in excitement. The riders thundered down on them, firing guns, and they stampeded.

For a moment it looked as if they would plunge straight into the Indian camp. But someone intercepted them, headed them off. Then they were running for the creek.

Jameson watched the horse guard raise his rifle. Half a dozen bullets ripped the Comanche apart.

Pandemonium struck the camp. Warriors burst out of the lodges, rifles and bows in hand. Some shouted in confusion. Some took wild shots at the raiders who swept away their horse herd. Those who had horses tied or hobbled nearby ran to them. Even some of these horses jerked free in panic and stampeded through the camp, galloping after the herd. While the warriors ran after the raiders in helpless fury, squaws and children hurried out of the lodges to see what was taking place.

Jameson lifted his binoculars and watched that second lodge. Then he saw her. She stepped through the flap and stood watching the dusty, pounding scene of wild confusion.

"There she is," Jameson said quietly to Pruitt, shoving the binoculars back into his saddlebag. "You ready to get that Texas woman out of there?"

Pruitt nodded gravely. They swung onto their horses. Jameson jabbed with his spurs. The mount burst forward in a lope, out of the brush, racing swiftly toward the woman. She was about two hundred yards away. Or was it two miles?

Rifle steady in his hand, Jameson spoke tensely under his breath and realized suddenly that he was praying. He kept spurring. He could hear the clatter of hoofs behind him and knew the other three were right with him.

They hadn't been spotted yet. Jameson couldn't see a warrior anywhere who might oppose them. They had all run toward the other end of camp. But a man couldn't dismiss those squaws. They could fight like so many wounded panthers if they needed to.

The captive white woman saw them. For the space of two or three seconds she stood numb, not believing. Then she broke into a run toward them.

Squaws saw them now. They waved their hands excitedly, most of them turning to flee, shooing the children before them. But one, with a knife in her hand, started running after the white woman. The woman saw her and tried to run faster. But the squaw was fleet-footed and gained rapidly. Jameson raised his rifle but realized he couldn't fire accurately at the speed he was riding. He might hit the wrong woman. His heart clutched in dismay. He knew he couldn't reach her before the squaw did.

Then, just as the squaw closed the gap and raised the knife, a gunshot roared behind Jameson. The squaw stumbled, rolled in the grass and lay still.

Reb Pruitt had slid his horse to a sudden halt, thrown his rifle to his shoulder and fired. It was a perfect shot.

Heart racing, Jameson pulled to a stop, kicked his left foot free and reached down for the woman. She put her foot in the empty stirrup. He gave her a quick boost up behind him. Then, as her arms clasped tightly about him, he spurred the horse again.

Arrows began to whisper past them as some of the closer warriors saw what was happening. Even a couple of squaws had bows and were stringing arrows, letting them fly at a speed Jameson would not have believed if he hadn't seen it. He kept spurring. They were out of effective range already. If an arrow struck them now it would be by sheer accident. A few rifles sounded behind them, and Jameson could hear the deadly sing of bullets.

Jameson took one quick glance over his shoulder. He could see the tense, shock-pale face of the woman—a young woman she was—and her long blond hair streaming in the wind. He could see his three riders close behind him, not one appearing to have been hit. It had gone off so quickly that it had been over before the Indians could act by anything other than reflex.

Now Jameson put his horse into the creek, splashed across, and spurred out on the other side again. They broke through the tangle of brush, then were out on the open prairie, running free.

{ TEN }

To his right Jameson could see the horse herd still running, necks outstretched, legs reaching to gather in the miles, the dust rising up from the dry grass. He reined that way, staying in a hard lope. He couldn't see behind him well, but he knew there was certain to be immediate pursuit on any horses the Indians had managed to keep in camp.

Through the patchy brush he could see Comanches on horseback, pushing across the creek in a splash of water that flashed a spangled reflection from the rising sun. He couldn't count them, didn't try.

"You all right?" he asked the woman behind him, speaking to her for the first time. Her answer, in a voice strained almost to breaking, was barely audible. "I think so."

He caught the wood-smoke smell of Indian and knew it was from her frayed old deerskin clothes. He could feel her body against him, trembling, but it might well have been because of the cold. She had no coat against the chill of the morning. Even the sleeves were gone from the old squaw dress she wore. They had splashed a lot of icy water moving across the creek.

He had caught only a fragmentary glimpse of her face,

but now he could see her hands, clasped tightly to the front of his coat. They were young hands—red, raw and bruised—but they were strong hands, hands that knew work.

Shad Blankenship edged out from the horse herd and angled his mount toward them at a run. Relief washed over his rough old face as he saw the woman and noted that none of Jameson's group was hurt.

"We got company comin', young'un," he shouted against the wind and the hammering of hoofs.

Jameson looked back over his shoulder at the line of Indians. Fifteen or eighteen of them. They were making a gain, for the hide hunters were hard-pressed to keep the horse herd moving on.

He got another look at the woman, too. He saw deep blue eyes etched with pain, a face haggard from hardship and taut with the remnants of fear. A mouth with lips drawn in tight, a chin firm and strong, indicating the fortitude to face up to what might come.

Ahead Jameson saw a buffalo wallow, not deep but good enough for at least some protection. He pointed to it, and Shad saw, nodding. Shad waved his hat. The men with the horse herd began pulling toward him, letting the Indians' horses run on. Pushing hard, they converged on the buffalo wallow. The Comanches were coming in, making it a tight race.

Jameson slid to a stop in the wallow and let the woman swing to the ground. The place was a depression, possibly thirty or forty feet across, where the louse- and fly-ridden buffalo came to wallow in the dust for relief from the constant itching.

Jameson motioned the woman to lie down against the bank for protection. The other hide men rode in and jumped from their horses and mules. Urgent though the situation was, not a man failed to stop long enough to glance at the white woman. Even Ransom King.

"Hold onto those mounts," Jameson yelled. "This is no time to be set afoot."

Kneeling, lying prone, some of them standing, they waited. Bridle reins were tight in their hands or looped over their arms, the rifle barrels bristling at the edge of the buffalo wallow.

The Indians closed in, shrieking and yelling.

"Hold your fire till they get close," Jameson said loudly. "Then get the horses, that's the main thing. Don't let a horse get away."

He raised his saddle gun, lined the sights on the Indian in the lead. This man, he realized suddenly, was the chief he had watched through the glasses yesterday. He waited, his breath held until a slow fire kindled in his lungs. Then he squeezed the trigger. The rifles on either side of him roared. Some of the hunters' horses and mules broke loose in terror and plunged away.

He saw the chief jerk back, clutch desperately at the horse's mane, then tumble off to struggle out his last breath on the ground. Other men's bullets tore into the charging line. Horses stumbled and went down. Indians rolled in the grass. Some jumped to their feet, some lay cramped and still where they had landed. Men and horses screamed in pain. The murderous gunfire went on. Jameson fired again and again, each shot bringing down a horse.

In seconds every Indian horse was hit. The vicious fire had riddled the Comanche line like a scythe whispering through wet grass. Few of the Indians had had time to loose an arrow or fire a shot. Now many were dead or wounded, and the rest were afoot, their fallen horses thrashing.

The surviving ones tried to return fire, bellied down in

the cover of grass or behind the fallen mounts. In the wallow a mule screamed and went down kicking.

But the hunters poured out a fearful hail of lead. They didn't have time to let themselves get pinned down here, Jameson knew, and he figured the others realized it, too. Given time, the Comanches would have reinforcements afoot from the camp.

Half the hunters had lost their mounts, either from their jerking away and running or from the Indians' fire.

One man lay on his face in the wallow. Jameson felt of him and shook his head. He had skinned his last buffalo.

"Mount up double," he ordered. "We've got to clear out of here."

He and Shad and a couple of others kept up fire while the rest mounted. Then they swung up, too, and they moved out in a run.

This time the woman was in the saddle and Jameson was behind, protecting her. The few remaining Comanches fired after them. Jameson heard a man cry out. Reb Pruitt drooped in the saddle, an arrow in his arm. Thinking the Texan might fall, Jameson pulled in beside him and caught him, holding him in the saddle.

"I'll make it," the little cook said through gritted teeth. "Nobody ever had to hold me on a horse yet."

They rode a mile. Then, knowing there could be no pursuit, Jameson reined in and stopped Pruitt's horse. He slipped off and helped the cook down. The woman swung to the ground.

"Bleedin' like a stuck hog," Pruitt breathed painfully, as if ashamed of himself for getting hit.

"Through the flesh part of the arm," Jameson said. "Arrowhead went through clean."

Shad Blankenship took one man to each mount and went after those horses and mules that had run away.

Jameson took out his knife and cut the arrowhead from the shaft as carefully as he could. It was a steel one, he noted in anger. Something from the Comanchero trade.

"Can you help me hold him?" he asked the woman. Tight-lipped but looking as if she knew what she was about, she put her arm around Pruitt's shoulder and held tight.

Jameson gripped the shaft and said, "This is going to hurt, Reb. Grit your teeth and cuss or say anything you want to."

Pruitt nodded, white-faced. "Just get on with it."

Jameson jerked. The shaft came out clean. Pruitt's head rocked back, his eyes shut, his jaw clamped hard. Slowly he expelled his breath and opened his eyes. They were moist with pain. But he managed a semblance of a grin at Jameson, and at the woman.

"Wasn't so bad. First time I've had a woman's arms around me in I don't . . . know . . . when."

He slumped back, unconscious.

"Shock," Jameson said. "We'd better stop the bleeding."

With her help he pulled off Pruitt's coat and rolled up the sleeve. The other men crowded around to watch. Blood flowed slowly, sticky and warm. Jameson searched his hip pocket for a handkerchief. He frowned at it. Not clean, but the best he had. He bound it tightly around Pruitt's arm. The cook was beginning to stir again. The woman held his head, keeping him as still as possible.

"That'll hold it," Jameson said at last. "We can do better when we get him to camp."

He really looked at the woman for the first time now,

admiration warm in him at the calm way she had helped him with Pruitt.

"You've got a steady nerve," he said.

"The Comanches taught me that," she replied.

It was hard to guess at her age. She might have been anywhere between twenty and thirty. Captivity had ground harsh lines into what must have been a pretty face, or close to it. The fear was gone from her eyes now, but a lingering of pain was still there. Her lips were dry and cracked from the sun and wind. Her long blond hair was wind-tangled but freshly washed, and it appeared to have been combed out not too long ago. The thought came to Jameson that it was lucky she hadn't been killed way back yonder instead of being kept captive. Many an Indian would give his right arm to own a scalp like that one, to keep it brushed down so it would glisten in the firelight at night as he bragged to other warriors about the many scalps hanging from the point end of his lance.

She was shivering again. The morning air was still cold. Jameson took off his coat and held it out to her. "Here. Put this on."

She took it hesitantly. "What about you?"

"I've got a heap to do. Being busy will keep me warm."

The coat was twice too big for her, but he could see the relief in her eyes at the warmth of it.

"We don't even know your name yet," he said.

"Westerman. Celia Westerman. And yours?"

"Gage Jameson. Where did the Comanches capture you?"

"Down on the San Saba, in September."

September. Two months and more. She had been through it, all right.

"A great many women would have died before now," he said.

She nodded gravely. "That might have been the easiest way," she replied.

Shad Blankenship and some of the others had brought back the runaway mounts and had rounded up the Indian horse herd again. Jameson looked it over. He picked a few of the best-looking to replace the animals that had been killed in the buffalo wallow.

"Brands on most of them," Shad observed. "Been stole, almost every hoof in there."

Ransom King's eyes glowed as he looked at them. "How many would you say there are, Blankenship?"

"Two hundred, a few more or less."

"They'll fetch a price in Dodge," King commented enthusiastically, the dollars shining in his eyes.

Gage Jameson frowned and checked his saddle gun. "We're not taking them to Dodge. We're shooting them."

He thought King was going to burst, the way anger made his neck veins stand out. "You're crazy, Jameson! Think what they'd be worth in Dodge!"

Jameson said flatly, "We've got no right to sell them. They're stolen horses."

"What owner is ever going to get a chance to claim them? They were lost when the Comanches got their hands on them. It's salvage now, Jameson, same as a sea captain salvaging a wreck."

"I don't know anything about salvage laws. But I know these are stolen horses. We've got no right to sell them."

King's voice went almost shrill in anger. Here was money, easy money, untainted by blood and grease and the smell of dead buffalo. And it was slipping from his grasp.

"Then what right have you to shoot them?"

"Just this: afoot a Comanche isn't much. Let him get on horseback and you're in trouble. They'd steal these horses back from us, King. We've got all we can do to keep them from taking what stock we already have. Take this many more and we'd likely lose them all, our own stuff, too. Then we'd be in it for sure. As long as these horses are alive, they're a millstone around our necks."

King declared, "I don't care what you say, Jameson. If you're going to shoot them, I'll claim them. They're mine."

Short of patience, Jameson flared. "Take them, then. Take your wagons, too. Cut out for Dodge the quickest way you can."

That stopped King. He stood stiffly, hands clenched in fury. But he was whipped and he knew it. His wagons were not yet half full of hides. He had come after hides, not horses. Alone with his small crew of men, he wouldn't stand a chance of getting to Dodge with those horses. They would be stampeded before he could travel thirty miles, perhaps his own stock with them.

He shrugged, anger still splotched red in his face. But he was helpless to alter the situation. He forced a smile that wouldn't stay.

"Shoot them, then. You're the wagon master."

He started to walk away, then stopped to look at Celia Westerman. His narrowed eyes swept over her, head to foot. A lingering of malice was in his voice. "What about *her*, Jameson? Now that you've got her, what'll you do with her? She's a little like the horses, isn't she? A millstone around your neck?

Jameson glanced at Celia Westerman, then quickly looked away as he saw a sudden tightening in her face.

King had hit him squarely. He had been so busy trying

to free her that he had given no thought to what he would do afterward. The hide camp was no place for a woman. Yet what could he do about her?

Hating the horse-killing job and now confronted with another problem, he spoke to Shad a little curtly, and instantly regretted it. "What're we standing here for? Let's get this job done and move out."

With his saddle gun and a pocketful of extra cartridges, he walked out toward the horses. He flinched, his stomach coiling in revulsion at what he had to do. Then he raised the rifle.

{ ELEVEN }

Jameson was glad to be on the move again, to get away from this place with its gagging stench of gunpowder and blood, the screams of the dying horses still in his ears. Someday men would come upon this gaunt stretch of bleaching bones and wonder what great massacre had occurred there.

Celia Westerman rode beside him, knowing what put the bleakness in his face. "There's no point in worrying yourself about it."

He nodded grimly. "I know. But I've never had a job I hated so much. A man gets a feeling for horses, depending on them the way I have. Shooting them is almost like shooting people."

She was silent a while, studying him as the group rode westward, driving the few animals they had chosen to keep.

"I don't know how to start saying thank you. I don't know any words half strong enough."

He eased a little then. It had been many weeks since he had heard woman-talk. He liked the way she spoke, slowly, deliberately, not quite a drawl like Reb Pruitt's, but slow anyway.

He said, "I know what you mean. I've been in the same kind of fix myself."

"But why did you do it? You didn't even know who I was. It was a terrific risk to take for a stranger."

"You were a woman, a white woman. That's why we did it."

"That seems mighty little reason, looking back on it."

Jameson said, "Several times in my life I've been in a tough spot, something I couldn't get out of by myself. Somebody always came along. Most often it was a stranger, somebody I never saw before or ever saw again. Seems like we go through life owing gratitude to strangers. The only way we can ever repay them is to help some other stranger. It all evens up, in the long pull."

Then he said, "To your family, I suppose it'll be as if you'd come back from the dead. Married?"

She shook her head. "Not married."

"Father? Mother?"

"I still have my father and a couple of brothers. I lost one in the war."

She studied him gravely. "I haven't figured out yet what you men are. You're not Rangers. You're not Comancheros. What are you?"

"Buffalo hunters. We're down from Kansas."

"From Kansas." He caught the disappointment before she managed to cover it up, and he knew what she was thinking. She had hoped they were Texans, that they could take her home.

"We'll find a way to get you home," he promised.

Some of the pain went out of her deep blue eyes, and a brightness came to them, shining warmly. "Home." She spoke the word softly, caressing it.

He watched her, and Ransom King's words came back to him. A millstone around his neck. He felt a nudge of anger at King for saying it, yet he realized that in a sense it was true. He had Celia Westerman now. But what could he do with her?

The circled wagons looked deserted. Gage Jameson reined up to study them, for caution was second nature to him. He motioned Celia Westerman to hand him the saddle gun from the scabbard beneath her leg. She did, and he signaled her to pull back. The other riders approached warily too, rifles ready.

Then there was movement at the wagons. The men who had been left on guard stepped out into sight, holding guns. They stared curiously at Celia Westerman.

"We couldn't tell at first." Fat Blair Farley spoke with nervousness. "You might of been Injuns."

The stock was all inside the circle. Camp was broken. The wagons were loaded. The only thing still to be done was to catch up the mules and hitch them to the wagons. But Jameson looked at the men around and saw the fatigue heavy in their faces from the long night ride, the hard action, the strain and the fear. Hunger gnawed at him, and he knew it must be the same with the others.

"We could do with a strong meal before we get moving," he said. He looked at Reb Pruitt, stretched out now in the shade of the chuck wagon. Reb hadn't lost much blood. Most of what ailed him was shock. Two or three days, he'd be doing a one-handed cooking job and talking his head off. Right now, he wasn't in much shape to talk or to help.

"Shad," Jameson said, "you're a good hand with a coffeepot and a Dutch oven. Let's see what we can fix to eat."

Celia Westerman had been kneeling beside Pruitt. Now she stood up and came to the chuck box. "Here," she said, "I'll help."

Jameson said dubiously, "You've been through a lot. Don't you think you ought to rest?"

She shook her head. "No, I can't afford to sit still right now. If I ever did . . ." She held out her raw hands for him to see. They trembled a little. "I might go to pieces. I've got to keep busy till I can steady down."

Jameson nodded. "I guess so. But cooking for a bunch like this isn't exactly a woman's job."

"I grew up on a cattle ranch. Lots of times I've cooked for a big crew. Just help me find what I need."

Jameson built up the fire again while Shad Blankenship put fresh coffee in the pot.

"Ignorant hide skinners," Shad grumbled, "they throwed out the old grounds. Can't make good drinkin' coffee without the old grounds."

Jameson climbed into the wagon and cut fresh hump meat. Watching Celia Westerman handle the Dutch ovens and the big pots, he knew she hadn't been bluffing. She had done all this before.

Presently the coffee was boiling and fresh meat was frying deep in bubbling grease inside a lidless Dutch oven over the fire. Reb Pruitt always kept biscuit dough made up for days ahead. Celia Westerman broke the dough into biscuit-sized wads and put it in ovens, setting them on live coals. Jameson heaped more coals on the lids when she finished.

There wasn't much to do now but wait. Jameson sat on his heels close by the chuck wagon and watched Celia Westerman. Occasionally his eyes drifted to the eastern horizon, but no anxiety was in them. Having left these Comanches afoot, he had no fear of immediate pursuit. Still, he knew it was high time to clear out of this part of the country. They wouldn't be afoot forever.

Something was worrying Celia Westerman. She carried it a long while, then looked at Jameson. "I keep thinking about that man who died back there in the buffalo wallow. He died for me, Mr. Jameson."

"It was a risk we all took. We all knew it before we started."

"But he died, and I was saved. I can't help thinking about it. What was his name?"

"Andregg. Milt Andregg."

"Milt Andregg." She tried the name. "What kind of man was he?"

Jameson shrugged. "A good buffalo skinner. Beyond that, I don't know much." He knew a little, but it was pointless to bring it up. The man was dead now. The manner of his death compensated for whatever he might have been or done before.

"Did he have a family?"

"None that I knew of."

"I hate to think of him lying back there unburied. You know what the Indians will do."

"You couldn't help that. None of us could."

"No, I guess not. But someday I'm going to put up a marker for him, in a Christian cemetery. It'll tell his name, and what he did. Then he'll always be remembered. As long as a man is remembered, he's not really dead, is he? I mean, as long as he lives in somebody's mind . . ."

"I don't know. I've never thought about that kind of thing very much."

She lowered her head. "I have, lately. I've had lots of time to."

Jameson could see a little of the pain come back into her eyes as she remembered.

"You want to talk about it?" he asked. "Maybe it would help."

She nodded. "Maybe." Her face seemed to grow older as she thought back on it, and the harsh memories crowded into her mind. She hesitated a little, then she started to tell it.

"Times haven't been easy, these last few years in Texas. The carpetbag government took our ranch away from us. I'd been to school, so I got a job teaching. It was a small log building at the edge of town. Hadn't been any Comanche trouble there in a long time. We never even thought about it anymore. One afternoon a storm came up just as I was letting out school. Most of the kids ran for it. But there were a little boy and girl—brother and sister—who had to ride five miles home. It wasn't more than a good thunderhead. I figured an hour or so and it would be over. So I told them to stay.

"They came in the rain, the Comanches did. They were in the schoolhouse before we saw them. We didn't even have a gun there. One of them, his name was Kills His Enemies, took a liking to my hair. He had a hatchet in his hand and was about to kill me when the leader came in. I found out later his name was Buffalo Finder. He looked me over, and he made Kills His Enemies turn me loose. Later, Buffalo Finder told me he'd wanted me for a wife. They took us out and put us on horses.

"They had made quite a foray. It was a big raiding party, no squaws or children along. They had perhaps four hundred horses that they had stolen from the ranches. They knew white men were after them, so they pushed hard.

"Some of them spoke a little Spanish, and so could I. It was rough on all of us, but especially on that poor little boy. He was sickly. He couldn't keep up. The first day in the rain was too much for him. He got sicker and sicker and was holding back the bunch. They wouldn't even let me help him.

"Kills His Enemies kept beating him with a mesquite limb. The third day, two of the warriors took the boy out in plain sight of us and pitched him into the air. And when he came down, Kills His Enemies was waiting with his lance. . . ."

Celia Westerman closed her eyes. A tear squeezed out and found its way down her cheek.

"He's a devil," she said, her voice tight, a deep hatred rising in her face. "A devil out of hell.

"Somewhere up on the cap rock we joined the squaws and children they had left behind. Then we came on up here to the high plains to a deep canyon, bigger than anything I've ever seen. A creek runs down the middle of it, and in places the walls go straight up for hundreds of feet. We camped there a little while. Mexican traders—Comancheros—came in and traded for about half of the stolen horses.

"One of them tried to trade for me. He said he wanted to return me to my own people, but that wasn't it at all. I could see it in his eyes. He offered a lot of trade goods, but Buffalo Finder wouldn't give me up. Then after him came an older man, named Felix Alvarez, and he was a kind one. He took pity on us, the girl and me. He said he had lost a daughter about my age. He traded for the girl.

She's on her way home by now. He offered everything he had to get me free. But the chief still wanted me for wife. And Kills His Enemies still hoped to get my hair. The old man stayed until he knew it was getting dangerous for him. And when he left, there were tears in his eyes.

"The day they left, I stole a knife. I walked down to the creek, and I tried to kill myself. But I couldn't do it, Mr. Jameson. I was either too strong or too weak, I don't know which. Life is hard to turn loose of, even when there's little left in it. I tried to hope Felix Alvarez might still find a way to rescue me. But I guess I knew he couldn't. It would have been suicide to try, and the little girl would have died, too.

"The chief started trying to get me to consent to be his wife. He didn't have to do it that way. He could have forced me. But he wanted it to be of my own will, I guess. I held off, hoping. And all the time, I knew I would die if I didn't. He had other wives. The number-one wife was jealous. If anyone tells you a Comanche woman can't make life miserable for her husband, he just doesn't know.

"And Kills His Enemies was working on him, too, trying to trade for me. A few days ago we moved here to set up a permanent winter camp. I knew the time was getting short. Either I had to submit to Buffalo Finder or let my hair hang from Kills His Enemies' lance."

Celia Westerman looked darkly at the ground.

"I've always been taught that death is better than dishonor. But it's easier to say it than it is to face the decision and die. I should be ashamed to admit it, but it's the way it was. I had just about made up my mind when you came. I didn't want to die.

"You killed Buffalo Finder this morning. I saw him fall. Kills His Enemies will take over now. He won't stay afoot long. He'll get horses and he'll be after you if you're anywhere on these plains. That's the way he is. He's not human."

Jameson looked into the cook fire a long time, admiring her strength, trying to make up his mind. "How far would it be to a Texas settlement?"

She shook her head. "I don't know. Perhaps a couple of hundred miles. If you're thinking about trying to take me, don't. No white man has ever done it, so far as I know. Only the Indians know the way."

"Couldn't you find the trail back, the way you came?"

"We made it too fast, and we made a lot of it at night. You have to know the waterholes. A quarter-mile miss on some of them and you're lost. I couldn't be sure I could find them again."

Grimly Jameson said, "Then the only way out is Kansas. We can take you to Dodge. You catch a train to one of the trail towns, and then you can get one of the Texas cow outfits to carry you home with them when they go back."

She looked over the wagons, and her shrewd blue eyes quickly sized up the situation. "It's a long way to Kansas, too. And those wagons aren't more than half loaded with hides. If you take me now, you'll hurt yourself, won't you?"

He would ruin himself, he knew. But he wouldn't tell her that. "We've got to get you home."

She shook her head again. "Not at that price, Mr. Jameson. It's been a long time. I can wait a little longer."

"A hide camp is no place for a woman."

He looked around at the men. As he had expected, most of them were staring at Celia Westerman. A woman in a hide camp could cause as much trouble as a woman at sea, if luck took that kind of a turn.

"I know what you're thinking," she said. "But there won't be any trouble. I won't let there be any trouble."

Judgment told him to say no. But he couldn't keep from looking at his hide wagons, only half loaded.

"You sure you want it this way?" he asked her, wanting her to say yes but afraid that decision would not be the right one.

"You'll hardly even know I'm here," she told him. Then she stood up and walked to the fire, to lift the lids off the ovens of brown bread and to take up the buffalo steaks.

A crinkle came to the corners of Jameson's eyes. There she was wrong. Never for a minute would he forget she was here.

{ TWELVE }

Five days they angled westward, working generally up the Canadian, and a little to the south of it. They crossed several creeks and streams of varying sizes. Along most of them Jameson found ample sign of buffalo. The land took on a sandier texture as the wagons moved westward. There was more bunch grass in places. But mostly it was still the short, thick turf of buffalo and mesquite grass, strong feed that kept his horses and mules fat on a minimum ration of corn.

Five days, and he thought they had gone far enough.

Reb Pruitt was cooking again now, with help. He remained pale, his left arm tightly bound. But his feet were as active as ever, and his mouth, too.

Because of Pruitt's bad arm, Jameson had suggested getting one of the other men to drive the chuck wagon for him.

"I can do it," Celia Westerman offered. "I've handled wagons almost ever since I was big enough to climb up on one by myself."

So Reb Pruitt rode beside Celia Westerman on the chuck wagon seat, his eyes taking on the glow of a pet dog's. He would have thrown the coffeepot at anyone who had offered to take over Celia Westerman's driving job.

"Handles that wagon better than I could," Pruitt told Jameson in admiration, watching her pull it into place. "I always could make a hand with a bronc, but I never was no great shakes with a team. That there's a woman, Jameson."

The little cook frowned. "Just one thing worries me, and that's them squaw clothes. They ain't fitten for a white woman. We got to do somethin'."

Jameson agreed but didn't know what they could do about it. "I don't know what she could make a dress out of. All we've got is a wagon sheet, and that wouldn't be of much account."

Pruitt reached into the chuck wagon bed and fetched down a canvas bag. "I got some extra clothes with me. Little as I am, it might be some of my stuff would fit her."

Jameson smiled. "I don't know that a shirt and pants would be much more proper than what she's wearing now."

"At least they didn't come from no heathen." Pruitt gave second thought to that and grinned a little. "No heathen *Comanche*, anyway."

Celia Westerman's presence in camp was making some difference. Reb Pruitt wasn't the only one who had taken up shaving almost every day. Even old Shad took to washing the tobacco out of his beard and combing his rusty hair regularly until one day he studied himself a while in the cracked mirror he used, then pulled a gray hair out of his head and scowled. He grunted something about a chuckle-headed old fool and lapsed back into his accustomed habits.

The new hunting grounds were as good as those they

had been forced to vacate, far to the east. Jameson was still bringing down twenty to thirty buffalo at a stand, most days. One time, when there were enough in one bunch for him and Shad to shoot together, they brought down fifty-three head without having to move more than three hundred yards.

November was well along, and he expected a howling blizzard to come streaking down across the plains almost any day. When it finally came, it wasn't so bad. Only one day was it so cold that they had to stay in camp, and there were only a few flurries of dry snow that never even settled on the ground, blowing about like so much powder. Soon the weather was warm and the hunting was good again. Even better than before.

In spite of this, Jameson found himself getting restless, wanting to go somewhere else, do something else, though he didn't know what it was.

He sat at a distance, watching the skinners work through the buffalo he had shot. First, with their straight-bladed ripping knives they would rip down the belly, starting at the throat and working all the way back to the tail. Then they circled the legs below the knee, slitting down to the belly. They cut the hide up to the ears, leaving the thick mat of curly black hair that grew on the huge head.

Taking their curved skinning knives, they then began to slice beneath the hide until the neck and legs were skinned free and the hide had been worked at least half-way down from belly to backbone. They used pritch sticks with a nail in one end to prop the carcass, feet up, so they could work down the tallowy sides.

This much done by knife, they rolled up a big flap of hide at the neck and tied it to a rope, with a pair of mules hitched on at the rump end of the buffalo. They shouted and flipped the reins, forcing the mules to peel the hide backward off the carcass.

Shad Blankenship rode up and dismounted, stretching himself, then squatting down beside Jameson. "What's the matter, Gage? You got a nervous look."

"It's just those skinners. Seems to me they're getting almighty slow lately."

Blankenship watched them a little. "Ain't nothin' slow about that. It's just you. You got the itch to get back to camp, and it ain't for supper, either. That Texas girl has got you goin' in circles, young'un, the same way she has Reb Pruitt."

Jameson felt the color rise in his face. Shad was striking mighty close to home.

Jameson had felt it coming on for several days. He would look at himself in Shad's mirror and snort the way Shad had. Thirty-five years old, already getting a fair sprinkling of gray in his hair. What was he doing, thinking about Celia Westerman?

But he liked to watch her, liked to listen to that gentle, slow way she had of talking.

As the days went by, the harsh lines in her face began to fade. She seemed to get younger. She moved with a new buoyancy, her captivity drifting into the past like a nightmare after the awakening. Occasionally now she even sang a little as she worked around the wagon, helping Pruitt cook as he had never cooked before.

She still wasn't really pretty, if a man wanted to look at her with a critical eye. But she had a way of making a man think she was.

To Shad Blankenship, Jameson said, "I was worried about her. I was afraid she might bring trouble in camp. It looks like I was wrong."

Shad said dryly, "We ain't in Dodge yet. They're all watching her, don't ever think they ain't. And Ransom King—you take a look at his eyes sometime when he's got them on her. That feller has more on his mind than buffalo hides, I'm tellin' you."

The days went by, and the hides piled up. Dried hides had to be taken off the ground to make room for green ones coming in. Jameson watched with satisfaction as the handlers pitched these flint hides onto a wagon. After a while it was loaded, lashed down securely with thick strings cut from a green hide.

Another load finished.

"We haven't got far to go now, Shad," he said. "We've got to move camp in a day or two. I think we'd just as well work over the Canadian, start drifting north a little."

Shad nodded without enthusiasm. Jameson could see what was working on him. Shad didn't relish going back to the settlements. It would be the same old story with him, soon as he got there. He knew it, and he was fighting it.

Jameson had something to worry about, too. Usually, with the prospect of an early return to town and the payoff, a hide crew got a new spring in its step, got to feeling jolly. But not this one. A tension was building, something hard to trace, hard to put his finger on. More than once he had to step in and stop a fight.

Even Reb Pruitt commented on it.

"Maybe it's the Indians," the cook volunteered. "You don't see any, but the air's got an Indian smell to it, someway. They're around. You can feel it."

To make it worse, Blair Farley had gotten brave and gone back to playing poker. And he was winning. A majority of the men in camp had fallen victim to his skillful fingers to one degree or another. Some already had lost more than they could hope to earn out of the whole expedition. Trencher was one of these. He stalked around the camp like an angry bull, brooding over his losses. Everyone stayed out of his way.

One morning in the first flush of dawn Jameson sat up straight in his tent. He had heard someone shout. He listened a moment and heard it again. Pulling on his boots, he hurried out. He saw several men moving toward the edge of camp.

Someone was calling, "Get Jameson!"

He quickened his step, and the men moved aside for him.

On the ground, a hundred feet past the stock corral, a fat man lay sprawled in his own blood. It was Blair Farley.

A skinner named Darcy Crosson stood by the body, excitement flushing his face. "Injuns," he said breathlessly. "Blair didn't come wake me for guard duty like he was supposed to. I found him thisaway."

Jameson knelt beside the dead man. Farley had been killed with a knife, a cruel ripping job that had laid his stomach open. And he had been scalped. It was rough, crude work that made Jameson's belly tighten, just looking at it.

"Bloody Comanches," somebody breathed in anger.

"Maybe," Jameson said. "And maybe it wasn't Comanches at all."

The men looked sharply at him. He said, "There's hardly a man here who didn't owe him money, lots of money. Now nobody owes him anything."

He could see the idea strike them like a hot iron. They

looked furtively at one another, each wondering if the man standing next to him had been the one who had wielded the knife.

Shad Blankenship came up. Jameson asked him, "He always kept those IOUs in his pocket, didn't he?"

Shad nodded. Jameson knelt and went through Blair Farley's pockets one at a time. They were empty, all of them.

He left all the pockets turned wrong side out, letting the men see them, letting them answer the question for themselves.

Someone went for a shovel, and someone else brought out a tarpaulin to cover the body. No one seemed to mourn Farley. Lately he hadn't had a friend in camp.

Shad Blankenship stood with eyes narrowed, watching Trencher lean idly against a wagon.

"Gage," he said, "you got any ideas?"

Jameson nodded. "One or two."

Blankenship's lips drew thin. "I reckon they're the same as mine."

One morning Celia Westerman walked out of her tent and moved toward Jameson.

"Do you know what tomorrow is, Gage?"

He shook his head. "Thursday, I think. Or maybe Friday. I haven't been keeping much track."

"It's Thursday. Thanksgiving. I wish we could have something special to fix for the men tomorrow. They've been brooding a lot the past few days. Maybe a good Thanksgiving meal would cheer them up."

Jameson brightened a little. How many Thanksgivings had he gone through and not even given them a thought?

"You might have something there. Yesterday I flushed

a bunch of wild turkeys in a chinaberry thicket up the creek."

Next morning he dug out a shotgun that he had shoved away among the gear in one of the wagons. Filling his pockets with shotgun shells, he motioned Shad Blankenship to him.

"Shad, how about you doing the buffalo shooting this morning?"

Shad looked him up and down, eyes dwelling on the shotgun.

"I'm going to get a few turkeys for Celia," he explained. "She thinks they might go over good with the crew for Thanksgiving."

Shad's eyes took on a glow of humor. "Now you're gettin' some sense. I only wish that when I'd been younger there'd been somebody for me to shoot turkeys for."

Jameson saddled his bay, sliding the saddle gun into the scabbard. The shotgun was all right for turkeys, but that saddle gun would always be handy in case something else showed up over the hill.

Celia Westerman walked out to the corral, wearing one of Pruitt's coats buttoned up to the neck against the winter wind. "Could you use some help? I'd like to go."

He hesitated, liking the thought of her company but a little skeptical just the same. "Always a chance of Indians."

"You'd be there, Gage," she smiled. "I really would like to go. I'd like to get out of camp a little while, just for a change."

He relented, knowing how monotonous it had been for her. "I can get another shotgun, if you want it."

"All right. I used to be a fairly decent shot."

He wasn't surprised. He had quit being surprised at the things Celia Westerman could do.

They rode out together, past Ransom King's wagons and hide grounds.

King stood and stared at them as they went by. He nodded at Jameson. Then he tipped his hat to Celia, and his eyes followed her. There was a trace of hunger in them. Time King was getting back to Rose Tremaine, Jameson thought.

Celia looked behind her once, but she didn't speak until they were well away from camp.

"I'm not sure I like your friend King," she said.

"King's all right," Jameson replied. "He just takes a little getting used to. He's up on a cloud one day and deep in darkness the next. He's wild, he's brash, and maybe a little selfish. But I guess it's selfishness that has made people stick with this country. Nobody would put up with it all, unless he thought he could get something out of it."

Celia frowned. "I know this—that if it had been up to him, I never would have been rescued from that Indian camp."

That blabbermouth Pruitt, Jameson thought with sudden impatience. "Who told you a thing like that?"

"Nobody. I just know it, that's all. I know that if it hadn't been for you, Gage, I'd still be there. Or I'd be dead. I'll always be in your debt."

Jameson found himself pulling closer to her, wanting to touch her but not doing it.

"You don't owe me anything, Celia. It's me that owes you. You don't know what it's been worth, having you in camp. In a way I'm going to hate to see you go home."

She nodded, and her blue eyes met his. "I know. In a way I'm going to hate to go. Sometimes I find myself wishing I could stay here. This is a good country, Gage. It'll be a good country to live in, someday."

They looked at each other until Jameson felt a warmth rising in his face, and a strong compulsion to reach across and pull her to him, to kiss her with all the hunger that was in him.

Suddenly he brought himself out of it, self-anger rising in him. Damn it, this isn't some dance-hall girl like King's Rose. What am I thinking of?

He rode silently a while, trying to put his mind on other things. But she was too close to him.

"You said you aren't married," he said. "Are you promised to anybody?"

She looked at the ground, her eyes absently following her shadow. "Not exactly. There's a man there—we grew up together. We've talked about it some."

Jameson drew up within himself. Well, he thought, that puts an end to it. Now maybe you can get your mind back on the buffalo.

{ THIRTEEN }

~~~

R eb Pruitt put water on to boil as soon as he saw
them coming, turkeys flung across their saddles.
Jameson had no desire to get into the work of
cleaning the birds. But he stood and watched as Pruitt and
the girl did it. The Texas cook handled the job with ease.
Jameson finally asked him:

"How did you ever come to be a camp cook, anyway?"

Pruitt looked up, laughter in his eyes. "Well now, I used
to have to ride a lot of rank broncs, back there on that ranch
where I worked. One day they fetched me one I couldn't
ride, and they had to leave me at the wagon to heal up. I
got to watching that fat, lazy cook. Come to find out he
was makin' fifteen dollars a month more than I was, and
he didn't have no saddle rubbing a callus on his rump,
either. So right then I knowed I'd missed my callin'."

Shad came in and unsaddled. He'd had a good stand.
Now he sat down, back to a wagon wheel, gun kit in hand.
He stripped down his big buffalo rifle, swabbing its barrel
clean and wiping a thin trace of oil on it before putting it
back together.

Jameson brought the empty cartridge cases he had been
soaking in vinegar to get all the burned powder out. Now

he set the cases up on end and poured black Dupont powder out of a can into a bowl. He started filling the shells with powder, stopping half an inch from the top. He tamped it down with the rammer, put the wad in, and spilled a little more powder atop the wad. He wrapped a piece of paper around the base of the bullet, then forced it into the shell, clamping it down tight.

"Get your turkeys?" Shad asked.

Jameson nodded.

Shad said, "Great country for game, ain't it? Man wouldn't never starve here, if he had powder and lead, and a little salt. He could live fine, the way we done a long time ago."

That far-off look was in Shad's eyes. He was back into times long past, savoring some elusive fragment of fond memory. "It's like the rest of the country used to be before they come and ruined it." He considered that and added, "Before *we* ruined it."

"I know what you mean, Shad," Jameson replied. "It's been that way with me. I get a feeling about this country, a feeling that maybe this is what I've been looking for all my life. You ever look out across it at sundown, Shad? Sundown's the time to look at a place, if you want to see the beauty in it. I get a feeling I don't ever want to leave. I want to stay here, and I want the country to stay just like it is."

Shad grunted, some bitter taste coming in his mouth. He spat and rubbed a greasy sleeve across his red beard.

"But it won't. Three, four years, the buffalo'll all be gone, the way they was from the Republican and the Arkansas. What would there be to stay for? How would you make a livin'?"

"I don't know for sure, Shad. I've thought about cattle. I guess Reb Pruitt put it in my head, always talking about the Texas cow business. This would be a fine cow country, Shad, as good for cattle as it is for buffalo."

"You'd have to get the Comanches off first, and they might not see it just your way."

"When the buffalo are gone, Shad, there won't be any more trouble with the Comanches."

Shad nodded. "But you've never had any experience with cattle, other than maybe popping a whip over a bull team. Takes more than bulls to run a cow ranch, I expect."

Jameson smiled. "A man can learn. *We* could learn, Shad, you and me together. The frontier is going. This would give us something we could both tie to."

Shad Blankenship's wrinkled old face held the beginning of a smile, and his pale eyes were looking far off again, far back into memory. Then, slowly, the smile faded. The memory was gone. The present was here again with its jarring reality. The present, and the future.

"Won't work for me, Gage. I'm too old to change over. The only hope I got is that when my time comes I can die out here someplace and be buried where I can listen to the wind blow and the wolves howl, instead of in town where all I can hear is a piano clinkin' and somebody bellyachin' about the price of beans."

He pointed his finger at Jameson, jabbed it at him.

"But *you* can make the change, Gage. Make it before it's too late. Get you those cows, and grab onto some of this land. And get you a wife, young'un. I never had one, and that's where I made a mistake. Life gets pointless for a man when he ain't got a home, ain't got a woman of his own. One of them dance-hall gals is all right for a young man still sowing his oats. But comes a day he needs to settle. You've come to that day, Gage. You watch or you'll pass it up, and then it's too late. You need a good woman, like that Celia Westerman. If I was you, I wouldn't let her get away."

Shad was right, Jameson admitted to himself. He wanted Celia Westerman. He needed her. But it seemed she already had gotten away, even before he met her.

The whole crew was waiting when at last the turkey was done. The sun was going down. The stock had been fed, and all the work had been finished. Nothing was left but to sit down and enjoy the Thanksgiving meal.

The anticipation of it was having the effect Jameson had hoped. The tension had eased.

Even the burly Trencher showed a semblance of a smile as he roughly shouldered his way into the line, digging a fork into one of the turkeys and knifing off a huge section of it.

But something went wrong. The first man to fill his plate shoved a big bite of turkey into his mouth and started to chew, grinning. The grin suddenly left him. His mouth twisted. He spat it all out, choking. Seeing that, another man judiciously tested a small piece of the turkey on the tip of his tongue. His face stretched awry in dismay.

Not seeing them, Trencher bit off a big chunk. He spat turkey for six feet, coughing. He looked up then, a flash of rage in his eyes. He flung the plate to the ground and stalked toward Reb Pruitt.

"You miserable, dried-up Johnny Reb, you're tryin' to poison us all!"

Pruitt stared at him, uncomprehending, until Trencher made a grab. He stepped aside quickly. But Trencher kept coming. He pinned Pruitt to the chuck wagon, swung his big fist and knocked the cook to his knees. He grabbed the little Texan by the shoulder and jerked him erect again. He slammed him against the wheel.

Jameson took long strides across to the wagon. He grabbed Trencher's arm and held it. "Stop it, Trencher!"

Trencher struggled with him, trying to free himself. "I'll kill the little whelp!" he grunted.

Finally, seeing he couldn't pull free, he whirled on Jameson.

"All right, Jameson," he breathed, "I been wantin' to do this for a long time." His eyes glowed with a wild fever of rage. He rushed at Jameson, his arms reaching forward from his heavy body. Jameson did not try to dodge. Instead, he lowered his head and drove straight into Trencher's hard belly. He made Trencher overreach, while his own fists pounded into Trencher's ribs. The big man grunted at the shock, and he reeled a step or two sideways. Jameson kept pushing, pressing this initial advantage, driving at Trencher's belly and ribs.

But the surprise lasted only a moment; then Trencher had his wits back. He plowed in now, his rage driving him on. He was apparently oblivious to the worst punishment Jameson was able to give him. He fought only to win, his heavy feet grinding down on Jameson's toes, his knee trying at Jameson's groin, his fingers grasping and twisting Jameson's ears. Pain rocketed through Jameson, pain and desperation. He knew Trencher would kill him if he could.

Somehow he managed to bring up his knee, hard and quick. His heavy boot smashed against Trencher's shin, taking the hide as it drove downward. Jameson saw an opening and arched a fist into Trencher's ear. The big man cried out and turned away from him. Jameson's fist slammed into Trencher's kidney, once, then again. Trencher doubled over. Jameson jerked Trencher's head up and hit him hard in the throat. Trencher fell heavily to the ground and lay there gasping.

Jameson took a couple of steps backward, heaving for breath. The chuck wagon was behind him. He moved to it and leaned on it for support, his chest rising and falling rapidly as the breath came back to him. He wiped a dusty coat sleeve across his forehead, and it came away wet.

For a moment his eyes were off Trencher. He didn't see where Trencher got the gun. Suddenly there it was, in the man's trembling hands, and Trencher was standing spread-legged, grinning with his lips while his eyes crackled with hatred.

"Now, Jameson," Trencher breathed heavily, and the barrel tilted upward.

Jameson could only stand there, his back to the chuck wagon, staring helplessly at the six-shooter. His mouth went dry. All he could think was, Where did he get that gun?

He sensed a sudden movement beside him. Trencher jerked aside, but not in time. A heavy iron pot hook from Pruitt's chuck box slammed into the man's head. Trencher fell heavily, the gun dropping from his fingers. Before he could grab it, someone else had it. Messick, the skinner. Jameson looked around and saw Pruitt still bent forward, the way he had been when he let the pot hook fly away, singing.

"Thanks, Reb," Jameson whispered.

As suddenly as it had begun, it was over. Ransom King helped Trencher to his knees. "I'm sorry about this, Gage," he said. "Trencher has a bottle hidden away somewhere, and he's been working on it. I'll get him sobered up. It won't happen again."

Jameson tried to speak, but his throat was leather-dry, and no sound came out. He watched narrow-eyed as King and one of Jameson's own men helped Trencher stagger away.

Angrily Trencher jerked free of the men who were holding him. He turned half around, his hate-filled eyes on Jameson.

"I'll get you, Jameson. Your time is about run out. I'll get you and don't you forget it!"

King took hold of the man and roughly yanked him away. "You're drunk, Trencher. Come on."

Celia Westerman hurried to Jameson. Her fingers anxiously explored the cuts and bruises on his face. "I'll take care of those," she said.

He waved his hand. "Never mind. I'm all right."

But she went anyway to the chuck box, hunting for antiseptic. The rest of the crew melted away, chewing on bread, sipping coffee, but leaving the turkey alone. Pruitt stared at it, puzzled.

"I can't figure it out. I know it wasn't nothin' we done. But that meat's so bitter it makes you sick."

It struck Jameson then, as Celia painted his wounds with iodoform. The chinaberries. He hadn't thought of it before. The turkeys had been feeding on chinaberries. That had tainted the meat.

"Dandy Thanksgivin'," Pruitt said disconsolately. "Nothing much here to be thankful about."

Jameson slowly shook his head. "One thing, Reb. We can be thankful we've got those wagons about loaded. I think it's high time we headed for Dodge."

{ FOURTEEN }

Rainin' way yonder," Shad Blankenship said, watching the heavy clouds scurry across the morning sky. "It would rain here too, if a man was to look at them clouds a little cross-eyed."

Jameson could smell the promise of rain in the sharp wind searching across the prairie. Riding beside Shad, holding the Big Fifty in his lap, he frowned at the skies. "Maybe. Been hoping it would hold off a little. Three or four more days and we'd have all the hides we can pack."

"We got plenty now," Shad said. "She starts in to rainin', we better settle for what we got and move out."

Shad spat, and his big black dog jumped aside. Shad let his pale eyes lift to the horizon. "Something else too, and that's that Injun, Kills His Enemies. I'd just as soon not have to mess with him. But there's Injuns around, Gage. I can feel them in the back of my neck."

When Jameson smiled, Shad said quickly, "Don't laugh. Dodge them as many years as I have and you get so you don't have to see them anymore. You can smell them, like a hound dog."

Jameson looked back toward the two wagons that trailed them, slackening his pace when he saw that they were getting some distance behind. Like Shad, he was getting that uneasy feeling, wondering each day if it might not be smarter to pack up and string the wagons north than to ride out for another day's bag of green hides.

They didn't have to ride far to find buffalo, for a big herd had drifted in along the creek where they were camped. The animals grazed in scattered bunches up and down it for miles. They were almost black now with the thick coat of winter hair that made them look bigger than they had a few weeks ago. These winter hides would bring more money. With that heavy hair they could be turned into robes instead of being cut up for leather.

It was this that had kept Jameson here, the robe hides and the ease of the kill. Had the buffalo been hard to find, he would have started north a week ago.

"Well, Shad," Jameson said, "let's split up and get this over with as soon as we—"

He broke off, for Shad had stiffened. Jameson turned quickly and saw what Shad saw—Indians.

Ten warriors swept down the crest of a hill toward them, whooping and yelling as they came. Ten warriors against two men, with the wagons still behind.

"We can't get back to the wagons, Shad!" Jameson exclaimed. "They'll cut us off."

Desperately he began to look for a hillock, a buffalo wallow, anything for cover. But there was nothing.

Shad stepped out of the saddle and dropped prone to the ground. He began to dig in his pocket. "Good a time as any to see if that man was right about these squallers," he said. He was as casual as if he were about to try a new gun on the buffalo.

Jameson had almost forgotten about those bullets Shad had bored the holes in. Now, dropping down beside Shad and ramming one of his own cartridges into the breech, he remembered.

Shad raised the rifle and fired. The bullet screamed as it sped through the air, the bored hole catching the wind. Shad put another one in and fired again.

"Squall like a banshee, don't they?" Shad said.

The Indians hauled up short, and Shad put a third one over their heads.

"I only got two left," Shad complained. "If they don't work, I'm gonna have to tell that feller he's an awful liar."

He fired the fourth one. Now the Indians began to pull back, gesturing excitedly. Shad balefully eyed the last bullet, then slipped it into the breech. It was even louder than the rest, one of the weirdest sounds Jameson had ever heard. It made the hair stand on his neck.

It did the job. The Indians wheeled their horses and took out across the hill again. Jameson lowered his own rifle, still unfired.

Shad grinned and spat tobacco juice out across the grass. "Superstitious lot, Injuns are. Come up against them with somethin' they ain't seen or heard before, and they don't hardly know how to take it. Come to think of it, somebody shot one of them things at me, I wouldn't know how to take it, either."

They stood up, catching their horses.

Jameson looked at the hill over which the Indians had come and gone. And he made a decision.

"I think we've got all the hides we'd better try for. We're heading north, Shad, while we still can."

Swinging back into the saddle, Shad nodded in agreement. "Now, young'un, you're talkin' sense."

They rode quickly back to the two wagons, not knowing if the Indians had been frightened enough to keep away, or if they might come back over that hill at any minute.

The men at the wagons had pulled up together and jumped to the ground, rifles ready. They still stood there as Jameson and Shad rode up.

The tall, thin skinner Messick solemnly shook his head. "We thought sure you was goners, both of you. And we wasn't even sure about us." His eyes went to Shad. "What in the name of heaven was that you shot at them? Not even a Comanche can make a sound worse than that."

Shad explained the squallers. "Worked this time. But they'll probably figure it out. Next time they won't be so easy fooled."

Jameson said, "Turn the wagons around and head for camp. There won't be a next time if we can help it."

They had not ridden three minutes before they heard other gunfire, farther away. Ransom King's. You could always tell by the sound of the guns who was doing the shooting. No two of these buffalo rifles made quite the same report.

Suddenly Jameson straightened, his ear turned toward the sound. The first tremor of alarm moved through him. There were more guns than there ought to be, and the firing was getting faster. That wasn't the way you shot buffalo. Jameson glanced at the other men and saw that they were listening, too.

"They've hit King," Jameson said. "Let's roll."

Messick and the other driver flipped their reins. The mules lunged forward, jerking roughly against the traces, bouncing the wagons. Jameson spurred into a lope and took the lead. Shad Blankenship fell in just behind him. Jameson leaned forward in the saddle, listening to the crackle of guns.

He looked back and saw the wagons trailing behind him, moving as fast as they could without bouncing the wheels off.

A mile. A mile and a half. The shooting was close now. They topped out over a ridge and there the battle was, below them. King and Trencher and two skinners were barricaded behind an upturned wagon. Around them lay four dead mules and King's sorrel horse.

A dose of our own medicine, Jameson thought.

Around and around the men fifteen or eighteen Comanches circled, whooping, yelling, letting arrows fly into the flimsy barricade. Three or four Indians and as many horses lay fallen on the prairie. And inside the barricade Jameson saw a man lying still, on his stomach.

He signaled the wagons to pull up, for he saw no practical way to get them down off the steep ridge in time to be any help.

"We'll do a better job shooting from up here anyway," he said to Shad. The skinners piled out and came running, bringing their rifles. Jameson signaled one man to hold the horses and mules, the rest to spread out in a line. He bellied down in the grass, put up the rest stick for his Sharps and drew a bead. The first shot sent an Indian horse plunging into a somersault. Beside Jameson, the other men opened fire. Two more horses went down, and Indians fell.

The Comanches hauled up in surprise. While they stood there, trying to locate the source of fire, well-aimed bullets cut down two more. One Indian made a signal, and the others followed him, leaving the battleground in a run. Jameson sighted down the barrel, held his breath and squeezed. The Indian who had signaled pitched to the ground. The others kept riding.

The hide men on the ridge continued rapid fire, and the

men behind the barricade were doing the same. Another horse fell. The rider jumped up limping. Two Comanches turned back, leaning down and drumming heels into their horses' sides. Riding on either side of him, they picked him up and carried him off between them, holding him that way until they thought they were out of bullet range.

Presently Jameson stood up, pulling the rest stick out of the ground, wiping the dirt off it onto his pants leg.

"Looks like it's over, Shad."

"Maybe. And maybe it's just started."

A drop of water struck Jameson's hat brim. He looked up, and another hit him on the cheek. His gaze went to the horizon. He saw that it had faded out into a gray pall of rain.

"Fixin' to get wet," he said. "Let's see what we can do down there."

Without going back for their horses, Jameson and Shad walked down the ridge toward King's upturned wagon. Messick followed behind them, using his rifle to help his balance as his long legs hurriedly worked down the steep slope.

One of King's skinners walked shakily out to meet them, his face gray as an ashbank, hands trembling. "Man alive, but you fellers came just in time. They had us, I'll tell you, they had us."

King stood beside the upturned wagon, rifle in his hand, the sprinkle of rain striking its hot barrel and turning to steam.

"You saved our hash, Jameson," he said levelly.

Jameson shook his head. "That evens us up. You saved mine once, in Dodge."

But Trencher glared angrily, his hatred for Jameson still burning in his eyes. "We was doin' all right," he said sullenly. "We'd have whipped them off without you." He turned sharply and trudged out to look across the field of battle.

Jameson knelt beside the man who lay facedown in the grass. One of King's crew. He touched him, then stood up. The man was dead.

Jameson looked at King. "There'll be more dead if we don't haul out of here. I think I've got all the hides I need. How about you?"

King looked up at the horizon over which the Indians had poured down upon him. "I'm satisfied. Those boys will be back, and I'd just as soon not be here."

The lean Messick was walking around over the battle scene. At length he paused to look down on three Indians who lay still within twenty feet of each other.

Trencher strode that way, taking a skinning knife from his belt.

"I'm gonna count coup this time," he said brutally.

He knelt by the first Indian, cut a crude circle around the top of the head with the sharp knife and roughly took off the scalp. He moved to the second. But this one wasn't dead. When the half-conscious Indian cried out at the fiery touch of the blade, Trencher jerked back as if he had touched something hot. Then he lifted the knife and plunged it into the Indian's throat. He grinned savagely as he brought it up and stabbed down again.

A moment later Trencher was wiping the knife in the grass and dangling three gory specimens of crude butchery, the grin cutting across his broad, bewhiskered face like a knife gash itself.

Messick stood watching him, his back stiff, some of the color drained from his cheeks. When Trencher had gone, Messick glanced toward Jameson and beckoned him with his sharp chin.

"What does that remind you of, Gage?"

"Blair Farley?"

Messick nodded and said tightly, "Yeah, and even farther back than that. Remember George Hobart, and those two men we found dead with him that last trip out for Miles and Posey?"

Jameson knelt and looked closer at the scalped Indians, remembering how it had been with the white men, wondering if possibly . . .

"Nathan, it couldn't have been . . ."

"But it could. The thought struck me when I saw Blair Farley, but I didn't believe it then. Now I do."

Jameson protested, "He works for Ransom King. How could he have killed Hobart?"

"He doesn't work for King all the time. They tell me sometimes he goes out for himself, when King doesn't need him. Who knows what he does when he's out that way? He's no hunter, Jameson. Man hunter, maybe, but not a buffalo hunter."

"We'd have to be sure."

"That knife he had—I caught a quick look at it. I'd swear it was George Hobart's. George made his own knives, and there never was anybody else ever made one just the same as his."

A chill passed through Jameson. He had to concede that Messick might be right. There was a brutality, a killer instinct about Trencher. Jameson had seen it often enough to know. He'd even been pitted against it.

"We'd still have to have proof before we could do anything."

Messick's eyes were narrowed in cold fury. "I'll get you the proof. I'll get my hands on that knife someway. And if it's George's . . . I'll put it in Trencher's throat, the way I'd do a buffalo."

Jameson closed his eyes, remembering last year when he had helped run down three hide thieves who had murdered a hunter and stolen the hides he had worked months to get. They had gone so far as to scalp the victim, trying to shift the blame onto Indians. But another hunter had stumbled upon the scene and run for help.

Jameson would never forget how they had hanged the thieves one at a time, out on the treeless prairie. They had used the upended tongue of the stolen wagon. The last two had watched ashen-faced and trembling as the first one had choked and slowly died.

And later, when it was all over, somebody had scalped all three of them.

Messick said, "I'll get that knife. Then we'll see what we do."

The rain was falling steadily as they hurriedly broke camp. They took up the half-green hides from the drying grounds and loaded them on the last empty wagons that had been used to haul each day's bag in from the killing grounds. At the first sign of rain Reb Pruitt had stretched a wagon sheet over the hoops of the chuck wagon to keep the remaining supplies and bedding dry. Then he had stretched a tarpaulin out overhead to give the men a place to stand out of the rain while they wolfed down a quick meal.

Gage Jameson stood on the creek bank, watching the angry swirl of mud-brown water. The creek was rising steadily. A couple of hours more and it would be out of banks from the rain which had already fallen farther upstream.

Shad Blankenship pointed his rusty chin toward the chuck wagon. "You better grab you somethin' to eat so we can drag it out of here."

Jameson shook his head. "In a minute. Just looking at that creek, Shad. Think we could put the wagons over it right now?"

Shad frowned, watching the brown water rush past. "Maybe, maybe not. Another hour or so and nothin' will get over it."

"That's what I was thinking. If we could get across it now, it would give us a lot of protection from the Comanches, at least till it went down. And we could get a long way by then, if we kept traveling."

Shad rubbed his chin. "It'd sure be some gamble. We might lose every wagon we got."

"No telling what we'll lose if we have to fight those Comanches. We'll try it with one wagon—*I'll* try it. If it works, fine. If it doesn't . . ."

He let it drop there. He turned and hurried back to camp. He sought out the wagon with the smallest load of hides on it and called a pair of teamsters.

"Let's hook a team to this wagon, quick."

He disconnected the trail wagon while they caught up the mules and put the harness on them. This would be the way, one wagon at a time, then come back for the trail wagons. Seeing what he was about to try, the other men gathered to watch anxiously. They all knew what this meant—a chance to avoid a battle.

Jameson shed his coat, his boots and his hat in case he had to swim. He started to climb up to the wagon seat. Celia Westerman caught his arm. Her blue eyes were big with fear.

She said, "Gage, I . . ." Her lips went tight, and she choked off the words. "Gage, be careful."

He squeezed her hand, then crossed two of her fingers. "Keep them that way," he said. He climbed to the seat and flipped the reins.

"Hya-a-a-a-a!"

The mules jerked against the traces and the wagon lurched forward, the iron rims slipping in the slick mud. Jameson swung the mules around, straightening the wagon before it reached the levelest part of the creek bank. The mules seemed to sense the danger. They began to falter. He took the long whip and lashed far out with it, popping it over the ears of the leaders, yelling as he went.

The leaders plunged into the water. Jameson kept the whip talking, kept the other mules pulling hard. The foamy water lapped up against the wheels of the wagon as they splashed down off the creek bank.

"Hya-a-a-a-a! Keep on moving there! *Hya-a-a-a-a!"*

The mules angled with the powerful current. For a moment Jameson's hopes soared high. It looked as if they would make it to the far bank without a hitch.

Then the full force of the water hit the flat side of the wagon. He felt a sickening lurch. He saw panic sweep through the swimming mules. He found himself wishing they were horses. Mules almost always were the most sensible in a tight situation, but in the water horses had them bested.

The wagon began to tilt, top-heavy with its load of hides. The mules were fighting, plunging up and down. One went under water, came up, then went down again.

He's lost, Jameson thought fearfully. Let him get his ears full of water and he's lost.

He felt the wagon begin to heave over beneath him. He jumped from the seat into the brown foam, his hands tightly clutching the lines. Over the heavy roar he heard the splash as the wagon went over on its side, then over again, the wheels up out of the water. He heard the snap of the tongue.

The wagon was doomed now, and the mules threshed in terror. Another was out of sight, adding its dead weight to drag the rest down. Jameson managed to grab the bridle of one fighting mule and hold while he drew the knife from his belt. He cut at the harness, trying to free the mules from the wagon.

But the heavy pull of the current wrested the harness from his hands, and somehow he lost the knife. He felt himself being pulled away from the wagon, away from the mules.

All was lost now, he knew, hopelessness sweeping through him. The mules, the wagon, the hides—all of it. All he could do now was try to save himself.

He swam desperately, managing to keep his head above water as the raging current carried him on. He fought to return to the bank. He was working nearer. But his mouth was full of the muddy water. He choked, swallowing some of it. His arms were afire with pain, heavy as anvils.

He realized suddenly that he was drowning, that he would never make it to the bank. Swallowing water, his arms giving out, he was done.

But he kept fighting, trying for the bank.

Then he saw someone out there on horseback, rope in hand. The horseman rode into the water, as far as he could without being swept into the current. Going down, Jameson saw the rope swinging. He fought to the surface again, and he felt the rope settle and jerk tight about his shoulders. Instinctively he grabbed it. He felt it burn cruelly into his flesh as he hit the end of it. Then the rope began to pull him against the current. He swung slowly but surely toward the bank. He felt the slick mud underfoot and tried to help himself ashore. But no more strength was left in him.

The rope dragged him onto the bank, out of the water. He stayed there on hands and knees, coughing up muddy water, nausea sending the world reeling about his head. He was conscious of the clean rain beating down on him.

Reb Pruitt jumped from Jameson's bay horse, dropping his end of the rope. He rushed to Jameson's side. He took off his coat and threw it over Jameson's wet shoulders.

"Go on now," he said gently, "bend over there, keep coughin' that water up. You'll be as sick as a horse if you don't."

Jameson kept coughing. Gradually the world stopped spinning and he could see. "How far . . . how far?"

Pruitt shrugged. "Quarter mile, maybe. That's a mighty fast current."

Jameson caught Pruitt's hand. "Thanks, Reb."

The little Texan grinned, recoiling the wet rope. "You're a pretty decent kind of a Yankee, Jameson, and I figure we better hang onto any of that kind we can get. There ain't many."

Men came running afoot, the quarter mile down from camp. Men, and a woman. Celia Westerman rushed to Jameson. Breathless, seeing he was all right, she threw herself into his arms.

Jameson held her tightly, his cheek against hers.

The rest of them were staring, and he didn't care. He held her a long time.

"Celia," he said at last, "we've got to go. It didn't work. All we can do now is travel, and travel fast."

{ FIFTEEN }

～～～

Moving the wagons out, Jameson tried to ride his horse. But the muddy water he had swallowed made him lean over and heave until at last he was too weak and head-spinning sick to stay in the saddle. So he moved to the seat of the chuck wagon, beside Celia Westerman, and let the cowboy cook ride the horse.

He had changed to dry clothes. Now the cold, steady rain had soaked even those, and he hunched up in a miserable knot, a raw chill penetrating him to the bone.

He looked back often to the long line of heavy-laden hide wagons strung out behind. Their wide rims cut through the brown cured grass and squeezed dirty water up into deep muddy ruts that ribboned out in their wake.

A blind Indian could have followed them, he thought darkly.

Celia Westerman touched his arm. "Look, Gage, yonder."

He glanced up where she pointed. His eyes still burned from the muddy water, but he could see the eight or ten horsemen far off there in the rain, hunched under blankets, watching the wagons.

"We can't get away from them," Celia said. "They'll follow us until they're ready. And then they'll come."

They kept rolling all the rest of the day and well into darkness. Shad Blankenship and Reb Pruitt rode in front, feeling out the low places for soft spots that might bog down the wagons. The rain was letting up some, for which Jameson was thankful. Much more of it and the ground would become so boggy the wagons couldn't move.

Jameson looked often to the right, and usually he saw the Indians there, following along patiently out of range.

Men in the other wagons were watching them, too. Someone said angrily, "Why don't they come on and get it over with?"

"They're just waitin'," came the answer in Nathan Messick's even voice. "Injuns don't like the rain. They'll come down in their own due time."

When they didn't come before dark, Jameson felt some relief. At least they weren't likely to strike before daylight.

Reb Pruitt came up, and Jameson called him. "Let me have the horse a while, Reb."

Celia Westerman caught Jameson's hand. "Gage, are you sure you can ride?"

"I feel a lot better now. Anyway, this shouldn't take long."

With Shad Blankenship, he rode along the creek bank, looking for a likely spot for camp, a spot that would help them present a good defense. The rain had stopped, but the creek was still running high.

"You ain't thinkin' about tryin' to cross her again, are you, Gage?" Shad asked worriedly.

Jameson shook his head. "No, thanks. I already had my bath."

He found what he wanted, a place where the creek bank had caved back far enough from the water itself so that the stock could all be herded down there out of reach of the Comanches.

"Reb," he said as he rode back to the chuck wagon, "I've found a good place where we can line the wagons up in a row right on the edge of the bank. We'll put the horses and mules down below. That'll give us the water at our backs so they can't circle us. Follow me."

The cave-off was perhaps a hundred yards long and the sharp bank about five feet high, a kind of pocket against the creek. Carefully they pulled the wagons up within feet of the edge, angling the tongues outward so the front of one wagon was almost touching the tail gate of the next. As the teams were unharnessed they were turned loose below the bank.

Working in darkness, the men cut timber and threw up a barrier at each end to keep the stock inside. Reb Pruitt built his fire below the bank with wood he had kept dry all day under the wagon sheet. Shivering with cold, their clothes thoroughly soaked, the men filed by to fill their cups with hot coffee, then went back to work. They shoveled wet earth high under the beds of the wagons as protection against bullets and arrows.

Only when the work was finished did they stop to eat. The hot coffee and the buffalo meat brought strength back to Jameson. His head was clear, and he was no longer sick at his stomach. He could almost forget the soggy clothing sticking to his skin, the cold that stiffened him and turned his lips blue.

Ransom King walked over and sat on his heels beside Jameson and Celia Westerman. "What now, Gage?"

"Nothing, just wait. I don't believe we could find a better place to make a stand. No more running. We'll wait here for them."

King looked worriedly back toward the water, which

still roared in the darkness. "What if that creek rises some more?"

Jameson's lips drew tight. "Then our bread just turns back to dough."

Waiting, Jameson reloaded all the empty cartridges he had. Celia Westerman sat beside him, brooding. "Gage," she said finally, "it's all my fault. If it hadn't been for me, you wouldn't be in this."

Gage shook his head. "It's not your fault. You weren't captured by your own choice. You didn't know we were going to try to free you until we'd done it. There wasn't a thing you could have done or changed. Besides, we'd likely have run up against them sooner or later anyway. We knew when we came down here we'd have a fight getting out. So now we have it."

"What do you think of our chances?"

He shrugged. "We've got a good defensive position here. We've got buffalo rifles that can shoot farther and straighter than anything these Comanches have ever seen. We've got powder and lead, and plenty of food and water. Whatever happens, they'll have a run for their money."

The glow from the faraway campfire barely lighted her face. She was looking at Jameson, her eyes soft. Presently she touched his hand.

"Gage," she said, "do you have a girl waiting for you somewhere?"

"No," he replied. "There's never been one."

She leaned to him a little. She said, "I told you once that there was a man back home. . . . I thought there was, Gage. But I know now that there never was enough between us."

She tilted her head upward. "Gage, whatever happens, I want you to know . . . I love you."

His arms went around her. He pulled her to him, and their lips met in the darkness.

Daybreak, and every man was up, peering anxiously out over the earthwork defense they had piled up beneath the wagons.

"Nothin' there," Shad Blankenship said. "Maybe they want us to sweat."

"Maybe they think we're going to move again," Jameson commented. "They want to catch us strung out in the open. But we'll fool them on that. We wait right here."

Reb Pruitt called out, "Grub's ready. Come and get it!"

The men filed by, and Jameson watched their faces, wondering how well they were going to hold up. In most of the faces he saw a tenseness, but if there was real fear, he failed to detect it.

Suddenly he became aware that someone was missing. Nathan Messick!

He climbed up on the bank and looked over the camp. "Anybody seen Messick?" he called.

Nobody replied. Most began looking around for him. Reb Pruitt had the loudest voice. He called again and again. But Messick was gone.

"Them Comanches," Pruitt muttered angrily. "They must of snuck up here in the night."

Puzzled, Jameson glanced at Trencher. He noticed that Trencher's knife was gone from the scabbard on the man's belt. And he remembered what Messick had said:

"I'll get you the proof. I'll get my hands on that knife someway. And if it's George's, I'll put it in Trencher's throat, the way I'd do a buffalo."

It hadn't been Comanches, Jameson knew. Messick *had*

gotten hold of that knife, sometime during the night. But something had gone wrong.

Jameson looked down at the flooded creek, still rolling and foaming. He knew where Nathan Messick was. He choked back the fury that welled up inside him.

When this is over, he promised himself, I'll get you, Trencher. I don't know how, but I'll get you.

After breakfast they sat and waited, an hour, two hours, three. Jameson watched the clouds lose their heavy gray. Slowly they thinned, the glare of sunlight showing in weak spots. By mid-morning there were definite breaks in them. The rain was over. The sun would be out soon, and the mud would begin to dry. The wagons could move faster.

"Here they come!" Shad Blankenship called.

Men scrambled for their places beneath the wagons. Most lay prone on their blankets to keep out of the mud. They had their ammunition lying beside them, ready.

Jameson looked up and caught his breath. The Indians came in a body, riding at a lope. The solid group spread out fanwise, and suddenly the Indians began to yell.

Jameson was held by the deadly magnificence of the sight. Never had he seen its equal, and he knew it was something he was likely never to see again. Shrieking and yelping, the Comanches came rushing across the rain-soaked ground, waving their bows and lances and guns, their heavy bull-neck shields. The bodies of Indians and horses alike were splashed with red and yellow. War bonnets streamed in the wind. The barbarically painted bodies glinted with metal ornaments and charms. In horses' manes and tails there fluttered bright red cloth, plaited to stay.

Jameson felt the hair lift at the back of his neck.

"Get down, Celia," he said. "Stay down."

She shook her head. "I'll help you reload."

"All right, then. But keep low." Then he yelled for the men, "If they get too close, shoot for the horses. Don't let a horse come through."

He flopped down on his blanket then. He rested the barrel of the rifle across a wagon spoke.

The Indians were bearing down on them, two hundred yards away.

"Trying to ride over us the first time," he said. He drew a bead on one of the nearest Indians and fired. The Indian spun half around and fell off the horse, blown open by the heavy bullet of the Big Fifty. Other rifles roared. Indians tumbled. Horses sprawled, other horses stumbling over them and crashing down.

The buffalo hunters kept up a rapid fire, lacing the Comanche line. Behind them, under the bank, their own horses and mules milled excitedly. When some of the Comanches appeared to be breaking through, the rifle muzzles tipped downward, and the horses rolled. Two Indians who fell near the wagons jumped to their feet and came running, only to be torn apart by bullets before they reached the breastworks. Others turned and fled afoot, some falling under fire, some managing to swing up behind other Indians who had not lost their horses.

The first attack was broken. The Comanches retreated in a ragged line, leaving the plain dotted with fallen horses. Some of these animals threshed and screamed in pain until merciful bullets sought them out.

The Comanches tried to pick up as many of their dead and wounded as they could before they rode away. Jameson counted ten warriors carried off. He could still see six or eight lying in the grass, too close to the wagons for the Indians to recover them.

One fallen Indian raised up on his elbow and began

dragging himself away. A rifle cracked, and he fell face-down in the mud. Jameson saw Trencher lower his rifle to reload it, grinning.

The Indians rallied far out yonder on the prairie, milling around, arguing. They would be a little while.

Jameson pushed to his feet and slowly made the rounds to see how the crew had fared.

"Any dead?" he called.

There was no answer to that, and relief lifted a heavy weight from his broad shoulders. "Any wounded?"

From two places came an answer. One of King's skinners held a rag to his shoulder, stopping the flow of blood from a flesh wound. Face a shade pale, the man said, "I've had mosquitoes do worse."

He found the other man kneeling over, pants pulled down, while Reb Pruitt grinned and poured antiseptic into a cloth, daubing it on an angry red streak across a tender part of the man's anatomy.

Reb said, "You Yanks taught me a long time ago that you had to keep more than your head down."

Jameson asked, "Think you'll be ready to fight again when they come back?"

The skinner nodded darkly. "Just as long as I don't have to sit down."

Jameson walked to Ransom King's place. "How's it going over here?"

King looked up and grinned at him. "Just send us more Indians."

Trencher lay beside King on a spread-out blanket. He wouldn't look up at Jameson, just kept scowling out over the muddy mound in front of him. Jameson looked down at the empty knife scabbard at the big man's belt. The anger came back to him.

But he had to bide his time now. They needed every man they had, even Trencher. It might be that the Comanches would get Trencher and Jameson wouldn't have to.

Jameson returned to his own place and found Celia waiting there, rifles loaded and extra cartridges laid out neatly. He touched her hand.

"I still wish you'd get down below the bank," he said.

She shook her head. "I'll stay by you."

He stood beside the wagon and watched the Indians milling far off in the distance. The group began to move forward again.

"Get ready," Jameson called. "They're coming back."

The tactic this time was the same as before. The Comanches fanned out and came riding in a lope again, shrieking and yelling, their line ragged but unwavering. Brown bodies glistened in the sun, war paint shining. Feathers streamed.

This time Jameson did not wait for them to get near. Lying down, he again rested the rifle barrel over the wagon spoke and took careful aim. At four hundred yards his bullet brought a horse down. The other men began to fire. Long before the Indians were near enough to use arrows or their own guns, the hunters' fire had cut another ghastly swath through their lines.

The Comanche attack this time was halfhearted. Two hundred yards from the wagons the Indians began hauling back before the deadly fire of the hunters' long-range guns. Gathering their dead and wounded again, once more they fled the field.

Jameson had been holding his breath until his lungs ached, cold sweat breaking out all over him. Now he stood up again to breathe heavily. Celia Westerman stood with him, leaning her head wearily against his shoulder. Black gunpowder streaked her cheek.

"Think perhaps they're leaving?" she asked him.

He shook his head. "I doubt it. They'll probably try again."

Once more he made the rounds to check casualties. He was pleasantly surprised that there hadn't been any this time. The Comanches had never gotten close enough.

Shad Blankenship took a fresh chew of tobacco and patted his black dog. "They probably don't know what to make of these big buffalo guns. The way you picked that Indian off a while ago was enough to set them to thinkin'. Turn them back one more time like that and I'd bet we've seen the last of them."

Jameson was grim. "I hope so."

He went back to Celia and sat down beside her. Her presence strengthened him. He poured water down the Big Fifty to cool the barrel and carefully swabbed it out to remove the burned powder.

"Pretty rough," he said to her presently. "Still think you like this country?"

She picked up the ramrod and used it on his saddle gun. Firmly she said, "It won't always be this way. A few years from now people will be moving onto these plains to stay, to ranch and to farm. There won't be any buffalo or any Comanches."

"What about *you*, Celia? Would you come back here, with *me*?"

Her eyes lifted to him and warmed. "I would, Gage."

"I've thought about it a good many times," he said. "A few more hunts and I'll have enough money saved back to go into whatever kind of business I want to. I've thought that as soon as this country opens up, I could bring cattle here. Shad Blankenship with me, and maybe Reb Pruitt, too. Reb knows the cattle business. And after what's happened this trip, I'd want Reb with me wherever I went."

He took Celia's hands and held them. "I've spent a lot of time thinking about the place I'd build. Lately it seems like you're always there with me."

She leaned to him, her head against his chest. "I *will* be there, Gage."

Shad Blankenship yelled, "Get set, boys. They're comin' back."

The Indians began to move toward the wagons, slower now, cautiously. Just outside effective rifle range they broke into three groups. One rode north, one south. The other waited.

Shad Blankenship squinted. "What're they up to now?"

Alarm began to tingle in Jameson. "I'm afraid I know. We've got two weak points, Shad, the ends of the line. They're going to outflank us on both sides."

The worry settled deeply into Shad's pale eyes. "And the other bunch will hit us in the middle, just like they been doin'."

"We've got to pull some of the men out of the middle and use them to strengthen the ends," Jameson decided quickly. He walked down the line, singling out men to move.

"Ammunition is no problem right now," Jameson told them loudly. "So use all you need. Start shooting as soon as you see a target. Thin them out as much as you can before they get here. There'll be more than enough of them left to go around."

He found himself sweating, and he rubbed his hand across his face. It left the acrid taste of burned powder from the rifle-cleaning job. Then he thought of something else.

He dug out four cans of gunpowder from below the bank, where he had placed them to keep stray bullets from striking them. Two he handed to Reb Pruitt. "Run those out there a couple of hundred feet and drop them. When the Indians get on top of them, put a bullet in them, blow them up."

Jameson hurried to the other end of the line with the remaining two. He climbed over the bank and ran out into the grass, a can of gunpowder under each arm. He dropped them off thirty feet apart and ran for the wagons. The shrill cries of the Indians came up behind him. He picked up speed, plunging down the steep bank almost on top of the hide handler, Ludlow.

"When they get on those cans of powder, be good and sure you shoot straight," he yelled.

He sprinted back to his own position and dropped down on the blanket, grabbing up the Big Fifty. He started to open the breech.

"It's loaded," Celia said.

The men along the line had already begun to fire. Jameson drew down on the Indians coming into the center of the line and squeezed the trigger. A horse went down, but the Indian line never faltered.

"They're coming on in this time, I think," he told Celia. "They're going to get us or give up."

The flanking Indians were the closest. They moved in a run, shouting, firing what guns they had even before they were within range. Jameson counted thirty or more coming in on the left flank. As many more came on the right.

Choking gun smoke rose over the buffalo hunters, hovering like a dark gray cloud. Horses and Indians went down, but there were more to take their places.

Jameson felt his heartbeat quicken. The flank charges

were going to overrun the defenses. There were too many of the Indians to stop. They were three hundred yards away now, two hundred. Now arrows began dropping in behind the wagons. Hunters feverishly worked their breechblocks, keeping their rifles blazing.

On Pruitt's side the Comanches were nearly upon the wagons. Suddenly one of the powder cans went up in a fierce blast, hurling half a dozen Indians to the ground, sending their horses rolling in a cloud of smoke. Other horses near the blast began to jump and pitch, squealing in panic. The second can exploded. For a moment then, that charge was broken. Bucking horses threw their riders and raced away. Indians left afoot made a run for the wagons, but they were easy marks for the rifles. Those still on horseback gathered themselves for another rush.

One Indian slammed his horse into a wagon, jumped onto the stack of hides and dropped down upon a skinner, knife blade flashing. Reb Pruitt swung his rifle barrel up against the Indian and shot him point-blank through the lungs.

Then the Comanches were coming in on the other flank. Heavy rifle fire had thinned them, but many still were mounted. Someone fired too soon at the first of the powder cans. Its blast set a couple of Indian horses to pitching in terror, but it did little to slow the charge. The Indians came streaming in.

Ludlow pushed to his feet to fire at the second can. It went up almost in the middle of a tight group of Indians.

But a handful of Comanches came on. They sent their horses running headlong at the timber barricade. Two came leaping over. Rifle fire caught one horse in mid-leap and he came down dead, falling on his rider and pinning him helpless against the ground. Ludlow lifted his rifle as the second Comanche came over. The Indian's lance caught him, spun him around. He fell, the lance driven through his body. The Indian whirled, raising his bow and whipping an arrow out of the quiver at his back. Bullets cut him down, even as someone grabbed up Ludlow's fallen rifle and brained the trapped Indian with the butt of it.

Jameson was still firing at the Indians who charged headlong into the middle of the wagon line. They were close now, what was left of them, making a last desperate attempt to overrun the hide men. Bullets ripped into the beds of the wagons, buried themselves in the hides: They puffed up dust and mud from the earthen breastworks. Behind him Jameson twice heard men cry out and knew that this time the casualties were running high.

Heart in his throat, he saw that the Indians were going to overrun the line. He fired so rapidly the gun barrel was red-hot in his hands.

"Get down!" he shouted desperately at Celia. "They're coming in!"

A Comanche tried to jump his horse between two wagons. The animal wedged. Jameson whirled and shot the Indian off the struggling mount's back.

Another Indian came over a load of hides and dropped to his feet behind the wagon. He fell upon a hide man with his knife and plunged it into the man's body. Ransom King brought the Indian down. He swapped ends with his rifle and clubbed another Comanche crawling under a wagon.

Relieved of the pressure at the ends of the line, men came hurrying back to bolster up the middle. Withering fire began throwing the Indians back. Jameson raised up to fire a shot.

Suddenly a bullet struck him with the force of a sledge. He fell back, dropping his rifle, grabbing at his left shoulder.

Celia was instantly at his side, desperately seeking the wound.

"Look out," Jameson cried. "Another one."

She whirled and grabbed up the rifle he had dropped. "It's Kills His Enemies," she breathed. She raised the heavy barrel, propped it against a wagon bed. The painted Comanche came streaking in, his war bonnet strung out in the wind behind him. He saw her and raised his lance, screaming.

The rifle belched fire. Kills His Enemies fell back, a gaping hole in the streak of red paint that crossed his chest. He rolled over in the muddy grass and lay still. Then only the war bonnet moved, the feathers still fluttering in the wind.

The gunfire slowed and finally dwindled to silence.

Celia Westerman knelt over Jameson and began to work his coat off his left shoulder. "They're gone," she said gravely. "I don't think they'll be back, not after all this."

The retreating Indians were almost out of sight now. Behind them they left a bloody battlefield strewn with fallen horses and fallen men. There would be wailing in the lodges tonight, Jameson thought grimly.

Celia tore away Jameson's shirt. He grimaced, clenching his teeth to keep from crying out. "It went through," she said. She pulled her shirt-tail out of the trousers Pruitt had given her and tore off a large piece of it to stanch the bleeding.

Jameson lay back weakly, trying to hold himself firm, trying to keep the sky from starting to spin. His head ached unmercifully.

"What about the others? How many casualties?"

Shad Blankenship and Reb Pruitt came up in a moment. "We got three dead. One of them's Ludlow," Shad said.

"Several wounded. They can all walk but one. He may not live. Arrows brought down six or eight mules we may have to shoot."

Jameson nodded weakly. "All right. Let's move, quick as we can."

They buried the three dead men a few yards from the creek bank, carefully moving the sod back, then replacing it to hide the grave. Sitting down, Jameson read over them from the old Bible he always carried. He felt a deep touch of sorrow, especially at the loss of Ludlow. The brooding, dark-bearded hide handler had been one of the best, when the time came.

Celia bandaged Jameson's shoulder and bound it tightly. The crew harnessed the mules and hitched them to the wagons. In a while they had them strung out, ready.

Jameson tried to stand, but he could not. He leaned weakly against a wagon, Celia holding his arm. "All right, Shad, let's get them rolling."

Shad moved away. Ransom King stood there, and Trencher. It suddenly occurred to Jameson that almost everyone was there. Trencher held a shotgun in his hand. Jameson's shotgun. He was glaring at King.

"You gonna tell him, King, or do I have to?"

They had been arguing. King said, "It's not the time."

"For what?" Jameson demanded weakly. "Time for what?"

"Time to tell you you're stayin' here," Trencher declared. "We're takin' your wagons!"

{ SIXTEEN }

Jameson felt his knees give way as the meaning soaked through his drumming brain. He held harder to the wagon.

"King," he said tightly, "I can't believe it."

In a rough voice Trencher said, "You can believe it, Jameson. We had it hatched out before we ever left Dodge. He was ready to call it off after you helped us out of that fight yesterday. But *I'm* not ready. And I'm not goin' to be."

King looked half defiant, half sour. "Sorry, Jameson. It looked like a good idea at the time. I didn't know I was really going to get to like you."

Jameson looked angrily down the line of hide wagons. "But you like money better."

King smiled wryly. "These hides, the wagons and mules, will fetch a fancy price. I'll be able to clear out of this country and never have to look at a stinking buffalo again."

"The minute you set foot in Dodge they'll have you. They haven't forgotten these wagons."

"We won't go to Dodge. There are places west of Dodge, like Granada, where they buy hides and mules and wagons. Then I'll fade away, Jameson. I won't be seen again."

In the grinding of futile anger, Jameson's hand clenched

the rim of a wagon wheel. Realization came to him. "You've been a hide thief all along, haven't you, King? I'll bet even these wagons you got for me were stolen. That's how you were in with Budge. That's why he didn't fit the part."

He looked at the men. They were backing King now. He knew he had no one left but Shad Blankenship and Reb Pruitt. Pruitt wouldn't be any help. One of the men held a gun on him.

And Shad . . . where was Shad?

Celia was pleading with King. "You can't leave him here, wounded like this. He'll die."

Trencher grinned viciously. "Who you think it was put that bullet in him? It wasn't no Injun. I just didn't make as good a shot as I aimed to."

King glanced quickly at Trencher. "You didn't. . . ."

"I did."

King's face darkened as he glared at Trencher. Then he turned back to Jameson. "I didn't plan on that. But it can't alter things now. We've got to leave you—you see that, can't you, Jameson?"

Fury welled in Jameson, fury that gave him a sudden strength. He stood clear of the wagon, swaying a little.

"I see you'd better kill me now, King, because if I *do* get out of this I'll hunt you down. I'll find you if it takes years. You can't go far enough to get away from me."

Trencher leveled his shotgun. King struck it down.

Trencher said angrily, "You heard what he said."

King nodded with grimness. "But he *won't* find me, Trencher. We're leaving him alive, like we agreed."

Then Shad Blankenship's voice cracked like a whip. "Put them guns down, King!"

Shad stepped from behind a wagon, his big Sharps in

his hand. Surprise in his face, then dismay, King dropped his gun. Trencher made a motion as if to lay the shotgun down. Suddenly the muzzle tilted upward and spat flame. Shad jerked back, slamming against the wagon. His rifle slipped from his fingers. He crumpled.

"Shad!" Jameson cried. He lurched toward the old man and fell to his knees beside him. "Shad!"

But Shad Blankenship had lived out his days. Now he was gone . . . gone the way of the other mountain men.

Jameson arose, fury ridging his paled face. He made a grab for Shad's rifle but never touched it. Something struck him across the back of the head. There was a burst of fire in his brain, and he pitched forward into darkness. . . .

"Gage!" Celia Westerman's voice broke in anguish. King grabbed her arm. She whirled back to fight him. In sharp impatience he brought up his fist and sent her sprawling.

"Blast you," he exclaimed, "I never wanted you here in the first place. I knew you'd get in the way when the time came. I've got a good mind to leave you here with him. But I won't."

He turned to one of the men behind him. "Pitch her in the wagon yonder."

Then he faced the other men, his fists knotted. "Anybody changed his mind and want to stay here?" No one moved. He glared at Reb Pruitt. "You weren't in on it, Pruitt, but you can be. Which had you rather do, stay here with Jameson or go on with us?"

Pruitt looked at Jameson, lying unconscious across Shad Blankenship's body. Then he glanced at the wagon where Trencher and another man had carried Celia Westerman. He chewed his lip, studying hard.

"I reckon I'll go," he said.

* * *

Consciousness was slow in coming back to Gage Jameson. The wound had drawn him down even more than the blow on the head. He raised up on his good elbow and heard whimpering. A hairy body touched him. It was Shad Blankenship's old black dog.

"Easy, Ripper," Jameson said softly. "Easy."

He sat up, his head seeming to whirl around and around, throbbing unmercifully. He blinked until his sight cleared. The black dog nuzzled him and whimpered again.

Jameson turned painfully and looked down at Shad's slack body. He turned the old man over onto his back and stared into the wrinkled face until the tears welled hot and stinging into his eyes. Tenderly he picked the caked mud from the rusty beard and smoothed it out.

"Shad," he whispered, his throat so tight it felt as if a knife blade were cutting into it. "Shad, you shouldn't have tried it."

The black dog nuzzled Blankenship's face, whimpering. Jameson reached across and patted Ripper on the head. "Both of us, boy," he said. "Both of us."

He looked about him then. The wagons were gone. He had no way of knowing how long it had been. An hour anyway, perhaps two. He tried to push to his feet and fell back. The second time he made it. He stood there swaying until some strength returned to him.

The dead Indians and horses still lay where they had fallen in that last wild charge.

Jameson knew the Comanches wouldn't leave these dead out here to rot. They would be back for them. And if they found him here . . .

"They didn't leave us anything, did they, boy?" he said

to the dog. "No gun, no food, nothing." His hand dropped to his belt. They had taken his pistol. And he had lost his knife in the flood.

"Lot of good it'd do me if I had one," he commented painfully. "I couldn't catch a turtle."

Even his hat had blown away, probably down into the creek. So had Shad's.

Shad. Jameson knelt beside the old man again. He couldn't just leave him here. He knew what vengeance Indians sometimes took on a dead body. Revulsion rose in him at the thought of leaving Shad here for that kind of treatment.

He couldn't bury him. He had nothing to dig with, even if he had the strength.

He listened to the roar of the creek. It was falling now, but it still carried a lot of force.

Jameson caught Shad's arm with his good hand and began to drag. He got him four or five feet the first time before he gave out and had to sit down to rest. The next time he got him to the edge of the cave-off. After resting again, he eased Shad's body down the steep bank and finally got it to the edge of the creek.

"It's a long way from a Christian burial, Shad," he said regretfully. "But it's better than the Comanches would do."

He took Shad's knife and stuck it in his own belt. He pulled Shad out into the creek, wading as far as he could hold up against the current. Then he gave the old man a hard push, out where the current would pick him up and carry him away.

Perhaps down there somewhere the creek would find Shad a grave in the deep sand. He remembered what Shad had said:

"The only hope I got is that when my time comes I can

die out here, and be buried where I can listen to the wind blow and the wolves howl."

He watched Shad disappear, and a terrible loneliness swept over him. For more than half of his life, Shad Blankenship had been his teacher, his guide. He had been even more than that—a father.

Now he was gone.

Yet Jameson realized that Shad had outlived his time, that he had dreaded this new, unknown world that would come as the frontier faded. Maybe he would have wanted it this way. Maybe it was meant to be.

Jameson waded out of the creek and reached down to touch the shaggy black dog. "Come on, Ripper. It's you and me now."

He climbed up the creek bank, having to stop and sit a while because of the shock of blinding pain. Setting out to follow the deep wagon ruts, he could feel the fever building in him. He ached until he was numb. His legs cried out for him to stop, to fall down and rest. But now he had a job to do, and he kept walking, his feet dragging heavily in the mud.

On the battlefield lay Indian guns and knives and lances, weapons he might have used. But the fever was numbing his brain now. All he could do was keep moving. All he could think of was to get Ransom King.

"Get some sense, King; take it easy," Trencher said irritably. "It's dark already, and you been drivin' these mules like the devil was after you. You'll kill them all if you ain't careful."

Ransom King turned nervously in the saddle and looked toward the wagons. Because of darkness he could see only those closest behind him. Grudgingly he said, "All right, then, let's make camp."

"About time," Trencher grumbled, and turned back to bring up the rear wagons.

"Swing into a circle, Pruitt," King said sharply. "You know how."

Pruitt never nodded, never answered. But he swung the chuck wagon around in his accustomed manner. Without a word he dug a pit and began to build a fire.

"Damn you," King exploded, "put that out!"

"We can't cook without a fire."

"We'll eat it cold."

Chilled, hungry, worn out after losing a night's sleep, going through the battle, then driving the wagons hard far into darkness, the men grumbled about not having a hot supper. Most of all they missed the coffee. But King would not relent.

They ate cold biscuits, as far as they went, and jerky. Then wearily the men began hauling down their bedrolls.

"Double guard tonight," King said.

Groaning, one of the skinners commented, "Man, we need sleep. After today we ain't fixin' to have any more Injun trouble."

King swung his fist and knocked the man to the ground. "I said double guard. I'll shoot the next man who opens his mouth!"

Even after the guards were posted, King stood in the darkness at the edge of camp, peering intently out into the black, straining to hear.

Trencher came up behind him. "Forget it, King. He won't be comin'."

King turned quickly. "What do you mean?"

"I know what's eatin' you. Been eatin' you all day. You

think Jameson will be after us. What you think he is, some kind of devil? He's dead by now. If that wound didn't kill him, the Injuns have. Now forget it."

King clenched his fists. "Maybe he's dead and maybe he isn't. If he isn't, he'll be after us."

Trencher grunted and looked back into camp, where Reb Pruitt was putting up a tent for Celia Westerman. "It ain't Jameson that worries me. It's them two."

He drew his knife and tested the cutting edge with his thick finger. "We ought to have left that woman with Jameson. We got to do somethin' about her before we get anywhere near the hide camps or they'll string us up. What do you say I walk her out into the dark a little ways, her and that cook both? It's got to be done, sooner or later."

King shook his head. "The men won't stand for killing her," he said. "We've got to figure something."

Disgustedly Trencher spat. "She's gettin' to you, that's what's the matter."

Sharply King responded, "You're getting too big for your britches, Trencher. I'm still the boss here, and don't forget it."

Trencher straightened, angrily holding his ground. "She's yours then, for now. Do what you want to. But before we get to the hide camps, we got to get rid of her."

{ SEVENTEEN }

The second day Jameson knew he was losing his mind. The sun hammered down from a cloudless sky, steam rose from the damp ground and wrapped the heat around him like some angry fiend. Long ago he had ceased to feel hunger, but the torture of thirst continued. His mouth was locked open, his lips dried and cracked, his tongue swollen and afire from the fever that burned in him. The little potholes of water had all dried out.

A maddening ache drummed in his bare head, and through his whole body. Soon now even his sight would be gone. He could see only the wavering image of the prairie ahead of him, dancing and shimmering, an endless reach of grass . . . grass . . . grass like the pitch and roll of the boundless sea.

Long ago he had strayed away from the wagon ruts, away from the creek. He dragged his heavy boots, knowing within reason that he was weaving aimlessly. He knew that soon he would fall to his knees again as he had done so many times already—that next time perhaps he would be unable to rise and would lie here forever in the short grass of the buffalo plains.

He had no idea now where he was going, little hope any

more of getting there. The grass looked soft and cool, and he longed to lie down and give it up . . . lie down and sleep and never waken again.

But a single stubborn thread of will remained, and he kept going . . . going . . . going until his mind in its torture seemed to sink back into sleep, and only his legs still moved.

At his side the black dog walked, stopping when Jameson stopped, licking Jameson's face when Jameson fell. Staggering along on the brink of unconsciousness, Jameson tried to force his mind to work. He knew the dangers he faced. At any time now Indians might ride up over the horizon. He wouldn't see them, he knew. Maybe he wouldn't even feel it. Maybe it would be the merciful thing.

Or if it wasn't Indians, it might be a blue norther, with its frigid winds that could cut down even a strong man caught out here in the open. This was early December, and here on these high Texas plains the temperature might plunge murderously fifty or sixty degrees.

Yet somehow he hardly cared. Only two thoughts kept him moving—the need to find Celia Westerman, and his hatred of Trencher and King.

Unable to see, he felt himself suddenly lurching down an incline. His feet went out from under him. He pitched forward on his face—into water.

Water. His fevered body cried out for water. His mouth and throat were leather-dry.

But somehow within him a single sentry of alarm still watched. Go easy, it told him. Go easy, for the first taste of water may leave you unconscious. You may fall into it and drown, unable to help yourself.

He pulled back, cupping his good hand and lifting a few drops of water to his fever-parched lips, holding himself back by firm will. At the taste of the water he lapsed into darkness.

After a while he came to again, now stronger than he had been. He felt the dog nuzzling him, licking his face. Once more Jameson cupped his hand and drank slowly, cautiously. He sat on the edge of the waterhole a long time then, feeling the strength slowly return. Cool water drove the fever back. His sight gradually cleared. In time he was able to regain his feet.

Thirst quenched, Ripper began to nose around in the grass for food. Presently he jumped a rabbit that had come up out of its burrow. He ran the rabbit down and brought it in his mouth, its stout hind legs still kicking.

Hunger had come back to Jameson as the fever had diminished. He took the rabbit from Ripper's jaws and slammed its head against the ground to complete the kill. He skinned and gutted the little animal awkwardly, having only one hand to work with. While Ripper worried the castoff parts, Jameson dug in his pockets and found dry matches. He felt of the grass. Away from the waterhole, the sun had dried it again so that it would burn. He found many buffalo chips there, but they were still wet from the rain and of no use as fuel.

He pulled up dry grass and twisted it as tightly as he could, setting some of it afire, feeding grass twists into the flame and holding the rabbit over them on the point of the knife.

Ravenously hungry, he was unable to hold himself back long. He began to tear the rabbit apart and wolf it down half cooked.

It wasn't enough, but it partially satisfied his hunger and added to his growing strength. He lay down to rest a while, knowing he had to get moving soon, had to find that wagon trail. It must be to the west of him, for he knew he had not crossed the creek. He could only have strayed eastward.

Sleep settled over him. Sometime much later he awakened, hearing Ripper growl. He pushed up quickly with his good arm, ice in the pit of his stomach. He knew without looking.

Indians.

Cautiously he pushed to his knees and peered out over the rim of the waterhole. Yonder, still hundreds of yards away, came a lone rider. But it might as well have been a thousand of them, for Jameson had no defense except the knife. And with his wounded shoulder, that would do him little good.

To his right was a little hummock. Keeping low, Jameson crawled behind it and lay still, the ripping knife gripped tightly in his hand, his heart thumping rapidly.

It was a single Comanche warrior, perhaps out scouting for buffalo. He carried a rifle instead of a bow, and a white man's leather cartridge belt instead of an arrow quiver. One feather was fastened in his straight black hair. There was no paint on his round, hard-boned face.

The Indian came straight for the waterhole, knowing where it was. He rode over the rim of it and dropped his leather reins, lifting his left leg over the horse's neck and slipping off to the ground to stretch. He went to his knees to drink of the water. Then his gaze touched the burned grass and scattering of rabbit bones. He turned suspiciously, eyes darting, rifle lifting in his hand.

Cornered, Jameson thought in despair. But he had one chance.

"Sic him, Ripper!" he shouted at the growling black dog. Ripper bounded over the hummock and dove straight at the Comanche's throat. Caught by surprise, the Indian went down under the hurtling weight of the big dog. Ferociously Ripper tore into him, fighting to reach the Indian's throat. Unable to straighten and fire the rifle, the Comanche desperately tried to club the dog with it.

Jameson moved in with the knife. He raised it quickly, and brought it down.

Later he patted the dog's black head. Ripper continued to grumble, hide still rippling with nervousness.

"Good boy," Jameson said quietly. "Now we've got a horse and a rifle. Now we can travel."

With his bad shoulder he had a hard time mounting bareback. Pain knifed through him, and once he thought he had broken the wound open. But finally he managed to get on the horse. His good right hand holding the rifle and the rawhide reins, he pulled the mount around and headed him west.

Ransom King tipped the bottle up and drank long and hard.

Resentment burned in him as he looked at the men scattered about in their blankets. Rebellion, that was it. The badly wounded Crosson had died late in the afternoon. The men had halted the wagons at dusk, ignoring King's orders to keep them moving. Silently they had buried Crosson, their eyes flashing anger at King for not stopping to ease the dying man's pain. They had built a fire, and Reb Pruitt had cooked them a hot supper. Now King had ordered another double guard and no one had paid him any attention. The men had dropped wearily into their blankets, worn out by the hard drive and loss of sleep. Even Trencher.

King walked to the edge of camp and gazed out into

the darkness, wondering about Gage Jameson, wondering at the chill that came to him. Trencher was right. He *had* to be right. Jameson *was* dead. He couldn't have lived this long with that wounded shoulder, with no gun, no food.

Even if alive, he couldn't be following them. He would be holed up somewhere, hiding from Indians, nursing that shoulder and slowly starving to death.

Sure, it was foolish to worry about him. Better for King to spend his time planning how to spend the money he'd get for all these hides, and the stock and wagons. With any luck, he could find a way to avoid having to pay the rest of the crew their share. That, with the rest he had stashed away, would set him up big in Mexico, or in Central America. He could feel the gold in his fingers already. It gave him a warm glow just to think about it.

All his life he had dreamed of pulling off a coup like this one. Now here it was, safe in his fist.

He raised the bottle again and walked back into the wagon circle. Fools. They hadn't even pulled the wagons up tightly. There was a three-foot gap between the chuck wagon and the next vehicle where a mule could walk right out without scraping a rib.

"Pruitt," he said irritably, finding the cook still up, "plug that gap."

Pruitt made no sign of hearing him. King scowled. They'd have to do something about that cook, sure enough. He sat down against a wagon wheel and looked about camp. Under the wagons men slept exhausted, rolled up in their blankets. Not a man on guard, he'd bet.

Well, he'd stay on guard. He'd stay up all night if he had to. But they'd remember it later. They'd remember it when he got away with all the money.

His eyes drifted then to Celia Westerman's tent. The

whisky was warm in his stomach, and he felt a lighthead-
edness he hadn't allowed himself in a long time. His mind
had dwelt on Celia Westerman a lot lately. He hadn't
thought of much else but her, and Gage Jameson, and
all those wagons loaded with hides.

It wasn't that she was so extra good-looking. In a big
town a man wouldn't give her more than a second glance.
She didn't have the blood-stirring beauty of a Rose Tremaine, for example. But she *was* a woman, an attractive
woman, and she was here.

He sat and pulled on the bottle, staring at her tent.
The hunger grew in him. There was no movement about the
camp. He took a last drink, emptying the bottle, and let it
drop to the ground. Then he pushed to his feet and walked
carefully toward the tent. The whisky had really gotten to
him now. He found himself weaving.

He ducked to push through the tent flap, finding to his
annoyance that the strings were tied. They gave way. It was
dark inside, but his eyes quickly adjusted themselves. He
could see Celia Westerman lying in her blankets, awake,
watching him.

He whispered, "I want to talk to you."

"Get out," she said. "I don't want to hear it."

"They're going to kill you," he said. "Trencher's afraid
to leave you alive, to talk."

She made no answer, gave no sign she even cared. He
could feel her hatred of him like an electric charge, even
though he could not see her eyes.

He said, "Say the word and I'll get you out of it. We'll
go off together, you and me. You'll live like you've never
lived before."

She pushed the blankets aside and stood up. She was
still wearing Reb Pruitt's clothes. "Get out, I told you!"

He grabbed her shoulders. "Listen to me. I want to save you. I'm in love with you, can't you see that? I want you."

She struck at his face. He grabbed her wrist and shook her violently.

"Stop it, Celia!"

She fought with him until she lost her footing. She fell backward, and he went down with her. The contact with her body set his pulse to racing. In the darkness, he found her lips and kissed her roughly, crushing her down.

Too late he saw her hand come up, the wrench in it.

She's been ready for this, he thought, helpless to move away. His brain seemed to explode with the impact. He went down on his elbows. He felt her move away from him, heard the wrench swing again. This time he tumbled forward into darkness.

Celia Westerman paused then, listening, wondering if the struggle had been heard.

She heard nothing. She picked up her coat and began to move toward the front of the tent on her hands and knees.

She stopped abruptly as the tent flap moved. She raised the wrench again, heart in her throat.

Reb Pruitt cautiously poked his head in. He held a six-gun, ready. He saw her poised there to strike him, and his eyes widened. His gaze dropped to Ransom King, lying unconscious.

"I ought to've known a Texas girl could handle herself all right," he whispered. "Now come on, and let's get out of here."

Gage Jameson saw the two horsemen as they came down over the rise far ahead of him. Heart quickening, he pulled the Indian pony back from the dried-out wagon ruts and eased down into a hackberry thicket on the creek bank.

"Come on, Ripper," he said to the dog. "Get down."

He slid down off the horse and checked the Comanche's old needle gun. It had been stolen out of some Texas home or off some luckless white man after a battle, he figured. The barrel was half plugged with powder, for Indians knew little about taking care of a gun. But it would still fire. Tensing, he went down on one knee and rested the rifle across the other, wondering how he was going to hold it steady with one good hand.

The two riders came into plainer view and he nervously licked his dry lips. Most of the fever had burned itself out, but a little still remained. He saw that one of the two was leading an extra horse.

Suddenly Jameson lowered the rifle and stood up, blinking unbelievingly. It couldn't be. But it was!

He walked out, leading the Indian pony, letting them see him. He saw Reb Pruitt swing a rifle up, then lower it in recognition.

Celia Westerman stepped down from her saddle and ran to meet him. He quickly moved toward her. He caught her with his good arm and crushed her to him, dropping his cheek down against the top of her head, her long blond hair.

"Gage, Gage," she said softly, holding him as tightly as she could. He could feel the hot tears on her cheek as he brought his hand up to her chin.

Reb Pruitt stood there first on one foot, then the other. Finally he took the sack of grub down from Celia's saddle.

"May not be the best time to mention it," he commented dryly, "but if you're hungry . . ."

Jameson devoured food out of the sack while Reb and

Celia told him what had happened, how they had gotten out of the camp with three saddled horses, some grub and several guns.

"I didn't have any hope of findin' you alive," Pruitt admitted. "I tried to talk her into heading north to find some hide outfit. But she wouldn't have it that way. So we come south, riding in the edge of the creek to keep them from tellin' which direction we went."

Hunger satisfied, Jameson grimly looked at the guns Reb and Celia had brought. A pistol apiece. A rifle. And his shotgun.

It was the shotgun Trencher had used on Shad. Looking at it, Jameson clenched his fist.

"I'm going to get them," he said tightly. "I've *got* to get them—for Shad."

Reb said, "I don't aim to take up any for King, he don't deserve it. But it was Trencher who shot Shad. It wasn't King."

Jameson said through gritted teeth, "When a man cuts loose a wolf, he's got to answer for whatever that wolf does."

"What're you going to do?" Celia pressed anxiously.

"Going to trail after them. Going to cut the ground out from under King a little at a time. Going to make him sweat while I take everything away from him. And finally, when he's lost everything, I'm going to ride in there and get him. Get him for Shad Blankenship."

{ EIGHTEEN }

⟨⟩

Jameson and Pruitt sat their horses on a small promontory and gazed down at the hide wagons, strung out like a long snake far below them.

"Still pushing hard," Jameson said. "Been like that every day, daylight to well after dark. Wonder he hasn't killed half the stock by now."

Reb Pruitt nodded. "And half the men, too. Stirred up as they were when we got out of there, I'm surprised they haven't run off and left him. Somethin' was eatin' at him pretty bad. I think maybe he sensed that you were following after him."

Jameson swung down from the saddle to rest a while, never taking his eyes from the wagons. His left shoulder was stiff and sore, but the fever was several days gone now. He had lost much weight. Still, his strength had returned, for the most part.

His beard was a week or more long, black and wiry. His clothes were crusted with mud and dirt. He was still bareheaded.

"Not over a couple of days' ride now to the Arkansas," he estimated. "They're going to be jumpy as cats down there, afraid you and Celia went after help and will be bringing a hanging party down on them."

"You think they might run if we was to prod them a little?"

Jameson shrugged. "I don't know. But we're fixing to find out."

At nightfall the three of them moved in toward Ransom King's camp. Working up close while Celia stayed back and held the horses, the two men watched the teamsters circle the wagons and drive the stock inside. Ransom King rode up and down the outside, shouting orders with a fury born of desperation.

"I'll bet he ain't caught much sleep since we been gone," Reb whispered. "Nor let anybody else get much, either."

They stayed out there until the camp quieted down. Then they moved up close to seek out the guards. Satisfied, they crept back out to Celia.

Jameson asked, "Reb, do you think you could move that chuck wagon a few feet, with that horse and your rope?"

Pruitt nodded. "I reckon. Wagon's not heavy loaded any more."

"Then you're going to open a hole in that wagon circle. And I'm going to run out all the horses and mules I can."

They remounted their horses. Celia walked up and pressed against Jameson's leg. "Don't take chances, Gage. Be careful."

"We won't crowd our luck too much," he promised.

Moving their horses in a walk, they worked carefully up toward the wagons, the black dog trotting at their heels. They split, Jameson riding far around the circle and coming in toward a spot where he had seen no guard. On the other side, Pruitt was moving in at the chuck wagon.

Jameson halted near the wagons, looking for a hole where he might put the horse through, listening for Pruitt's rope to sing. But it was silent.

Suddenly he heard the creak of the chuck wagon as a horse lunged against a rope. He saw the wagon lurch, then wheel out, leaving a gap in the circle.

Six-gun in hand, Jameson fired into the air and yelled. Horses and mules within the enclosure began to mill and stomp. Then, seeing the opening, they broke out, running. Jameson kept shouting and firing until he saw men rushing toward him. He started to spur away.

Then he recognized the bulky man who came in the lead. He heard the man's roar, saw the gun in the man's hand.

Instead of running away, Jameson touched spurs to the horse and headed straight toward the man. It was Trencher. He saw the spurt of flame from Trencher's gun, felt the heat as the bullet cut by his ear. He brought his own six-shooter down level and squeezed the trigger. He saw Trencher stagger back, and he fired again.

That, he thought, is for Shad.

He pulled aside as the other men began firing at him. He leaned low and pushed the horse into a lope. He circled around and met Reb Pruitt riding away, driving a sizable string of horses and mules. The black dog was running too, barking at the animals' heels.

"We got maybe half of them," Reb shouted, "before they cut them off."

Half of them. Jameson felt a glow of triumph. That would hit King where it hurt the most.

"Let's keep them running," he said.

He half expected pursuit, but it didn't come. Next morning they moved in cautiously and found the train already pulled out. Six wagons loaded with hides sat there, deserted for lack of mules to pull them.

"This," Jameson said, "is what will kill King, having to leave these hides."

They found Trencher lying unburied, just where Jameson had left him. They had all hated Trencher.

All day they trailed along well behind King's wagon train, pushing with them the horses and mules they had captured last night. Along in mid-afternoon they came up over a rise and saw a pair of wagons sitting there. Two men had a wheel off the tongue wagon.

"King must be getting panicky," Jameson commented. "Went off and left them." He checked his six-shooter and looked across at Reb Pruitt. "Want to take them?"

Pruitt nodded.

Jameson said, "You stay back with the stock, Celia."

They moved into a lope. They were almost upon the wagons before the men saw them. One man made a run for a rifle propped up against a wagon wheel. Jameson fired a pop shot at him. Dust puffed under the man's feet. He stopped abruptly and raised his hands.

The other man stood limply, his face drained of color.

"Jameson," he breathed. "I told them it was you last night. You and that black devil of a dog. I told King and he knocked me down. He said it was Indians. Said he'd kill the man who mentioned your name again."

Reb Pruitt grinned through his scraggly growth of beard. "Panicky, Gage, like I told you."

Jameson nodded and frowned at the two men.

"What should we do with them, Reb, shoot them right here?"

The two began to tremble. One pleaded, "Look, Jameson, we didn't know how it was going to turn out. We didn't expect any killing. They said all they were going to do was set you afoot."

Jameson scowled at them. "We ought to shoot you, but we'll give you a chance. Start hiking. If you're ever seen in this country again, you'll hang."

Reb Pruitt unhitched the mules while Jameson watched the two walk eastward out across the prairie, no rifles, no bedding, just a canteen of water from under the wagon seat and the knives in their belts.

Jameson frowned. "It'll give King some more to think about when these two wagons don't come in tonight. Eight wagonloads he's already had to leave behind him. That's half of them, Reb."

They watched from afar as Ransom King made camp. There weren't enough wagons left now to circle. Instead, King left them strung out and tied the remaining animals on picket lines, the lines secured to the wagon wheels.

"Won't be anybody asleep down there tonight," Jameson guessed. "He'll keep them awake, watching the stock."

No fire was built in King's camp that night. For a while Jameson considered working down there and trying to cut some of the picket lines. But he knew they would be closely watched. It wouldn't be worth the risk.

"We'll worry them a little, just the same," he said. Taking the needle gun, he fired a shot down toward the camp. He heard a burst of shouts and the squeals of animals, then a pounding of hoofs leading off away from camp.

"There went a picket line," Pruitt laughed.

Jameson lay down on the ground to rest a while, his eyes on Celia Westerman. He felt a stirring of pride at the way she had taken all this, the help she had been.

Occasionally during the night he would get up and move around, looking off toward King's camp. At the back of his mind lurked a worry that the men might come out looking for him. But he doubted, really, that they would. They couldn't know for sure who was stalking them, or how many.

Reb Pruitt shook him awake at daylight. "Gage, there's somethin' goin' on down there."

Jameson arose, pausing to smile at the sight of Celia Westerman still lying asleep beneath a blanket that they had taken out of one of the hide wagons yesterday.

Reb pointed. "What do you make of it?"

The hide men were knotted up together in a group, facing one man. That man could only be Ransom King. Jameson wasn't sure, but he thought King held a rifle.

He watched King gesturing angrily. The men milled back and forth, and occasionally some of them used their hands in violent argument. King raised the rifle, leveling it at them.

Someone threw something at King and he stepped aside, off balance. Then the men were on him. Jameson thought he saw a flash, and he heard the delayed report of a gun. The melee ended. The men scattered, catching up horses and mules. They streamed out of camp, heading east, abandoning the wagons.

"They're gettin' away," Pruitt said anxiously.

Jameson shook his head. "Let them go. We wouldn't know what to do with them if we had them, and we know they'll never dare come back. The one we want is still down there."

Only one man remained. He was stretched out on the ground. Watching from afar, Jameson thought for a while that they had killed him. But presently King stood groggily and staggered to a wagon. He held himself up against a wheel, letting his strength return.

"Want to go down and get him?" Pruitt asked.

"No, let's wait a while. Let's see what he's going to do. I want to see if he sticks with his wagons or if he gives up and runs."

King wasn't running, yet. Jameson could only imagine the frustration in King's mind as he leaned against the wheel, looking helplessly at the hide wagons strung out there, each pair laden with a thousand dollars and more in flint hides. All this he had held in his grasp. Now it had slipped through his fingers.

It was still there, its very presence a mockery of his extravagant dreams, his well-developed plans.

The hides were there within his reach, but worthless to him now because he could not move them.

This was what Jameson had been waiting for, to let the ground slip away from under King's feet and leave him with nothing but the gray ashes, the dark knowledge of defeat.

"We better get him, Gage, before he runs."

"He won't run," Jameson told Pruitt, "not so long as he thinks he can salvage a little of it."

Four mules remained on one picket line. King harnessed them one by one and hitched them to a pair of wagons. He popped the whip, and the mules strained so that the muscles bulged on their chests and on their legs. The wagons moved, but slowly. The mules would wear out before they had gone a mile. It was too heavy a load.

King pulled them up and sat there, looking back dejectedly at the wagons he was leaving. Finally he climbed down and unhitched the trail wagon, leaving it there with the rest.

All he had now was the tongue wagon, with no more

than three or four hundred hides. Only this, where once he had had fifteen wagons, every one loaded.

"Like the dregs at the bottom of the cup," Jameson thought aloud.

King cracked the whip again. The mules strained, and the wagon rolled out.

Jameson watched him a while, then rose to his feet. "Let me have that shotgun, Reb. I think it's time now."

Celia Westerman pushed back the blanket and got to her feet. "Gage, what are you going to do?"

"I'm going to get Ransom King."

Dismayed, she looked at the shotgun. "With that?"

"It's what they used on Shad."

Celia caught his arm. "Gage, please let the law handle him. Take him alive. Take him in."

He looked at Pruitt. "Let me have a couple of extra shells."

Reluctantly Reb handed them to him. "You ought to listen to her, Gage."

Celia pleaded. "You're not a killer, Gage. Don't make yourself one by doing this. You'll have it with you as long as you live."

But Gage Jameson could still see Shad Blankenship's broken body the way they had left it there on the prairie. That Trencher had paid for it wasn't enough. There was still the man who had cut loose the wolf.

He leaned down and kissed Celia. "Wait for me," he said. "I'll be back."

He rode out, paralleling King's wagon.

Later he could see a brushy creek far ahead, cutting diagonally across his path. He knew King would have to move over it. That would be the time to get him, while he had his hands full in crossing the stream.

For Jameson's shoulder was still stiff. He had only one hand with which to handle the gun. He had to take all the advantage he could get.

He rode on in an easy lope, splashing into the creek, pushing across and reining up on the far side. The water had been deeper than he thought, two and a half or three feet. Staying in the brush, he watched impatiently for King's wagon.

And at last it came.

King angled his mules toward an open spot on the brushy bank. There was a two-foot drop-off into the water. King hauled the mules up to a slow walk, easing them out into the creek slowly so the wheels would take the drop without breaking spokes or coupling pole.

Watching him from the cover of brush, Jameson felt his heart pound.

It's time, he thought.

Shotgun ready, he pushed his horse into the water with a splash. King reined up suddenly, whip in his hand, the front wheels of the wagon just starting to slide down the drop.

He stared at Jameson openmouthed, his face blanching. "I guess I knew it was you all the time," he said in resignation.

Jameson gripped the shotgun. "You're going to die, King. Die the way Shad did."

King's voice lifted. "*I* didn't kill him, Gage. It was Trencher."

Jameson's voice crackled with fury.

"You planned the whole thing. You set it up. You got Shad killed just as much as if you had pulled the trigger."

Moving out into the creek, closer to King, he lifted the shotgun.

"Gage," King exclaimed, "I haven't got a gun. Honest to God, they took them away from me. They left me unarmed."

Jameson hesitated, wondering if King might be lying. Somehow, he knew he wasn't. And he knew he couldn't shoot King down in cold blood.

Instead of feeling cheated, he felt a vague sense of relief.

"Then I'll take you in," he said at last, lowering the shotgun. "But you know what they'll do, King. They'll hang you!"

King sat motionless on the wagon seat, his eyes sick at the contemplation of such a death.

"That," he said in a strained voice, "is no way for a man to die."

Suddenly his arm moved. He lifted the whip.

Before Jameson could bring the shotgun up again, the searing whip wrapped around him. His horse reared and plunged in panic. Grabbing at the horn with his one good hand, Jameson accidently fired the shotgun into the air. The kick of it set him off balance. He tumbled from the saddle into the cold water.

In desperation King hauled his mules around, trying to turn. But the front wheels slipped in the mud, and the right hind wheel skidded from the drop-off. The wagon tilted. For a moment it stood balanced precariously on two wheels while Ransom King struggled to keep his seat.

He slipped off and fell into the muddy creek. An instant later the wagon tipped over and crashed down on its side in a huge splash of water. It lay there then in the brown stir of mud, the left rear wheel spinning.

King never came up.

Jameson waded hurriedly to the wagon. He couldn't see

for the mud. He dropped down under the cold water, feeling around for King. He caught King's hand, felt the man threshing wildly, pinned beneath the load of hides.

Jameson braced himself and pulled hard with his one good hand. He felt the hides shift just a little, but not enough. He pulled desperately, feeling King's struggle growing weaker. He pulled until the world went black before his eyes. But his own strength had been drained by the wound in his shoulder.

He heard horses running. He saw Reb Pruitt and Celia galloping up to the creek.

"Reb," he called in desperation, "come help me! Come quick!"

By the time Reb got there, King was limp. With Reb's help Jameson pulled him out from under the heavy hides. They dragged him to the bank. But it was no use.

"Too late," Reb Pruitt said quietly.

Jameson knelt, breathing heavily. "If it hadn't been for this shoulder . . ."

Regret touched him then, and he said evenly, "There was a lot that was likable about him. If he'd been honest . . . What gets into a man like that, Reb? What is it that sets him wrong?"

Reb Pruitt shook his head, looking at the overturned wagon in the creek, then at the lifeless body of Ransom King.

"Who can say, Gage? Stolen hides, stolen wagon. Only one man to help him, and that man crippled because of what King himself had done. Strange, ain't it, the way a man's life catches up with him?"

Celia took Jameson's hand. "I'm glad *you* didn't have to do it, Gage."

He nodded solemnly. "So am I. I wanted to, but now I'm glad I didn't."

He looked northward then. "Somewhere up yonder, past the Arkansas, we ought to be able to find some buffalo hunters out of luck and looking for something to do. We'll bring them and get the stock and wagons."

Reb said, "You'll have King's wagons, too. I reckon you've earned them."

Jameson shook his head, thinking of Nathan Messick, and the sister who was left with no one to provide for her. "I don't want them," he said. "But I know where they'll do some good."

Looking southward again, he said, "Someday we'll go back to Texas together, Reb, you and Celia and me. And we'll stay there."

"That'll be a good day for all of us," Reb replied. Then he turned back to figure a way of getting the overturned wagon out of the creek.

CLOUDY
IN THE WEST

To
Debbie and Darrell, Shane and Shea,
our grandchildren

Cloudy in the west, and it looks like rain,
My danged old slicker's in the wagon again . . .

"The Old Chisholm Trail," TRADITIONAL

{ ONE }

HENDERSON COUNTY, EAST TEXAS, 1885

All afternoon Joey Shipman had been killing his stepmother with the hoe, chopping her to pieces an inch at a time. His small hands were raw from his angry grip on the wooden handle. A water blister was rising on his right palm. Sweat from beneath the band of his floppy felt hat burned his blue eyes and fueled the banked coals of his resentment.

Two rows away in the shin-high corn, an aging black man paused in his own labor to wipe his brow and dry a sweaty hand against stained old trousers that bore new patches on top of old. He studied Joey with a bemused gaze. "Young'un, you goin' to blunt that hoe plumb down to the handle. You could chop them weeds without bein' half so fiercesome."

"I wouldn't enjoy it half as much."

"Don't look like enjoyment to me." Reuben shook his head. "It's Miz Dulcie, ain't it? She sharp to you again at dinnertime?"

From as far back down his twelve years as Joey could remember, Old Reuben had been able to see through him like he was store-window glass. "All I done was tell her I thought Pa was lookin' worse. She taken it to mean she wasn't carin' for him proper, and she flew all over me. She's held a grudge against me ever since Pa brought her here to live."

Reuben tamped tobacco into the bowl of a foul old black pipe and lighted it. Joey had often wondered how it kept from poisoning him, but Reuben seemed to take pleasure in it. Life didn't afford him many material pleasures.

"She is a grudgin' woman, right enough. She takes hold of a grudge and nurses and coddles and feeds it like it was a baby." That was as near criticism as Reuben was likely to get. It was his custom to tread lightly on dangerous ground. "Just the same, she's your pa's wife. He'd want you to show her proper respect."

"If it wasn't for Pa, I might just light out . . . leave this place and nary once look back."

The old man shook his head. "Boy, you'd be like a cottontail rabbit amongst a pack of wolves. The world out yonder'd eat you alive."

"I can run pretty fast."

"So can a rabbit. But theys mighty few wolves ever starve to death."

A peacock began a shrill cry of alarm, as it always did when someone approached on the town road. A movement caught Joey's eye. "Buggy yonder. Doctor again, I expect."

Reuben made no comment, but Joey caught a grave look in his eyes before the old man covered it up. Reuben's edge-sitting station as a hired man, and a black one at that, had made him skilled at concealing what was on his mind. He turned away from Joey and went back to his hoeing.

Joey said, "Pa did look awful bad at dinnertime. You don't reckon he's fixin' to die?"

"The Lord's got everybody's future wrote down in the

book of reckonin', but ain't nobody can read it except Him."

By rights, Pa could as well already be dead, bad as the accident had been. He had been coming home from Athens by himself with a load of staple goods in the wagon when, the best anybody could tell, something had spooked the team. They had run away, flipping the wagon over on top of Pa at a fence-corner bend in the road. Doctor had said his ribs were busted bad, and one had evidently punched a hole in his lung. Now, on top of his injuries, Pa had pneumonia so bad he could barely breathe.

Joey watched the buggy pull to a stop in front of the white frame house Pa had built for Mama before Joey was born. Fear clutched at his throat. "Doctor says pneumonia's the old folks' friend. Takes their pain away and puts them at rest. But Pa ain't old, not by a long ways."

"It ain't for us to question the Lord's will." Reuben pointed with the stem of his pipe. "You'd best get back to your job. Miz Dulcie steps out onto the porch and sees you not workin', she's apt to serve you a cold supper."

Joey felt a stirring of rebellion. "Ain't hungry noway." However, he put the hoe back into motion. "Looks like somebody came with the doctor. I believe it's Dulcie's cousin, Mr. Meacham."

Reuben squinted, trying to see. He had lamented often that his eyesight was no longer what it used to be. But his eyes betrayed disapproval.

Joey said, "I don't know what you got against Mr. Meacham. He's always smilin', always got somethin' funny to say."

He had sensed that Pa didn't care much for Blair Meacham either. Pa had never been much for stories and idle gossip and such. Easy laughter was not in his makeup. But Dulcie's cousin had always been friendly to Joey, telling him jokes and riddles, even bringing him stick candy from town occasionally. Not many folks were that thoughtful.

Joey worked his way to the end of the row and hearing an angry snort, glanced across the fence. A dark, tight-hided bull ran up to the wire, stopping inches short of the barbs. It pawed dirt and bellowed a challenge at him, its bulging brown eyes belligerent.

Joey took that as a personal insult. This bull had been trying to get at him for five or six years. He walked past the turnrow, picked up a rock, and hurled it, striking the bull just above one eye. The animal slung its head, another angry bellow rising from deep in its throat.

Reuben shouted, "You'd best not agitate that old bull. One of these days he'll come right through the fence at you. Ain't nothin' on this earth meaner than a bad Jersey bull."

"He ain't got any horns, hardly."

"But he could get you down and tromp on you and bust your bones with that head of his. I don't know what it is makes a cow brute hate young'uns so."

It was true that the bull seemed to vent its hostility most strongly against youngsters. Being smaller, they probably appeared weaker, Joey guessed. The animal would threaten men but turn away if they stood their ground. Pa or Reuben had only to raise a hand and the bull would back off, its bluster gone. But it had put Joey up and over a fence several times. Joey knew that in his case it was not a bluff, that the bull would kill him if it could. It also pawed dirt and threatened darkly whenever it saw Dulcie. He supposed it classified women and children as natural prey.

Somebody ventured out onto the front porch and waved an arm. It wasn't Dulcie or the doctor, so it had to be Blair Meacham, who seemed to be shouting. Joey said, "We better go see what he's hollerin' about."

The grave look returned to Reuben's black-button eyes. "You run on. These old knees can't move as fast as yours, but I'll be comin' along behind you."

Mindful of Pa's ruling about taking proper care of tools, Joey held onto the hoe instead of dropping it in the dirt. He carried it down to the barn and set it just inside the door before he trotted the last fifty yards to the house.

The doctor had stepped out onto the porch with Meacham. His voice was like a minister's at benediction. "Your daddy's asking for you, boy. If you've got anything you want to tell him, you'd best be doin' it."

Blair Meacham placed a gentle hand on top of Joey's head. He offered no joke this time, nor was he smiling. "Don't look like there's much time."

Joey's throat felt as if he had swallowed a knife with its blade open. He walked into the house, struggling not to cry. He was too big for that, he thought. But his resolve came near falling apart as he entered the bedroom and looked through the iron bars of the bedstead. His father lay thin and drawn, his face flushed with the fever that was taking him. His breathing sounded like a rasp filing a horse's hoof.

Dulcie Shipman stood beside the upper end of the bed, arms folded. In Joey's mind she was already getting pretty old, somewhere in her mid-to-late thirties. He had heard men refer to her as handsome, but he supposed they hadn't seen the severe side of her face like he had. Compared to his memories of his own mother, she was skinny and thin-lipped, and he had never heard her sing to herself.

No tears showed in her gray eyes. Instead Joey saw a pinched look he had always interpreted as resentment. He assumed he was a constant reminder that Pa had loved another woman before her and that she was jealous of the attention Pa paid to him. But Pa had always had a great capacity for love. He could give it generously to Joey without taking anything away from Dulcie. Why couldn't she see that?

"Pa . . ." Joey said.

Pa seemed to have trouble seeing. "Joey? You there, Joey? Come here to me."

Joey moved closer, on the opposite side of the bed from Dulcie. His father had always had large, strong farmer hands. It seemed a supreme effort for him to extend one of them to Joey. Time was when Pa could have crushed Joey's hand like an eggshell. Now waning strength barely allowed him to close his fingers around the boy's. The hand was hot with fever.

"Son . . . I'm sorry."

Joey was puzzled. He didn't see any reason for Pa to be apologizing. It wasn't his fault the fool mules had stampeded, that he lay here helpless, his life ebbing away. It was Joey who should be sorry. Pa had offered him a chance to ride with him to town that day, but Joey had wanted to go down to the creek and try to catch a catfish. Maybe if he had been along he could have done something. At least he would have been there when Pa got hurt. As it was, Pa had lain out on the road for hours before Reuben got worried and went looking for him.

Pa tried to speak but broke into coughing. When he recouped enough, his strained voice bespoke pain. "You're a good boy. I want you to grow up . . . and be a good man."

Reuben appeared in the doorway, breathing heavily

from the hurrying. Pa beckoned weakly. The old man glanced apprehensively at Dulcie, then moved around to Joey's side of the bed, dragging his feet a little.

"Reuben . . . you help Dulcie look out for Joey."

"I'll do that, Mr. John. I sure will do that."

Pa's eyes closed. His rough breathing trailed away, then stopped. The doctor laid the flat of his hand across Pa's chest. "He's gone."

Dulcie blinked, looking a moment at the man who had been her husband, then across the bed at Joey. She spoke bitterly, "I'm his wife. You'd think the last words out of his mouth could've been for *me*."

Blair Meacham said, "Don't take it to heart. He probably meant to say more but time ran out on him."

"Another woman's son, and he expected me to raise the boy like he was my own."

The doctor said, "He's left you this good farm to do it with. Many a widow has been left with far less."

Joey could no longer hold back the tears. He leaned over his father and let them all go. He felt hands on his shoulders and knew by the feel of them that they were Reuben's. They should have been Dulcie's, perhaps, but she had left the room with Mr. Meacham's arm around her shoulder.

In a little while Dulcie called from the kitchen. "Reuben!"

The old man gave Joey's arm a squeeze and left the room. Joey took a lingering look at his father's face, then followed.

In the kitchen, Dulcie stared through the window toward the barn. She seemed to be trying not to look at anyone. "Doctor said he'll notify the preacher to come out in the mornin'. You'd best get started diggin' the grave, Reuben. You know where."

"Next to Miz Molly?"

Joey's mother was buried along with three of her babies in a small family plot up on a gentle hill that overlooked the field. Joey had been the only child to survive beyond the first days.

Dulcie did not answer the question directly. "Take Joey with you. He needs to be out of this house, not in here where his daddy just died."

Reuben nodded solemn assent. "Sunshine and fresh air will help ease his grievin'."

Dulcie turned her back. "Tell Mr. Meacham I want him to come in here."

Meacham was on the narrow front porch, watching the doctor leave. Joey sensed that Reuben was disturbed over Meacham's staying behind. Dulcie would need kinfolks around her now, and she did not recognize Joey as kin; he was painfully aware of that. But that was all right; he didn't see her that way, either.

Reuben said with a curtness unusual for him, "Miz Dulcie wants you."

Meacham seemed to overlook the attitude. His voice carried some comfort. "Too bad about your daddy, boy."

Joey did not know what to say. He grunted acknowledgment and followed Reuben to the barn. Reuben fetched out a pick and shovel and started up the gentle slope toward the tiny cemetery. "Doctor'll tell the neighbors on his way to town. There'll be some of them over here later to help with layin' out your daddy."

"Now that he's gone, am I goin' to have to live with Dulcie?"

"Young'uns got to live with somebody."

"I don't think I'll want to live in that house. I'd rather come out and stay with you."

Reuben lived in a twelve-by-twelve box-and-strip shack beside the barn and windmill. Most of the time he cooked his own meals on a small cast-iron stove and toted his water by the bucketful from a cistern filled by runoff rain funneled down from the roof of the larger house. The water always seemed to carry a flavor of cypress shingles, but it was better than the mineral-laden stuff brought up by the windmill.

Reuben said, "Ain't room in that shack for a mouse-catchin' cat, much less a half-grown boy. Besides, ain't much tellin' how long I may still be here."

Ever since she had come to the farm, Dulcie had been agitating Pa to fire Reuben and hire somebody white, like her cousin Blair Meacham. "I don't like livin' this close to a nigger man, not even an old one," she had complained. But Pa had held firm. Back in slave times, Reuben had belonged to Joey's mother's folks, and Mama had promised that he had a home here for the rest of his days. A promise from Mama had been like gospel to Pa.

Now that Pa was gone, though, and Dulcie was in charge, old promises might wind up buried in this cemetery like the folks who had made them. Joey suspected that thought was tracking through Reuben's mind.

"You promised Pa you'd look after me. How you goin' to do that without you keep livin' here?"

"We'll have to trust in the Lord."

Joey had often thought Reuben would have been a good preacher if he had turned his mind to it and if he had been able to read. Growing up a slave, he had been denied any book learning. What he knew of the Word he had absorbed from listening to other people and to the inner voices of his own gentle soul. He kept a copy of the Bible on a wooden box beside his cot. He often studied the pictures, and he claimed he could sometimes feel the power of the book warming his rough old hands.

Reuben took off his hat and stood a moment before the gravestone that marked the resting place of Joey's mother. "There was a blessed woman."

Time had faded and blurred Joey's memories of her. More than what she had looked like, he remembered the warm comfort of her arms and the soft music of her voice. He remembered the pain of losing her, a pain that returned to him now in the loss of Pa.

Reuben said, "Her and your pa, they're probably huggin' one another right now in heaven."

Joey's eyes burned. "I wish I was there with them."

"Don't say that. Remember that your mama went through some mighty sad times to bring you into this world." He motioned toward the three small stones that bore the names of the lost babies. "You were a glory to her. She'd want you to live long and happy."

"How can I be happy livin' with Dulcie, without Pa?"

The old man offered no answer. Joey turned away from him, seated himself on the stone fence, and wept quietly while Reuben dug a grave in the soft ground.

When Reuben stopped to rest and smoke his pipe, Joey took up the pick and shovel. The physical exertion helped ease, or at least mask, his pain. The hole was almost as deep as he was tall when he heard Reuben say, "Somebody comin' down the road."

Joey climbed out of the hole and made a halfhearted attempt at dusting himself off. He heard the peacock and saw a wagon. "Looks like Mr. Hayworth and his wife, come to help. Maybe I better go tell Dulcie so she can get the coffee started."

He ran more than he walked, so that he was gasping by

the time he reached the house. He leaned against the wall, trying to regain his breath. Through the window he heard Dulcie's voice, and her cousin's. Meacham was saying, "You can't run this farm by yourself, Dulcie. You was always a town girl. You don't know the first thing about cotton and corn. You don't even know how to milk a cow."

"I don't figure on stayin' out here very long. Soon's the lawyer reads John's will and gets the papers fixed up, I'm sellin' this place. It ought to fetch a pretty price. I'll move to Waco or Dallas or someplace where there's life and people."

"What about the kid?"

"What *about* him? He's not mine."

"The law'll say you've got to take care of him."

"By the time the law finds out I'm gone, I'll be so far away they won't know where to look for me."

"John'll turn over in his grave."

"I don't see where I owe him anything. He married me just to have a mother for that kid. Made me all kinds of promises to get me out here, but there never was a day he ever stopped grievin' over his first wife. So whatever I can get out of this place, I've got it comin'."

Joey felt as if a mule had kicked all the wind out of him. Dulcie never seemed to lack for excuses to whip him when Pa wasn't around, but this was worse than any whipping she had ever given him. He put aside his intention of telling her that company was coming. If he went into the house now she was likely to suspect that he had overheard. He ducked down so she would not see him through the window, then retreated. He tried not to cry, but a few sobs escaped him unbidden as he made his way back to the cemetery.

Maybe Reuben would know what he should do.

The old man had made considerable progress. He stood shoulder deep in the hole. Wiping a patched sleeve across his face, he climbed out and relighted his pipe. His eyes narrowed. "By the looks of you, Miz Dulcie must've give you what-for again."

"She didn't see me." Joey found it painful to speak. He gathered up what strength he could muster and blurted, "She's fixin' to run off and leave me."

Reuben almost lost his pipe.

Joey went on, "I heard them talkin', her and her cousin. She figures on sellin' the place and takin' the money and goin' off where they can't find her."

Reuben chewed hard on the pipe stem. "First place, boy, he ain't really her cousin."

"She always said he was."

"Sayin' and bein' ain't the same thing. Your pa, he knowed."

"Then why . . ."

"There's man-and-woman stuff a boy your age wouldn't understand, nor need to know about." Reuben took the pipe from his mouth and pointed the stem at Joey. "Your pa and Miz Dulcie, they was both expectin' more from one another than they had any right to. After your mama died, your pa done his best at raisin' you, but it's almighty hard in a house where there ain't no woman. He probably told Miz Dulcie he loved her, and all that, but in tryin' to do right by you he done wrong by her.

"And Miz Dulcie, she never had much in the way of decent fixin's. She was raised dirt poor, scratchin' like a banty hen for whatever little she got. To a woman hungry as her, your pa must've looked mighty well off. So when he offered her his name and a place in his home, she grabbed at the chance. They both wound up holdin' a sack with a hole in it."

Joey knew it was customary for friends and relatives to take turns sitting up with the body through the night prior to the burial. He tried to sleep but found he could not. He judged that it was after midnight when he arose from bed, slipped into his overalls, and went out into the modest parlor where Pa lay in a pine box a couple of the neighbors had fashioned. The box had been placed across two wooden chairs. A lamp burned dimly, its wick turned down as low as possible without snuffing out the flame.

Overhead, suspended just below the ceiling, was Mama's old quilting frame on which she had sewn bedcovers for her family as well as for neighbors and friends. Dulcie had never used it. She did not favor that kind of meticulous, artistic work.

Blair Meacham slept on a pallet on the wooden floor. Reuben sat in a rocking chair that Pa had always favored.

"You oughtn't to be up," he whispered. "What you need most right now is sleep."

"I kept thinkin' about Pa." Joey studied the still figure in the box. A desperate hope touched him for a moment. "Maybe he's just unconscious. He looks like he could raise up any minute, wide awake."

"No, boy, he's gone to a better life. Ain't nothin' in that box but the empty shell he used to live in." Reuben arose from the rocker and put an arm around Joey. "It's a hard thing and a test of our faith, sayin' goodbye to folks we love. You'll see your pa again someday when your own time comes. Your mama too."

The wooden floor creaked. Looking up through his tears, Joey saw Dulcie standing in the door that led to the bedroom she had shared with Pa. Her voice was severe. "Joey, you've got no business bein' up. You get yourself back in bed."

Joey shrank away from her. "I just had to come and see Pa again, while I still can."

"You can see him in the mornin'. Now get to bed."

She turned away. Reuben silently indicated that Joey should obey his stepmother. Joey started to comply but paused again beside his father. Anger welled up in him at the injustice of it all. "We ought to shoot those fool mules!"

Dulcie faced around. "You'd just as well know, Joey. Your daddy left town dead drunk, like he'd been doin' for a long time. Chances are he did some fool thing that made them mules run."

"No!" Joey shouted. "That's a lie!" He ran at her and pummeled her with his fists. "Don't you be tellin' lies about my pa."

Reuben grabbed him. Through his own anger Joey could see fury in Dulcie's eyes. She drew back a hand to slap him, but Reuben pulled him away.

"Whoa there, you've got no call to act thataway." He turned to Dulcie. "The boy ain't hisself."

"He's himself, all right. But I ain't puttin' up with no more of it."

The commotion had awakened Meacham. He cast a blanket aside and arose. He had been sleeping in his clothes, except for his shoes. "Now, Dulcie, you calm yourself down before you say somethin' you hadn't ought to. And Reuben, you better take Joey out to your house. I'll sit up with John the rest of the night."

Reuben held firmly to Joey. "Yes sir, Mr. Meacham.

Sorry, Miz Dulcie. I'll get the boy calmed down. His thinkin' just ain't straight right now."

Joey glanced behind him as they walked toward the shack beside the barn. Through the window, in the dim lamplight, he saw Meacham put his arms around Dulcie.

"It ain't true what she said about Pa."

Reuben opened the door. He fumbled in the darkness until he struck a match and lighted a lamp. The cooped-up smell of sweat and tobacco and grease from Reuben's cooking hit Joey in the face like a wet saddle blanket.

Reuben said, "You lay down on my cot and try to get some sleep. I figured on settin' up the rest of the night anyway."

Joey knew his father had been drinking some lately; the evidence of it had been on his breath, and sometimes he stumbled in his walking. But he wasn't a drunk.

"Why would she tell a big lie like that?"

Reuben took the pipe from his pocket and lighted it, staring toward a picture of Jesus on the wall. "Your pa was carryin' a heavy load of grief. He tried to lift it off with whiskey, but whiskey is the devil's snare. Him and Miz Dulcie never had the true feelin's of a man and wife, sure not the feelin's him and your mama had. He was just lookin' for a new mama for you. Miz Dulcie was lookin' for a home and an easier row to hoe. They didn't neither one of them find what they was lookin' for."

"So now she figures on sellin' the place and runnin' off and leavin' me. What am I goin' to do, Reuben?"

"When the time comes, the Lord always shows us the way."

"He'd better show us pretty quick."

{ TWO }

⟨⟩

The funeral was like a bad dream from which Joey hoped he would awaken and find had never happened. But it was all real. He had never realized how many friends Pa had. All of them came by to shake Joey's hand or to hug him and tell him everything would be all right and he would understand it by and by.

He understood well enough. Pa was gone, like Mama before him, and Dulcie was fixing to leave him to shift for himself the best he could.

Preacher Johnson's calm voice gave him some comfort, though part of what he said went past Joey like the soft west wind that moved across the cemetery during the services. He had always found pleasure in listening to ministers, even when he didn't understand them. Reuben had told him that God spoke directly to men who preached the Bible, so listening to a man of the cloth was almost the same as listening to the Lord Himself.

Johnson labored for wages during the week but did battle for the Lord on Sundays and between times when there was a funeral to be preached or a sinner to be prayed for.

Just before giving a final prayer, the minister read a small poem:

"The glass is dashed.
The wine is spilt.
The sword is broke,
And left the hilt.
The powder's burnt,
That spent the ball.
The soldier's gone
To his recall.
May Him whose will
Controls the whole
Call the body,
Receive the soul."

The visitors began trailing away in buggies and wagons and on horseback. The lawyer Wilson, an old friend of Pa's, had ridden out from Athens with the doctor. As they started to climb into the physician's black buggy, Dulcie and Meacham caught up to them.

Dulcie said, "Mr. Wilson, could you stay a little longer? I'd like to talk to you about John's will."

The attorney seemed surprised. "I'd think you'd want to wait a few days to compose yourself."

"I am composed, Mr. Wilson."

Blair Meacham smiled easily. "It's just that it's a ways out here from town, and she wants to save you an extra trip."

The attorney seemed a little put off, but he said, "Very well." He sought out the old man with his eyes. "Reuben, you'd best bring Joey."

Dulcie gave Joey a hard glance. "He's just a boy. He wouldn't understand."

"This will concern him."

Reuben deferentially touched blunt fingertips to the brim of his hat. "I'll fetch him along, Mr. Wilson."

Dulcie and Meacham climbed into Pa's wagon, which Reuben had repaired after the wreck. Dulcie jerked her head, and Meacham put the team into motion behind the black buggy. They left Joey and Reuben to walk. Joey thought he saw a ripple of resentment flit across the black man's wrinkled face, but it was gone in an instant, covered as he always covered any ill feelings.

Joey could easily have outdistanced the old man, but he held to an untaxing pace. The former slave wore his black go-to-meeting suit, older than Joey. The cuffs of the coat were fraying, and the knees had been patched, for Reuben knelt often when he felt the presence of the Lord.

Joey asked, "What do you reckon Mr. Wilson wants with me?"

"I got a feelin' he's fixin' to dump a load of disappointment on Miz Dulcie."

Meacham stood on the porch, waiting. He gave Joey a thin smile.

In the house, Dulcie pointed to the two chairs across which the casket had so recently rested. "Have a seat, Mr. Wilson. I want to talk to you about this farm."

"A mighty good farm it is. John knew how to run it properly."

"Somebody around here ought to be willin' to pay me what it's worth. I want you to take care of the lawyer work so I can sell it."

Wilson and the doctor frowned at one another. "Dulcie, did you ever see John's will?"

"No. He just told me him and you wrote one up."

"We did. And the way it's written, the farm belongs to Joey."

Dulcie's eyes flashed dismay, then a rising anger. "To Joey? But he's just a kid."

"He won't always be. John wanted to make sure the farm would be secure for him when he comes of age. He stipulated that you have a home here until Joey is grown, provided you remain and take proper care of him."

Dulcie's face reddened. She stared at Meacham. He seemed as surprised as she was. "You're sayin' I can't sell?"

"Not without Joey's consent. And Joey can't legally give that consent until he comes of age."

"You're a lawyer, Mr. Wilson. You could find some way around all that."

"I might, if I so chose, but I won't. John Shipman was my friend."

Joey felt the old man's fingers tighten on his arm. Reuben was trying hard not to smile. Joey was not certain there was much to smile about. "You mean I got to keep livin' here with Dulcie?"

The lawyer said, "She is your legal guardian."

Meacham considered the proposition. "Sounds logical to me, as far as it goes. But what if somethin' was to happen to Joey before he comes of age? Where would that leave Dulcie?"

"She is the secondary heir. But nothing is going to happen to Joey, not if he is properly cared for."

"And he will be. Dulcie'll see to that. But we've all seen sickness carry kids away . . . typhoid fever and diphtheria and such. I was just thinkin' about what'd come of Dulcie."

The doctor said, "It'll be my job to see that none of that ever happens. John was a friend of mine too."

Joey asked, "What about Reuben? Did Pa say anything in his will about Reuben?"

"He said Reuben is to have a home here the rest of his life."

Joey looked hard at Dulcie. "And nobody can run him off?"

"It's in the will."

Reuben squeezed Joey's arm again. "I told you. The Lord will provide."

"With help from Pa."

Dulcie turned her back and faced the window. Her fists were clenched. "Damn that man! Even in the grave, he's got a chain around my neck. Why didn't he just sentence me to life in prison?"

Wilson said, "There's not a better farm within twenty miles. It will make you a living."

"If a livin' was all I wanted, I'd've left here a long time ago."

The lawyer shrugged. "Life usually gives us whatever we need. It doesn't guarantee us all we *want*."

"I can't run this farm with just Reuben and the boy. I'll have to hire a man."

"I'll see if I can find someone for you."

"No need. I'm hirin' Blair Meacham."

Wilson gave a nod of approval. Folks in town seemed to regard Meacham as a hail-fellow-well-met. People were always offering to buy him drinks so they could listen to his jokes and stories. "A good choice. Being your kin, he will take an extra interest in doing things properly."

The doctor jerked his head at Wilson. "We'd best be leaving. I have a sick woman to visit on our way back to town."

Dulcie stalked into her bedroom and slammed the door. Joey and Reuben and Meacham followed the two towns-men out onto the porch. Wilson turned to Meacham. "I hope you will stress to her that she must take *proper* care of the boy. The doctor and I will be the ones who define proper care."

"I'll see to it, or you can call Blair Meacham a liar."

Wilson turned to Reuben. "And I'll be depending upon you, just as John always did."

"I been watchin' the boy ever since the day his mama give birth to him."

As the two men rode away, Meacham walked back into the house to join Dulcie.

Joey said, "Of course Mr. Meacham ain't nothin' like Pa, but I feel better knowin' he'll be here."

Reuben's voice held a sharp edge. "No, boy, he sure ain't nothin' like your pa."

In light of her disappointment, Joey expected Dulcie to be hell on wheels the next few days. Her attitude was a pleasant surprise. It was not truly friendly but more or less detached, as if other matters had taken priority and she had more to do than pick on him.

Perhaps the amount of time Meacham spent with her was keeping her in a better humor than Joey could have hoped. He seemed to be in the house a lot while Joey and Reuben were working in the fields or garden or with the farm's few cattle. Dulcie had suggested that Reuben be moved into the barn, but Meacham had declined the use of the small shack. He said he didn't want to put Reuben out. Joey thought that was nice of him.

Supposedly Meacham was sleeping in the barn, but some nights Joey heard him quietly enter the house and go into the bedroom where Dulcie was. He never heard him leave, and Meacham was always at the table awaiting his breakfast when Joey got up.

Hand-pulling weeds from among the garden's young tomato plants, Joey glanced toward the house. Meacham had not left there since they had finished the noon meal an hour or so ago. Reuben was breaking out new rows with a moldboard plow and a mule.

Joey told him, "Dulcie ain't said a cross word to me in two or three days. You reckon she's sick or somethin'?"

"Not unless sick means givin' in to the ways of the flesh."

"What do you mean by that?"

Reuben's face furrowed. "When you get a little older, you'll know."

Joey already understood more about such goings-on than the old man gave him credit for. But he did not want to disillusion Reuben about his innocence. In any case, it did not matter to Joey why Dulcie seemed in a better humor; it only mattered that she was.

Meacham came to the garden fence. "Joey, that milk-pen calf has got out and joined its mama. I'd like you to go fetch it in. Else it'll take all the milk, and the cow won't give us none tonight."

"I'll saddle old Taw."

"You're young and wiry. You don't need a horse. Just walk out there and drive that calf and its mama back."

Joey was disappointed. He liked to ride horseback when he could find an excuse. As for missing out on the milk tonight, he would not have minded. The twice-a-day milking chore had been his since he was eight years old, and it had become eternally tiresome. But even walking out into the milk-cow pasture was preferable to pulling weeds.

"What about that mean Jersey bull?" he asked.

"That old gentle pet? He's shut up in a pen, snug and safe."

Pet? Maybe for a man full-grown who could run a bluff, but that bull had taken Joey's measure and found it short.

He climbed over the garden fence and jumped down, not taking time to walk to the gate. Reuben was always cautioning him that this was a good way to break his leg if he happened to slip, but youthful impatience had little time for such considerations. To be on the safe side, he made an arc around the barn to satisfy himself about the bull. The gate appeared shut. Joey whistled a happy tune as his gaze swept across the small pasture, seeking the cow and calf.

He found them no more than three hundred yards from the barn, contentedly celebrating their happy reunion. The cow was filling her paunch with spring grass while the calf punched her udder, trying to coax down more milk. It would be difficult for Joey to separate the two until he got them into a pen. He circled around them and shouted, waving his arms. The calf ignored him, and the cow gave him a blank bovine stare until he moved closer, shouting again. Reluctantly she turned and began plodding toward the barn. The calf twisted its tail over its back and hopped along after her, its muzzle white with milk foam. Joey began whistling again. It was an old church song, but he gave it a jaunty bounce that Preacher Johnson might not have approved.

A hundred yards from the barn he stopped suddenly, his attention caught by a dark movement, then a bellow. The bull was loose.

Joey's breath stopped; his heartbeat quickened. He looked toward the pasture fence. If the bull made a determined run at him, Joey would never reach the wire in time. He dropped to his knees, hoping the bull would be interested enough in the cow that it would not notice him.

His hopes were short lived. The bull circled the cow, unceremoniously bumping her calf aside, but after a moment's inspection found her not to be in heat. Its interest rapidly waned and transferred to Joey, who tried to flatten himself on the ground out of the bull's sight. The bellowing resumed. The bull began to sling its head and paw dirt back over its shoulder.

Joey saw no choice. He had to try for the fence, for any moment now the bull would make a run at him. He jumped to his feet and sprinted. From the edge of his eye he saw a blur of movement. The bull was cutting across to intercept him, snorting at every step, head low to the ground. Joey cried out in fear.

He did not reach the fence. The bull rammed into him from behind, a glancing blow that shot a bolt of pain from his legs to his head. The bull's horns had been sawed off years ago, but the stubs were still sharp at the edges. The impact sent Joey stumbling and rolling, then he flipped himself over onto his back so he could see what was coming. The bull's huge head was so close he could reach out and touch the snotty muzzle. The belligerent bellow froze him along his spine.

He shouted and waved his hands, but that only seemed to stir the bull to more of a frenzy. That brown-black head, hard as iron, connected with Joey's nose, and he nearly strangled on a sudden flow of hot blood. The bull hooked at Joey's chest, the stub horns cutting into his flesh. He felt the breath mashed out of him. One of the cloven hoofs pressed down on his leg. Pain seared him as the bull brought its full weight to bear.

In his panic he knew it would take but a moment now to crush the life from him.

He heard a cry that was not his own. Through a haze of pain he saw Reuben climbing over the fence with the alacrity of a youngster. He had never seen the old man's creaky legs move so rapidly. Reuben came running, waving his hat, shouting at the bull.

The animal raised its head at this new distraction. It pawed dirt in response to Reuben's challenge and made a threatening sound deep in its throat. It feinted as if it were about to charge, then lost courage and turned. It ran off thirty feet or so and wheeled back around, offering an empty bluff. Reuben made a run at it, throwing his arms into the air and yelling. The bull retreated.

Joey's heart pounded in the aftermath of panic. He choked, lungs ablaze for want of air. He fought to regain the breath the bull had knocked out of him. Blood and dirt burned his eyes. His sides ached from the pounding his ribs had taken. He tried to arise, but Reuben gently pushed him back down.

"Slow, boy, slow. Get your breath first, then raise up easy. Got to be sure you ain't got no ribs caved in, less'n they punch a hole in your lungs like happened to your pa."

Gradually Joey regained his breath. Reuben pressed carefully upon his ribs, first one side and then the other, testing. "Looks like the Lord set an angel on your shoulders, else that old bull would've killed you dead."

Joey wheezed. He tried to tell Reuben that no angel would ever be half so welcome as the sight of him coming over that fence, but his breath was too ragged. He could not speak the words.

Reuben's gaze fastened on Blair Meacham, trotting out from the direction of the barn.

"How's the boy? Is he bad hurt?"

Reuben's eyes flared. "You said that bull was safe in the pen."

"I can't for the life of me figure how he got out."

"You think he unlatched the gate all by hisself?"

Joey recognized the oblique accusation, but Meacham either did not see it for what it was or did not want to acknowledge it. "We better get the boy to the house."

Reuben cautiously helped Joey to his feet and dusted him off the best he could. "You able to walk?"

Joey felt of his ribs. He could not tell if anything was broken. His lungs still ached like fury, and he worked up saliva so he could spit dirt and blood from his mouth. "Someday I'm goin' to take a shotgun to that damned bull."

Reuben chided, "The bull was just the devil's instrument. And you watch the words that come out of your mouth, boy, or the devil may claim you yet."

Meacham said, "I'll trot ahead and tell Dulcie."

Joey strongly suspected that Dulcie already knew. That bull was smart, but he doubted it was smart enough to unlatch the gate. And how was it that the calf had gotten out in the first place?

He limped a few steps but gave in to the pain. He protested to no avail as Reuben picked him up. "You may be hurt worse than you think, young'un."

He was amazed at the old man's strength, the result of lifelong heavy labor. The bull stood off at a safe distance, pawing dirt, but it made no attempt to charge. Joey could only imagine what kind of thinking process a bull had, but it probably remembered the painful outcome of some previous indiscretion with Reuben.

Meacham and Dulcie waited on the porch. Meacham showed concern, but Dulcie seemed resentful at the interruption of whatever she had been doing. She followed Reuben as he carried Joey into the tiny room where he slept. "I'll bet he's puttin' on a lot worse than it really is. Boy's been spoiled too much."

The criticism rolled off Reuben like rain. To Meacham he said, "Which a-one of us is goin' after the doctor, me or you?"

"Doctor?" Dulcie complained. "The old quack'll charge us three dollars just for comin' out here. And he won't find anything but a bruise or two. That old surly is mostly bluff."

She always spoke of the bull as a *surly*. It was not considered respectable for a woman to say the word *bull*.

"Boy could have some stove-in ribs. You can take the three dollars out of my pay." Reuben wasn't paid much, but he didn't spend much except to buy tobacco for that foul old pipe and an occasional new suit of working clothes when his old ones began falling apart. The merchants in town counted him as a nice old man but not much of an asset to business.

Meacham said, "Ain't no use arguin' when we've got a hurt boy to see after. I'll fetch the doctor."

Joey took Meacham's attitude kindly, especially when he contrasted it to Dulcie's. He figured her tears wouldn't wet one corner of a handkerchief if he died. She had controlled her grief mighty well after Pa's death.

Dulcie shrugged in resignation. "You'd best give the boy a good washin', Reuben. We wouldn't want the doctor to think we let him go around dirty as that all the time."

Dulcie left the room. That suited Joey fine. He was getting too big to let a woman see him without his clothes on, even his stepmother. Reuben fetched a wash pan and a rag and carefully gave Joey what Pa used to call a Tuesday bath, considerably short of a Saturday-night immersion. Joey flinched as Reuben's careful hands touched the torn and bruised places. He still spat up dirt and blood. Reuben was concerned about the blood, which he feared might be coming from a punctured lung. But Joey felt it was probably inner bleeding from his nose, which the bull had tried to flatten.

Reuben lamented, "I promised your pa I'd look after you, but I wasn't doin' a good job of it when I let this happen."

"Wasn't your fault."

"I'm goin' to take me a good look at that gate after a while."

Joey wondered if Reuben's thoughts ran along the same lines as his own. He asked, "You think somebody messed with it?"

"This farm is worth a right smart of money. Folks can do some awful things when there's money in it."

Most people would think this was just a foolish notion. Everybody knew that kids and old folks sometimes developed a lot of such notions. Joey doubted that anyone would listen if he and Reuben were to voice their suspicions. Reuben *was* old, but Joey could not remember many times he had been wrong.

Reuben spoke in a low voice, careful that Dulcie not overhear. "Worst comes to worst, I may have to take you away from here."

"Where would we go?"

"Your pa used to have a cousin name of Beau. Remember? He come here to visit one time. Didn't stay long because him and your pa never saw eye to eye about nothin'. Mr. Beau was heedless as a wild mule. Never did give much thought to anything past quittin' time."

"I remember him and Pa arguin'."

"Ain't heard of him gettin' killed, so I reckon he's still livin'. He's at a town called Bastrop, if they ain't run him off."

"I don't know where Bastrop is."

"A long ways southwest, down close to Austin City. If it come to that, Mr. Beau might know a place where nobody could find us."

"Why would they try to find us if all Dulcie wanted was to get me out of the way?"

"Because the farm is in your name. Only way to change that is to see you dead. *Gone* ain't enough. She'd have to show the court a dead body."

Joey remembered a story he had read about the wicked brother of a dying king trying to kill the young princes so he would be the one to inherit the throne and rule the kingdom. It had seemed unreal to him that anybody could be so mean. That had been a long time ago and a long way away. This was here and now. But the old story didn't seem so far-fetched to him anymore.

Still, this was the only home Joey had ever known. He would have to give the matter a lot of study before he went off and left it.

The doctor wrapped Joey's ribs tightly and painted his cuts and bruises with something that had a fearsome burn and a worse smell. "If it doesn't hurt, taste bad, or burn," he said, "it's not doing you any good."

Joey thought it must be mighty beneficial.

Reuben watched worriedly. When Dulcie and Meacham left the room, he quietly hinted to the doctor about his suspicions. "I checked the gate. Wasn't nothin' busted. I don't think it was latched proper in the first place."

The doctor's gray eyebrows arched. "Do you know what you're saying?"

"I ain't *sayin'*, exactly. I'm only suspicionin'."

"I would not want to pay a nickel for the difference." The man's eyes narrowed. "I'll forget what you said, Reuben, and you'd better forget it too. You know what could happen if you were to make such accusations in public? They could flay the hide off of you, and the law would not do a thing."

"I'm just fearful for the boy."

"I can't believe the boy is in any danger. But *you* might be, if what you told me should reach the wrong ears."

Meacham walked in. Joey suspected he had heard at least part of it. Meacham said, "Reuben, we'll all be better satisfied when you go down to the pen and put a stronger latch on that gate, one no animal can open for itself."

"I'll be takin' care of that right now." Avoiding Meacham's eyes, Reuben walked out of the room.

The doctor's gaze followed him with a look that bespoke pity. "You have to take his age into account."

"His old mind has commenced to drift. I don't take offense."

Joey had not noticed that Reuben's mind was drifting, but perhaps he had lost some of his old sense of caution. It was not like him to accuse people out loud, even by the vaguest implication.

Meacham said to the doctor, "You can tell the sheriff to come out and look things over . . . satisfy himself if there's any doubt."

"I'll tell him, but there's no suspicion on my part. Just in case I've missed something, you and Dulcie keep an eye on Joey for any undue rise of fever."

"Joey's tougher than a boot." Meacham gave Joey an easy smile and a wink. "Ain't you?"

"I've already quit hurtin', almost." That was a sinful stretch of the truth, but Meacham's endorsement stirred his pride. He hadn't cried no matter how bad the pain had been, and he was not going to let them know how much it still hurt.

He thought Dulcie might come and look in on him after the two men had gone out onto the porch, but she did not. She was probably disappointed that he had not been killed.

If that old bull ever knocks you down, see if I care, he thought.

He had assumed that when the initial pain faded that would be the end of it, but he had not counted on the residual soreness that set in on him hours later and intensified during the night. He was hurting in places he did not even know he had. He slept fitfully, waking each time he tried to turn over or change position in bed.

At daylight he surrendered to the soreness and sat up, swinging his legs carefully over the side of the bed. He was sure every joint in his body ached. Given the opportunity, he would gladly shoot that bull, taking him down one leg at a time and then making the final grace shot right between those two bulging, evil eyes.

Slowly he stood up, testing his weight, flinching at the soreness. He found he could walk, though not without pain. Pa had always said the best cure for soreness was to go back and do more of whatever had caused it in the first place. Joey did not care to go that far. He had had enough of the Jersey bull.

He dressed and went out into the larger room that served as kitchen, dining room, and parlor combined. He was not surprised to see Meacham eating breakfast, looking as content as a horse in an oat bin. Meacham seemed to take pleasure from many things, and mealtime was among the foremost of them. It puzzled Joey that he was not fat. Probably had worms.

"Mornin', Joey. You ready to wrestle Ol' Bully again?"

"I'm still ready to shoot him."

Dulcie stood at the stove. "You feel like eatin'?"

The bull had not injured Joey's stomach. "Yes'm." He knew he should add *please*, but that seemed like bowing down. If she were his real mother, and she treated him like a son—well, a lot of things would be different.

Meacham smiled sympathetically as the pain of walking caused Joey to wince. "Maybe you'd better lay around the house today."

Dulcie turned away from the stove. "Best thing for him is good hard work to exercise the soreness out. Last thing you want to do is give a boy an excuse to be lazy."

Maybe she would be more understanding if that old bull ever caught *her* without a place to run or a club to protect herself with, Joey thought. It was a show he would gladly give up a week of school for, to see her scramble up a fence with that bull blowing snot all over her sitting-down place. She would probably whip him for laughing, but the satisfaction would be cheap at the price.

She fried a slice of ham and scrambled a couple of eggs, setting the plate in front of him without ceremony. She acted angry, as if it had been his duty to let that old bull kill him. He managed to grab one biscuit before Meacham took the last one and swabbed up a helping of butter and molasses from his plate.

"Ain't no fresh milk," Dulcie said. "It taken all that calf left us to make biscuits. Reuben said he'd do the milkin' in your place this mornin', but we ain't seen hide nor hair of him."

Reuben had his own chores to do. He had probably forgotten about the milking because that normally was Joey's job. But Joey remembered how concerned Reuben had been yesterday. He thought it strange that Reuben had not already been to the house this morning to see about him.

"Reckon he's sick?" he asked.

Dulcie snickered. "He ain't been sick in his life. Except maybe sick of work."

The remark aroused Joey's resentment. Nobody worked harder than Reuben, considering his age. Pa had said that in his prime Reuben could pick half again more cotton than anybody he had ever seen. He must have been a sight to behold. But Dulcie wouldn't appreciate that. She had known him only as an old man who strained what little patience she had.

Joey said, "He's probably been worryin' about me. I'll go show him I'm all right."

"You finish that breakfast first," Dulcie commanded. "Your pa never gave much thought to waste, but I don't abide it."

The eggs and ham had lost their flavor. Joey put them down hurriedly anyway, then left the table. He took half the biscuit with him to eat on the way. He paused at the door of the barn to finish the final bite while he looked around. He did not see Reuben there or in the milk pen. The cow and her calf were separated by a fence. A glance at her udder told him she had not yet been milked.

"Reuben!" Hearing no answer, he walked to the old man's shack. The door was ajar. He pushed it open and stepped inside.

Reuben lay on the cot, one black arm across his chest, the other dangling off the near side. Odd, Joey thought, finding him still asleep this late in the morning. Often as not, Reuben woke up the rooster. The old man appeared peaceful, but the room did not. The patchwork quilt barely covered his feet, most of it hanging haphazardly off the far side of the cot. The wooden box beside the cot was turned over, and Reuben's Bible lay on the floor.

Alarm struck Joey like a dash of cold water in his face. "Reuben!" Three long steps brought him to the edge of the cot. He reached out to touch Reuben's hand, then hesitated. Instinctively he knew what he was going to find. He forced himself to it. The hand was cold and lifeless, like Pa's had been as he lay in his wooden coffin.

Reuben was dead.

{ THREE }

The doctor had made several trips to the Shipman farm in recent days. His first remark was, "It looks as if I may have to build me a room onto the Shipman house."

Sheriff Lawton rode in the buggy with him, for this was a sudden and unexpected death. Many lawmen wouldn't go to this much trouble for an old black man, Meacham said, but the sheriff accepted his duty like a religious calling. He had known and respected Reuben since his own boyhood.

Joey stood outside the door of the shack, leaning in just enough to see and hear. The adults might send him away if he called attention to himself.

The doctor was saying, "I believe he suffered a heart seizure during the night. Those can be violent sometimes. That would account for his kicking the cover around and knocking the box over."

The sheriff gravely accepted the explanation. "Not a bad way to go. Quick, anyhow."

Meacham left the shack and started back toward the house. Joey worked up his nerve and stepped through the door. He heard the doctor saying, "Looking back to Reuben's state of mind yesterday, I can readily understand. The excitement and exertion of rescuing Joey from that bull, then carrying him to the house . . . And he was considerably agitated afterward. The stress was too much for his old heart."

Joey blurted, "What if somebody killed him?"

The doctor and the sheriff turned, surprised. The sheriff said, "No one killed Reuben, son. The doctor and I both looked him over. There's no sign of a wound, nothin' like that."

Joey demanded, "What if she poisoned him? That wouldn't leave no bullet hole."

"You're lettin' your imagination run away with you. Why would anybody want to poison a good old man like Reuben?"

"Dulcie always wanted to run him off, but Pa wouldn't let her. And Lawyer Wilson told her she couldn't."

The sheriff patted Joey's shoulder. "If Dulcie poisoned everybody she didn't like, half the people in town would be dead. Me included, I expect. No, son, don't let such a notion sour your mind about your stepmother. The Lord decided He needed Reuben, so He called him home."

Joey blinked away tears. He needed Reuben worse than the Lord did.

The sheriff eased him out of the shack. "While I'm here, why don't you show me the gate where that bull got out?"

Joey did. He found a heavy chain had been added since yesterday's excitement, and a large bolt had been inserted solidly into the post to keep the chain tightly fastened. That must have been Reuben's final piece of work.

Joey lamented, "First Pa, then Reuben. I don't know how I'll get along without them."

"You'll always carry them with you in your memory, and they'll keep on pointin' your way."

Yesterday Reuben had said they might have to leave this place for Joey's own safety. Now Reuben was dead, and Joey could not feel confident in the sheriff's assurances. He could not shake off a dark suspicion that Dulcie was somehow responsible for Reuben's dying. He didn't see how she could have rigged Pa's accident, but once he was home she might have done something to make sure he never recovered from his injury.

First Pa, then Reuben. Who next?

Who else, except me? With me dead, the farm belongs to her.

Fear began to build a small, cold knot in his stomach. Dulcie didn't like him any better than she had liked Reuben. Not much, anyway.

At the edge of the barn, the sun shining through a spider web made the thin strands look like threads of silver. A freshly caught fly struggled vainly for its freedom. A black spider was moving down to devour it.

Joey had no use for flies, but the thought of a creature entrapped and doomed made a chill run along his back. He picked up a short stick and poked at the web, freeing the fly. He watched it disappear but felt only partial relief.

At least the fly had wings. Joey had none, and the black widow spider was closing in.

They buried Reuben just outside the family cemetery's stone fence. It wasn't fitting, Dulcie declared, to bury a black man inside, where white folks lay. To Joey, Reuben was family, but any argument from him would set her mind even firmer. It probably didn't matter too much anyhow. By the time all graves were opened on Judgment Day, that fence wouldn't still be here. Preacher Johnson said the ages would melt the mountains down. A little old fence like that wouldn't stand any kind of chance.

Joey watched the mourners depart, mostly a few near neighbors and a handful of people from town. As the last of them rode away, he felt abandoned, alone as he had never been. He watched Dulcie go back into the house, Meacham's arm around her shoulder. He had not seen any mourning on her part. Reuben's dying had probably been a relief to her, like pulling a thorn out of her foot.

He felt Meacham was the nearest thing to an ally he had left, and not even Meacham was likely to believe Joey's suspicions. Nothing less than Joey's death would prove them true.

Soon after Reuben was laid to rest, Joey began plotting his escape. He stole food in small amounts he didn't think Dulcie would miss—a little sugar at a time, a little flour and salt—hiding them in the barn. He did not customarily drink coffee, but he supposed that when he was on his own he would have to learn to like the stuff. Pa used to say that when he went off to the big war as a gangling boy, he had sometimes gone for days without more on his stomach than black coffee and a handful of parched corn. There was already corn enough at the barn, feed for the working stock. Joey would sneak off and try to learn how to parch it. He knew he should have listened closer to Pa, because he never could make it taste like anything but scorched horse and mule feed.

He wished he could bring Meacham in on his plans; he felt a need to confide in someone. But Meacham's first loyalty would be to Dulcie. He would probably tell her, and that would be the end of the scheme—and probably the end of Joey, because anyone wicked enough to plan the deaths of Pa and Reuben would have no compunctions when it came to eliminating a small nuisance like a boy twelve years old, going on thirteen.

Pa had never let Joey overfeed the stock, but he began slipping extra oats to his horse Taw. He figured to fatten him up a bit and give him stamina for a long trip. Taw was far from young. He had already been grown and broke to the saddle before Joey was born. He didn't know much, and half the cows on the farm could outrun him, but at least he was docile and responded well to the reins. The saddle was an old one left over from Pa's own youth. Joey considered Pa's much newer saddle but knew it was too large for him. He would bounce around in it like a ball on a string.

Pa had taken him nowhere much except to town, and never more than twenty or thirty miles from home. Joey had but little notion what lay beyond that limited range of travel. He had read books, of course, lots of them. While they aroused his curiosity, they also triggered a great deal of uncertainty. His imagination was not expansive enough to accommodate lands so distant or cities so large as those he had read about.

He had heard of people running off to Mexico, usually when they found themselves at cross purposes with the law. But it was his understanding that Mexico lay a considerable distance to the south, and that he would have to make his way through a lot of thirsty desert and stickery cactus to get there. A school friend had told him people in Mexico did not even know the American language. He had encountered Mexicans in town and marveled at their ability to understand one another even though he could not comprehend a word that passed their lips.

The world would be a simpler place, he thought, if everybody talked the same as he did.

Mexico was out.

He knew his mother had kin somewhere back in Arkansas to whom she had occasionally written, but Dulcie had long since burned up all of Mama's old family letters. Pa had originally come out of Georgia; Joey was hazy as to just where. None of those kinfolks had ever come visiting, so far as he could remember. They would be strangers to him even if he could find them. They would probably not believe when he tried to tell them about Dulcie. Chances were they would let her know where he was, and she would send some sheriff to bring him back. In handcuffs, like as not, as he had once seen them bring in a man accused of murdering a farmer for his mule.

Joey remembered that the steel cuffs had rubbed the culprit's wrists until they were raw and bleeding. Joey had heard in school later that the prisoner had beat his head against the stone wall of his cell until his brains began to seep out and he died. Folks had said it was better than hanging, but Joey hadn't seen that either choice had much to offer. He was sure of one thing: he did not want to run afoul of any sheriffs. He was glad the local one was a family friend.

But even Sheriff Lawton would not believe Joey's suspicions about Dulcie. He would just pat Joey on the head to humor him, treating him like a kid.

Joey strained his memory, trying to recall what Reuben had said about Pa's cousin Beau, living somewhere to the southwest. What was the name of the place? Bassett . . . Bastard . . . couldn't be *that*. Bas*trop* . . . that was it, Bastrop. He had only the vaguest idea where it was. He could not afford to ask anyone around here because when he turned up gone they would remember his asking and know where to start looking for him.

If he were in school he might find Bastrop on the Texas map tacked to the wall, but school had let out for planting time. Most farmers agreed that their children—the boys, at least—were benefitting themselves and their families more by working in the fields than by studying Webster's Blue Back Speller or practicing arithmetic. In their futures as farmers they were unlikely to have to add up large sums anyway.

Once he got away from here he could find Bastrop. It was not going to move anywhere. Nor was it likely to be more than a temporary refuge for him. From what Reuben had said, cousin Beau was not exactly a pillar of the community. But perhaps he would help Joey get a little farther down the road to some place where Dulcie could not find him.

Farther west or southwest were places with interesting names like San Antonio, San Angelo, El Paso. . . . They sounded as if they would be worth seeing. He began to itch with impatience to be on his way. But he would await the right opportunity, a fortunate combination of circumstances that would give him a good head start before anyone had time to miss him.

A couple of weeks after Reuben's death, Blair Meacham gave up any pretense about sleeping in the barn. He moved his stuff into the house and began sleeping in the same room with Dulcie, the room Pa had shared with her. It had only one bed.

Joey wondered what Preacher Johnson would say about such goings-on, and them supposed to be cousins. Reuben had said they weren't, and Joey guessed Reuben had known. Cousins or not, the whole thing was more than a little odd to him, especially considering how short a time it had been since Pa's death.

The saving feature about the arrangement was that Dulcie stayed in a better humor most of the time. She hadn't whipped Joey lately or even hounded him about being slow in doing his chores. He decided he could overlook her indiscretions if she was going to treat him decently for a change. He even began wondering if he might have been wrong about her intention of killing him. Perhaps, like the sheriff had said, his disliking for her had caused his imagination to run away with him.

One night after supper he sat down to read a book by the light of a kerosene lamp in the parlor. He tried not to notice the way Meacham and Dulcie kept looking at one another, making little signals, touching each other and trying to make it appear to be unintentional. Their faces began to flush. Joey pretended he did not see, but he was a long way from blind.

At length Dulcie said, "Joey, ain't it your bedtime?"

He glanced at the clock over the fireplace. "It's early yet."

"You look tired. You'd better go to bed anyway."

Experience had taught him not to argue with her. He took the book with him; he could light the lamp in his room and finish the chapter.

She said, "No more readin'. You go to sleep."

He wasn't just a kid anymore. He knew what they were about. He laid the book down on a table and walked toward his room. He noticed that the door was closed. He usually left it open in the evening to try to draw in fresh air. Perhaps the breeze had pulled it shut.

He opened the door. The room was dark except for a little reflected light from the lamp in the parlor. He started to unbutton his shirt when he heard a faint buzz that made the hair tickle the back of his neck. The buzz suddenly became louder, and he knew instantly what it was.

Rattlesnake!

His heart hammered frantically, his skin prickling with a thousand needles of panic. Scary as that Jersey bull had been, a rattlesnake was ten times worse. Instinct told him to run for the door, but he did not know at first where the snake was. Any direction he stepped might carry him to it. He froze in place and tried to pinpoint the deadly sound.

The snake was coiled atop his bed. It looked as big around as a tree trunk. Forked tongue darting wickedly, it was poised to strike.

Joey gave a shriek, then flung himself toward the door. From the corner of his eye he saw the snake hurl its body toward him. It was fast, but he was faster. He raced out into the parlor, shouting at the top of his voice.

He stumbled and fell headlong upon the floor. Meacham knelt beside him. "What the hell, boy?"

"Snake!" Joey managed the word in a wheezing voice. He pointed toward his room.

Meacham picked up the lamp by which Joey had been reading and cautiously made his way toward the door, holding the lamp out in front of him. Joey heard him say, "My God, that's a big one."

Dulcie didn't say anything. She stood near the eating table, hands at her sides. She didn't seem to have a great interest in snakes.

The reptile crawled out into the larger room. Meacham fetched a broom from the corner behind the stove and poked at the snake, which set up a fearsome rattling. He began hazing it toward the front door. As it finally slithered out across the threshold, he shouted, "Dulcie, bring me John's rifle."

She brought him the weapon from her bedroom.

The shot shook the wooden walls. Joey flinched. He

found himself trembling as if he were freezing to death, though the night was agreeably warm.

He wanted to cry, but he had prided himself on not letting Dulcie see him do that except at Pa's deathbed, and once over Reuben.

Meacham came back into the house, carrying the rifle. The smell of burned powder clung to him. He handed the weapon to Dulcie and bent over Joey. "Are you bit?"

Joey found it difficult to summon voice. "It missed me."

Meacham frowned darkly. "Must've come from under the house. Probably a hole in the floor someplace. Come daylight, we'll find and patch it."

Dulcie had not said a word.

Joey hoped his eyes did not show what was running through his mind. He didn't know how, but he was certain Dulcie had placed that snake in his room, then had closed the door to make sure it did not get out. She had acted eager for Joey to go to bed so she and Meacham could proceed with whatever they were up to together, but what she had really wanted was to get Joey snakebit. He would die, and everybody would say what a poor, unlucky family the Shipmans were.

They would also say how lucky Dulcie was, because this farm would be hers.

"Excitement's over," she said. "You can go on to bed."

"No ma'am," he declared. He could not quite bring his trembling under control. "I'm not sleepin' in that room, not tonight. I'll go out to Reuben's shack."

"Suit yourself. But you're liable to find a rattlesnake anyplace."

Anyplace Dulcie was, he thought. But it was not likely she would try the same stunt again tonight. And he wasn't going to give her many more chances. He made up his mind he wouldn't stay around this place much longer.

His break came a couple of mornings later. Meacham finished his breakfast coffee and wiped his sleeve across his mouth. He was always given to good humor, but today he smiled as if he knew a secret and was busting to tell it. "Joey, reckon you can take care of things around here a day or two? Me and Dulcie are fixin' to make a little trip. We won't be back 'til tomorrow evenin', maybe even the next day."

Dulcie seemed in a fine mood too. She actually smiled, placing her hand on Meacham's arm. Her eyes held a sparkle Joey had not seen before. "I've cooked you an extra pan of biscuits and some salt pork so you won't go hungry. And you can always fix you some bacon and eggs."

Joey's heart leaped. He had not expected such a wide-open opportunity. He tried not to betray his enthusiasm lest she become suspicious. "I reckon I can make do."

He helped hook the mule team to the wagon and followed afoot as Meacham drove up in front of the house. Dulcie came out onto the porch, carrying a colorful carpetbag that once had been Mama's. She made no false pretenses about loving Joey. She did not hug or kiss him or anything like that, though she did give him the biggest smile he had ever received from her. "You watch out for things now, Joey."

"I've *been* watchin' out."

Meacham took her arm and helped her up onto the wagon seat. "You take care of yourself," he told Joey.

"I sure figure on doin' that."

He imagined he could feel the throbbing of his pulse as he watched them move along the town road. He turned toward the barn. The milk-pen calf stood at the fence, looking between the boards at its mother grazing a couple of hundred yards out in the pasture. It would be cruel to let the calf's belly go empty a couple or three days until Dulcie and Meacham came back. Cautiously, Joey looked around for the Jersey bull. It was grazing a considerable distance away, beyond the cow. He unlatched the gate. Tail raised high, the calf gave Joey a wide berth as it trotted away, bawling and racing toward its mother.

Joey threw out some extra grain for Dulcie's chickens, then went to the house to put his few belongings together. He spread the quilt Mama had made for him, rolling it up inside two blankets to protect it. He put his extra clothes in the war bag Pa had brought home from the fighting. It was old and thin and patched in places, but it was Pa's, and Joey wanted to carry it with him.

Hidden in a bureau drawer, rescued from a pile of things Dulcie had discarded when she came here, was a tintype of his mother and father, made at the time of their wedding. Joey took it out with reverence and tucked it inside the old Bible Reuben had never been able to read. That went into the war bag along with a few other items, including Pa's straight razor and twelve dollars Joey had saved up in small change Pa had given him. He had no use for the razor now, but folks said he already resembled Pa in many ways. A few more years and he would probably have Pa's whiskers.

Itching to be on his way, he rummaged in the kitchen, sacking up the food Dulcie had prepared for him as well as some extra flour and sugar and coffee. He left the blanket roll and war bag on the porch while he trotted to the barn to put on a pair of cheap OK spurs and throw his saddle on Taw. The old horse stood with his head down in infinite patience. It probably thought they were just going out to bring in the cows.

"Like as not, you'd run off if you knew how far we're fixin' to travel," Joey said. "But I ain't tellin' you."

He rode up to the house for the blankets and bag. The blanket roll was a long way from neat, bulging on one end and thin on the other. It was awkward when he tied it behind the cantle. He hung the war bag off one side and the sack of food off the other. They did not balance well. He imagined he and Taw looked a sight with their lopsided load, but appearance was not a major concern at the moment.

He rode up to the cemetery. He removed his hat but did not dismount because it was a struggle to throw his leg over the thick roll of blankets. He felt a catch in his throat as he stopped at Mama's grave, then the fresh mound that marked Pa's. There was no stone yet. He wondered if Dulcie would ever bother to put up one.

"I'll come back some day when I'm grown, and I'll fix things proper," he promised. A haze came before his eyes, and he decided it was time to ride on. He forded the creek, which lapped against Taw's belly. The morning sun was at his back, so he decided he was headed in the right direction.

{ FOUR }

B y midafternoon Joey had passed beyond the
neighboring farms with which he was familiar. He
had avoided roads and made broad detours around
fields where he might encounter someone who knew him
or who might remember him later when he was reported
missing.

He found it difficult to sort out his conflicting emotions.
On the one hand he was uplifted by a sense of escape, of
being on the road to adventure, to new discoveries. On the
other he harbored an unsettling doubt about the unfamiliar. Never had he ventured off alone. The little traveling
he had done had always been with Pa. He had felt protected beneath Pa's long shadow.

He had no watch—he had been unable to find Pa's—so
he could only guess at the time. He had begun feeling hungry long before noon, so he had dug out a couple of biscuits and sliced off a piece of the pork Dulcie had cooked
for him. By the middle of the afternoon he did it again.
He realized that at this rate he would empty the food sack
considerably sooner than he had planned. He had not realized how traveling could stimulate the appetite. Or per-

haps it was just knowing he had the food with him and could eat any time he took the notion.

He noticed that the biscuits were taking on the flavor of horse sweat. He tried shifting the food sack so that it did not rub against Taw, but it seemed to have an affinity for horse hide. He decided to eat the biscuits now, before they became inedible.

Though he had hoped to avoid people, he came upon a stranger so suddenly that he had no chance to change course. A large-bellied man in dirt-stained overalls appeared without warning from beyond an oak thicket, astride a big Missouri-looking mule built along the same generous lines as its rider. Joey checked an impulse to break and run. He thought that might look suspicious.

The stranger hauled up on the reins. He spat a stream of tobacco juice, a little of it trailing down into his gray-splotched whiskers until he rubbed a sleeve across his lantern-sized chin. He looked beyond Joey as if expecting to see someone else trailing along behind.

"Boy, you lost?"

"No sir."

The man gave him a moment's silent, critical study, a wad of tobacco pooching out his left cheek. "Ain't seen you before. You ain't from around here."

"No sir. From back yonder a ways."

"Where's the rest of your folks?"

Joey pondered a lie. He had never been good at lying. He always turned red in the face and gave himself away. But he decided he would have to learn if he intended to get plumb away from Dulcie. "Back yonder at home. I'm on my way to visit my aunt and uncle."

He felt his face warming. The man would have to be

blind not to catch on, and his steady gaze indicated good eyesight. He surveyed the uneven blanket roll and the food sack. "Runnin' away from home, ain't you? Just about every boy does it, some time or other. I must've run off five or six times myself."

Joey had no idea how to reply.

The rider said, "I learned one lesson real early, though. When I found my food supply half gone, I always turned around and started back." He motioned toward the food sack. "How's yours holdin' up?"

Joey could not admit that he had already used up the biscuits and had cut heavily into the pork. "I'm all right."

A jovial smile spread across the broad face. "Well, if you're hungry on your way back, my house is over yonderway. Old missus has always got somethin' on the back of the stove."

Joey was tempted to say *I ain't comin' back*, but all that came out was, "Much obliged." He watched glumly as the man set the mule into motion again, its belly sloshing from a goodly fill of water. The stranger stirred a concern Joey had suppressed from the beginning. It was easy not to dwell upon such mundane things as food when there was plenty to eat. But hunger could change the complexion of this whole trip.

He wondered why he had not thought to take a ham or two out of the smokehouse. He considered going back for it; Dulcie and Meacham were not supposed to return for another day or two anyway. But to retreat now would mean a waste of all the miles he had put in and all the miles it would take him to get home again. He wished he had Reuben along. He could always depend upon Reuben for advice.

When Reuben didn't know a better answer, his stock reply had always been, "The Lord will provide." But Joey was not where the Lord was accustomed to seeing him. What if the Lord was looking for him somewhere else?

He was not ready for nightfall. It came much too soon and a long way from water. Reluctantly he made a dry camp, staking Taw to graze at the end of a cotton rope. He ate a little of the pork that remained and thought wistfully of the biscuits he had used up earlier. Any satisfaction they had given him at the time was long gone. He rolled out the blankets but found they did little to cushion the hard, uneven ground. Lying with eyes wide open, he studied the stars. The longer he lay there, the harder the ground seemed to get. Worse, he imagined he could feel a hundred tiny critters crawling around on his body, punishing him for usurping their piece of ground. And he could not escape the notion that somewhere out in the darkness a rattlesnake was looking for him.

It was the first time in his life he had ever spent the night completely alone. He listened to the distant yipping of coyotes and the challenging reply of a farm dog somewhere in the darkness. He had no fear of coyotes. They were harmless to people, unless one happened to be infected with hydrophobia. Folks said hydrophoby coyotes didn't howl, so as long as they were talking to each other he needn't worry about them. He worried a lot more about what he might eat tomorrow and all the other tomorrows down the road.

Sometime during the long night weariness overcame the loneliness, and he drifted off into a troubled sleep. Pa and Reuben came to him and seemed to be trying to give him advice, but he could not understand what they were saying. Their voices were muffled. When Dulcie appeared, he understood her well enough. She wanted to kill him, and stated her intentions in plain American.

Once he thought he heard some kind of rustling noise and a snort from Taw, but it was not enough to bring him all the way out of a deep sleep. Eventually the faraway crowing of a rooster summoned him to rise up from his blankets and stare into the rising sun. Taw stood with feet braced and head down, sleeping while the world awakened around him. The old horse had seen a lot more sunrises than Joey, and they held no surprises for him. Joey had slept with his clothes on, except for his boots. Those he found wet with dew. He realized he should have tucked them beneath the edge of the blankets to keep them dry.

A lesson of the road, one he would remember.

His stomach growled, reminding him of another road lesson he was rapidly learning: to stretch his food supply. He reached for the food sack to quiet the rumblings. It was not where he had left it, beside his saddle.

He walked a slow circle around the camp and found the sack ten or fifteen paces from where it should be. The smaller cloth bag holding the coffee beans lay near the larger, empty one. The sugar was scattered on the ground like a white powdering of snow, its paper sack torn open. The pork was gone. Small canine tracks indicated that a couple of coyotes had helped themselves. Sneaky little devils, they had known he was harmless. Folks claimed a coyote could smell a gun, and Joey didn't have one.

It was just as well he had eaten all the biscuits when he did, for now he would have none anyhow. Not counting the coffee, he had nothing left to eat except the corn which he had done a poor job of parching. The coyotes could have had that with his blessings.

A cottontail rabbit watched him from beneath a bush thirty feet away. It would be breakfast if he had a way to bring it down. Had he planned his trip better he would have fetched along Pa's rifle. He picked up a rock and hurled it in the rabbit's direction but missed. He saw a flash of white tail disappear down a hole.

He had a canteen, but he had drunk up the last of the water when he had made camp. He thought of a couple of times yesterday he could have refilled it but had not bothered.

More lessons of the road.

He remembered Pa saying that soldiers had sometimes survived for days without anything to eat, that they lived off of their own stored fat. Trouble was, Joey had always been on the skinny side.

He managed to roll his blankets into a neater bundle than yesterday. He hoped he would look a little better organized and less like a runaway kid. He saddled Taw and set out, the early-morning sun behind him again as he traveled in a southwesterly direction. He could not stop thinking of the breakfast table back home. If things had been different, he would be sitting there now. Whatever her shortcomings, Dulcie had been a fair-to-middling cook.

He tried to focus his mind on bigger matters, like where he was going and what he would do when he got there, but the thought of a breakfast missed kept getting in the way. At length he came upon a farmhouse that appeared to be abandoned. At least, some of the shingles were missing from the roof and the windows had all been removed, leaving wide-open holes in the weathered log walls. He approached it cautiously, for the coyotes had been about as much surprise as he wanted in one day.

He found nothing of interest or use except an open well, which reminded him that neither he nor Taw had had a drink of water since last evening. He turned the windlass and was pleased to find a bucket at the end of the rope.

Though no one lived in the house anymore, they evidently used the well on occasion. He lowered the bucket until he heard a splash and felt the weight as it filled with water. He drew it up. The water looked all right. At least it didn't have a drowned bird or anything like that in it. He dipped a little of it in his cupped hand and sipped carefully. It tasted all right, so he drank what he wanted, then held the bucket for Taw.

He imagined the lecture he would get from Dulcie if she saw him letting a horse drink from a bucket meant for people. He almost wished she *could* see him. He felt a flush of independent spirit, even rebellion.

Joey filled his canteen. Only now did it occur to him that he should have done it before Taw had drunk from the bucket. Well, he didn't figure the horse had any dread disease that it could pass along to him. A traveler could not afford to be narrow-minded in such matters.

The water was only a temporary substitute for food. The abandoned log house was still in sight when hunger began gnawing at Joey again. Reuben had always said adversity helped shape a man's character. Much more of this, Joey figured, and his character ought to be in pretty good condition.

Toward noon he saw a farmer leaving his field, heading for his house. A woman stood on the front porch, banging a piece of metal against a large iron ring, tolling him in for dinner. Joey reined up, running his tongue along his lips and imagining what kind of fixings waited on the kitchen table. It would be biscuits, surely, and pork or beef roast, and probably red beans, topped off with pie that had meringue six inches deep. He watched, arguing with himself. The argument went on a while, but eventually caution won out over hunger. He rode on, looking back over his shoulder. He ate a little of the parched corn and came near gagging on it.

By evening, caution was no longer a primary consideration. He felt weak, even a little faint. When he saw a campfire flickering in the dusk, he headed toward it. By now he was hungry enough that he was almost willing to go back and take his chances with Dulcie. At least, he would risk getting caught if he could just get something to eat.

He heard children's laughter before he was able to make out any details about the creek-side camp. He saw the dim form of a wagon with a canvas top and a team of mules staked on grass nearby. As he approached, a small girl watched him a moment, then turned and ran, shrieking.

Probably thinks I'm an Indian or something, he thought. The notion gave him a momentary sense of power, until he heard a man's voice. The shout carried a hint of threat.

"Who's that out yonder?"

"It's just me," Joey shouted back. He thought afterward that they had no way of knowing who *me* was.

Nearing the wagon, he saw a man cradling a weapon in his arms. Joey could not tell whether it was a rifle or a shotgun, not that it made a nickel's worth of difference. He felt a chill. A woman and three children waited distrustfully beyond the wagon tongue, barely touched by the flickering light of the campfire. The little girl who had given the alarm peeked out from behind her mother, exposing only her left eye.

The man took a few steps forward, giving Joey careful scrutiny before he lowered the weapon. He was large framed, but that frame was not fleshed out. He had probably spent a lot more time at hard labor than at the dinner table. "You ain't nothin' but a boy. Who's with you?"

"Nobody. I'm by myself."

The man moved closer. Distrust faded, and his face began to warm with a smile. "Kind of short in the britches to be travelin' alone, ain't you?"

Joey considered repeating the lie he had told the stranger yesterday about visiting an aunt and uncle. That man had seen through him immediately, and this one probably would too. Joey either had to improve his storytelling technique or quit trying to lie. "I'm runnin' away from home."

That was the last answer the man would have expected. He reacted with surprise, then a degree of pleasure. "At least you're honest. Most boys would've made up some fool yarn. By the looks of things you didn't get off very well fixed for travelin'. Bet you're hungry."

"Ain't had nothin' to eat all day."

"Well, you won't founder yourself here, but you're welcome to share in what little we got. You see, we been out west, tryin' to farm. Now we're headin' east, back to the wife's kinfolks." The man turned toward his family. "Wife, we got another hungry young'un here."

Reluctance tinged the woman's voice. "We already had three. How far do you think them two squirrels'll stretch?"

The man ignored her negative attitude. To Joey he said, "You can look at the campsite and tell which direction folks are travelin'. Goin' west, they'll leave ham bones and coffee grounds and empty airtights. Comin' back, they don't leave nothin' but rabbit skins and squirrel tails." He motioned toward the food sack hanging almost limp from Joey's saddle. "What you got in there?"

"Nothin' much but a little corn and some coffee."

"We run out of coffee a week ago. Boy like you has got no business drinkin' coffee anyway. It'll stunt your growth and turn your skin black, and then white folks won't associate with you."

Joey would trade it all for a square meal. "You folks are welcome to it." They could have the parched corn as well as the coffee. He untied the sack and handed it to the farmer before he climbed down from the saddle. The man pointed at the mules. "Stake your horse yonder and come on to the wagon. We'll be eatin' directly."

At home Joey was sometimes choosy about what he ate, but here he would ask no questions. He saw two steaming pots suspended from an iron bar over the small campfire. One held a stew of some kind, the other a plentiful supply of red beans. The woman lifted the coal-covered lid from a black Dutch oven and exposed a batch of browning cornbread. Cornmeal was the poor man's flour. Anybody who could raise a crop of corn could grind his own rough meal without having to haul it to a mill. Wheat flour was harder to come by.

The woman gave him a reluctant look, then turned to her husband. "George, the blessin'."

The big farmer bowed his head. "Lord, we'd rather it was beef and biscuits, but we thank Thee for them squirrels just the same. Bless this poor runaway boy, and show him the road to righteousness. Amen."

Badly as he wanted to dive right into the fixings, Joey managed the good grace to stand back and let the three youngsters fill their tin plates first. His stomach was talking loudly, but he imagined he could hear Reuben speaking even stronger, reminding him that no matter how hungry he thought he was, someone else was worse off. Joey remembered how hungry he often got when *he* had been a kid.

The three children shyly gave him room even as they stared at him with undisguised curiosity. He surmised that they were not used to strangers. Country kids often hid from visitors and would not reappear until the company left or it was time to eat.

He could see that the squirrel stew was badly depleted, so he took only a little of it and made up the difference in beans and cornbread. Pa had always maintained that though Texas since the big war had gained a reputation as beef country, the pioneers who settled it had subsisted largely on beans and cornbread, augmented by rabbits, squirrels, and poke salad.

Joey felt kinship to those pioneers, venturing off on his own this way.

The farmer ran some of Joey's coffee beans through a handcranked grinder attached to the wagon. With a look of eager anticipation, he suspended a coffeepot over the fire. Wistfully Joey watched the children divide up what was left of the stew. He could have handled a second helping, but manners prevailed over appetite. These folks looked as if they were ready to throw open the gates and declare surrender after a long siege of hard luck.

"You-all been out west," he said. "What's it really like?"

The farmer jerked his head toward the old wagon. "Just look at this used-up outfit. That about says it all."

The woman said, "That country ain't good for nothin' but heathen Indians and heathen cowboys. I'm hard put to say which one is worse."

The farmer gave her a look of reproach. "Now, wife, we never even seen an Indian. They're all on the reservation up in the Territory. And there never was a cowboy done us any harm either. There was even a couple of them brought us a quarter of beef when we needed it most. It's just that the Lord never intended that country for farmin', or He'd've let it rain once or twice. Grass is all that country's good for, and weeds. I swear, you plant one grain of corn and three weeds come up."

Joey's interest quickened. Two or three young men in town had claimed to be cowboys, but he had been unable to tell them from everyday farmers. "I've heard about cowboys. What're they like?"

"Like everybody else, only a little different."

The woman put in, "They're a hard-drinkin', hell-raisin', uncurried lot. Beyond redemption, most of them. A boy like you has got no business goin' amongst them. They'd turn you away from your mama's teachin's."

The farmer frowned. "What *about* your mama? Don't you know she's worryin' about you?"

"My mama died a long time ago. Pa died a little while back. I got nobody but a stepmother, and she don't like me." He thought about telling them the rest of it, that Dulcie had been trying to kill him, but he doubted they would believe it. They would probably take it as a sign to disbelieve everything else he said.

The farmer sympathized, "It's a hard world for orphans."

His wife motioned toward her children. "It's a hard world even for kids that've got their mama and daddy."

It took Joey a while to go to sleep, for the ground was as hard as the night before. As he lay wide awake, his mind ran back to Pa, and even farther, to Mama. The nearness of this family brought a crushing weight of loneliness down upon him. Poor though these people were, at least these children had a mother and a father. He wanted to cry a little but would not allow himself. He was getting too old for that sort of weakness.

He made up his mind not to abuse this family's hospitality by imposing further on their scanty food supply, though he stayed for a breakfast of cornmeal cakes and even drank a little of the black coffee made from his beans. Its bitterness required some forcing down but got better after the first couple of strong swallows. It warmed his stomach. With time, he thought, he might learn to like it. That would be a sign of manhood.

The farmer gravely watched him saddle Taw. "Son, I'm not your daddy, so I can't tell you what to do. But what you *ought* to do is go back. Get three or four more years on you before you set off by your lonesome again."

Joey did not want to tell him he might be three or four years dead by then. "I ain't wanted back yonder."

"I hope you find yourself wanted where you're goin'."

Joey had decided this man could be trusted not to give him away. "Do you know where there's a town called Bastrop?"

"You'll need to keep travelin' west and maybe edge south the least bit. I hope you got kin there."

Joey's eyes burned a little. "My daddy used to have a cousin in Bastrop. All the other kin I know are in the cemetery."

The farmer blinked some himself. "I wish we could take you with us, but I don't even know where *we'll* end up. Choppin' some other man's cotton, like as not." His handshake was so strong it hurt all the way to Joey's elbow.

Though the woman fretted about how to feed her own, she gave Joey what was left of the cornmeal cakes from breakfast. She also gave him ground corn with instructions for preparing rough hoecakes from meal and water. "They won't make you fat, but they'll hold you 'til you find somethin' better."

"Much obliged, ma'am."

"You got a Bible?"

"Yes'm, in my war bag. It's pretty old."

"The Word never gets old. Read a little in it every night. Feed your soul as well as your body."

The body wasn't likely to be fed very much, he thought, not unless his luck took a sharp turn for the better. The family started eastward in their wagon, and he rode westward, turning once to wave.

Remembering how Taw's sweat had flavored the biscuits, he took pains to keep the food sack hanging atop his leg. That did not present a serious challenge, for it was much smaller than the first sack he had carried.

{ FIVE }

Joey ate a couple of the cornmeal cakes at noon to quiet the rumbling in his stomach. Shortly afterward he came upon a well-beaten east-west wagon road that paralleled a clear-running creek. He felt less nervous about meeting strangers, now that his encounter with the farm family had produced no serious effort to send him back. He and Taw had traveled a lot of miles. He felt that distance had decreased the chance of anyone getting word back to Dulcie. Perhaps he would be fortunate enough to come upon a kind soul who would invite him for supper.

Luck brought him into a freighters' camp as the sun was setting. He saw dust stirring before he came upon the big high-sided wagons and teams of mules. The drivers were unfastening the leather harness, dropping it on the ground where the mules stood. One of the young mules was acting up. The man at the singletree expressed displeasure in words that would have launched Reuben into a sermon about the perils of blasphemy.

Joey surveyed the crew, picking a tall, lanky fellow with a gray beard who appeared to be the oldest in camp and most likely to be the boss. "Mister, reckon I could help some way and earn a supper from you?"

Graybeard pointed to the youngest man Joey could see. "You'll have to ask the kid yonder. He owns the outfit this trip."

The "kid" did not look as if he would have to shave often to keep his beard in check. Joey guessed he was no older than his early twenties. He would have thought a man had to be thirty at least, and therefore middle aged, before he could own an outfit like this.

The young man said, "You can help me lead these mules down to the water." His eyes turned quizzical. "I'll bet you're not out of the fourth reader. How come you're not in school?"

Joey recognized this as an oblique way of asking why he was on the road in the first place. "School's out. Reckon how far it is to Bastrop?"

"You might make it in four or five days if that horse don't die of old age on you."

Joey felt a flare of resentment. Nobody had any call to insult a man's horse. "Taw's all right."

The young man grinned, recognizing that he had touched a raw spot. "We'll give your horse a bait of oats after a while. Looks like he could stand a good fill."

"He's come a long ways," Joey admitted.

The teamsters all gave him a suspicious looking-at while he helped water the mules. They probably had him pegged rightly enough as a runaway. There wasn't any point in trying to lie to them. But nobody asked. Some had an outlaw look, the kind of men Pa would have said weren't using the names their mothers and fathers gave them. These men wouldn't want their own pasts inspected closely, so they were given to tolerance of others who posed no threat.

Joey didn't see how he could appear a threat to anyone, except perhaps to Dulcie.

After they had fed the mules and Taw, the young boss said, "You might help Ol' Shiloh yonder start fixin' our supper." Shiloh was a big-shouldered man with rheumy eyes and red-veined face. Joey guessed him to be a heavy drinker when the opportunity presented itself. He looked as if he could wrestle a bear but had lost his last match. He had not shaved in a couple of weeks, nor was there evidence that he had washed in at least that long. Joey decided he had better not look too closely at his supper.

The cook dug a fire pit with a dull shovel and piled some dry wood into it in a haphazard manner. He poured coal oil from a can onto the wood. He tried to strike a match on the patched seat of his old cotton trousers but had to lift one foot and use the sole of a well-worn boot instead. Flames shot up with a *whoosh*. Backing away from the burst of heat, Joey noted that Shiloh recklessly held the coal-oil can in his hand while standing close to the fire.

Reuben would have said he risked burning himself up before the devil even had a chance at him.

Shiloh rigged an iron bar across the fire. On a small table lifted down from the wagon he began mixing a batch of bread dough without taking time to wash his hands. He pinched off pieces of sourdough and laid them into a greased Dutch oven, which he placed over glowing coals as soon as the fire had begun to burn down. He pointed toward the wagon. "Boy, fetch me that bucket of beans hangin' under yonder."

The bucket was suspended beneath the wagon bed. Joey found it heavier than it appeared, but he supposed it took a lot of beans to feed a freighting crew. Shiloh said, "I let a fresh pot simmer over the fire every night so it's ready by mornin'. All I got to do is heat it up for dinner and supper."

Joey feared at first that beans would be the main course, but Shiloh unwrapped a blood-stained tarp to reveal a hind quarter. "You like mule meat, boy?"

Joey had never tried it and didn't want to now. He saw a fleeting smile and realized Shiloh was teasing him. This was beef. Wielding a butcher knife, Shiloh carved off enough thick slices to go around and dropped them into a deep pan of melted lard bubbling over the fire.

He still had not washed his hands, but Joey's appetite was strong enough to overcome any squeamish reservations. Anyway, the grease was hot enough to kill anything it touched.

When Shiloh hollered that supper was ready, the freighters crowded around, wasting no time on ceremony or manners. Joey would have thought they should defer to the boss, but some of them stiff-shouldered him aside to fill their plates first.

Standing back with Shiloh, Joey made a quiet comment about the lack of respect for authority. The cook said, "He just won the outfit a few nights ago playin' poker with Ol' Fontaine yonder." He pointed a thumb toward the older man Joey had first assumed was the head teamster. "Like as not Fontaine'll win it back before we get to where we're goin'. With this outfit, you never know from one game to the next who you'll be workin' for. Not that it makes much difference. Ain't none of them much smarter than their mules."

Joey could not imagine Pa ever risking what he owned in a poker game. Whatever he had acquired, he had held with the tenacity of a tick in a cow's ear. The main thing Joey remembered about cousin Beau was of listening to him and Pa argue over the sanctity of property, over the virtue of hard work and frugality. Pa had said Beau was improvident. Beau had declared that a shroud had no pockets—whatever that meant.

Joey watched from outside the circle of firelight as the men played poker on a blanket spread upon the ground. They were using matches instead of chips. Joey did not understand the rules of the game. Pa had never indulged in card playing, and Reuben had always maintained that cards were the devil's invention, a means of increasing the population in hell. But Joey was fascinated to watch the young boss's pile of matches shift gradually over to the gray-bearded Fontaine.

When the final hand had been played, the young man shrugged with indifference. "Well, I reckon I'm workin' for you again."

Fontaine seemed less happy over the situation than Joey might have expected. "You sure you wasn't cheatin'?"

"Naturally I was. How else do you think you won?"

The men began walking off toward their bedrolls. Joey felt he owed it to the young former boss to express his regrets over loss of the outfit.

The answer came with a smile. "This is a money-losin' operation anyway. I make more money workin' for him than ownin' the whole works."

Joey was tired enough that he quickly dropped off to sleep, feeling safe in the company of these men. They looked and talked rough, but he sensed that there was no harm in them for a boy of his age. They might even go out of their way to protect him should they see harm coming his way.

He awakened sometime during the night to the sound of snoring. He had heard snoring before, but none as harsh as this. It came from the area where the mules were tethered to picket lines. Nobody had ever told him that mules could snore.

It was amazing the lessons a person could learn on the road, though he doubted that this one would ever be of much use.

The next morning he pitched in to help feed and water the mules. He kept waiting for Fontaine to invite him to share breakfast. The man never did, so Joey quietly invited himself. He dried utensils, cups, and plates after Shiloh washed them in a tin tub. He decided the only time Shiloh ever got his hands clean was when he did the dishes.

Fontaine cracked a whip and the mules quickly found their individual places in front of the several wagons. Joey had never seen mules trained like this. Harnessing them was a relatively easy matter. One young mule's rebellion earned it a quick kick to the belly. The mule tried to retaliate with its hind foot. The teamster anticipated the move, stepped out of the way, then kicked the animal again. The rebellion was quelled.

Shiloh gave Joey the few biscuits and some thickly sliced bacon left from breakfast. "You been a right smart of help, not to be no bigger'n a watch fob. You may not run onto anybody else as generous as us down the road."

Joey drew back to avoid the dust and watched the wagons lurch into a ragged start eastward. He had not set his mind on his life's work yet, having always assumed he would remain on the farm. But he thought the mule skinners' life might not be so bad. Most of the time they rode on their wagons, and the mules carried all the heavy load. But to fit in he would have to learn to cuss, and it might be helpful if he could play poker.

He could still hear the popping of the whips and the sharp voices of the skinners as he turned Taw southwestward.

* * *

He rode through a considerable pine forest before he broke free of the timber and saw the town spread before him. He supposed this had to be Bastrop. A farmer a few miles back had paused in his plowing to tell him it was no longer far. Joey had asked if he knew Beau Shipman. Giving him a strange look, the farmer had nodded in the affirmative and had shouted for his mule to *giddyap*, biting the point of his moldboard plow into the soft ground. He left Joey standing there choking on several more questions he wanted to ask.

Pa's first stop when he went to town was usually the livery barn, where he left his horse or his mules to be fed while he took care of whatever business had taken him off of the farm. The hostler usually brought him up-to-date on whatever news there might be. It was seldom much, for not a lot happened around Athens. Joey considered it reasonable that a livery barn might be a logical place to find out something about cousin Beau. After passing a number of houses along the wagon road, he saw a red barn and a layout of corrals with horses and mules standing around several hay racks. Half a dozen wagons and buggies had been left standing outside.

Taw poked his ears forward, interest sparked by the other horses or perhaps by the smell of feed. Taw would have enjoyed a bucket of oats, but town stables were not in the habit of giving those away. Maybe Beau would have some.

A hostler came to the wide-open door, carrying a pitchfork. He gave Joey a momentary glance, then looked beyond him. "Where's the rest of your family?"

"I'm all there is."

The man's eyes said he knew: Joey was a runaway. Joey wondered how everybody seemed to know that right off.

"It'll take fifty cents to put your horse up and feed him. You got fifty cents?"

"Yes sir, but I ain't spendin' it. I'm lookin' for Beau Shipman. Know him?"

"Everybody knows Ol' Beau. What you want with him?"

"He's about all the kin I got left. Him and my Pa were cousins. Where do you reckon I can find him?"

"I can guess. You see that tall buildin' yonder, the one with the cupola standin' up so high? That's the court-house."

"That's where Beau is at?"

"No, there's another buildin' just back of it. The jail-house. I expect that's where he'll be."

"Is he the sheriff or the jailer or somethin'?"

The hostler made a little smile that said he knew a joke Joey didn't. "No, he's one of the reasons we *have* a sheriff and a jailer. He's one of the steadiest customers they've got."

The bottom seemed to fall out of Joey's stomach. He had counted on cousin Beau's help, but he wouldn't be much help from the wrong side of the iron bars. He grasped at a fragile thread of hope. "You sure that's where he's at right now?"

"If it ain't, just wait around."

Joey thanked the man for the information, unwelcome though it was, and reined Taw toward the courthouse. Several people on the street stopped what they were doing to look at him. They might be seeing him as a runaway, or they might somehow sense that he was kin to Beau Ship-man. He wondered which they would rank the lowest.

As he approached the courthouse, he saw the jail in back of it, smaller but built of the same sort of stone. Back home, he had always regarded the jailhouse with some dread, and that feeling prevailed now. He would rather take a beating from Dulcie than approach that somber-looking building with its iron-barred second-story windows. But he had come this far. He swallowed hard and climbed down from the saddle.

He remembered from home that it was common for the jailer, or perhaps the sheriff, to live on the ground floor of the jail and keep the prisoners upstairs. Joey tied Taw to a post and walked reluctantly to the open door. He could smell food cooking inside, but he would not enter without an invitation. He rapped his knuckles against the door facing.

A woman appeared, her broad middle covered by a white apron. Her expression seemed pleasant enough, though a little reserved. She reminded him of the teacher he had had in the first and second grades, before she up and married the widowed owner of the general store and became a woman of property.

"Ma'am, can you tell me if you've got Beau Shipman in jail?"

"*I* don't."

His momentary relief was dashed when she added, "My husband does, though. He's the sheriff. Of what possible interest could Beau Shipman be to you?"

"He's my cousin, and I've rode a long ways to see him. Reckon I can talk to him?"

"You'll have to ask the sheriff about that. He's off somewhere in town right now." She frowned, studying him. "You look to me like you might be hungry."

He admitted that he was. The smell of baking bread made his stomach growl like a quarrelsome dog.

She said, "Well, then, you come right on in here. I've

got my husband's supper cookin', and he weighs too much anyhow. Won't hurt him to share it."

"I'm obliged, ma'am, but I'd like to see Beau Shipman first."

"I have no authority above this floor. But here I do, and I say you're goin' to eat. A couple of hot biscuits should hold you 'til the sheriff comes for supper."

As she opened the oven, the smell of fresh bread overwhelmed any disappointment over postponing a reunion with cousin Beau. She lifted down a jar of jam from a crude cabinet that had its legs standing in cans of water to thwart the foraging ants. "Any more than this might spoil your appetite," she warned.

He doubted anything could do that. He had finished off Shiloh's sack of grub days ago. Later he had summoned the nerve to visit a farmhouse where a kindly woman had questioned him carefully before refilling the sack. Nothing remained of that food now but a warm memory.

While she bustled around the kitchen the sheriff's wife asked him the same questions everybody else was asking, either directly or by implication. He told her about losing his mother, then Pa. He did not tell her about Dulcie trying to kill him. She wouldn't believe it anyway.

The sheriff came along after a while. The woman told him he had company and that he had best watch what he said and did.

The sheriff seemed an affable sort at first. He gave Joey a quick study and declared, "Why, you ain't big enough to be an outlaw. Way she talked, I thought you might be Miller Dawson or somebody like him."

"Who's Miller Dawson?"

"One of the worst badmen that's ever left his tracks in

these parts. Holds up stores and banks. Folks claim he's killed fifty men. But I can tell that you ain't him."

"No sir, my name's Joey Shipman. I come to see my cousin Beau."

The sheriff's expression changed with the abruptness of a door slamming. He bored a hole in Joey with his eyes. "You don't look anything like Beau. I hope you *ain't* anything like him, either."

Joey flinched from the look. "What's the matter with him?"

"His mama ought to've drowned him when he was a baby. Works hard when he's sober, but that ain't often enough. Soon as he gets a few dollars in his pocket he goes on a tear, and he don't stop 'til I shut the cell door on him. One of these days I'm goin' to forget to ever open it again."

Joey tried to picture Pa doing such things. The image was alien to all of his memories except the drinking part. Pa *had* taken to drinking after Mama died. Joey figured that he must not have been sober when he chose Dulcie to be his second wife.

The sheriff said gruffly, "I'll take you up to Beau, but I'm eatin' my supper first."

His wife said, "I've set a place at the table for Joey."

"We've got no responsibility for any kin of Beau Shipman."

Her voice was stern. "He's a boy, and he's hungry, and we're feedin' him."

The sheriff surrendered to the inevitable, but not in good grace. "If Beau is all the kin you've got, you're in a bad way."

The stairway to the second floor was uncomfortably dark as Joey followed the lawman. He had never been inside a jail. The atmosphere was oppressive, even hostile.

He quickly resolved that he would travel miles out of his way to avoid ever getting locked up in a place like this. Because whiskey seemed to have a lot to do with people going to jail, he decided he would allow it no part in his future plans.

The sheriff declared, "Beau, got some company for you."

A voice answered from a dark cell in a back corner. "I never promised her nothin', Sheriff. If she claims I did, she's a liar."

"Got a boy here says he's your cousin."

"Second cousin," Joey said quickly. Given the sheriff's attitude toward Beau, the more distant the kinship the less prejudice there ought to be.

Obscured in semidarkness, a man arose from a cot and moved uncertainly toward the barred door. Joey recognized him despite the poor light and several days' uneven growth of whiskers. The only time he had seen Beau he had studied that face, vainly seeking some resemblance to Pa. Cousins should look at least a little alike, he had thought.

"Remember me, Beau? I'm Joey."

Beau Shipman looked as if a team of mules had dragged him across a rocky field. His voice bordered on belligerency. "I don't know no Joey."

"Joey Shipman. John Shipman was my daddy."

Beau seemed to have difficulty bringing Joey into focus. "I don't remember John havin' a boy your size."

"Last time you saw me was when we buried Mama. I wasn't this size then."

"You ain't got much size on you now. Where's your daddy at?"

"He died too. I'm all that's left. Except you."

A spark of hope lifted Beau's voice half an octave. "Did John leave me somethin'?"

"I don't remember him ever mentionin' your name again after you left."

"Then why the hell are you here pesterin' me?"

The sheriff said, "Looks like the boy's got nobody to turn to except you, Beau. That sure don't speak well for his prospects."

Beau's expression ran the gamut from fear to denial to anger. "I hope he don't expect me to finish raisin' him."

Joey flared. "I don't expect you to do anything. I wasn't stayin' noway. I just came to let you know about Pa."

"I'm sorry about John, but I ain't in no position to take on any added responsibility."

The sheriff snorted. "*Added* responsibility? When was the last time you had any responsibility at all?"

The hostility rolled off Beau without a trace. "I ain't takin' on no kid to raise."

"The boy's your kin."

"I could always choose my friends. I never had no choice in pickin' my kinfolks. Tell him to go find somebody else."

"You want out of this jail?"

"I never was crazy about the place."

"Maybe if you *did* have some responsibility, I wouldn't be havin' hell with you so often. I might be persuaded to turn you loose if you'd take this boy home with you and do right by him."

"I don't know the first thing about takin' care of a kid. That's why I never had none of my own."

"You never had any kids because no woman of a sound mind would have you. If I saw a better way out, I wouldn't be givin' you this chance, but I can't keep the boy here. Jail ain't no place for a young'un. Take him home with you for a few days 'til I get things figured out, or I swear to God I'll keep you in here 'til Christmas."

"Stayin' in this place, I could be dead by Christmas."

"Maybe even sooner if you keep grindin' on my patience. What do you say?"

Beau glared at Joey as if he had brought him this load of trouble with malice aforethought. "It's a stacked deck either way."

The sheriff smiled wickedly. "And I'm the dealer."

Beau said a few words that would have done credit to a mule skinner. "All right, then. But the first time he gives me any of that sass . . ."

Rattling the keys, the sheriff swung the door open. "You got anything to eat in that shack of yours?"

"Damned little."

The lawman considered a moment. "Well, the county would have to feed you anyway if you stayed in here. I reckon it can afford to set you up to a few groceries." He took five silver dollars out of a desk drawer and started to hand them to Beau. He thought better of it and gave them to Joey instead. "Here, boy. Don't buy anything with this but good solid grub. Beau don't need nothin' stronger to drink than coffee."

Joey started to tell him he had a few dollars of his own, but he decided he had better hang onto those for an emergency. Someday, when he had a regular paying job, he would send the sheriff's money back with maybe an extra half dollar or so for interest. Pa had always held that a man should go into debt only with great reluctance and regard that debt like a rattlesnake in his pocket until he paid it off.

Beau demanded of the sheriff, "Where'd you put my horse?"

"Turned him out on grass. County don't need the expense of keepin' him at the wagon yard."

"That means I got to walk all the way home."

"I wish it was twice as far. Come on over to my desk and I'll give you back your stuff." It did not amount to much—a pocketknife, a few coins, a couple of scraps of wadded paper.

Beau declared, "Seems to me like I still had half a pint or so of whiskey left. Where's it at?"

"Don't you remember watchin' me pour it out? You bleated like a lost sheep."

"You got a streak of cruel in you, Gardner. You'd pull the wings off of a butterfly."

"Not as cruel to you as you are to yourself. One of these days I'll probably have to drag your pickled carcass out of a muddy ditch someplace and see to your buryin'. If I don't kill you first."

"Just leave me lay. It'll be a lesson to wayward youths." Beau turned to Joey. "You comin', kid, or am I goin' to be lucky after all?"

Reluctance dragged like a heavy weight on Joey's legs. He thought he had an inkling to the reason Pa had never talked about Beau. If Beau was the best he had to show for kinfolks, he would be better off among strangers. A few days' rest for himself and Taw, a few solid meals, and he might decide to strike off on his own again. He was a freeborn American. He had put Dulcie behind him. He could leave Beau the same way.

But right now it was coming on dark, and he fancied the idea of having a roof over his head after all those nights under an open black sky.

{ SIX }

❦

Joey could hear the sheriff's wife arguing with her husband over the propriety of sending a little boy off with a bad example like Beau Shipman. The sheriff countered that Joey could learn from bad examples as well as from good. "Once a young'un touches a hot stove, he learns not to ever touch it again."

Joey could not help resenting being called a little boy. She must not have looked at him very closely. He *was* twelve, going on thirteen.

The sheriff said, "Beau's broke. He'll have to work a while before he can afford another binge. By then maybe somethin' better'll turn up for the boy."

Taw was still tied outside, where Joey had left him. Head drooped, he appeared to be asleep. Beau made a long, frowning study. "This the best horse you've got?"

"He's the *only* one I've got," Joey said.

"You're the next thing to bein' afoot." Beau tried to raise his leg high enough to reach Joey's left stirrup but could not. "Damned poor saddle you've got, too."

"It fits me all right."

Beau pulled himself up, dragging his leg across Joey's bedroll tied behind the cantle. His feet hung down far below the stirrups. "You're young and healthy. You can walk."

"He's my horse," Joey protested.

Beau reined Taw around and set off in a walk. Smoldering, Joey followed. He suspected that Beau would gladly ride away and leave him if he did not keep up.

Joey had never been in a saloon, but he knew what they were for. He saw a woman standing just outside the saloon door, smoking a cigarette, and he knew what she was for, too. She gave Beau a look that might cause cotton to wither and die. Beau seemed to make a concerted effort not to see her.

Joey said, "That woman don't appear to like you very much."

"She's got an odd notion that I owe her money."

Joey thought he knew, but he asked anyway. "For what?"

Beau ignored the question. "It's humiliatin', everybody seein' me ride a ewe-necked old nag like this."

The insult to his horse added fuel to Joey's anger. "Any worse than seein' you staggerin' drunk?"

"You've got a smart mouth, kid. Keep it shut, and the flies won't get in."

"The flies are all followin' *you*."

"My way of livin' ain't none of your business."

I guess not, Joey thought, *because I ain't staying very long*.

Beau reined up at a general store and swung down from the saddle, almost falling before he got his feet under him. He held out his hand, the palm up. "Sheriff gave you some money for groceries. Hand it here."

"He said for me not to give it to you."

"Give it to me before I hoist you up by your feet and shake it out of your pocket."

Reluctantly Joey reached into his britches. His fingers played over the five coins, then brought out three of them.

"That's all there is?" Beau demanded. "I thought it was more."

"You must've been seein' double."

"Can't cut much dust with three dollars." Instead of going into the general store as Joey expected, Beau walked two doors down to a saloon. In a few minutes he returned with a bottle of whiskey. "Ain't had my supper," he said.

After leaving the business section they passed through a nice residential area where Joey assumed the merchants lived. Most of the houses were larger and featured more gingerbread trimmings than the one Pa had built on the farm. Joey's hopes rose at the thought that Beau might have a house like this. Expectations flagged, however, as they passed smaller and plainer houses. Finally, at the edge of town, Beau reined up in front of a crude frame structure little larger than Reuben's shack. It lacked even a porch.

Beau seemed to catch the disappointment in Joey's face. "What did you expect, bay windows and a balcony?"

"I hope you didn't pay much for this place."

"Didn't pay anything. Folks that built it decided to leave. Nobody else claimed it, so I moved in."

Joey tried to make the best of a poor situation. "I guess it's dry inside."

"When it don't rain." Beau slid down from Taw and handed the reins to Joey. "He's your horse, take care of him. Ain't got no oats. He'll have to fill up on grass, same as mine."

Joey gave in to resentment. "At least he won't be fillin' up on whiskey."

Beau had to push hard on the door. It was bound against

the threshold because the shack leaned slightly northward. "Just unsaddle him and turn him loose."

"What if he strays off?"

"Wouldn't be no great loss."

Joey took the precaution of hobbling Taw. From the un-promising looks of things he might be leaving here sooner than he had expected. He didn't want to have to hunt for the horse all over the town section.

Beau had lighted a lamp and sat at a small, rickety ta-ble, the bottle in front of him, its cork gone. "If you're hun-gry you'll have to stir up your own supper. I've got mine."

"I done ate with the sheriff and his wife." But Joey looked around, for this trip had taught him to eat when-ever and wherever he got the chance. On top of the small cast-iron stove sat a blackened pot. In it he found red beans, soured and growing a coat of mold that resembled soiled velvet. In a small pan three remnant biscuits were dry and hard as stone.

He asked, "How long were you in jail?"

"This time? Three or four days, maybe five. I never kept count."

Rummaging, Joey found but little food in the cabinet: a tin container almost empty of flour, a limp burlap sack with perhaps a single potful of dry pinto beans, and a ba-con rind with just enough meat left on it for half a dozen thick slices. Breakfast would finish it and leave both of them hungry.

He wondered how much the sheriff's remaining two dollars would buy. He did not intend to benefit Beau with any of the little money he had brought from home.

A steel cot in the corner was the only bed, its blankets carelessly tangled atop a lumpy-looking mattress that Joey guessed was filled with straw or corn husks. "Where do I sleep?"

"You got your own blankets. Spread them on the floor or go outside; I don't care."

Joey had seen no sign of rain. The night air was probably a lot fresher than the shack's. At least it wouldn't smell like cigarette smoke and whiskey. He spread his blankets on the ground, moving them twice but finding no spot less hard than another. He lay staring up at the stars, wondering why he had bothered to hunt down cousin Beau. He was better off without any kinfolks if this was the best he had.

The tight door was almost too much for him to push open, and the scraping of wood against wood made enough noise to stir the dead. It did not stir Beau, however. He lay asleep on the cot, snoring like a freighter's mule and still wearing all his clothes except boots and hat. The cover blanket lay on the floor. The bottle stood beside it, uncorked and two-thirds empty.

Joey studied Beau's inert form, and last night's resentment boiled up again. It didn't seem possible that Beau and Pa had come out of the same family. Pa had always put a lot of stock in bloodlines when it came to farm animals. Joey supposed that just being cousins, Pa and Beau didn't share as much blood as brothers. He was glad *he* was only a second cousin.

He had it in mind to fix a little breakfast for himself, then ride off. Beau might sleep until noon. Even then, he would probably be relieved to find Joey gone. He was unlikely to say anything to the sheriff until the lawman came out and asked him. By then Joey would be miles away.

He gave his attention again to the whiskey bottle. Last night he had noticed a knothole in the floor, near the cot. He turned the bottle over, shoving the neck of it down into the hole. The whiskey gurgled as it disappeared.

Rattlesnakes often took refuge beneath houses like this. Joey grinned wickedly as he pictured how a drunk snake might act. Probably couldn't hurt Beau. He should have enough alcohol in his system to be well fortified against snakebite.

Joey built a fire in the small stove. He was not much of a cook, but he knew how to fry bacon. He could try his hand at whipping up a batch of biscuits because he had watched Dulcie make them many a time. She always mixed milk or clabber with the flour, though, and he doubted that there had been a drop of milk in this shack since Beau had lived here. Water would have to do.

The bacon was sizzling when he heard a creaking sound behind him. Beau sat up on the edge of the cot. He hit the whiskey bottle with his foot and sent it rolling. He grabbed it up and studied it in bleary-eyed dismay. "I thought I still had some left."

Joey was tempted to tell him the truth and revel in his mischief, but he did not know Beau well enough to gauge his potential for violence. "I guess you didn't."

"Where's the coffee?"

"I didn't find any. Reckon you're out."

"No whiskey, no coffee. Ain't much use in gettin' up." Beau lay back on the cot and brought both arms up over his face. "What's that you're fixin'?"

"Bacon. Got biscuits in the oven."

"Bacon. It smells terrible. God, kid, I'm sick."

"You wouldn't be if you hadn't spent the grocery money on whiskey. Now what you goin' to do?"

"Die, if I'm lucky."

Joey had no experience in handling people with a hangover. Dulcie had sent him away when Pa was like that. "Maybe you need to eat somethin', but there ain't nothin' except bacon and biscuits. It'll take all mornin' to cook beans."

"Don't you understand, kid? I'm sick, maybe dyin'."

Joey thought he ought to feel sympathy, but it wasn't as if somebody had poked a six-shooter in Beau's ribs and made him drink. "Pa always said if you hadn't climbed up, you wouldn't have fallen down."

"Your daddy had a mean streak in him. Appears he passed it on." Beau pressed his hand against his forehead. "Feels like there's three blacksmiths beatin' out horseshoes in there."

Joey could only imagine, and he didn't really care to. "You want some bacon or not?"

Beau got up again, arms pressed tightly against his stomach, and staggered toward the door in his sock feet. Joey had left it half open at the point where the bottom dragged so heavily upon the floor that he could not move it further. Beau bumped his shoulder hard against the edge of the door. Joey thought he felt the shack tremble. He could hear his cousin outdoors, retching.

He managed to eat a biscuit and some of the bacon before he was overcome by an imagined image of Beau Shipman vomiting. His own stomach made half a turn. He sat at the table a while, waiting. Beau did not appear.

I don't care if he never comes back, Joey thought. But in spite of himself he began to worry. He peered out the half-open door. Beau lay face down on the ground, not moving. Painful images of Pa and Reuben flashed into Joey's mind. "Beau!" He rushed outside and knelt beside his cousin. To his relief he could see little puffs of dust as Beau exhaled. He tried to turn Beau over onto his back but only succeeded in getting his face a little higher from the ground.

"You've been breathin' dirt," he said. "If the whiskey don't kill you, that probably will." He realized he could not lift Beau by himself. Beau had to help him. He tugged at his cousin's arm.

"Come on, get up. Don't you be dyin' on me!"

Beau tried to fight him off but lacked the strength. Joey provoked him into rising to his knees and crawling to the shack with Joey tugging on his arm. Beau made it through the door and to the cot. With Joey's help he managed to pull himself up and flop onto the mattress.

Breathing hard from exertion, Joey felt emotions pulling him in two directions at once. He still intended to leave, but he realized he should put it off until he knew Beau was going to make it. Left alone, for all Joey knew, Beau might lie here and die. "There's still some bacon and biscuits on the table. You'd better eat somethin'."

"I don't need no snot-nosed kid tellin' me what to do."

"You need somebody. You sure don't take care of yourself."

Joey realized that if he was going to stay here a day or two and see Beau get on his feet, he had better lay in a few more groceries. He started for the door.

Beau demanded, "Where you goin'?"

Joey did not feel that Beau had any right to question him, so he did not answer. He found the hobbled Taw grazing near the shed and corral. A brown horse stood nearby, the brand GO on its hip. Joey assumed it was Beau's. He saddled Taw and rode into town, stopping in front of the general store where he had thought Beau was going to buy supplies last night. He double-checked his pocket to be sure the two dollars were still there. Wrestling around with Beau, he might easily have lost them. The feel of the coins reassured him.

The sign over the door said *Casper Tatum, Groc*. Joey assumed that the merchant who met him at the door was Tatum. He was a middle-aged man whose girth showed that he had partaken well of his own merchandise. The broad smile on his face shone almost as brightly as his bald head. "Good mornin', sonny. What can I do for you?"

"Need some groceries." Joey fished out the two dollars. "Reckon how much that'll buy?"

The grocer rubbed his chin. "Well, not enough to give you a bellyache. Just what is it you need?"

Joey told him he thought they needed some bacon, beans, and flour, maybe a few potatoes and surely some coffee. "My cousin Beau needs lots of coffee."

"Beau Shipman? You're a cousin of Beau's?"

Joey wondered if he ought to try to lie out of it. Beau might owe the store money, and the merchant might simply keep the two dollars without giving him anything for them. But he owned up to the truth. "Yes sir. He's my daddy's cousin, anyway."

Tatum's voice softened with sympathy. "Most people like Beau, except for Sheriff Gardner and those that've had a fight with him when he's drunk. He's his own worst enemy."

"I sure couldn't argue none with that."

"Tell you what I'll do: Seein' it's for Beau, I'll give you my brother-in-law rate. We had a bad hailstorm a year or

so ago. Beat my roof into splinters. Beau helped me resh-
ingle it and wouldn't take any pay. I slip grub into his cabin
now and again when he ain't lookin'."

"I didn't know he was a carpenter."

"He's a carpenter, a jackleg blacksmith, a plowman, and
a pretty good hand with horses and mules. Beau can do
just about anything he sets his mind to. If he just didn't
like whiskey so much . . ." Tatum put the groceries into a
burlap bag. It was so heavy Joey could barely lift it. The
grocer carried it out for him and tied the sack to the horn
of Joey's old saddle. "Now, don't you tell Beau where you
got this. If he asks, just tell him you found it along the road
somewhere."

"I sure do thank you, sir."

"*Sir.*" The man smiled again. "Ain't every boy says 'sir'
anymore. Glad to see that there's a few of the younger gen-
eration ain't gone to hell in a handbasket."

Joey found Beau still lying on the cot, his face clabber
gray. But Beau was not too sick to scold. "What do you
mean runnin' off like that and not answerin' me, kid? I
figured you was gone for good."

"I thought about it. I'd be better off if I'd rode plumb
around Bastrop and never seen you."

"You ain't my notion of a life's companion either.
Where'd you get the money to buy groceries?"

"Found it layin' in the road."

Beau hurt too much to keep up the attitude. He lay back
and pressed his arm to his forehead. "Anyway, thanks for
comin' back, kid. I didn't think you would."

"Don't keep callin' me kid. I'm almost thirteen years
old. Name's Joey."

He decided he had better get busy fixing the coffee.
Beau looked as if it might save his life. Joey said, "I got

some potatoes here. I'll fry you one for dinner, along with some more bacon."

"I tasted what you fried up this mornin'. Who ever taught you to cook?"

"Nobody."

"That's what I thought. Boy your age ought to learn. Might save him and his cousin from starvation. Let me do the cookin', and you watch me." Slowly and painfully rising from the cot, Beau made his way to the little stove. He pointed to the coffee grinder. "You know how to crank that thing, don't you? I'll punch up the fire." He burned himself lifting a stove lid and muttered under his breath as he sucked on the scorched fingers.

A voice called from the doorway. "You-all alive?" The grocer Tatum stood with one hand braced on the door facing and peering around the door that was stuck half open.

Beau beckoned for him to come on in. "Just barely."

Tatum said to Joey, "The sheriff told me about his bargain with Beau. Glad to see you're still here. If you weren't, Gardner's got a cell reserved for Beau over at the jail."

Joey recalled how close he had come to leaving. That was still his intention, as soon as he and Taw rested up a little and Beau seemed able to stand squarely on both feet. "Beau's fixin' to teach me about cookin'."

"Good thing for an orphan boy to know. You did tell the sheriff you're an orphan, didn't you?"

"Yes sir."

"I thought that's what you said. Gardner seemed to have some doubt about it."

Beau said, "I was at his mama's funeral. As for his pa dyin', I don't see any reason he'd tell us a windy."

Tatum said, "I hope you two are gettin' along with one

another. The sheriff might take it kind of bad if he was to ride out here and find this boy gone."

Even in his weakened condition, Beau seemed to appreciate the grocer's concern. "Much as I hated to, I gave Gardner a promise. I do keep my promises."

"I wish you'd promise to quit drinkin'."

"The shock'd kill half the people in town. I'd hate to be responsible for that."

"I'd chance it." Tatum went to the door, then turned back. "You feel up to a job of work?"

"Doin' what?"

"I've had Luke Quincy buildin' me a new barn and pens out at the farm. He fell off of the ladder and stove in some ribs. There's probably a couple weeks of work left if you want it."

"I'll be out there tomorrow."

"Bring the boy. He can earn a little by fetchin' and carryin' for you."

Joey was elated. "You mean you're goin' to pay me?"

"Your legs are too short for full wages. How about fifty cents a day?"

That was fifty cents more than anyone had ever paid him. "I reckon it'll be all right." He did not want to seem overeager, but he could not help exclaiming, "It'll sure be all right." A few extra dollars in his pocket would be helpful when he struck out on his own again.

He would probably have to hide it, though, to keep Beau from spending it on a bottle.

Tatum frowned at Beau. "I don't want you takin' whiskey out to the job. Luke was cold sober and got hurt anyway. Drinkin', you'd fall off the roof and break your neck."

Beau frowned back. "You sure know how to take all the pleasure out of hard work."

Joey watched the merchant leave. Beau turned back to the stove, his hands shaking. He appeared ready to throw up again, but Joey doubted that he had anything left in his stomach.

Joey asked, "Why do you drink when you know it's goin' to do this to you?"

"Why do you ask so many questions that ain't none of your business? A button your age wouldn't understand even if I told you."

"You probably don't understand it yourself."

"What I *don't* understand is why you ran off from a good home and came here to bother my life. You've got a stepmother. Sure, she ain't your real mama, but she'd take better care of you than I can."

"She was tryin' to take care of me, all right. She was tryin' to kill me!"

The look on Beau's face was like the look Joey had seen on everyone else he had tried to tell. Beau said, "The devil's got a special place for kids who tell stories like that, and you're knockin' on his door."

"It's the truth. I think she let Pa die, and I know she killed Reuben someway. Then there was the bull that almost got me, and the rattlesnake . . ." He stopped, for the disbelief in Beau's eyes told him it was useless to go on talking.

Beau said curtly, "I wisht you'd go out and chop some wood. Ain't enough left in here to keep the coffee hot."

Joey choked off a retort and stomped outside. They would believe him someday if Dulcie got her way. They would look at him lying in his coffin, and they would be sorry. He would like to see their faces then.

{ SEVEN }

The Tatum farm lay just across the Colorado River an hour's horseback ride from town, beyond the last of the pine trees. Beau rode the brown horse with the letters *GO* branded on its hip. Joey asked if the horse answered to "Go." Beau said that was too short a name for a horse, so he called him Git Out.

He abandoned the meandering wagon road and cut across country. "We'll save us some time," he explained.

Joey suspected it was not time Beau wanted to save, it was his badly abused innards. The whiskey and the brown horse's rough trot were keeping them riled up. Beau's shortcut missed the road's shallow ford, so they struck the river at a point wide and deep. Taw balked until Beau rode up behind him and slapped his rump right smartly with a quirt. Taw jumped into the water with an alacrity that almost threw Joey out of the saddle.

Joey shouted, "You didn't have to do that."

"Sometimes you got to show a horse who's boss. Same way with a kid."

"I'm not a horse. And I'm not a kid, either." He worried that his blankets would get wet, rolled and tied behind the cantle, and that they might not dry out before night.

Beau said, "You need a bath anyway."

"I'll bet I've had one since you did."

"Won't hurt either one of us to slip down here after dark and take off a pound or two of dirt and sweat. Now quit your bellyachin' or go back to town."

Joey quickly decided he liked the farm because of its variety of livestock: horses, cows, pigs, sheep . . . also chickens, guineas, and a couple of peafowl that screeched at every disturbance and sometimes when the only disturbance was the one they created. It reminded him of home in happier days when he had been younger, when Mama had been there, and Pa, and the sun had laid a golden glow upon the Shipman farm.

"You know somethin'?" he asked Beau that night as they soaked in the shallow water at river's edge. "I'm goin' back home someday when I'm bigger. I'm goin' to take that farm away from Dulcie and fix it up a lot like this one."

The cool water had not improved Beau's disposition. "Why wait? You ought to go back now."

"I told you about Dulcie. She's set on killin' me."

"Never saw a boy with such a wild imagination. You'd be a lot better off at home."

"I'd be dead."

Tatum came out in a well-traveled buggy the second day to see if they had settled in and started work. He seemed pleased to find Beau on the barn roof, nailing down fresh cypress shingles. He hollered up, "I brought some extra grub for Emma, since she's got two more mouths to feed."

Emma was a black cook who lived on the place with her farmer husband. She sang to herself while she worked, like Joey remembered Mama doing many times. He had found the first day that she could bake a better cobbler pie than any he had tasted since Mama died. The man, called

William, reminded him a bit of Reuben, though he was younger and could read. He had a stack of newspapers Tatum had brought him and tried to talk to Beau about current affairs like the situation in Europe. That came to naught because all Beau knew about Europe was that it lay somewhere on the other side of the big water. He didn't know London from St. Petersburg. Joey knew, but his knowledge was only from schoolbooks. Those were not current enough to give him much ground for conversation. William knew who most of the kings and queens were, who was at war and who was fixing to go.

"I don't reckon you brought anything to drink," Beau said to the grocer.

"Only coffee. Emma broke William from drinkin' twenty years ago. Time you leave here, she may have you preachin' temperance too." He turned to Joey. "You doin' all right, sonny?"

"Yes, sir."

"Sheriff Gardner asked me to check on you, make sure Beau's treatin' you proper."

That rubbed Beau the wrong way. "And what if I wasn't?"

"I expect you'd be back in jail before dark."

"That Gardner's got a special rope saved up with my name on it. He'd've hung me a long time ago if he'd had an excuse."

The turn of the conversation made Joey nervous. He tried to change the subject. "I sure like your place here, sir."

"I'm glad you do. It's somethin' anybody could have if they're willin' to work hard and save their wages." He gave Beau a look that said the remark was aimed right between his eyes.

It bounced off. When the merchant moved on to the house to talk to Emma and William, Beau said, "It's some-

thin' anybody could have if they're careful to marry a
woman whose daddy has got money. That's the secret of
success: to marry into it or to pick a mama and daddy that's
already got it."

"He doesn't look rich. First time I saw him, he was
sweepin' out his own store. And look at that old buggy he's
ridin' in. The wheels are sprung."

"The way rich people stay rich is that they don't ever
spend nothin'. Their money just sets there and mildews.
When I've got it, I put it to work and spread it around. I
believe in havin' a good time."

"Like you were havin' the mornin' after you got out of
jail?"

Beau struck his thumb with the hammer and ended the
conversation. "I wisht you'd take the posthole diggers and
start workin' where William put down stakes for the corral."

They had been on the job a week when Blair Meacham
showed up. Joey did not see him ford the river, so he was
taken by surprise when one of the peacocks screeched to
announce the arrival of a stranger. Meacham drew rein
behind Joey, almost close enough to reach out and touch
him. Joey was holding a post in place while Beau tamped
the fill-in dirt around it with the tip of the shovel handle.

He had begun to feel that there might be some chance
for Beau if he could stay away from town and the tanta-
lizing lures it dangled to trap the weak willed. During long
days on the farm Beau had labored as if the place were his
own and everything would be lost if he slacked off for even
an hour while there was daylight to see by. The new barn
was finished, its pine siding bright in the sun and waiting
for paint. The new corral adjoining it lacked perhaps a

couple of days' labor to be finished. Casper Tatum had estimated the job would require two weeks, but he had not taken into account Beau's nervous-energy drive when the alcohol was burned out of him.

"See?" Joey had said. "You can do a good job when you stay sober."

"The sooner done, the sooner I get paid. There's several bottles of pure happiness waitin' for me in town."

Joey was beginning to realize that a man, like a coin, could have two sides. There was heads, and then there was tails.

He stared in open-mouthed amazement at Blair Meacham, sitting on his horse and staring back. A smile slowly spread across Meacham's face, but Joey had an uncomfortable feeling it was false as a lead dollar. He saw coldness in the gray eyes, and rebuke.

Meacham said, "Well, Joey, you've caused me and Dulcie a right smart of trouble and worry."

Joey swallowed, unable to answer.

Beau wiped a sleeve across his sweaty face and let the shovel fall, the handle thumping upon the ground. He asked Joey, "You been struck dumb or somethin'?"

Joey had to clear his throat before he managed to speak. "This is Mr. Meacham. He's Dulcie's cousin."

"Not cousin," Meacham said, "husband. Me and Dulcie, we went on a little trip and got ourselves married by a preacher. Then we went home and found you'd run off without a word. Now, that wasn't no thoughtful thing to do, was it?"

His mouth was still smiling, but there was no smile in his voice or in his eyes. He didn't seem the same Mr. Meacham who used to bring Joey candy and tell him jokes and stories.

"You married Dulcie?" Joey did not understand how any man could do that after seeing the way she treated Pa.

"I did."

"Bet you wouldn't if you'd known she was tryin' to kill me."

"Kill you? Now, what ever gave you such a notion?"

The words spilled out like water through a broken dam. "There was Pa. I don't think she wanted him to live. She just stood back and let him die. And Reuben . . . I don't know how she done it, but she killed him. And she turned that bull loose on me, and she put that rattlesnake on my bed. She wants me dead so she can have the farm."

Meacham shook his head in disbelief, like everybody else Joey had tried to tell.

Joey said, "You better watch out. She'll get tired of you, and then she'll kill you too."

Meacham turned to Beau. "Poor boy went through a lot, losin' his daddy and then the old darkey that helped raise him. Unsettled his mind, it looks like. I suppose you'd be the cousin Sheriff Gardner told me about?"

"Beau Shipman." Beau reached up and shook hands.

Meacham dismounted. "We sent letters to every county sheriff in two hundred miles. I've come to take Joey home where he belongs."

Joey hoped Beau might stand up for him. They had gotten along decently well the last few days, between occasional sullen spells on Beau's part brought on by his painful withdrawal from whiskey. But Beau only shrugged. "That's the best thing to do. I can't provide no fittin' home for him."

Joey protested, "Beau . . ."

Meacham took a firm grip on Joey's arm. "Come gather up whatever stuff you have and let's get started. We can make a good many miles before dark."

Beau volunteered, "His stuff is in the old barn yonder."

Meacham said to Beau, "Sheriff Gardner told me you're a man who likes whiskey."

"I've been known to indulge a little now and then."

"I've got a full bottle here in my saddlebag. It's yours if you'll go fetch up Joey's horse."

Beau said, "It won't take any time at all."

Joey tried to jerk free of Meacham. "No! You-all listen! She'll kill me if I go back!"

He dragged his feet, pulling against Meacham, but he was no match for the man's strength. He began to cry. "Please! Please! I don't want to go."

Meacham argued, "You'll see how wrong you are when I get you home. Dulcie'll bake you the biggest cobbler pie you ever saw."

And put poison in it, Joey was certain.

"Beau," he pleaded, "please talk to him. Make him see."

But Beau had turned his back and ambled out to catch Taw. Joey would bet he was already tasting that whiskey in his imagination. Damn him for the sot that he was!

Meacham stopped at the door of the old barn and pointed inside. With Beau out of hearing, he made no pretense at the kind nature and easy humor he had shown Joey in the past. His voice was gruff. "Throw your stuff together and let's be movin'."

Joey wished the barn had a back door, but it didn't. Even if it had, he could not run fast enough to elude Meacham's horse. Beau would probably even aid in his capture. What an awful fix this was, two men working together to carry him to his death and neither of them realizing his peril.

Joey rolled his few belongings in his blankets, tied them behind the saddle, then carried saddle and bridle out the door. Beau brought up Taw, leading him along by nothing more than a gentle grip on the horse's mane. Why couldn't the fool horse have taken a notion to run away? Joey wondered. Instead he had simply stood there and let Beau walk right up to him in the edge of the pasture. Gentle as a dog, but not half as smart.

About like Beau!

Joey gritted his teeth in frustration. Well, it was a long way home. Somewhere along the road, with any luck, he would catch Meacham off guard. The man had to sleep sometime. When he did, Joey would slip away. He wasn't going to his death without putting up the struggle of his life.

Beau saddled Taw and pulled the girth up tight. "You'll realize after a while that this is the best thing for you. If you stayed with me you'd probably grow up a drunk."

"You've been sober for more than a week."

"I won't be tonight. Go back to your stepmother, kid. She'll be so happy to see you that maybe she won't even give you a whippin' for runnin' away."

"She'll be happy all right." Joey's throat was painfully tight as Beau boosted him up into the saddle. He could not control the sudden flow of tears. "I'm tryin' to tell both of you if you'd just listen. She'll kill me."

Meacham shook his head pityingly. "You've got her all wrong, boy. Come on, let's go."

They started toward the river. Beau watched them a minute, then came running, waving his arm. "Hey! What about that bottle you were goin' to give me?"

Meacham pretended not to hear him. He put the horses into a long trot and quickly outdistanced Beau.

Despite the fear that put pain in the bottom of his stomach, Joey found satisfaction in the fact that Beau had been beaten out of the promised whiskey. Mr. Meacham probably didn't have a bottle with him in the first place.

It served Beau right.

Gradually Joey began pulling himself together, trying to bring his fear under control so he could think clearly. He realized Meacham was not heading toward the shallowest spot to cross.

Joey said, "If we'll follow the wagon road it'll take us to the ford. The horses won't even have to swim."

"Shorter this way. You need a bath anyhow. Look at the dirt on you."

"Been buildin' fence." A hopeful thought struck Joey. "We're goin' by town, ain't we? Mr. Tatum owes me some wages." It wouldn't be more than four or five dollars at best, but the grocer had seemed an honorable and intelligent man. He might listen if Joey could just talk to him. It was a chance.

Meacham did not reply. He rode down the long, slanting riverbank and stopped at the edge, looking back. Joey turned to see if Beau might be following in the vain hope of getting his whiskey. The house and barn were more than half a mile back and hidden by heavy timber that fringed the river.

The water appeared sluggish, but Joey knew it could be deceptive. The undercurrent was swifter than the surface. He said, "It's real deep right here. There's shallower water upriver a ways."

"This'll do. A little swim won't hurt the horses." Meacham took hold of Taw's reins, pulling them out of Joey's grasp and over the horse's neck. When Taw showed reluctance, Meacham circled behind him and slapped him across the rump with a quirt. Taw plunged in. Soon Joey sensed that the ground had gone out from under the horse's feet. Taw was swimming, fighting the current. Joey held the horn with both hands. It was a challenge to stay in the saddle.

He shouted, "We ought to've gone to the ford."

Meacham did not reply. Joey thought he was busy with his own struggle. Something bumped his leg hard, and he saw that Meacham had drawn his horse up against him. A chilling look had come into his stepfather's eyes.

Meacham grabbed Joey's arm. Joey shouted in alarm as Meacham dragged him free of Taw and plunged him into the water. Joey clutched at Taw's mane, at the saddle strings, at the horse's tail. But Meacham held his arm, pulling him away, pushing him under.

"Mr. Meacham . . ." Joey choked as he gulped a mouthful of water. "What're you doin'?"

What he was doing came clear in a blinding flash of panic. Meacham was trying to drown him. Many other things suddenly came clear, too.

Joey struggled to break loose, but Meacham grabbed a handful of his hair and pushed his head under. Trying to hold his breath, Joey swallowed water nevertheless. He kicked and tugged and came up gasping for air. He managed a cry like the desperate bleating of a lamb.

"Quit fightin'!" Meacham shouted at him. "Ain't goin' to do you no good." He pushed Joey down and tried to hold him. But the struggle threw Meacham's horse off balance and caused its nose to go under water. Terrified, it came up fighting the river. Meacham lost his hold, and Joey began swimming away.

Meacham cursed first the horse, then Joey. He brought the mount under control, and Joey felt a hand clutching at his arm. He dove to get out of reach and sensed the current taking hold, carrying him downstream.

Coming up for air, he heard shouting. The voice was not Meacham's. Beau was swimming his brown horse, waving his arm. "Here, Joey! Come to me!"

The weight of water-filled boots and wet clothes tried to drag Joey down, but he splashed toward Beau as Beau closed the distance. Choking, gasping for air, Joey grabbed desperately at Beau's outstretched hand.

"Hang on, kid."

Joey clutched Beau's sleeve. Beau got his arm around Joey's shoulder. He shouted at Meacham, "I've got him. It's all right now!"

Joey realized Beau had mistaken Meacham's intentions. He probably thought Joey had fallen off his horse and Meacham had been trying to rescue him. Joey managed to cry, "He tried to kill me."

Beau seemed not to have heard him. "I'll get you to the riverbank, then your Mr. Meacham had better have that whiskey."

From behind them, Joey heard Meacham shout. Joey turned his head, though he had to blink the water from his burning eyes before he could see. "Beau! He's got a gun!"

Beau was too surprised to move. Meacham pulled up beside him, pistol in his hand, and swung the barrel at Beau's head. The blow was deflected by Beau's upraised arm and softened by the crown of his felt hat. Beau wheezed, "Godalmighty!" and turned Joey loose.

Meacham's horse was already spooked. Joey's splashing and threshing frightened it more. Meacham cursed the animal and tried to pull its head up. Fighting restraint, the horse plunged forward, rolling over onto its side. Meacham yelled in surprise just before he went under. He came up floundering and no longer had the pistol. The horse swam away from him. Meacham splashed around wildly.

Beau managed to take a new grip on Joey's arm. Joey felt Git Out steadying himself as he took solid footing on the riverbed. On the bank, Beau let Joey slip to the wet sand amidst several broken pieces of driftwood. Joey's heart was hammering, and he coughed up water. He saw Taw climbing out downstream, stopping to shake himself like a dog. Incongruously, Joey's immediate worry was the roll of blankets tied behind his saddle. They were strung out halfway to the ground and thoroughly soaked. He would have to sleep wet tonight.

At least it would not be the long sleep Meacham had planned for him.

Beau seemed a bit stunned, struggling to understand. "What's the matter with him, anyway? He didn't have to pistolwhip me over a bottle of whiskey."

Joey managed to quit coughing for a moment. He fought for breath. "It would've been hard to explain a bullet hole in you."

Meacham was still splashing, reaching out his hands as if he sought something solid to grasp. There was only the water. His shout was a strangled cry for help.

Joey said, "You were a witness. He had to try and drown us both."

Beau slowly began to comprehend. He eyed Meacham without sympathy. "I don't believe the son of a bitch can swim."

Joey began to regain his breath. "This is three times him and Dulcie have tried to kill me."

Beau said, "They ain't very good at it, are they?" He pushed Git Out back into the river. "It'd be a great lesson to him if we let him drown. But the sheriff wouldn't see it like me and you." He drew up next to the gasping Meacham, took a handful of the man's wet collar and dragged him to the bank. He dropped Meacham in the mud at the river's edge. Meacham spat water, his shoulders heaving.

Beau told him, "What I ought to do is stomp hell out of you and throw you back in. But when you're done spittin' up mud I'll take you to town and let the sheriff treat you like he's been treatin' me for so long."

Joey clenched his fists. He could see the plan. His dying had to look like an accident. And Meacham had to get it done as soon as possible so Joey would not have a chance to escape on the long trail home. "I'll bet he was goin' to say I ran away from him and got drowned when I tried to cross the river."

"Pity the sheriff didn't believe your story in the first place."

"You didn't either."

"It sounded like somethin' a runaway kid would make up."

Joey began to feel the warmth of gratitude. "At least you came out to help me."

"I had no such notion. I came to get the whiskey he promised me. See if you can catch his horse and look in his saddlebags."

Joey's gratitude vanished more quickly than it had come. "You'd sell your soul for a bottle of whiskey."

"I already did, a long time ago."

A blur of movement caught Joey's eye. Meacham rushed toward them, a large chunk of driftwood swung back over his shoulder. Joey cried, "Watch out, Beau!"

The warning was too late. The club smashed against the side of his cousin's head with a solid thump. Beau staggered, instinctively throwing his arms up against a blow that had already struck. Meacham raised the club again.

Joey grabbed up a piece of driftwood, smaller than the

other but about as large as he could handle. Meacham struck Beau a second time. Beau's arm took the brunt.

Joey aimed for Meacham's head, but Meacham bent forward and the stick struck him in the ribcage, costing him some breath. Meacham hesitated, struggling to regain the air he had lost. Beau grappled with him for the heavy club. The two staggered and splashed back into the edge of the river. As he fought, Meacham kept swearing, his fury sweeping him out of control.

Both men had their hands on the club, the strength of one challenging the power of the other. Beau threw Meacham off balance, then thrust the club into the man's face. Blood burst from Meacham's nose. He stumbled but kept his hold on the club. Joey waded in and swung his stick again, hitting Meacham on the back of the head. Meacham faltered, and Beau jerked the club free. He brought it around hard and smashed Meacham across the jaw. Meacham staggered backward and fell. The current carried him away face down, blood streaming behind him before losing itself in the flow of the river.

Knee-deep in the water, Joey watched in shock as the body drifted downstream. Full realization set him to shaking.

"We killed him, Beau!"

"He was tryin' to kill *us*." But Beau was shivering too, and Joey knew it was not because of cold water. "Came within an inch of gettin' it done." Beau raised a hand to feel the place on his head where the first blow had struck. It bled a little.

Meacham's body disappeared around a bend.

Joey said, "We'd better go tell the sheriff."

"Tell Gardner?" Beau vigorously shook his head. "He'll call it murder. He's been sayin' all along that I'll get on a big drunk and kill somebody someday. He wouldn't believe a word I'd tell him."

"Maybe he'll believe me."

"Remember how much good it did to tell him about your stepmother? He'll figure I got into a fight with Meacham over him takin' you home. Probably say I was tryin' to make him give me money to turn you loose."

"But Mr. Meacham tried to kill you."

"Nobody knows it but me and you, and that sheriff's been itchin' for an excuse to salt me away for good."

"What'll we do? The body is sure to wash up somewhere." From what Meacham had said, the sheriff himself had sent him here, Joey thought. When the body was found, the lawman would know where to look for answers.

"You can stay here. Sheriff'll put the blame on me anyhow. Ain't but one thing for me to do, and that's to hightail it out of here . . . get as far away as I can before the law starts lookin' for me. I'll lose myself out west someplace where they can't find me. Arizona maybe, or California, whichever one is the farthest."

Joey visualized the map on the schoolhouse wall. "That'd be California, I guess. But it's an awful long ways."

"The farther the better. Ol' Gardner's heavy on his feet. He'll get tired of travelin'. I'd better catch up my horse."

They waded out. Taw had climbed to the high bank and had his head down in the tall grass. Joey was struck by the irony. His own world had just blown itself to pieces, but his horse was peacefully grazing as if nothing had happened. Beau had difficulty in catching the skittish Git Out. The horse turned and trotted away three times before Beau managed to sweet-talk it into standing still until he could grasp a rein.

Beau said, "See Meacham's horse anyplace? I sure could use a stiff drink of that whiskey."

"I don't think he had any whiskey."

"Then he was a liar on top of everything else."

Meacham's mount had evidently run off. Well, somebody would find it, just as they would find Meacham's body.

Joey spread his wet blankets and rerolled them into a neater bundle. He wished he had time to lay them out and let them dry. As Beau rode up to him, Joey asked, "We goin' by town to pick up the rest of your stuff?"

"Ain't nothin' in that cabin worth the risk. And *we* ain't goin' no place. You're stayin' here."

That's what you think, Joey thought. After all, he had struck Meacham a staggering blow. When he told them his story—and he wouldn't lie—they'd count him as a participant in the killing. Maybe they wouldn't hang him as they would hang Beau, but they would probably put him in a boys' reformatory until he was old enough to go to the Huntsville penitentiary and bust big rocks into little ones.

Beau rode to the old barn to gather his blankets and a few other belongings. William came in from the field, bringing his mule team. He said, "You-all look like you went fishin' and fell in the river. Thought you was buildin' a fence."

Beau frowned at Joey, who was tying his things to his old saddle. The look said for Joey to keep his mouth shut. Beau told William, "The job is all finished except a little of the corral. Tell Casper I hate to leave on short notice, but I got an emergency on my hands."

William could probably see that for himself, because blood had dried on the side of Beau's head. "What kind of emergency?"

"Best I don't tell you. What you don't know can't get you in trouble. You got any cash money you could lend me?"

William was slow to answer. "I got a little up at the house, maybe twenty, thirty dollars." Doubt insinuated itself into his eyes. Beau was notoriously unreliable. "But if you're leavin', how you goin' to pay me back?"

"Casper can pay you out of the wages I got comin'. Tell him I said it was all right."

Joey knew from past conversations that William had money, probably a lot more than any twenty-thirty dollars, stashed in various hiding places where no robber could find it all and no banker could euchre him out of it. He and Emma were of a saving nature, trusting no one else to take care of their futures. In that, they were different from Reuben, who had never shown much interest in money.

William accompanied Beau to the house, where Beau remained evasive in his reason for leaving. Joey held his silence. Emma insisted upon washing away the blood and putting something on the head wound that must have burned like hell's hinges, from the way Beau hollered. She accepted on faith that whatever mess they had gotten into, it had not been of their choice. She sacked up most of the groceries she had. "Mr. Casper'll bring us some more next time he comes," she said.

William said, "If anybody asks us where you went, Mr. Beau, what you want we should tell them?"

Beau swung up onto his horse. "Just say that the last time you seen me, I was headin' for the moon." He set the brown into a long trot.

Joey had to spur hard. Beau turned in exasperation as Joey pulled up beside him. "How many times have I got to tell you? You're stayin' here."

"No I'm not."

"You ain't ridin' with me."

"Yes I am."

"That old horse of yours travels like a sore-footed cow. Me and Git Out'll leave you behind."

"But you've got to stop and sleep sometime. When you do, me and Taw'll catch up to you."

Beau let fly some curse words Joey did not think he had heard before and set his horse into an easy lope. Joey tapped Taw with his OK spurs. He fell behind and knew Taw could not match Git Out's brisk pace. But if he could keep Beau in sight he would be able to catch up with him eventually. And if he lost sight of him, he could follow tracks.

After a couple of miles Beau stopped and waited. He pointed his thumb toward a darkening sky. "It's cloudy in the west and fixin' to rain misery. You sure you want to face that?"

"If you can stand it, I can."

"The first time you start to crybaby on me, I'm leavin' you."

Joey made a vow to himself that the sun would come up out of the west before Beau would see another tear in Joey Shipman's eye. "Are we goin' to travel, or are we just goin' to sit here and talk?"

Beau muttered under his breath and gave Joey a look meant to sting, if not actually to bring blood. He put Git Out into a trot.

After a while the rain started. Joey hunched his shoulders against the chill of it, for he had no slicker. He had only a light cotton jacket, and it was wrapped in the roll of wet blankets. He set his jaw, determined not to let Beau see the pain he felt in his body and in his soul.

{ EIGHT }

B eau said, "We'll follow the river west as far as
Austin, but we won't tarry there. That town is full
of lawyers and people studyin' to be lawyers. It's
no place for an honest man."

Joey thought back to the nice Mr. Wilson, who had
always been a friend of Pa's. "What's wrong with lawyers?"

"They rob you without a gun, and charge you for doin' it."

"We ain't got much worth stealin'."

"They'll take it anyway just to keep in practice."

Beau rode a long time in silence. Joey might as well
have been talking to Taw for all the response he received.
The rain had stopped, but the sun had not emerged from
behind the clouds. A light wind cut through Joey's wet
clothes and made him shiver. It also reminded him how
long it had been since he had eaten.

He told Beau, "I'm gettin' hungry. Ain't you?"

Beau snapped, "There you go crybabyin' on me. I got a
lot more to worry about than your empty belly. I'm travelin' as long as there's daylight, and maybe after there
ain't. Turn back if you want to. I wish to hell you would."

"Me and Taw'll still be goin' after you quit."

Beau did not stop until at least a full hour after darkness had fallen. He halted then only after Git Out cut sharply to the right to avoid stumbling into a steep and muddy washout Beau had not seen and which almost lost him his seat. It occurred to Joey that the horse probably had the most sense.

"We'll stop," Beau said. "Can't afford to cripple an animal."

Joey thought some bacon would taste real good, broiled on the end of a stick. "I'll build us a fire."

"And have the law spot it? You ain't got a lick of sense. Besides, where you goin' to find any dry wood?"

The tone of voice stung Joey. Defensively he declared, "This mess wasn't my doin'. If you've got to blame somebody, blame Dulcie and Mr. Meacham."

"It's part your fault. I'd never laid eyes on you but once 'til you came ridin' into town and dumped all this aggravation on me. Why couldn't you have picked on somebody else?"

"There wasn't anybody else. Not kin, anyway."

"We ain't kin. Second cousin don't count. I was livin' happy and free 'til you came along."

"Not very free. You were in jail."

He had touched a raw nerve. Beau snapped, "That's a smart-aleck way to talk to a man that saved your life."

"I saved yours too. He was about to stove your head in when I hit him with that stick."

"None of it would've happened if you hadn't come here. I ought to've rode off and left you. I still got a mind to do it."

"Go ahead then. I got along by myself all the way to Bastrop."

"The law would probably have you before sundown tomorrow, and you'd tell them where I was headed."

"I don't *know* where you're headed. And I don't think you do either."

"Didn't have time to plan ahead, or I'd've done a better job of it. And I wouldn't have you hangin' on my back like a dead weight."

Joey stewed in silence, for he was weary of an argument that was not going anyplace. He ate some of the food Emma had sacked for them, then rolled himself in his blankets. They were still damp, so he never got warm. He lay thinking about the trouble he and Beau were in, more or less making up his mind that he would sneak away before daylight and leave Beau to manage by himself, and probably do a poor job of it. But he eventually dropped off to sleep, dreaming of rattlesnakes in his bed and of Mr. Meacham. He saw Meacham's blood-smeared face rising up out of the reddened water like some avenging demon, raging at him that he was fixing to die and go to hell.

When Joey opened his eyes he found himself blinking at the rising sun. For a moment, despite his own earlier intention of going off and leaving Beau, he had a momentary sinking feeling that Beau might have ridden away and left *him*. He looked around desperately.

Beau had a small fire burning and a tin bucket of coffee sitting precariously on small pieces of blazing driftwood. Joey wondered how he had ever gotten them lighted.

"You goin' to sleep all day?" Beau demanded. "Sheriff Gardner has probably been on the trail for two hours."

"I didn't sleep hardly any. Must've dropped off just before sunup."

"You snored all night." Beau had some thick slices of bacon impaled on a couple of sharpened sticks, dripping fat into the fire. The aroma awakened Joey's hunger. Beau said, "I'm figurin' to make many a mile today, so you better get yourself fortified if you're goin' with me. You sure you're old enough to drink coffee?"

Joey had been coming around to an easier tolerance of the stuff, though it was black as tar the way Beau boiled it. "You think I'm just a schoolboy?"

"Yes, and I wish you was still in school."

"School's out."

"Not here it ain't. You'd better be a fast learner."

Joey found his blankets still about as damp as when he had spread them last night. He had no choice but to roll them that way. Reuben's old Bible was damp but not soaked. It had protected the picture of Mama and Pa. For that, he was thankful.

They ate hastily, Beau's gaze going often to their back trail. As he mounted he said, "You better keep up. I ain't waitin' for you and that burro you're ridin'."

"Taw ain't no burro."

"Ain't much of a horse, either."

"Go on and leave me if you want to. I'll be all right."

"I laid awake most of the night, studyin' on doin' just that. But I owe somethin' to John. He *was* my cousin."

Joey saw no reason to tell Beau that he had considered the same option and probably would have taken it had he not gone to sleep. He made it a point not to fall behind, though sometimes he had to spur Taw more than he liked. Beau would put the brown into a lope at intervals then slow to a trot again to avoid wearing the animal down.

By midday Taw required more spurring to make him match Beau's pace. Joey was glad when Beau said, "We've got to rest these horses a while or we'll run them into the ground."

They had been avoiding the road, following the course of the river. Joey could often see horse and wagon traffic at a distance, however. The increasing frequency indicated to him that they were nearing Austin. He knew from school that it was the capital of the state. The governor lived there, and the legislature. Pa had said most of the laws were made in Austin, so what Beau had told him about the place being infested with lawyers rang true.

They rode down off the river's high bank where they would not easily be seen. Beau staked the two horses to graze and parceled out Emma's food sparingly. Joey could easily have eaten twice as much as Beau allowed him, but he would not show weakness by complaining. He noticed that Beau took no more for himself.

Killing somebody probably dampened a man's appetite, Joey thought, though his own hunger was not noticeably diminished.

Beau said, "I didn't get much sleep last night. I'm fixin' to catch me a few minutes' nap. You keep watch."

Joey resented the order but did not want to start another argument. He had not won one with Beau yet. At best, their set-tos had come to a draw.

As Joey walked up onto the bank where he could see for some distance, Beau hollered after him, "Don't you go to sleep."

That was just what Joey did. The shade was a pleasant refuge from the warmth of the sun, and the high-pitched singing of insects in the trees was like a lullaby.

Hoofbeats awakened him. Opening his sleepy eyes wide, he saw five horsemen approaching from the east, so close he could have thrown a rock and hit one had he not been paralyzed by surprise. He could only stare and wonder how they had slipped up on him so easily. He felt ashamed for his dereliction of duty.

He was also scared, for he saw a badge on one man's vest. It was round with a star inside. A Texas Ranger badge, he realized.

"Well, son," the rider spoke, "you're not out here all by yourself, are you?"

Joey considered lying that he was, but his throat tightened so that he could not speak.

The lawman said, "We've been followin' the tracks of two horses." He eased carefully to the high bank and looked down where Beau slept. The officer drew a pistol, motioned with it, and led his four followers down toward the water. Joey managed to find his voice. "Beau! Look out!"

Beau jumped to his feet, but it was too late for him to do anything. He saw the lawman's six-shooter and raised his hands. His jaw dropped with dismay. "I give up. Don't shoot."

Joey reached his cousin's side. Beau's eyes burned with accusation. "You went to sleep, didn't you?"

"So did you." He knew that was an empty excuse, for Beau had stated his intention of catching a nap.

The lawman gave Beau a long study, then lowered the pistol. "Sorry we gave you a scare. You're not the man we're lookin' for."

Beau swallowed. "I'm not?"

"I'm Sergeant Curtis Wheat, Texas Rangers. We're huntin' for Miller Dawson, the outlaw. We got a report he was seen over this way yesterday. Of course that may not mean much. People claim to've seen him in Dallas and El Paso both the day before. We came across your tracks and thought you might be him."

"I ain't."

The lawman holstered the pistol and leaned forward in the saddle, bracing both hands on the horn. "What *would* your name be?"

Beau's answer was quick. "John Smith."

The lawman glanced at Joey. "And you?"

Joey was surprised at the speed and ease of his own reply. "Joe Smith." St. Peter was going to call on him for a full explanation someday, but surely the good angel would consider extenuating circumstances.

The officer appeared to doubt. He extracted a small notebook from his shirt pocket and thumbed through it. "You'd be surprised how many people named Smith I've run into in seven years of rangerin'." He ran his finger down several pages. He said to Beau, "You may be in the book someplace, but I haven't got time today to read the whole thing. We've got bigger fish to catch than you and your son."

Beau said, "He ain't . . ." He caught himself. "We ain't no fish at all. We're just farmers on our way to town."

"Then we'll be about our business of catchin' Miller Dawson. Chasin' him, anyway. Should you run across him by some accident, give him plenty of room. He is a dangerous man."

"I promise you, we won't bother him none."

Joey could not stifle his curiosity. He had heard Sheriff Gardner mention Miller Dawson's name. He asked the ranger, "Ain't he some kind of a Robin Hood, or somethin'?"

"Robin Hood took from the rich and gave to the poor. Miller Dawson takes from the rich and poor alike, and I ain't heard of him givin' any of it away."

Beau said, "The boy has read too many books. Too much readin' ain't good for anybody. It clouds the mind."

The lawman agreed. "Some people make a romantic figure out of a brigand like Miller Dawson. But they're not the people that've seen him over the muzzle of a six-shooter." He put the book back into his pocket. "One piece of advice: If you *are* in the book, I would advise you to keep ridin' 'til you wear your horses' feet off to the knees. Texas law has a long memory and a long arm."

The posse rode up the riverbank and quickly disappeared. Beau turned on Joey. "You like to've got me hung that time."

"He wasn't lookin' for you."

"He could've been, for all you knew. And where'd you learn to lie like that? I'll bet you've been keepin' bad company."

"Not 'til lately."

Beau unstaked his horse and motioned for Joey to do the same. "They've rested enough, and so have you."

"Whichaway we goin'?"

"Whatever direction that ranger took, we'll take another."

Joey's pulse had not quite returned to normal. "I sure thought he had us."

"We've been travelin' faster than the news. But we'd better not slow down or it'll catch up with us."

The more Joey thought about it, the more troubled he became about their riding where no one else traveled. He said, "That ranger followed our trail easy because there was just two horses. Sheriff Gardner could do the same thing."

"That's why we're travelin' fast."

Joey pointed southward to the distant road, where he could see a freight wagon and a couple of riders. "Seems like it'd be harder for him if our tracks was all mixed up with a lot of others."

"But on the road, people would see us."

"What would they see? Like you told the ranger, just a farmer and his son on their way to town. There's probably a lot of them."

"I don't know where a boy like you comes up with such damn fool ideas." But soon Beau began edging southward and fell into the main road. They met a farm wagon going east, a man and a woman sitting on the seat. Groceries and other supplies were stacked in the bed of the wagon.

Joey was nervous about stopping to visit, but Beau told him it might look suspicious if they didn't.

"How far on in to Austin town?" Beau asked the couple.

"We been about two hours in this wagon," the farmer replied. "You'll make it some sooner a-horseback." He gave Taw a critical study. "Or maybe not."

As the wagon moved on, Joey looked back. Its wheels were obliterating part of the tracks left by his and Beau's horses. "A few more wagons and there won't be a sign we passed this way," he said, indirectly telling Beau he had been right.

Beau could not let him off free. "But if anybody asks that farmer and his wife, they'll remember us."

As they came to the top of a gentle hill, Joey saw a town spread out before them, most of it lying north of the river. A lot of the buildings were of stone or brick. It was the largest town he had seen, larger than Bastrop. He reasoned that it must be Austin.

Beau said, "We'd better lay in a few more supplies before we head off to the west." He licked his lips. "And I sure could use a drink."

"You said we weren't goin' to tarry long."

"It won't take long to buy a bottle of O Be Joyful."

Joey could visualize the outcome. "If you do, you won't get two miles down the road. I'll go and leave you where you fall."

"You're a millstone around my neck anyway."

"The millstone around your neck isn't me. It's that damned whiskey." He surprised himself, using a word like *damned*. He supposed it was the company he had been keeping.

Beau colored. "When men are talkin', children keep their mouths shut."

"I'll keep my mouth shut when you start talkin' like a man."

Beau descended into a sulking silence that he did not break until they found themselves looking northward up a wide and busy street. At the far end of it, behind scaffolding, Joey could see a large construction site. A dozen or so wagons and teams of horses and mules were clustered about it, and a couple of dozen men worked against or atop the walls.

"Must be the new capitol," Beau said. "Old one burned down. They're buildin' this one with stone."

Though only the first-story walls had been raised so far, Joey could tell that this would be a huge structure. "Looks bigger than Pa's cornfield."

"Folks'll be sorry they didn't let the thing stay burned down. Politicians bring nothin' but misery. Like Sheriff Gardner." Beau gave the capitol no more of his attention. He sought out a general store. "I'll go get us some more bacon and flour and stuff. You watch the horses. Town like this, somebody's liable to try and steal them and get a crooked lawyer to swear they were his in the first place."

Joey was relieved that Beau was going for the groceries

first, before he went after any whiskey. Otherwise the groceries might never be bought. He looked uneasily in all directions, wondering if he and Beau were being watched, if someone on the street might remember them when the Bastrop sheriff came asking questions. Telegraph wires across the street reminded him that news today could outrun the best horse that ever lived.

He was startled by a voice from behind him. "Well, young man, I see you and your father made it to town all right."

Joey's mouth went dry when he saw Ranger Wheat, still on horseback. "Yes sir. He's takin' care of some business."

"And what did you say your name is?"

Joey struggled to remember. "Smith. We're both Smith. My name's the same as my daddy's." He realized he was babbling, and trembling a little too. He tried to steady himself. "Did you find the outlaw you was lookin' for?"

"Miller Dawson? No, the report was probably false. Most of them are. But we'll catch him eventually. No wanted man gets away forever."

"None of them?"

"One way or another, every guilty man pays his debt." Wheat started to leave but paused. "That's a good lesson for every boy to learn. Wanted men must always keep lookin' back. Stay out of trouble, and you can keep your eyes on the green hills ahead."

Joey watched the ranger ride up the street, then turned his head to see what might be behind him.

Coming out of the store with two sacks, Beau tied the larger to his own saddle and the smaller to Joey's. "That takes care of luxury," he declared. "Now for the necessities." He reined in at a brick building where a sign declared *Spiritous Liquors*. He said, "In a town full of lawyers you'd think they'd at least know how to spell proper. Supposed to be a *k* in *liquor*, ain't there?"

"I don't know. The word never came up in school." Joey knew it was useless to lecture Beau directly. He said, "You promised we wouldn't be here long. No tellin' how near the law is to catchin' up with us."

Beau shot back at him, "You think I've forgot? I don't need to be lectured by a ten-year-old boy."

"Twelve. Goin' on thirteen."

Despite being ill at ease, Joey found much of interest in the passing traffic—horseback riders, buggies, wagons, people afoot. By Joey's standards, many of the men were dressed expensively. Coats were much in evidence, though the weather was warm, and necks were decorated by ties or scarves. Men carried themselves as if they had too much business and too little time to attend to it. Lawyering must pay better than farming, he thought. But then, most any-thing did.

Beau came back sooner than Joey expected, though his breath indicated that he had taken time for a quick drink, or maybe two. He carried a bottle. "They say there's a lot of snakes in that western country." He took a long drink before he deposited the bottle in his saddlebag and mounted Git Out. Watching him, Joey had a bad feeling. With Beau, one drink led to another and another and another until the bottle was empty or Beau was on his back, whichever came first.

They rode south down Congress Avenue. Followed far enough, Beau said, the street became the San Antonio road.

Joey commented, "I've heard of San Antonio all my life. I sure would like to see it."

"Go if you want to. I ain't stoppin' you."

"I didn't mean right now. Someday, maybe."

"I was there once. Long's you've got money to spend they've got a glad hand stuck out for you. But go there broke and nobody wants to know you. Except the *po*lice."

Joey wondered whether to tell him about seeing the ranger. That might arouse Beau's cautionary instincts. On the other hand, it might just make him drink more.

Beau needed no encouragement to drink. He stopped at the edge of town and took another long drag on the bottle, then reined onto a westerly wagon road. Joey looked back. He did not expect pursuit this soon, but one never could be sure. That Ranger Wheat seemed like a man who knew his business.

In a while they were beyond the town, moving into rough limestone hills and through extensive cedarbrakes which seemed to choke off whatever wind there might have been, trapping the heat into stifling pockets.

This road appeared less beaten out than the one east of town. Joey realized that population was thinner to the west, where the land was more suited to livestock grazing than to farming. The only cultivation he saw was in narrow valleys where soil had washed down from the hillsides and left deposits deep enough for plowing. Anywhere else the limestone rocks would probably cause a farmer to spend as much time sharpening his plow point as breaking sod or planting a crop.

They met a couple of sturdily built wagons and pulled out of the road to make room. Drawn by extra spans of big mules, each wagon carried a heavy cargo of large limestone blocks, edges and corners neatly trimmed.

Beau said, "Those must be goin' into the new capitol."

A little farther on they came within sight of the quarry from which the blocks had been cut. Men with rifles guarded other men, some white but most of them black, in dirty prison garb. Beau stopped briefly to watch and to take another drink.

"Convict labor," he explained. "The whole legislature ought to be out here sweatin' in that rock pile instead of back yonder passin' laws to tax the workin' man."

Joey thought the biggest levy Beau had ever paid was probably the liquor tax, but judgment prevailed against his expressing that opinion.

A thought chilled him. If they caught and convicted him for his part in killing Mr. Meacham, he might wind up in such a place as this. He tried not to look at the quarry again, but some morbid fascination made him turn in the saddle to stare. He saw prisoners straining to hoist a large square stone onto a wagon with block and tackle. "Poor fellers."

Beau shook his head. "There's poorer ones, them that go to the rope."

They had traveled perhaps a mile when Joey heard three popping sounds in rapid succession behind them.

"Guns?" he asked.

Beau did not even turn to look back. By this time he had made heavy inroads into the bottle's contents and was not seeing well. "Somebody tryin' to get him a venison supper. Must be a poor marksman, havin' to shoot at it three times."

"I hope the deer got away."

"You'd look at it different if you was the one hungry."

Joey heard hoofbeats. Turning to look, he said, "Somebody's comin' up fast behind us."

"That damned Gardner." Beau turned out of the trail,

but it was already too late to hide. The horse was in plain sight, running. "Well, we tried."

It became evident that the horse was carrying double. The man in the saddle was not Sheriff Gardner. He was a broad-shouldered, dark-complexioned man with as big and black a moustache as Joey had seen in a long time. Joey did not get a good look at the other man until the blue roan horse came to a stop. He realized that the man behind the cantle wore the work uniform he had seen on prisoners at the quarry. The man in the saddle trained a pistol on Beau. His eyes were like flint.

"We have need of your horse," he declared. "Would you kindly step down?"

Beau had a sudden burst of courage. Joey suspected it had escaped from the bottle. Stiffening, Beau declared, "Hell no! This is my horse. Go find you another one."

The man behind the saddle slipped to the ground, looking anxiously behind him. "We got no time to argue. Shoot him, and let's be gone."

The gunman said evenly, "I don't like to shoot a brave man, but a fool is somethin' else. Which are you, brother, brave or foolish?"

Joey was afraid Beau's false courage would get him killed. "He's been drinkin', mister. He don't know what he's sayin'. Please don't shoot him."

Through his whiskey fog Beau seemed suddenly to grasp the seriousness of the situation. His belligerence evaporated. "The law's after us too. If you leave me afoot, what chance have I got?"

"Better than if I have to shoot you." The man's knuckles bulged as he tightened his grip on the pistol.

Beau dismounted unsteadily. He cursed the man who

held the pistol. "Maybe I'll run into you again sometime, and you won't have that six-shooter in your hand . . ."

"Perhaps when that day comes we'll have more time for pleasantries. Right now we're a little busy."

His companion in the prison garb grabbed the reins from Beau's hand and swung into the saddle. He untied the blanket roll and war bag, letting them drop to the ground, lightening the load on the brown horse.

The tall man shoved the pistol back into its holster. "There'll be some people along directly, askin' after us. Tell them we're sorry we couldn't stay and be sociable." He spurred away. The other man had no spurs, but he beat the heels of his heavy shoes against Git Out's ribs and fanned the horse's rump with his cloth cap, trying to catch up.

Beau stood swaying in the middle of the road, his arms stiff and fists clenched. "Damn, but I hate a horse thief." He stepped over to where his blanket roll and war bag lay in the dust. The saddlebags had gone with the horse. "Not only took Git Out, but they got off with my sippin' whiskey and most of our grub."

Sipping whiskey. Joey doubted that Beau had ever *sipped* whiskey in his life. Gulping it was more his fashion. Loss of the bottle was the only positive element Joey could see in what had happened. "That sure is too bad," he said, holding down a smile that he knew was badly out of place. Beau's being afoot would slow them dangerously.

Beau picked up his blankets and war bag and tied them on Taw along with Joey's stuff. It made for an unwieldy load. "I don't know if Taw can carry all this," Joey complained.

Beau was in no mood for argument or sympathy. "Walk if it bothers you. I'm havin' to." He set off down the road afoot, not looking back to see if Joey was following. Joey had little choice.

Pursuit was not long in coming. Joey and Beau drew off to the side of the road. Four horsemen rushed past, giving them no more than a glance. They appeared to be guards from the quarry.

Joey said, "I hope they don't shoot your horse."

"They're so far behind they won't even see him."

Beau was not accustomed to walking much. His shoulders began to droop, and the steady pace he had set at the beginning slowed to a painful trudging. Step by step, Beau had to force one foot to move past the other. Joey said, "You want to ride Taw a while? I'll walk."

"Your legs are too short for walkin'. They barely reach the ground."

"I can walk faster than you've been doin'." Joey tried to raise his leg high enough to clear all the belongings tied behind the cantle but could not. He had to swing it forward over Taw's neck, then jump to the ground. Beau dropped any pretense at argument. He managed to lift his right leg over the blankets, but once he was in the saddle both legs hung down halfway between the stirrups and the ground. Taw looked back reproachfully at the extra burden.

Beau grumbled, "I still say your horse is half burro."

Joey considered a response but saved his energy for walking.

The four horsemen returned, no longer running their mounts. Their dejected attitude told Joey they had not caught up to the fugitives. An older man who appeared to be in charge gave Beau a critical study.

"Ain't you ashamed of yourself, ridin' and lettin' a boy walk?"

Beau grunted. "He's younger than I am. You ever see anything of them fellers you was after?"

"Nothin' but their dust. We shot a horse out from under one of them when they left the quarry, so they were ridin' double. Now they have two again."

"They stole mine. I'll be watchin' for the gink that took it. I'll make him wish he'd never seen me."

The horseman frowned. "I don't know as I would do that, were I you."

"He's got it comin'."

"He's got a lot comin', but you wouldn't want to be the one who gives it to him. Didn't you recognize Miller Dawson?"

Beau almost choked, his Adam's apple bobbing up and down. "That was Miller Dawson?"

"Sure was. He came and busted out a confederate that we had workin' in the quarry. He's too desperate a man for any farmer to be tanglin' with. If you happen across him, I'd advise you to go around. *Way* around."

Miller Dawson. Joey was intrigued. "How many men has he really killed?"

"If all the stories are to be believed, fifty or sixty, maybe seventy. I expect there's been a little exaggeration." The horseman jerked his chin as a signal to the other three. "We'd best go make a report. Boss is goin' to be real put out about this."

Beau said hopefully, "I don't suppose you'd want to lend a man a horse?" The men rode on. Beau said, mostly to himself, "I guess not." He turned to Joey. "My God, boy, I cussed out Miller Dawson." He shook his head in disbelief. "I sure could use a drink of that whiskey."

"If you push, you might catch up to Dawson and get it back."

Beau shook his head. "I wouldn't want to hurt your horse."

{ NINE }

The farther west they went, the more rugged and unfamiliar the terrain to Joey, broken limestone ledges jutting out from rough hillsides, dry creek beds yearning for a rain. Dark green mottes of live-oak timber and thickets of dense cedar offered plenty of places for Miller Dawson and his fugitive friend to have evaded pursuit across the trackless ground. Joey suspected that the four who had given chase had taken care not to get too close. Some might regard that as cowardice, but Joey recognized it as a strong aversion to suicide.

Much earlier than Joey expected, Beau said, "We'll stop pretty soon. I reckon you're tired from walkin' so long."

Joey was, but he would not admit it. He did not know if Beau was genuinely concerned about him or if he was probing for weakness.

Beau said, "I've got to think about the horse, too. There's a line of timber just ahead, so maybe there's a creek. I need a cup of coffee worse than any man ever did."

Irony crept into Joey's voice. "Don't you want to catch up to Miller Dawson? You said you intended to give him a good whippin'."

"I've thought it over. I'm a forgivin' sort of feller."

They were surprised to come upon a camp where a small creek crossed the wagon road. A buggy stood beside a pyramid-shaped tent, the canvas too new to bear much stain. A black man knelt before an economical campfire, skillet in his hand. A gray-haired, blockily built white man stepped out of the tent and walked to the edge of the road, motioning with his hand. "Welcome, friends. Come share our camp for the night."

Beau studied the place distrustfully. "We need to be makin' some more distance before dark."

The stranger gave Joey a sympathetic study. "But this boy appears to be worn out." His eyes held silent accusation, for Joey was still walking, and Beau was riding.

Beau seemed to read his mind. "We been takin' turn about on the horse."

That was true as far as it went, but in Joey's view it had been much too long since they had last traded places.

Sizzling meat in the black man's frying pan gave off an aroma that set Joey's stomach to grumbling. "You-all fixin' supper, are you?"

"Venison," the white man replied, "and plenty of it. Samuel bagged a nice fat doe."

The black man smiled, showing a row of perfect white teeth. "Everybody'd just as well eat all they want. The leavins'd just spoil."

Joey walked to the fire, leaving his cousin little choice. Dismounting, Beau had to swing his leg high to clear the rolled blankets. He took a few stiff-legged steps to ease the cramping that came from the ill fit of Joey's saddle. "The boy's doin' fine, but I expect the horse has traveled enough for one day."

The man shook Beau's hand. "Welcome, then."

"Our name's Smith," Beau offered, his eyes telling Joey not to contradict.

"That's a coincidence," said the gray-haired stranger. "So is mine. I am Henry Smith—Judge Henry Smith."

Beau swallowed. "Judge?"

"Yes, district judge. I make a circuit through this hill country. I am on my way to Austin for a conference."

Beau dropped his gaze to hide the momentary panic in his eyes. "We appreciate your hospitality, Judge, but maybe we'd better see if we can go a few more miles."

"Nonsense. Tomorrow is another day, and this boy looks tuckered, not to mention hungry. Come, lad, by the time you wash your hands and face in the creek, Samuel will have this first mess of venison ready for you."

Joey saw that he and Beau were trapped. To leave now would only arouse suspicion if suspicion did not already exist. He went on his best behavior. "I'm much obliged, sir. So is my daddy."

The judge said to Beau, "I congratulate you, sir. So many today do not coach their children in good manners."

Beau's voice was not quite steady. "I do the best I can."

The judge's easy manner assured Joey that he knew nothing about the trouble they had left behind them. The thing to do, he thought, was to play out the game the best he and Beau could, trying not to say or do anything that might later cause the jurist to put two and two together.

He wolfed down the venison.

Sticking a fork into a second slice of meat, the judge said, "I suppose you have a farm somewhere around here?"

Beau replied uneasily, "No sir, we're just sort of lookin' for a place. We ain't found the right one yet."

"These rough hills cause many prospective settlers to

turn back too soon. There is good valley land around Fredericksburg suitable for cultivation. The German farmers have proven it quite productive for the man who is willing to work."

"We'll take a look at it."

"I must say, I find it strange that you have only one horse between you."

Beau said, "We had another, but a couple of outlaws stole it. One of them was Miller Dawson."

The judge's eyebrows went up. "Miller Dawson? Are you sure?"

Beau explained briefly what had happened after they passed the stone quarry.

The judge's jaw set grimly. "Those misguided souls who romanticize the likes of Miller Dawson are deluding themselves. I hope someday to have him and all his confederates stand before me. It will be a swift and terrible judgment." His eyes flashed with the zeal for vengeance. "We have been much too lenient with the criminal class. We should chop off the right hand of every thief. We should round up every man who has done murder and stretch his neck at the end of a rope—exterminate them with no more thought than we would give to burning a wasp's nest, until every last one is gone from the face of the earth!"

He slammed his tightened fist into the palm of his left hand. Beau flinched.

The judge demanded, "Do you not agree, sir?"

Beau seemed to have trouble with his voice. "What if a man done a killin' without meanin' to?"

"Murder is murder. There is no excuse and no redemption short of the gallows."

Joey wanted to ask *What about a kid?* But he remembered a saying that used to hang in a frame on the school-house wall: Silence is golden. It had never meant so much to him as it did now.

He slept fitfully that night, for he kept seeing himself standing before Judge Smith, begging for mercy and finding none. After a quick sunrise breakfast Beau pleaded urgency and departed the judge's camp as if it were a den of snakes.

"Talk about a hangin' judge . . ." he said, when they were out of earshot.

Joey asked, "What do you think he'd do to a kid?"

Joey did not know which bothered him most when they stopped that evening, his weariness or his hunger. One of the items in the sack Beau had hung on Joey's saddle in Austin was a box of crackers. Joey appeased his appetite by devouring some of those while he waited for the coffee to boil over a meager campfire. He wished they had some of the leftover venison Samuel had offered. In their haste to depart the camp they had left it behind.

Joey asked, "Where does the road lead to?"

"I've never been this far west. Judge talked about Fredericksburg, so it must be somewhere out yonder."

"Suppose we run into Indians?"

"Been years since the last Indian trouble. You're more apt to have a rattlesnake crawl into your bed."

"I already had one *on* my bed." Joey shivered at the recollection, and again as that led him to remember Blair Meacham floating down the river, trailing blood.

Taw was staked on a level spot where grass was plenti-ful. It had worried Joey to see the little horse carrying not only Beau's weight but all of their belongings as well. "What're we goin' to do about gettin' you a horse? Taw can't keep this up all the way to California."

"I ain't got the money to buy one, and they can hang you for stealin'. Maybe when we get far enough west to feel safe from Gardner for a while, I can get a job and earn one."

Joey spread his blankets on bushes, hoping the air would dry them before he had to crawl into them for the night. They were still damp from the soaking in the Colorado River. He seated himself beside the small campfire and opened Reuben's old Bible. He took out the photograph that he had placed between its pages.

"What you got there?" Beau asked.

"A picture of Mama and Pa." He handed it to Beau.

Beau studied it. "I never did get to know your mama much more than to say howdy to her. Me and your daddy, though, we used to run together some as kids. One way or another, we never did get along very good after we got grown. He thought we were put on this earth for nothin' but labor."

"He did believe in work," Joey agreed. "But he was always good to Mama and me." He felt his eyes begin to burn. He took the photograph back from Beau. "This is all I've got left from them, just this old picture."

"It's not all. You've got some good memories. That's more than I have from *my* folks."

"No good memories?"

"More like bad dreams. I'll bet your daddy never told you much about me, did he?"

"I don't remember that he ever did."

"My daddy wasn't married to my mother. He already had him a wife, and folks said my mother was kind of a sportin' woman. She didn't want me so she unloaded me and ran off before I was old enough to remember much about her. My daddy's wife never wanted me either, and the old man was always tellin' me I never would amount to nothin'. I reckon I showed him he was right. When he died, the family lawyers saw to it that I didn't inherit nothin'."

"You *could* amount to somethin'. You've just got to want to, is all."

"Maybe when we get to California."

In the middle of the third afternoon from Austin, Beau walking and Joey riding, they approached a small settlement. Beau said it ought to be safe enough to stop there a bit because he saw no telegraph lines and no courthouse where some sheriff without enough to do might become nosy about their business.

A farmer in dirty overalls was stacking rocks, building a fence along the edge of a field. He wore no gloves, so his huge hands were rough as sun-dried leather. Sweat rolled down his stubbled face, cutting muddy trails through the dust. He paused in his work as Beau and Joey approached. He removed a straw hat and wiped his brow with the tattered sleeve of a homespun shirt.

"*Grüss Gott*," he said.

Beau asked, "They got a place here where a man can get a drink?"

The farmer seemed not to comprehend. He replied in words Joey could not understand. Beau asked him to say it again. The second time was as unintelligible as the first. The man was speaking something besides American. The only other language Joey had heard was Spanish, and the farmer did not look Mexican.

Beau said, "This must be one of the German settlements the judge talked about."

Joey thought it just as well. "Maybe you won't find a drink here after all."

"I'll find it. Whiskey sounds the same in any language."

The word brought a nod of understanding from the farmer. "*Ja*, visky." He pointed and said something more.

Beau thanked him and set off at a pace slightly more brisk than he had managed most of the day. Joey followed on Taw, resigned to the probability that Beau would be dead drunk before the sun went down.

A dozen or fifteen stores and houses fronted on the road to form the settlement's main street. Several were constructed solidly of limestone blocks, smaller but otherwise similar to those being used in Austin's new state capitol. The rest were of lumber with fancy gingerbread trim decorating porches and eaves, a touch of civilization in a land still largely raw.

Joey's gaze was drawn to four horses tied to posts in front of a frame building. They switched their tails, trying to ward off flies. One was a blue roan. Another was a familiar-looking brown with a GO brand on its hip.

Trying to control his excitement, Joey said, "Looky yonder, Beau. Ain't that Ol' Git Out?"

Beau had not been looking at the horses; he had concentrated his attention on the building, for it appeared to be a saloon. He stopped dead in his tracks. "Damned if it ain't."

"Looks to me like you're not the only man who's worked up a thirst. Miller Dawson must be inside."

"I reckon so."

"You goin' to walk in there and tell him you want your horse back?"

Beau did not consider long. "I don't like to bother a man when he's busy drinkin'." He eased up to Git Out, rubbing his hand along the animal's rump, then its neck. After carefully looking around for anyone who might challenge him, he untied the reins, eased his foot into the stirrup, and swung up. He backed the horse away from the post slowly so he would not disturb the others tied nearby and attract attention. He motioned quietly to Joey and rode between the saloon and a store that stood next to it. Glancing back, he eased Git Out into a smart trot, then a lope. When they had gone a hundred yards, he put the brown into a hard run. Though Joey pushed Taw for all the speed he could get, he lagged far behind.

Beau reined the horse to a stop once he had moved into a stand of cedar dense enough to mask him from the settlement. Joey caught up, turning in the saddle to see if anyone might be coming after them.

The sack of groceries Beau had bought in Austin was missing. Ruefully he said, "They ate up the grub or lost it. My whiskey's gone, too."

Joey grinned. "Thought you were fixin' to get a drink back yonder."

Beau did not grin. "Sometimes you're not near as funny as you think you are. I doubt Miller Dawson'll laugh much either when he comes outside and finds this horse gone. We'd better put some miles behind us."

Joey had read about Robin Hood. He thought if the merry bandit of Sherwood Forest had ever found the joke turning upon himself in this way he would probably get a chuckle out of it. But Texas Ranger Custis Wheat had stressed the point that Miller Dawson was not Robin Hood.

Several miles farther on they saw another settlement, considerably larger than the last.

Joey said, "I'm awful hungry."

"And I'm thirsty." Beau turned, looking back for sign of pursuit. "But I wouldn't want a bullet in my gut."

Joey was gratified that Beau was able to put temptation aside in the interest of self-preservation. "Maybe if you wanted to bad enough, you could give up drinkin' for good."

"If I wanted to. But I *don't* want to."

Joey guessed the place was Fredericksburg. It had the solid look of a town meant to endure, more buildings of stone than of wood, and a couple of the tallest church steeples he could remember seeing. He was especially taken by a large structure fronting on the wide main street. It resembled pictures he had seen of a steamboat. The sign said *Nimitz Hotel.* Farther north, an odd-shaped hexagonal building fitted Judge Smith's description of the "coffee mill," the first church built after the early immigrants had founded their town.

All Joey knew about Germans was what he had learned in school, that they had come from a distant country across the ocean and spoke a language he probably could not understand if he worked at it until he was forty years old. But Reuben would have approved of any people who built so many churches. He would have understood them as he had understood a Bible he could not even read.

Beau dug a few coins from his pocket. "I sure am dry."

"And I'm still hungry. Don't you think the first thing you'd better do is buy us some grub?"

"Boy, when you get a notion stuck in your head, you don't let go of it." But Beau stopped in front of a store that had one small sign reading *Eisenbach Gen'l Merchandise* and a larger one with words Joey could not decipher. He said, "I don't know if they understand American, but I'll bet they understand money. You watch the horses."

When Beau came out, he hung one sack on his saddle and handed another to Joey. "You'll find some sardines in there." He dug into his pocket for a coin and nodded toward another building which had a sign reading *Bäckerei*. "Go get you some bread to eat with it. I got a little business next door."

Next door was a dramshop. Joey protested, "You been doin' real good—you don't need to be goin' in there."

"You're just a boy. You've got no idea what a man needs." He terminated the discussion by walking away. Joey's feeling of helplessness gave way to anger, which in turn gave way to his hunger. He went into the little bakery shop and found the aroma of freshly baked bread almost overpowering. He felt as if he had not eaten in a week. He showed the coin to a portly woman behind the counter. "I need to buy me some bread."

He could not understand her reply, but he pointed to a shelf of dark brown loaves. She handed him one of them and took the coin, giving him back two smaller ones in change. "*Danke*," she said.

Walking out, he wondered why she hadn't thanked him. Most storekeepers would, just out of common courtesy.

He sat on the edge of the wooden sidewalk and hungrily set to work upon the bread and a can of sardines from the sack. He had almost finished both when he became aware of two horsemen stopping in front of him on the street. Joey skipped a breath as he saw that one horse was a blue roan. He recognized its rider by his heavy black moustache.

The other declared, "Miller, you see what I do?"

Joey dropped the little left of the sardines and pushed quickly to his feet. The can clattered on the wooden walk, spilling oil and a remnant of tiny fish. The man who had spoken got down from a fine-looking sorrel. Miller Dawson still rode the horse Joey had seen him on before. The younger man had exchanged his prison garb for a farmer's overalls and a homespun shirt, neither of which fitted him. Joey suspected he had stolen them from somebody's clothesline without attention to size. A Mexican sombrero sat squarely on his head. Joey could only guess where he had taken that, and how.

The man declared, "That's the horse I lost yesterday."

Dawson said, "Forget it, Hull. You've got a better one now anyway."

"And come near gettin' shot over it. Somebody here needs to be taught a lesson." An ugly anger darkened Hull's face, accenting a long scar down his right cheek.

Dawson warned, "Last thing we need right now is to call attention to ourselves."

"If there's anything in this world I hate, it's a horse thief." The escapee's eyes bored into Joey. "I remember you, kid. Where's that horse-stealin' partner of yours?"

Frightened, Joey found it difficult to speak. "I ain't got no partner."

"You ain't ridin' two horses." The man walked to the door of the general store and peered inside. Not seeing Beau, he turned back, his gaze going to the door of the dramshop.

Dawson called, "Hull, if you start a ruckus . . ." The words trailed off as his confederate passed through the door.

Joey dropped the bread and ran for the dramshop. "Beau! Beau, look out!"

A strong hand grabbed the back of his shirt, and a stern voice said, "Whoa, son. A boy your age has got no business in a place like that. It ain't respectable."

Joey wiggled free from Miller Dawson and hurried through the door. He saw Beau sprawled back against the bar, blood trickling from the side of his mouth. Hull swung his heavy fist again. The blow hit so hard that Joey feared it might have broken Beau's neck.

"You stop that!" Joey shouted. He made a running leap and landed on the man's broad back, wrapping his legs around Hull's waist. "You leave Beau alone!"

Hull pitched like a horse, trying to throw Joey off, but Joey clung, clamping one arm around the man's head, covering his eyes. Hull's Mexican hat rolled across the floor. Joey was dimly aware that half-a-dozen bystanders watched in surprise, none moving either to help or to hinder him. He pounded his fist against the top of Hull's head. Hull roared and tried to dislodge Joey by slamming him against the bar.

Joey's anger crowded out reason. He bit down hard on Hull's ear, as he had seen men do to a horse they were trying to break. Hull squalled.

Beau seemed to be in a stupor. He staggered forward as if to help Joey, but Hull bumped into him and sent him reeling back.

Miller Dawson's voice was sharp. "Hull, you quit pickin' on that kid."

Joey felt strong hands take hold of him, wrenching him loose, pulling him away from the big man. Dawson spun half around, setting himself between Joey and the raging Hull. "That's enough. Enough, I say!"

"The little . . ." Hull reached for Joey, but Dawson blocked him. "I told you I wasn't goin' to stand for any ruckus. Now back off."

Hull did not back away. In a move so swift Joey barely saw it, Dawson drew a pistol from its holster on his hip and struck Hull a stern blow across the side of his head. Hull went to his hands and knees.

Dawson said, "Sometimes he won't listen 'til you talk to him kind of rough."

Joey broke free of Dawson and hurried to Beau, who was still groggy and disoriented.

Dawson caught Hull beneath the arm and helped him to a chair at a small table. "Bartender, draw him a beer. Draw us all a beer . . . except the boy, of course. You got any milk?"

Joey's blood still rushed hot. "I don't need no milk. I don't need nothin' from you, and neither does Beau." He tugged at Beau's torn sleeve, trying to lead him out of the shop.

Dawson said, "Hold on, boy. Let your partner get his feet under him first. And you better settle down a little yourself. No use leavin' here mad."

"I've got cause to be mad, him whippin' up on Beau just because Beau took back a horse that was his in the first place."

"What's your name, boy?"

"Smith."

"Funny. So's mine, sometimes." Dawson glanced at Hull to be sure he wasn't looking for more fights. "This Beau, is he your brother?"

"He's my cousin . . . second cousin, anyway."

"You-all must be pretty close, you jumpin' in on his side so fierce."

"Sometimes I've been mad enough to shoot him, but he's all the kin I've got."

"Nobody in my family ever took up for *me* like that. You've got grit, boy."

"I didn't want him hurtin' Beau any more. Me and him got too much travelin' to do."

"What's so important about travelin'?"

Joey glanced around to be sure nobody else could hear. With Dawson being hunted like he was, there shouldn't be any harm in telling him. "We're on the dodge."

Dawson smiled tolerantly. "What did you-all do, tip over somebody's outhouse?"

Dawson wasn't going to believe him any more than the others he had tried to tell. Well, he didn't owe an outlaw any explanation. He decided not to say anything else.

Dawson said, "You and your cousin had better come with us."

Joey felt a stirring of alarm. "What do you need us for?"

"Soon as he gets his feet back under him he'll want to complain to the law. We'd sooner he didn't."

"He won't go to the law. He can't. They're lookin' for us, him and me both."

Joey wanted to retreat from Dawson's probing gaze but could not take his eyes from the man. The outlaw seemed to be trying to believe him. "If that's truly the case, you'll both be better off ridin' with me and Hull."

Every lawman in this part of Texas was probably watching for Miller Dawson. To be with him would be like cuddling up to a lightning rod. Joey hedged. "I don't know what Beau would say."

"He don't look like he's in a shape to say anything right now. He don't even know which direction is up. Let's be goin' before the local law comes messin' in our business. I've never shot a Dutchman, and I don't feel like startin' today."

Hull tried to put on his hat but took it off again, flinching from pain. Blood was matted in his hair where Dawson's pistol had struck him. In his bleeding ear was a clear impression of Joey's teeth. Hull complained to Dawson, "Did you have to hit me so hard?"

"I had to get your attention." Dawson handed several greenbacks to the bartender. "Hope this'll cover any damage. And help make you forgetful."

The smiling bartender counted the bills. "For this much money I forget even my name."

Dawson pointed toward the bystanders. "Here's a little more to buy all them other fellers a drink. Won't hurt them to be forgetful either." He stopped at the door and carefully peered up and down the street before he stepped out onto the walk. "You-all come on."

Beau remained addled, but Joey reluctantly guided him by the arm to where Git Out was tied. He had to help Beau get his left foot into the stirrup. Joey untied Taw and mounted, then took Git Out's reins and led the horse into the street. He briefly considered trying to get away from the two outlaws but feared Beau would probably fall out of the saddle before they got halfway started.

Dawson and Hull were arguing. At least, Hull was. "What're we takin' them with us for? Last thing we need is a horse thief and an ear-bitin' kid."

Dawson said, "You got *your* horse awful cheap. Now let's ride out of here in a walk so everybody won't be lookin' at us."

Hull pointed back down the street. "At least we ought to stop in at that little two-by-four bank. We could clean out that place as easy as takin' the poor box in a Mexican church."

Dawson scowled at him. "Even a coyote knows better than to kill too close to its den."

He turned at the first corner to get away from the main thoroughfare, then followed a residential street until they

cleared the town. "Now, let's rattle their hocks a little."
Watching to be sure Joey and Beau stayed with him, he
swung into an easy lope. He cut into a wagon road that
trended in a northwesterly direction.

Joey asked apprehensively, "Where we goin'?"

"Llano River country. You could hide half the Confederate army in those mottes and cedarbrakes."

"The Confederate army lost the war, didn't it?"

Joey marveled at the strange turn of fate that had made
him a fugitive and suddenly put him to riding with outlaws.
Pa would not have understood, nor would Reuben. Joey
did not understand, either. The thought was at once frightening and exhilarating. He pictured himself telling the
story to wide-eyed friends in school, then realized he could
never go back to school, or to his home. Mr. Meacham's
unexpected demise had nailed that door shut.

Well, this was an adventure the likes of which he could
never have pictured in his wildest dream. He decided to
make the best of it for however long it lasted.

Someday he could tell about it in California.

{ TEN }

Their direction was westerly, through rough-hewn hills slabbed with brittle limestone outcrops and along narrow valleys where occasional green fields of tall forage and corn reflected the settlers' old-country diligence. The lowland soils were rich and deep, deposited layer upon layer as rainfall through the ages carried them down from the steep slopes where grass was thin and could not bind them.

Deer bounded away in a clatter of tiny hooves and a flash of white tails, disappearing into the dark-shaded protection of live-oak timber and juniper thickets. Wild turkeys, startled by the riders' approach, would gobble in alarm, soar short distances, touch the ground, and soar again. Except for the planted fields, Joey thought the land must still look as it did when the Indians had it. His imagination carried him into a fantasy that Indians might yet be hiding in one of the obscure canyons, that they might be watching him even now.

Dawson made a sweeping gesture with his hand. "See all that game, boy? Long as a man has got plenty of cartridges, salt, and a little coffee, he can live out here for months and never set foot in a store." He glanced at Hull. "Or a bank either."

Hull had said little that Joey could understand since they had left town. He had hung back, mumbling morosely to himself, nursing a grudge over the blow Dawson's pistol had struck him and perhaps over Dawson's refusal to transact business at the bank. Hull's prison-short hair was exposed to wind and sun. His head hurt too much for him to wear the sombrero that hung from the horn of his saddle. He made no reply to Dawson's comment.

Joey had an uncomfortable feeling that if it were left to Hull the man might shoot him and Beau as casually as he would extract a thorn from his flesh. His hostile glare indicated that he regarded them as he might regard such a thorn. He broke his brooding silence once to complain, "For all we know, these two may be rangers."

Dawson gave him the look he might give a puppy that muddied him with its paws. "A boy this age, a ranger? Use your head for somethin' besides a place to put your hat."

Hull withdrew into his prickly shell like a porcupine rolling up into a ball with its bristles out. Beau would probably say he was playing poker with a deck short on aces and long on jokers.

Beau was starting to shed the stupor he had carried out of the dramshop and the first miles from town. His nervous eyes bespoke severe misgivings. He told Dawson, "Me and Joey appreciate your kindness, but we got places of our own to go. If it's all the same to you, we'll be takin' our leave."

Dawson shook his head. "You don't know this country. Like as not you'd stumble into a bunch of rangers."

Hull grumbled, "And you might not remember to forget where we was the last time you seen us."

Joey suspected Beau would be willing to take an oath against whiskey if they could slip away from Dawson and Hull. It might be worth their lives—Beau's, anyway—to try to break loose before the pair was ready to let them go. Joey shared Beau's dread of Hull, but he was instinctively drawn to Miller Dawson. The man fascinated him, especially the contrast between his fierce reputation and the benign look in his eyes. Joey was unable to reconcile the extremes.

He was intrigued by the idea of a life free and unfettered in this wild land where the taming hand of civilization had made so little mark. It was unlike anything he had seen. He asked Dawson, "Do you really live out here in this rough country?"

"I live wherever I happen to be. Home is any place I lay my saddle down, from the Sabine River to the Rio Grande. I'm just a workin' man like anybody else. I go out and take care of business, and then I come back to camp in the Llano River cedarbrakes and rest up from my labors."

To Pa, work had been something a man did with a plow or a hoe or a shovel. He would have a different name for Dawson's version.

"You sure me and Beau won't get caught if we go with you?"

"I ain't never been caught."

"But Hull has, else you wouldn't have had to rescue him."

"Hull gets careless sometimes. I don't."

Dawson's casual self-confidence was reassuring. Joey said, "Maybe we'll stay with you for just a while, then. Me and Beau, we're headed for California."

"Why California? They've already dug up all the gold out there. A feller with ambition can find gold enough around here. You just got to know how to get it."

They camped for the night some distance from the wagon road and built a tiny fire in a ring of rocks that would hide the miserly flames from view. The men made their supper mostly on coffee and brown-paper cigarettes. Joey opened another tin of sardines and finished up with a can of tomatoes. They were a treat because Pa had never indulged much in food that came in airtights. He had said they were wastefully expensive and not nearly so good as a meal cooked fresh.

Joey thought the outlaw life might not be bad at all if he could have canned sardines and tomatoes whenever he felt like it.

Beau seemed to have no appetite except for cigarettes. He smoked several, one soon after another. He did a lot of looking around, as if seeking a place to run.

As the campfire died, Dawson said, "Boy, you sure you ain't just been loadin' me about the two of you bein' on the dodge?"

"It's true. They're lookin' for us."

Dawson's smile was faintly patronizing. "For burglari-zin' somebody's barn maybe, or some crossroads store?"

Joey considered long and hard. Perhaps it would ease the tension if Dawson and Hull knew he and Beau had so much in common with them. He blurted, "We killed a man."

That wiped away Dawson's smile. "You're just a boy. Don't you mean your cousin killed a man, and you just happened to be there?"

"I helped him." Joey explained at length about Pa and Reuben, about Dulcie and Mr. Meacham and the fight at the Colorado River. "That's why we've got to keep movin'."

Dawson had turned dead serious. "You're mighty young to be startin' down that trail. It's a narrow one, and hard to quit once you're on it. Believe me, I've tried."

"We didn't mean to. Things just happened."

"Things always do. Ain't many of us set out in life with the notion that we want to be a fugitive. We just kind of stumble into it."

"Is that the way you got started?"

"Pretty much. I had a preacher daddy who gave me a big dose of hellfire and brimstone with a razor strop every time the moon changed. I run off and took up with a rough crowd. Before long I had the devil by the tail, and I couldn't turn him loose."

Joey burned to know more. "They talk like you've killed a lot of men. Sixty or seventy, maybe."

"They've exaggerated a mite. It ain't been that many."

"How many?"

"Well, to tell the truth, not more than three. And they wasn't none of them deacons in the church. Just the same, killin' a man ain't somethin' you feel good about, even when they've got it comin' to them."

Joey remembered Mr. Meacham and felt cold. "Why do they tell such big windies about you?"

"The worse them sheriffs and rangers can make me look, the better excuse they've got for not catchin' me. Then there's the newspapers. They love a big story whether it's true or not. Somebody gets killed in El Paso and they don't know who done it, they say it was me. Somebody robs a bank the same day in Fort Worth, they say I done that too. I'd have to have my own private express train to get around as fast as they make out." He rolled a cigarette and lighted it with a burning stick from the campfire. "One thing about havin' a reputation: If people are scared enough of you, you don't *have* to kill anybody. They'll help you tote the money out of the bank."

Dawson fell into quiet meditation, not breaking silence for what seemed half an hour. "You remind me of myself when I was about your size, lots of grit and not enough luck. Reformatory ain't no place for you, but that's where they'll send you if you're caught. You and your cousin had better stay with me and Hull. You'll be safe where we're goin'."

"Where is that?"

"You'll know when we get there."

Later, when Dawson was seeing after his horse, Joey told Beau, "I like Mr. Dawson."

"Damn it, boy, he's an outlaw."

"So are we."

"Not like him and that Hull. We ain't robbed no bank or stole any horses. If we stay with them, we'll find ourselves in real trouble."

"I thought we already was."

"First chance we get, we're slippin' away. I am, anyhow. You can suit yourself."

Evidently Dawson sensed Beau's intention, for as they spread their blankets, Dawson casually warned, "Fellers, I wouldn't be gettin' up and movin' around in the dark, was I you. I sleep with a gun by my head. I've got a bad habit of wakin' up sudden and shootin' at whatever moves. I wouldn't want to be the cause of a bad accident."

Given that kind of notice, Beau did not stir from his blankets. Joey knew, for he lay awake all night worrying. He would not move if a rattlesnake crawled into bed with him.

The next morning they did not return to the wagon road. Dawson followed no trail that Joey could see. He picked his way through the hills, through the thickets, and down the centers of spring-fed streams whose clear waters and slab-rock beds would show no tracks. It was obvious why Dawson so easily eluded pursuing officers, especially if they were not eager to catch up to him anyway.

Joey asked, "How much farther is it?"

"Not far," Dawson told him.

"But how can you find it? These hills all look the same. One cedarbrake and one live-oak motte is just like another."

"There's landmarks if you know what to look for. We try not to come and go the same way from one time to the next. We don't want to beat out any trails the rangers can follow."

They came after a time to a wagon road that lay in a generally north-south direction but followed the vagaries of a restless little creek, meandering like a drunk trying to find his way home in the dark. Dawson studied the ruts, which showed recent horse and wagon tracks.

"Boy," he said, "down yonder just past the bend is a small store." He handed Joey a coin. "I want you to go buy you a piece of stick candy and look around. See if there's anybody totin' a badge. If there ain't, ask the storekeeper how long he thinks it might be 'til it rains."

Joey looked up. "There ain't a cloud in the sky."

"Ask him anyway, then come back and tell me what he says."

Joey sensed that the question and the answer were some kind of code between Dawson and the storekeeper. It felt wonderfully mysterious, carrying the message even though he did not understand the meaning of it.

He asked, "You comin' with me, Beau?"

Dawson said, "Beau needs to stay here with us. He might run into a ranger or somebody lookin' for him."

Joey knew what Dawson was thinking, that if the two of them got off alone they might keep riding. Beau was held hostage to guarantee Joey's return. There had been a time when Joey might have left him behind to wiggle off the hook the best way he could, but not now. In a way, he felt that he had become Beau's guardian rather than Beau being his. Joey set Taw into an easy trot along the road.

The store was a crude structure with cedar-picket walls and rough-hewn cypress shingles on the roof. A wagon stood in front, two sleepy-eared mules hip-shot in the harness. One saddled horse stood tied to a post in front. Chickens scratched amid fresh droppings, and two hounds came out to meet Joey with deep-throated barking that caused the tied horse to jerk its head up, straining against the leather reins. The mules took no notice. A mule was smart enough to conserve energy any time it could. Joey tied Taw's reins in a cinch ring wired to a post.

It took a minute for his eyes to adjust to the interior darkness and longer for his nose to adjust to the stuffiness. A man stood behind a crowded counter, a dirty apron tied around his middle. A farmer in overalls and a cowboy in high-topped boots gave Joey a long study. Joey was not sure how to tell a ranger from anybody else except by the badge, and he saw no badges here.

"What can I do for you, button?" the storekeeper asked, looking over the top of black-rimmed glasses perched low on his bent-over nose.

Joey showed him the coin Miller Dawson had given him. "I'd like to buy a stick of candy."

The storekeeper opened a large tin and let Joey take his pick. Joey asked, "How soon you reckon it might rain?"

The question startled the storekeeper, who walked to the door and looked out before he attempted an answer. Evidently he saw nothing. He said, "We had a little rain this mornin', but the sky's all clear now."

The farmer remarked, "I didn't see no rain."

"It was just here at the store." The merchant put the lid back on the can and said to Joey, "You tell your friend I don't think he'll need his slicker."

The farmer puzzled, "Ain't needed a slicker around here in quite a spell."

The storekeeper said, "It rains more on some than on others."

Joey returned to the waiting horsemen and told Dawson what the storekeeper had said. Dawson seemed pleased. "Then the way is clear for us to stop by and pick up some supplies before we go on to camp."

The farmer and his wagon were gone. Dawson left Hull and Beau outside to keep watch. Joey perceived that Hull was mainly keeping watch on Beau. Dawson asked Joey, "You like candy, don't you?"

"Yes sir, sure do."

"Well, then, we'd better lay in a supply that'll last you a while." He motioned for Joey to accompany him into the store. The cowboy was still there, drinking a bottle of warm beer. A flicker in his eyes told Joey that he recognized Dawson, and he moved aside to give the man plenty of room.

The four riders left the store with two canvas bags full of goods tied to the horns of Dawson's and Hull's saddles. Joey could hear bottles clinking together in rhythm with the horses' stride. Dawson had bought whiskey before he had bought flour and bacon and beans, salt and tobacco. Joey watched Beau with misgivings. If his cousin ever uncorked one of those bottles, he might not stop until he was flat on his back and oblivious to the world.

Late in the afternoon Dawson pointed to a small bluff that appeared suddenly, as if it had abruptly pushed up out of the earth. "There's a little pocket canyon back in yonder," he said. "Sign shows it used to be a Comanche hideout. The soldiers never found it, and the rangers won't either. Not unless somebody gets careless and leaves a trail they can follow into it." He gave Hull an accusing glance.

Hull turned defensive. "I wasn't careless, I was drunk. Can't blame me for what I do when I'm drunk. Besides, I didn't lead them to anybody but myself."

"If you ever do it again, I'll leave you in that quarry chiselin' rocks. You might learn a useful trade."

Joey caught the quick flash of a mirror from the top of a live-oak-covered hill. Dawson saw it too and reacted with satisfaction. "Somebody's seen us cross this stretch of high ground. Shows they're awake." He waved his hat over his head. "It's too pretty a day for gettin' shot."

Descending from the high ground, the four crossed a narrow valley and skirted partway around a cedarbrake. Dawson turned into the scrub timber and stopped. "Hull, we're leavin' tracks on that strip of bare ground. Get down and brush them out. There's rangers that can track a buzzard's shadow across a granite rock."

Hull betrayed silent resentment at being ordered around. He complied, though with little grace. Joey had already realized that Hull and Dawson were bound together by mutual need, not by any liking for one another.

Beau had acted anxious all morning, finding himself pushed into a situation from which he might never extract himself. He kept looking westward. "It's not like me and Joey don't appreciate your hospitàlity, but we need to keep on goin'."

Hull threw aside the cedar limb he had used to brush the tracks. His voice was heavy with threat. "You've seen too much to just ride away."

Beau shook his head vigorously. "I been lost since yesterday. I couldn't find my way back here in a hundred years."

Dawson warned Hull, "Don't you be scarin' Joey now. There ain't nobody goin' to bring the law in here, and there ain't nobody goin' to be hurt."

They came to a limestone ledge where clear water bubbled from between moss-covered layers of rock, forming a small spring that snaked out of sight into a narrow canyon. Above the seeps, clumps of prickly pear clung precariously to thin patches of soil. Joey was startled by the unexpected appearance of a youth on foot, carrying a rifle. His clothes looked as if he had been dragged across the rocks. His shirt sleeves resembled an assortment of ribbons, and his trousers were torn at the knees. Joey suspected he had made a fast ride through thorny brush at some time or other, probably with lawmen shooting at him from behind.

The guard was younger than Beau and not much taller than Joey. His grin was friendly. He seemed delighted to see Dawson. "Miller, you been gone so long we wondered if you'd played out your string." To Hull he showed surprise. "Last we heard, they had you behind the walls."

Hull answered in a low growl. "I busted out." He made it sound as if he had done the whole thing by himself.

Joey was tempted to protest but decided it might be wise

to let Dawson speak for himself. The young guard turned his grin toward Joey. "They're weanin' them awful young these days."

Dawson said, "Brought a couple of visitors, Tolley. Their horses need to recruit a few days."

Joey thought Beau perked up a little. By inference, he and Joey would be leaving here after a short rest. Joey hoped that was the truth.

Tolley said, "Farlow may raise hell about strangers in camp."

Dawson's eyes narrowed. "Farlow? Who gave him the big say in things around here?"

"Nobody, he just took it. You know Farlow . . ."

"I know him." Dawson's ironic response told Joey as much as he needed to know about Farlow. He did not look forward to meeting him.

Beau said, "If we ain't welcome, we'll gladly ride on. Just show us whichaway to go."

Hull glowered. "You ain't goin' no place."

The guard said, "I hope you brought some tobacco with you. I'm plumb out, and Farlow won't divide." His face twisted. "Whatever Farlow gets ahold of, he keeps for himself. He don't divide nothin'."

Dawson pitched Tolley a small sack from his shirt pocket. "Don't smoke it all at once. Damned stuff shortens your life."

Dawson seemed troubled as they walked their horses, paralleling the limestone ledge. More seeps and tiny springs yielded modest streams of water that trickled into the little creek, making it wider and deeper as it worked its way farther into the restricted canyon. Joey stared in awe, for he had spent his life in deep-soil farming country where a rise was called a hill and a hill was called a mountain. He had never seen rock formations courthouse high, tilted and buckled and standing aslant.

"I'd hate to've been here the day all this happened," he declared. "Bet there was some awful scared Indians around."

Dawson seemed preoccupied and did not respond. Beau gloomily studied the high canyon wall as if he were entering a prison. He gave Joey a fleeting look of resentment that said this was all Joey's fault and none of his own.

Joey had been unsure what to expect of the outlaw encampment, but even so he was disappointed. He had thought it might have the appearance of a small town, or at least a decent farmstead. Instead, it was a nondescript scattering of dirty-gray tents and four crude cabins spread haphazardly along the creek. *Cabin* might have been too exalted a term; *shack* would be more like it. One was of traditional construction, live-oak logs laid horizontally, one atop another. Three were picket-style, upright logs and branches forming the walls, the cracks between them chinked with mud. One leaned to the south, buttressed by two bracing logs, all that kept it from lying down like a lazy dog.

Joey did not see a cabin that a competent carpenter would want to carve his name on. He lost the exhilaration he had felt as he entered the canyon; it was gone like a moment of bright sunshine suddenly overwhelmed by dark clouds. In its place came revulsion, dread. Beau had been right; it was a mistake to come into this camp. But Dawson and Hull had allowed them no choice.

Several men emerged from the tents and shacks to stare in curiosity as if Dawson and Hull had returned from the dead. Only a couple extended greetings with any warmth.

Most were dressed no better than Tolley. Their clothing for the most part was threadbare and torn and badly in need of a washerwoman's stern attention. Joey saw no one he would call fat. Most of the men had a lank and hungry look, the gaunt ghost of poverty dulling their eyes.

He would have thought the outlaw life should pay better than this. Back home, he had seen field hands show more signs of prosperity. The men and the place repelled him.

Dawson pointed with his chin to the larger of the shacks, south of the others. "Looks like somebody's taken over my cabin. I'll let him finish cookin' supper for us, then throw him out."

Gray smoke curled from a crude rock-and-mud chimney that leaned precariously against the log structure. Joey was no judge of fireplaces, but he would consider this one a hazard. Whoever had built it was not a stone mason.

A tall, angular man stood in the open front door and anchored his hands on his hips in a way that told the world to go to hell. His thin face, days beyond its last contact with a razor, made Joey think of a hatchet blade. His pant legs were tucked into high boots once black but now mostly the color of the earth around the cabin. Joey's eyes were drawn to the butt of a pistol protruding from the top of the right boot. The man's mouth smiled, his teeth white against heavy black whiskers, but his eyes had the wild, sharp look of a hawk searching for something to attack. Joey suspected he was a little crazy, the same way Hull seemed to be. He had begun to wonder if most outlaws had something loose in their heads.

The usurper leaned back on his heels, giving a false outward appearance of laziness, but he was like a compressed spring, straining to snap free. Joey was instinctively afraid of him. He was glad when Miller Dawson edged forward, setting himself like a buffer in front of the others.

Dawson did not offer a *howdy*. He simply said, "Farlow."

"Miller. Thought they'd throwed you in jail, or maybe even planted you in a graveyard someplace."

"They'll get you long before they get me. That's my cabin. I want it back."

Farlow did not move from the door, nor did he relax his cold smile. "It was empty, and I didn't see your name on it. Besides, I ain't by myself. You wouldn't want to throw a lady out to sleep in the rain."

Dawson stiffened. "We agreed a long time ago that nobody was to bring a woman in here."

"I didn't agree to nothin'. You may cut a big swath outside, but you don't boss this camp. We're all free to do whatever we damn please as long as we're man enough." Farlow glanced back into the cabin. "Woman! Come show yourself!" When she did not appear immediately, his voice hardened. "Alta, I said git yourself out here before I take a quirt to you!"

She hesitated at the door, then came out blinking at the afternoon sunlight and wiping her hands nervously on a flour-sack apron. She was little and thin, as if it had been a long time since she had had enough to eat. Her plain gray dress had been torn down one shoulder and crudely sewn together with black thread that did not match the fabric. Her brown hair was badly in need of a good brushing. Somehow she reminded Joey a bit of Mama, except that Mama used to smile a lot. This woman looked as if she might not know how to smile. By Joey's standards she was middle aged, probably in her midtwenties or edging toward thirty. But her face had nice features, her nose thin, her mouth not overly large, her eyes blue.

He saw fear in those eyes, fear like he had seen in a rabbit trapped and huddling in a fence corner. He noticed a dark bruise on her left cheekbone.

Dawson declared, "Farlow, a woman in a camp like this can cause no end of trouble."

"I can handle any trouble that comes." Farlow turned to the woman. "You've heard of Miller Dawson. Well, yonder he is." He paused, waiting for her reaction, but she showed none beyond her initial fear. He added, "I can see you're disappointed. There ain't much to him."

Dawson seemed to flounder in search of a reply. Joey had thought nothing could catch Dawson on his left foot, but Farlow had, or perhaps it was the surprise of finding a woman in camp.

Dawson directed his question at Farlow. "How long has she been here?"

"Maybe three weeks. I brought her up from San Antone."

"Anybody been killed over her yet?"

"I've bloodied a couple of noses, but I ain't shot nobody."

"You will if you don't take her back where you found her."

Farlow exhibited no intention of following advice. "For a good-lookin' woman, she ain't too bad a cook. Come back for supper and see what she can do with a squirrel stew." He jerked his head toward the door. The woman quickly disappeared inside.

Dawson's hands knotted, braced against the horn of his saddle. "You'd better get her away from here before she busts the place wide open."

Farlow was defiant. "You may have all the sheriffs and rangers afraid of you, but in this camp you're no bigger than anybody here. Whenever you think you can whip me, you're welcome to come and try."

Dawson turned to the left down the creek, reining his horse a little rougher than was his custom. Joey kicked Taw into motion to follow him. He wanted to be away from Farlow.

Hull muttered, "I see now why Tolley complained about Farlow not sharin'. I'll bet he ain't sharin' *her.*" He straightened in the saddle, looking hopeful. "We're goin' to eat supper with them, ain't we? I'd like to see if she's as good a cook as he says she is."

Dawson's voice was gruff. "Ain't her cookin' you're interested in, or what he's keepin' her for. He'd just as well turn a mare loose amongst a dozen stud horses. Sooner or later there'll be blood and hair and strips of hide scattered all over the camp."

There already were, Joey noted, though not in the way Dawson meant. He had never seen a place so unapologetically trashy. Every shack, every tent had a pile of refuse behind it—bottles and tin cans, discarded bones, cattle and deer and rabbit hides, wild-turkey feathers—a perfect picture of sloth as Reuben had described it to him from his understanding of the scriptures. Half-a-dozen mongrel dogs had gathered, some barking at the horses and riders, others nosing futilely at the careless leavings which they had probably worked a hundred times already.

This was nothing like Joey's mental image of Sherwood Forest. He saw his own distaste mirrored in Beau's eyes.

Beau muttered, "Look what you've gotten us into."

"Wasn't anything I could do to help it."

"This is the grubbiest bunch of heathens I ever saw. Horse thieves and holdup men, bunko artists and hog rustlers. Might even be a lawyer in here someplace."

Dawson stopped a short distance below the cabin. "Ain't slept under roof or canvas for a spell. I can rough it another night or two 'til Farlow decides to clear out."

Perhaps Dawson hoped to outbluff him, but Joey had not seen any indication that Farlow considered vacating.

Beau pointed his chin southward, where the canyon appeared to close tightly. "This place looks like a trap to me. If the rangers ever find the openin', they'll catch everybody in here with no way out."

Dawson dismissed Beau's concern with a motion of his hand. "It only looks like a box canyon. The back door is so narrow you can't see it 'til you're right up on it. This creek runs out the far end and down into a bigger canyon where a hundred men could scatter into the brush and not be found." He paused, reflecting. "If you're thinkin' about ridin' out that way on your own, don't. Those canyons and cedarbrakes could swallow you up and have you wanderin' around in circles like a baby lost in the woods."

Hull added ominously, "Been men never seen or heard of again."

Dawson and Hull untied their gear and unsaddled their horses, turning them loose on green grass along the creek. Downstream Joey could see a crude brush corral, its gate lying open. Several horses were scattered along the canyon, grazing free. It occurred to him that if rangers *did* luck upon this outfit, they might capture the whole bunch before anybody could catch a horse. The fact that the mounts were allowed to run loose reflected the confidence of these men. He wondered where confidence ended and arrogance began.

Dawson seemed to read his thoughts. "There's a brush fence and ropes strung across the bottom end of the canyon to keep the remuda from strayin'. We keep a rustlin' horse staked so we can bring the rest in pretty fast. So don't you worry about the law catchin' us afoot. The guard'd hold them back long enough for everybody to get mounted."

When Dawson had drawn away far enough not to hear him, Beau muttered, "Ain't the law that worries me most, it's the *out*laws. They look like they'd skin their grandmothers if they could sell the hide for two dollars."

"I don't like it here either," Joey said. "But he may be right about us not findin' our own way. Like as not we'd ride all day and end up where we started. I almost wish the rangers *would* come."

"Don't let anybody hear you say that. Hull would gut you like a catfish, and if he didn't, Farlow would. There ain't a one of these old boys that's normal people like me and you."

"Dawson said we'd just be stayin' a few days."

"I don't trust Dawson much further than I'd trust any of these other ginks. But he seems to like you, so stay on his good side. Ain't much else we can do but keep our heads down and watch for any chance that comes our way." He added gloomily, "There's days when old Sheriff Gardner don't seem near as bad as I thought he was."

Joey wondered if Dawson would eventually try to eject Farlow from the cabin. That would be a show worth watching. But Dawson said, "We'll camp down here below the cabin 'til Farlow decides to take that woman out of here."

Hull said wishfully, "If she don't go, Farlow'll have to share sooner or later. The boys'll make him do it."

Dawson's face darkened. "That's when the blood and the hair'll fly. It ain't worth that grief to keep a woman in camp."

Hull said, "Depends on how long it's been since you had one."

"That's no way to be talkin' in front of this boy."

"This boy probably knows more than you think he does." Hull frowned at Joey. "Too much for his own good, and ours."

Joey perceived threat in his voice. Instinctively he pulled closer to Miller Dawson. Dawson laid a reassuring hand on his shoulder. "Don't you fret. Hull knows I'd skin him like a beef if he was to hurt you."

Tolley came down from his guard post and sought out Dawson's camp below the log cabin. He said, "Me and Hank have talked it over. You're welcome to our tent up yonder."

Joey could see respect for Dawson in the youth's eyes.

Dawson looked at the reddening sky. "Thanks, but it wouldn't be big enough for all of us to sleep in. I'll get my cabin back when Farlow takes that woman out of here."

"I don't think he's got any such notion."

"He will. I'll hound him 'til he does."

Tolley's gaze held morosely on Dawson's campfire. "This is the second woman he's brought here since you been away. He told us he was takin' the other one home, but he wasn't gone long enough to've traveled far. We figure he killed her."

Dawson jerked as if a spark had leaped out and burned him. "Killed a woman?"

"A woman don't mean much to Farlow once he gets tired of her. Dead, she'll never tell anybody where this camp is at."

Dawson's eyes were troubled. "Farlow's no Baptist preacher, but I never thought he'd do a thing like that."

"Flora was her name. Saloon woman out of San Antonio, like Alta, only a troublemaker. She got to messin' around with some of the boys, tryin' to set them against

Farlow, hopin' they'd kill him. I was glad to see her go, but murderin' her—that curdled my stomach."

"Farlow talked like he's already bloodied a couple of noses over this woman."

"One of them was mine. I told him he was treatin' her mean. He won't hardly let her out of the cabin without he's watchin' her." Tolley placed a chunk of wood on the fire. "Sometimes I hear her cryin'. God knows how he's abusin' her. I'd brace him again, but I know he's crazy enough to kill me. She's not like that other one. Any chance I get, I'm takin' her out of this place."

"Has she asked you to?"

"She hasn't asked me anything, but I can see it in her face. She knows Farlow don't intend to ever take her home."

"I'll talk to him."

"Somebody'll have to kill him sooner or later. I doubt that I can. I don't know anybody here who could except maybe you."

"Killin' is easy to talk about but hard to do. I don't owe this camp anything like that."

"Well, no matter what happens, I don't intend to stand by and let him murder this woman."

Dawson's baleful gaze followed Tolley as the youth walked back toward his tent, his head down.

Hull declared, "Farlow'll chew that kid up and spit him out like a plug of tobacco." He seemed eager to see the show.

Dawson shook his head. "Women sure can complicate a man's life, make him lose it if the cards fall wrong."

Hull said, "I've never seen you interested in one."

"I was once. Even got married."

Hull showed surprise. "How come you went and left her?"

"I didn't. She died givin' birth."

Joey's interest sharpened. "You've got a kid?"

"A boy. He was about your size last time I saw him. Even looked a right smart like you."

"Where's he at?"

"On a farm in Arkansas with his mother's folks. As far as he knows, his daddy's dead. It's better that way."

"How can he not know about you? Everybody's heard of Miller Dawson."

"I wasn't always Miller Dawson. I saw that name on a signboard. It's one thing I took that didn't cost nobody nothin'."

"But how could you have seen your boy if he doesn't know you're alive?"

"Pretended to be a stranger askin' directions. It was a hard thing to ride off and leave him, but I couldn't take him with me, or even let him know. This ain't no life for a kid." Dawson cleared his throat. "It ain't no life for *you*."

"I wish I knew a way out of it." Joey glanced at Beau. "For both of us."

{ ELEVEN }

D awson made no move toward taking up Farlow's invitation to share supper in the cabin. Hull went but was back shortly, disgruntled. "He didn't mean it," he grumbled to Dawson. "He knew you wouldn't go, or he wouldn't have made the invite."

Dawson added, "You just went because you wanted another look at that fancy woman."

Fancy? Joey hadn't seen anything fancy about her. She looked as if she had been dragged through hell and out the far end.

Hull complained, "Farlow acted like he thought I had intentions."

"You did, didn't you? You wished, anyway."

"Maybe, but I ain't goin' to have Farlow kill me on account of a woman. There's women everyplace. Except here."

"I'm afraid Tolley ain't as cautious as you are."

"Tolley's head ain't growed to match the rest of him. If he's got no better sense, then I won't cry over him."

"I don't remember you cryin' over anybody, ever."

"Ain't nobody ever cried over *me*."

That sounded reasonable to Joey, though he deemed it

wise to look away so Hull could not read the thought. Beau read it and gave him a frown that warned him to be careful. Even thinking could be dangerous in a place like this.

At dark they rolled out their blankets near the creek. The trickling sound of the water was comforting until Joey heard another sound, a woman's cry of pain from inside the cabin. He raised up on one elbow to listen. He did not hear it again.

He heard Miller Dawson, however. Dawson said quietly, "Best go to sleep, boy. Ain't none of your concern."

"You could do somethin'."

"Ain't my concern either. Farlow didn't kidnap her out of a convent. She left San Antonio of her own will."

"She ain't stayin' here of her own will."

Dawson did not answer. But Beau reached across from his blankets and pinched Joey's arm. "We ain't either," he whispered, "so, damn it, keep still."

Joey got another look at the woman the next morning. He had walked down the canyon, looking for Taw among the horses scattered on the curing grass. He saw several large circles of stones, the blackened remnants of long-dead fires in their centers. He thrilled to the realization that these were tepee rings, that he was leaving tracks where Comanche warriors once had walked.

He saw Farlow coming his way afoot and hurried back toward Dawson's camp, giving the lanky outlaw a wide berth. Farlow scowled at him but said nothing, going on down the canyon to inspect the horses.

Joey saw the woman emerge from the cabin and circle around to a pile of dry wood behind it. Picking up an ax, she began chopping dead branches into short pieces.

Tolley had been seated on a rough stool beside his tent, watching the cabin as though teasing temptation. Seeing the woman, he quickly got to his feet and walked down to join her. After passing a few words with her, he reached for the ax. She glanced anxiously in Farlow's direction, then handed it to him. Wind carried the broken sound of their voices as Tolley took up the chopping chore, though the pair were too far away for Joey to understand the words. She kept looking nervously down the canyon where Farlow had gone.

Beau's voice startled Joey. His cousin had walked up behind him. "Sometimes it pays not to see too much."

Joey recovered his composure. "I ain't seen nothin'." But he watched Tolley carry an armload of wood into the cabin. The woman followed him. He did not see them come out.

Beau said, "Keep watchin', then, and you're liable to see a hell of a fight. Farlow's comin' back."

Joey could foresee dreadful consequences. "We'd ought to warn them."

"Let them kill one another off. The more the better. Maybe we'd get a chance to sneak out of here."

"But Farlow's apt to hurt her. Maybe bad."

"He could hurt you too. That kind of woman ain't worth it."

Joey held his breath, debating whether to mix in something clearly none of his affair. It did not take him long to decide. He ran to the cabin door and shouted, "Farlow's on his way."

Tolley came out, then turned toward the woman standing at the threshold. "I don't know how, but I'll get you out of this place, Alta. First chance that comes . . ."

Joey moved so that the cabin hid him from Farlow until

he reached his tent. Joey took one more look at the woman's desperate face, at the fear in her eyes. He felt compassion, but he knew he had better find business elsewhere too.

Farlow stopped him with a challenge. "Boy, what was you doin' at my cabin?"

Other men in camp made Joey feel ill at ease, but Farlow scared him all the way down to his feet. Even so, he managed to lie with a straight face. "I wasn't at your cabin, Mr. Farlow. I just walked up the creek lookin' for a good place to go fishin'."

Farlow seemed undecided about believing him. He took hold of Joey's shoulders and gave him such a hard shaking that Joey feared his head would come off. "Boy, I'll give you the whippin' of your life if I ever catch you messin' around my cabin again. Ain't nothin' there that's any of your business. You hear me?"

Miller Dawson's voice was stern and loud, "And you better hear *me*, Farlow. You turn a-loose of that boy before I bend a gun barrel over your head."

Farlow eased his hold but did not let go. He turned an angry gaze upon Dawson. "You'd better bring plenty of help."

Dawson drew his pistol, and Farlow turned Joey loose. Joey hurried to Dawson's side.

Farlow pointed a finger in Joey's face. "You mind what I tell you, boy." He turned and entered his cabin. Joey heard a slap and a woman's cry.

He asked Dawson, "Ain't you goin' to do anything about that?"

"I brought you in here, so you're my responsibility. But that woman came of her own accord. Come on, you'd better get away from this place."

As Dawson went to his campfire and poured a cup of coffee, Beau moved close to Joey. "Didn't your daddy ever teach you that a boy who pokes his bill into other people's business ain't got near enough to do?"

"All I done was give them a little warnin'. The law says everybody's got a right to free speech."

"The only law around here is that the meaner you are, the longer you live. And Farlow looks like the meanest man in camp."

That afternoon two horsemen entered the upper end of the canyon, a pair of heavily laden pack mules trailing behind them. Curiosity carried Joey up to the first picket shack, where the riders dismounted. Other men from the camp gathered to greet them, most with more enthusiasm than they had shown Dawson yesterday. Dawson had not brought them anything.

Joey saw Farlow coming and moved far out of his path. Farlow pushed to the front, shoving aside everyone who stood in his way. "Did you bring me my goods?"

One of the new arrivals walked to the nearest mule and untied the diamond hitch that bound a stained tarp over a loaded pack saddle. "Sure did. We cushioned the bottles to where they wouldn't bust."

Farlow grumped, "Last time, you bought the cheapest stuff you could find and kept half of my money."

"This is prime sippin' whiskey. Me and Sim, we sampled it to be sure." He lifted off a burlap bag labeled *beans*, set it gently on the ground, and cut the string. The dry beans rustled as he ran his hand down into them and brought out a bottle. "Try it yourself and see if I ain't right."

Farlow worried out a cork and tipped up the bottle, taking two long swallows. He wiped a dirty sleeve across his mouth and declared, "Maybe this time I won't have to stomp on you."

Some of the men moved close, hoping Farlow would offer them a drink, but he did not. He ordered, "You-all bring the rest of my goods down yonder." He turned on his heel and walked back to his cabin, stopping once for another drink.

It was clear to Joey that the two men had been buying for several in camp. They began dividing up what they had brought. Someone asked, "You hear any news out there?"

Joey moved closer in case they might have heard something about a manhunt for him and Beau. "Not much," the newcomer Sim said. "There was a train robbery up on the T&P day before yesterday. They say it was Miller Dawson, and they've upped the ante on him again."

Day before yesterday. Joey had been with Dawson then, and they had been nowhere near anything called T&P, whatever that was. So Dawson had been right. Once they branded you an outlaw, they blamed you for anything bad that happened. He wondered what mischief he and Beau might be getting credit for. That Bastrop sheriff was probably clearing his books of every unsolved crime on record, pinning them all on him and Beau.

Dawson came up presently to watch the distribution of whiskey and flour, salt and bacon, cartridges and shotgun shells. None of it was for him; he had bought his supplies shortly before reaching the canyon. He inquired about the news, and Sim repeated the report about the train robbery.

Dawson's face twisted in wry acceptance. "I wonder if they'd pay me the reward if I was to turn myself in? It'd be more money than I've ever had at one time in my life."

Sim said, "Let *me* turn you in and I'll split the money

with you." Such a statement in earnest could get a man killed in company like this. Clearly he was joking. But just the same, Joey looked quickly at Dawson to see if he took it that way.

Dawson smiled thinly. "They might hang you before the money came in. Then where would I be?"

Joey thought it would be hard to dislike a man who could joke about his own fate.

It did not take long for the newly arrived whiskey to have its effect upon the camp. As darkness fell and camp-fires began to reflect their glow upon the limestone wall, Joey could hear laughter spilling from one shack, cursing and quarreling from another. Most men in camp were de-scending into various stages of drunkenness. Hull visited one shack and one campfire after another, sampling the whiskey other men had paid for. He came staggering back, barely able to move one foot in front of the other. He col-lapsed upon his blankets as if someone had broken an ax handle across his head, which in Joey's opinion would not have been a bad idea.

Dawson drank, but he did it slowly without allowing himself to lose control. Joey was moderately surprised at his self-restraint in view of the lack of it elsewhere in camp, but Beau surprised him more. Though Dawson offered to share his bottle, Beau declined. "Never was one for whis-key," he said.

If lying could get a man sent to hell, Beau was a goner. But Joey realized Beau was trying to keep his wits about him. Should luck provide a chance to take the two of them out of here, Beau intended to be sober and ready.

Tolley came down to Dawson's camp, looking wor-riedly back over his shoulder. "I'm hearin' ugly talk up yonder. Some of the bunch are tryin' to work up the nerve to come down to Farlow's cabin and take Alta away from him."

Dawson considered the situation, the campfire's flickering light playing over his somber face. "If Farlow gets as drunk as I think he will, it oughtn't to be hard to do. You've been wantin' to see her turned loose."

"Turnin' her loose ain't what they've got in mind."

Dawson scowled. "I knew there would be hell to pay over her, sooner or later. They'll bust up this camp." He pushed to his feet. "I never saw a sportin' woman who was worth this kind of trouble, but do you want her bad enough to take a chance?"

"A chance is all I ask for."

"Catch and saddle a couple of horses for you and her. I'll see that Farlow gets too drunk to know what's happenin'."

Tolley said, "I always knew you had a good heart."

Dawson grunted. "I don't give a damn about that woman; I'm just tryin' to save this camp. Be careful you don't cause any commotion. Drunk or sober, Farlow has got rattlesnake blood in him." He started for Farlow's cabin, carrying two bottles.

Beau whispered to Joey, "Bring our bridles. This is a chance for me and you to get out of here too."

"I don't think Mr. Dawson meant for us to go."

"I don't care what he meant. We're goin'." Beau trotted after Tolley. Joey grabbed their bridles and followed.

Away from the campfire, Joey's eyes rapidly adjusted to the bright light of the full moon. He saw most of the horses farther down the canyon, some standing, some lying down. Tolley welcomed the help. He said, "Let's push them into the corral. They'll be easier to catch."

Several saddles had been left atop the corral fence, along

with bridles, blankets, and ropes. Joey began shoving the sagging gate shut behind the horses. Crudely constructed of tree branches tied together with rawhide, it scraped heavily against the ground. Beau hissed for him to be quieter. Joey tried to lift the gate, but it was so heavy he could only drag it.

Beau bridled Taw and Git Out while Tolley saddled two other horses. Beau motioned for Joey to follow him, leading the horses back to Dawson's campfire. They worked quickly, rolling their blankets and tying them onto the saddles with their other meager belongings. Hull stirred and groaned a little. Joey held his breath, watching him, but Hull settled back down and resumed his snoring.

Beau started to mount, then noticed Hull's rolled gun belt with his pistol and holster near the upper corner of his blankets. He stooped to pick them up.

Joey said nothing, but Beau explained in justification, "He borrowed my horse without a by-your-leave. I reckon it's fair for me to borrow his six-shooter."

Joey saw someone running toward them in the shadows. He feared at first that they had been discovered, but the woman emerged into the moonlight. Urgently she told Tolley, "Farlow's pretty far gone. Miller Dawson is drinkin' with him to keep him that way. Said we'd better git while the gittin's good."

Farther up the canyon, the racket of whiskey-driven revelry continued, and the tone of shouting at the farthest shack indicated that there might be a fistfight. Beau said, "I don't see how we can slip past all them heathens without bein' caught."

She pointed southward. "Mr. Dawson said go out the lower end and follow the creek down to where it runs into a bigger canyon. He said Tolley knows the way."

Tolley boosted Alta into a man's saddle, which pushed her long skirt far up her legs. He said, "I've only been out that direction once. We're liable to wander around lost in them cedarbrakes."

Alta replied, "Mr. Dawson said if we travel south long enough we'll strike an old military road that goes east to San Antonio and west to El Paso."

They started in a walk, trying to make as little noise as possible until they were well away from camp. They had gone perhaps two hundred yards when Joey heard a loud commotion from the direction of Farlow's cabin and Farlow's gruff voice shouting into the night. His shout was followed by two gunshots that echoed and re-echoed like a ricochet against the canyon walls.

Joey chilled. For a moment he was unable to move, staring back toward the camp. He heard Farlow's angry voice again.

Beau shouted, "Don't just sit there! We've got to run them horses out ahead of us."

Joey broke free of his trance and grasped what Beau was saying. If they did not drive the horses away, much of the camp could soon be mounted and in pursuit. Some horses remained in the corral. Joey put Taw into a lope, entering the pen and pushing the horses out to join those that Beau had begun herding southward. A couple cut back toward the camp. One was Miller Dawson's. Beau shouted, "Let them go. We ain't got the time."

They reached the short brush fence that had been thrown up across the narrow end of the canyon to keep the camp's mounts from straying beyond easy reach. Exit by the creek had been closed off by a couple of ropes stretched across the water and tied to trees on either side. Beau and Joey held the horses while Tolley stepped down to cut the ropes.

The woman rode into the creek and passed through the opening, waiting on the other side while the loose horses spilled past her.

Farlow was chasing after them afoot, shouting, firing in their direction. A bullet ripped through the dry brush that constituted the fence. As Tolley swung into the saddle, Joey heard a thump and knew a bullet had struck something solid. Tolley jerked. Joey wondered if he was hit, but he was reassured when he saw that Tolley was still in the saddle and moving. Joey splashed through the narrow opening. Tolley followed closely behind him.

Beau was last to go through. He jumped to the ground, grabbing a handful of cured grass and twisting it, striking a match on the sole of his boot and holding it until the flame began to crackle through the wad of dry vegetation. Git Out did not like the fire and jerked the reins from Beau's hand. Joey caught him before he could run away. Beau shoved the burning material into a clump of dry grass that had grown up into the dead brush. The flames quickly spread along the fence.

Remounting, Beau declared, "They'll play hell makin' a horse come through there 'til the fire dies down."

Joey marveled. "Beau, how'd you think of that?"

"When you're sober you can think up lots of things."

They kept the horses running for a time, until a couple of the loose ones stumbled and fell on the rough ground. Beau said, "We'd better slow down."

Alta declared, "Farlow don't turn loose of anything easy. Soon as he can catch him a horse, he'll be comin'."

Joey added, "We didn't get them all. There was a couple cut back, and two or three more were staked close to the shacks."

Beau said, "If we cripple our horses we'll be afoot, and

then he'll *sure* catch up to us." He frowned at Tolley, hunched in the saddle. "Somethin' wrong?"

"Nothin' as bad as what's behind us. Keep movin'."

From far back, Joey heard a couple more shots.

Beau scattered the riderless horses out into the cedar brush where they would be difficult to find and harder to catch. Joey saw that he had been right about slowing down. The rough terrain prevented the riders from making good time, for gathering clouds were beginning to compromise the moonlight, obscuring the ruts and washouts, the tangles of fallen scrub timber. Joey was gratified that Beau took the lead, seeking the easiest course through the obstacles.

He was amazed at how much Beau had learned during their brief association. There was hope for him yet.

The occasional moments of moonlight and dark shadows cast by the cedar gave the landscape a surreal quality, as in a strange dream Joey occasionally had when he ate something like cucumbers that did not settle quietly in his stomach.

His short stay in the canyon had been bad dream enough to last him the rest of the year, he thought.

By daylight a blanket of gray clouds extended from the eastern horizon all the way to the west, hiding the sunrise. Joey could not even tell for sure in what direction the sun lay. The canyon walls had withdrawn and were not really walls any longer but simply long hills far away. Somehow in the darkness the fugitives had pulled back from the creek that was supposed to point their direction. He was not sure anymore where it was. He turned, but he could see little behind him in the way of landmarks by which he could retrace his steps. He saw no reason he would ever want to.

No one had talked much during the nighttime flight. Now Joey noticed that Tolley was trailing, hunched over so far that the horse's mane was brushing his face. He said, "Beau, somethin's sure enough wrong with Tolley."

Beau turned back, and Joey pulled in beside him. Blood had soaked Tolley's shirt and trouser leg, stained his saddle, and trailed down his horse's left side.

Beau told Tolley, "You should've told us you was hit. You've bled half to death."

Joey saw blood on Tolley's lips. He could hardly hear Tolley's weak voice. "We couldn't stop. We can't stop now."

"You ain't got another mile left in you," Beau said. "Joey, let's help him down." They untied Tolley's blankets from behind the cantle and spread them on the ground, then eased the young man down upon them.

The blood was warm and sticky. Joey tried to wipe it onto his pants, but it would not all come off. The stain on his hands made him want to gag.

Alta had dismounted. She led her horse to where Tolley lay. She choked off a cry as Beau ripped the blood-soaked shirt to reveal a dark and ugly hole still oozing blood. Beau said, "The bullet's in there someplace deep. It never came out."

Tolley's voice was almost too weak to hear. "Keep goin'. You know what they'll do to Alta if they catch her."

Joey did not understand the flush of anger that came over Beau as he glanced up at the woman. "It ain't like she's never had it done to her before."

Alta gave Beau a fleeting look of resentment, then turned her attention back to Tolley. "Can't you take the bullet out?"

Beau's voice was sharp. "What with? A pocketknife?"

Joey did not like the look in Tolley's eyes. He had seen

the same look in Pa, just before the end. Alta knelt to take Tolley's hands in her own and hold them. She leaned forward and kissed him on the forehead, tears running down her cheeks.

Tolley tried to smile at her, but the smile was lost in a fit of coughing. When the coughing stopped, his breathing stopped with it. Alta folded Tolley's arms across his chest.

Beau closed the young man's eyes, then cleared his throat and stood up, removing his hat and looking down at the still figure. "He was an outlaw, you can't get around that. But he was a game little rooster."

Joey shivered uncontrollably and turned away so they would not see the tears that burned his eyes. He had watched his father die. He had found Reuben lifeless in the shed that had been his home, and he had watched Mr. Meacham float away facedown in the Colorado River. Lately, life seemed to have become just one death after another.

When he turned back, Alta was still kneeling beside Tolley, her eyes deeply sad. He said, "You must've loved him."

"I didn't even know him, hardly. But he offered to help me get away from Farlow and that camp. I feel like I'm the cause of him dyin'."

Beau said, "You are. If you hadn't been there . . ."

Joey protested, "Wasn't her that shot him, it was Farlow."

Beau said, "We can't afford to stand around here arguin' about whose fault it was. We've got to figure that Farlow's back yonder someplace, catchin' up."

Alta said, "We can't just leave him lyin' here. The coyotes and the buzzards . . ."

Beau said, "We've got nothin' to dig a grave with."

"We can cover him up with rocks," Joey said. "There's aplenty of them around."

Beau stripped Tolley's gun belt, holster, and pistol from the body, hanging them from the horn of his own saddle. "We may need that six-shooter," he said. "And the rifle he carried, too."

The three gathered stones from nearby and stacked them over the blanket-wrapped body, finishing up with several so large that Joey and Beau had to work together to carry them. Beau said, "I don't think there's a coyote in the country big enough to push those away." He placed Tolley's saddle at the head of the grave. "A poor marker, but it's all we got."

Joey said, "Don't you think we'd ought to say some words over him?"

"I never was one to go to church much. I don't know what a man is supposed to say."

Alta said, "Ashes to ashes, and dust to dust." She bowed her head and began to recite the Lord's Prayer. Beau stared at her in amazement until Joey poked him to remind him he was supposed to bow his head too.

When she was done Beau demanded, "Where'd a woman like you learn to pray like that?"

Her voice was defiant. "A woman like me has got a lot to pray about. I doubt that *you're* any candidate for sainthood, or you wouldn't have been in an outlaw camp."

"I wasn't there because I wanted to be."

"Neither was I."

Joey feared they might waste an hour arguing. "We'd better be movin', or we're liable to see Farlow again."

That jarred them into action. Joey gave Alta a boost up into her saddle before he mounted Taw. Beau attached Tolley's scabbard and rifle to his saddle and said, "Joey, you lead Tolley's horse. Might be we'll need it." He began a winding path through and around the cedarbrakes. After a time Joey moved up even with him. "I thought we was supposed to keep ridin' south."

"We *are* ridin' south."

"No, we're goin' east."

"Boy, you've got no sense of direction. If we was goin' east we'd be facin' into the sun."

"We are, only you can't see it for the clouds."

"You're full of prunes." Beau kept riding. Joey burned with frustration but followed him; he saw no choice.

He could only guess how long and how far they had ridden, snaking their way through the thickets and around the hills. Beau finally reined to a stop and took a worried look in all directions. "I believe we've swung too far west."

Joey argued, "We've been goin' east the whole time."

Alta said, "I believe Joey's right."

Beau's face colored. "You think I don't know east from west? If you don't like the way I'm travelin', you're free to go your own way."

Joey looked to Alta for support, then gave up. He followed Beau, though he was convinced the cloudy skies had left his cousin disoriented. Much later, Beau hauled up suddenly and examined the ground. "Here's fresh horse tracks. Farlow must've got ahead of us some way."

Joey dismounted for a close look. He decided the tracks had been made by four horses. One looked familiar. He led Taw a few steps and checked the impressions the hooves had just made. They were identical to one of the other sets.

"That's our own tracks," he said. "We've gone in a circle."

Beau snorted. "That can't be."

"Look at them yourself. There's Taw and Git Out's, and them yonder is from Alta's and Tolley's horses."

Beau declared, "You're wrong." But his eyes betrayed

him. He knew. "All right. Just to prove you're mistaken, we'll go your way a while."

Joey pointed in the direction the old tracks led. "That's south." Alta nodded agreement.

Beau did not accept defeat with any grace. "If we wind up back in that canyon with Farlow and them, don't blame me."

Before long they approached the place where they had laid a cairn of rocks over Tolley. Breaking out of a cedar thicket, Joey saw too late that a horse and a man stood beside the grave.

"That damned Farlow!" Beau exclaimed. He seemed paralyzed.

Alta said, "You've got Tolley's rifle. Use it."

Beau made no move toward the weapon.

Alta demanded, "Have you never shot a man before?"

"I've felt like it a few times, but I never did it."

Bitterly she said, "Then give me the rifle. I can shoot him. I'd shoot *myself* before I'd let him get ahold of me again."

Beau said, "Maybe he'll decide to back away."

Joey doubted that. Farlow had seemed the kind who would charge into hell with a bucket of water and challenge the devil to fight. He might not be smart, but he was determined.

The man at the grave had seen them. He mounted and began moving their way. Reluctantly Beau drew the rifle from its scabbard.

Joey studied the oncoming figure. "Wait a minute, Beau. That looks like Mr. Dawson's roan horse."

Beau lowered the rifle and blinked. "You sure?"

Joey did not reply until he was certain. "It's him. And that's Mr. Dawson ridin' him."

Miller Dawson had come equipped for a long trip, blankets tied behind his saddle, a sack of supplies dangling from the saddle horn. He seemed relieved at the sight of the three riders, especially Joey. He said, "Boy, I'd about given you up. I was afraid you'd ridden off the edge of the earth."

"Seemed like it for a while. Beau got lost."

Joey caught a reproachful glance from Beau.

Dawson said, "I didn't figure on anybody but Tolley and this woman leavin' camp." He fixed an accusing gaze on Beau. "I suppose it was your idea to take Joey and go too."

"You know I never wanted to be there in the first place."

"You could've got this boy killed." He turned back to Joey. "Anyway, I'm glad it's not you in that grave. Everybody's here but Tolley. I suppose it's him?"

Beau replied, "He caught a bullet in his lung leavin' camp. Farlow's doin'."

If Dawson was much moved, he hid it well. "Too bad, but the business he was in, he didn't stand much chance to get a lot older. If it hadn't been Farlow it'd've been some sheriff or ranger." He gave Alta a dark look. "Too bad it couldn't be over somethin' worth dyin' for, like a sackful of silver."

Joey was puzzled. First Beau and now Dawson were acting as if the whole thing had been on account of Alta. Well, he supposed a person could look at it that way. If she had not been in camp in the first place, none of this would have happened. But he figured Farlow must have told her a lot of lies to get her to leave San Antonio with him, and then she was trapped with no way to get out on her own. Helping her escape was the decent thing to do, and to Tolley's credit he had chosen to do it. *Anybody* could have a streak of bad luck. Joey had been having one himself lately, a long one. That wasn't his fault and he couldn't see where this was Alta's.

People kept telling him he would understand things better when he got older. He wished that time would hurry up and get here.

{ TWELVE }

D awson leaned forward in the saddle, rebuke in the twist of his face. "You-all've been circlin' like a blind goose ever since you left this spot. I gave up tryin' to follow you. Damned poor way to treat this boy, ridin' around lost and hungry."

Beau said defensively, "It's hard to tell directions when the sun's covered up and you've got no landmarks. We ought to've had a compass."

"I never had a compass in my life, and I've been all over this country in fair weather and foul."

Joey pointed. "I kept tryin' to tell him that way is south."

Beau gave him a look that would have meant a paddling if it had come from Pa.

Dawson indicated with his chin, a little off Joey's direction and far from Beau's. "Yonder is south. If you're ready, we'll be gettin' started."

Beau was surprised enough to put aside his pique at Joey. "You're goin' with us?" He did not hide his reservations.

"Only for a while, to get you as far as the road. Then I've got some bankin' business to see about."

Joey could guess the kind of business Dawson intended

to transact. "Thought you was stayin' in camp a while to rest."

"Won't be much rest there after last night's ruckus. I'm afraid the camp may be done for."

Beau turned a concerned gaze northward, in the direction of the canyon. "Farlow ain't a man to give up easy. He's probably followin' us."

"He won't be followin' anybody unless it's as a ghost. He sobered up enough to figure out that I was lettin' his woman slip away. He came back on the fight and I had to shoot him."

Alta demanded, "He's dead?"

Dawson gave her another accusing stare. "On account of you, he didn't leave me no choice."

She seemed about to weep but broke into hysterical laughter instead. Beau looked at her askance. "A man bein' dead ain't somethin' to laugh about, even if he *was* a rattlesnake."

Joey realized she was not laughing because something was funny. Her kind of laugh was a form of crying.

Beau was puzzled. "Farlow could go fetch him another woman any time he wanted to. He was probably gettin' tired of this one anyway. We saved him havin' to get rid of her."

Joey did not like Beau's tone. He talked about Alta as if she were not beside him, hearing everything he said.

Dawson said, "You don't understand a man like Farlow and the way he saw things. To him she was property, like his horse. He might sell his property, maybe give it away or even destroy it. But for somebody to take it was like slappin' him in the face." Dawson was grim. "Farlow needed killin', but I never liked puttin' a man in the ground."

Beau said, "The rangers talk like you've done a lot of it."

"Tell a lie often enough and it's as good as the truth." Dawson turned to Alta, his voice severe. "If you hadn't come out to the camp with him, none of this would've happened."

Alta brought her emotions under control. "You've never been where I was. He didn't have to promise much to get me to go."

Beau gave her a look like a preacher confronting an unrepentant sinner. "I doubt that anybody held a gun to your head to make you do what you was doin' in San Antonio."

"They didn't have to. When you've been hungry enough, long enough, you'll do just about anything."

Joey was stirred to anger. "You-all quit pickin' on her. You act like everything's her fault."

Beau glared at him. "You're a boy. When grown men talk, boys listen."

Alta said sharply, "But sometimes men don't know what they're talkin' about. I can go on from here by myself. You men don't need to trouble yourselves about me any longer."

Dawson frowned. "You've got nothin' but the clothes on your back, and they ain't much. No blankets, no grub. Like as not you'd get lost and die, and you wouldn't even have anybody to bury you."

Her blue eyes flashed. "You've made it clear I'm not worth the trouble."

"The trouble's over with. I reckon there's no more damage you can do. So come on, I'll show you-all to where you can find your own way out." His sharp tone brooked no more argument.

Dawson took the lead, Alta following close behind him. Beau and Joey dropped back a little. Joey could tell that

Beau was peeved at him for what he had said. Well, that was all right. Joey was a little peeved too. He said, "I don't see why you've got to keep diggin' at Alta so."

"Boy, there's a lot you need to learn about the world and about women like her."

"I already know more than you think I do."

"But not half as much as *you* think. Most of what you know ain't true."

"I just want you to quit bein' so hard on her."

"Looks to me like you're in danger of comin' down with a bad case of puppy love. She's a way too old for you, and the wrong sort of woman at that. I've had my share of experience with her kind. Most of it took on a sour taste before it was over and done with. They ain't got true feelin's like normal people. They're all warped inside, like my mama was when she went off and left me."

"Alta's had a lot of bad luck, is all."

"Bad luck is when people like me and you get in trouble through accident. I expect she walked into hers with both eyes open."

Joey let himself stare at Alta, riding a length behind Dawson with her skirt pushed up and her legs exposed almost to the knees. He would not tell Beau, but she did look pretty good. "All the same, I want you to quit pickin' on her."

"We'll get her to the San Antonio road, and then we'll be shed of her."

Joey knew nothing about the geography of the land they traveled through. Dawson explained that rough terrain prevailed all the way south to the Rio Grande . . . cedarbrakes, broken hills, canyons, and hollows. Cutting through an otherwise dry land were many small creeks and such major rivers as the Guadalupe and the Frio and the Nueces as well as branches of the Llano. The cedar and live oak would prevail most of the way, replaced by cactus and huisache, creosote and other desert vegetation near the Mexican border.

"Ain't good for much except stock raisin'," he said, "especially sheep and Mexican goats. You'll find where people have broke out small farms in some flats and valleys, but most of the land has got too much up and down to it, and solid rock that reaches halfway to China. Lots of deer and turkey and javelina hogs, though. It was a great country for the Indians. They sure hated to give it up."

Joey asked, "How far this way are we goin'?"

"To an old emigrant and army road. When we get there, you and Beau can go west to Fort Stockton, then out to Fort Davis and El Paso. From there you can go to Arizona, California, wherever you want to. And this good lady can go east back to San Antonio." His ironic tone contradicted the term *good lady*.

Alta said nothing.

Joey said, "Mr. Dawson, how about you goin' west with us?"

"I'd like to. I'm tired of lookin' over my shoulder all the time. They say up in Oregon there's the prettiest cropland a man ever saw. Maybe I could go back to usin' my own name and fix a farm up real nice. Then I could send for my boy."

"Go with us then, why don't you? Oregon ain't far from California, the way I remember the map."

"A man's got to have money to buy a farm. I figure if I get real busy I'll have enough before long."

"The rangers might catch you first."

"They talk brave, but they ain't been all that eager to get real close."

They almost got too close while Dawson was talking. Joey's sharp eyes caught a glimpse of horsemen half a mile in front of them. He gave the alarm. Dawson pulled away toward a thick growth of cedar. "You-all keep goin' like you are. I'll catch up to you later."

Beau tensed. "Looks to me like a posse. They could be comin' for me and you, Joey."

Joey's skin prickled. "They might, but they're bound to've seen us already. Taw ain't fast enough to get away."

Beau's jaw set firmly. "We'll have to lie our way out. You've got so good at it, I worry about you." He turned to Alta. "You string along with whatever I say."

"Then you'd better talk like you had good sense."

Joey counted nine men. One wore a ranger badge, another a star that Joey supposed marked him as a sheriff. The rest had no badges that he could see. They were probably sworn in as temporary deputies to legalize whatever they might do.

The men reined into a semicircle around Joey, Beau, and Alta. The ranger moved closest, giving each of the three a hard scrutiny before he spoke. His gaze dwelt longest on Alta. Most women rode sidesaddle, and she was riding astride in a long dress not made for it. Obviously she looked out of place. He demanded of Beau, "Who are you, and what is your business?"

Joey could almost see the wheels of imagination grinding in Beau's head. Beau said, "Name's Smith. Me and my wife and our boy, we're on our way to visit her kinfolks."

"You're travelin' awful light."

"We're not goin' far, just down on the Frio."

The ranger studied Alta critically. "This lady's face is

bruised. Ain't many things I hate worse than a man that beats his wife."

"She fell off of her horse."

Alta backed him with a nod.

The ranger did not appear satisfied, but he seemed to have more pressing business. "We've been informed that there's an outlaw camp somewhere north of here."

"That might be so. Been some hard-lookin' characters come past our place from time to time."

"Where is your place?"

Beau jerked his thumb back over his shoulder. "That way."

"I don't suppose you'd know where their hideout is at?"

"Them canyons look pretty much alike. But if that camp is there, and you keep lookin', I'll bet you find it."

"We intend to do that. We mean to make this a fit country for raisin' families."

"That sure would be an improvement," Beau agreed.

The ranger had not shed all his suspicion. He gave Alta's face another study. "How long you folks been married?"

Beau said, "Since before the boy was born. He's ten."

"Twelve," Joey corrected him. "Goin' on thirteen. You never did learn arithmetic."

The ranger almost smiled. "Honor thy father and mother, son, even when they can't do sums."

The posse rode on northward, and Beau lost no time striking out to the south, looking back often to be sure the ranger did not change his mind. For the next couple of miles Joey kept looking for Dawson but could not see him. Then suddenly Dawson materialized beside him, popping out of a thicket.

He asked, "Them fellers say they was lookin' for anybody in particular?"

Joey said, "They're lookin' for your camp, and they're goin' in the right direction to find it. I suppose you'll want to circle back and warn your friends." He hoped not, for he would hate to see Dawson go.

Dawson gave the question hardly a moment's thought. "Them boys're friends to nobody but themselves. They're a bunch of crooks anyhow."

They came without much warning upon the wagon road, a pair of twin ruts which iron-rimmed wheels had ground into fine gravel and caliche powder through years of passage. Dawson was gratified at finding no fresh tracks. "Been a while since anybody's passed this way, so maybe you'll have the road to yourselves. I reckon this is where we part company." He lifted off a sack of food hanging from his saddle horn. "Girl, you take enough out of this to carry you a couple of days. The boys can have the rest of it."

Joey argued, "You'll need to eat too."

"I've got some friends to the south a ways. They'll see that I don't go hungry." Dawson took several silver coins from his pocket and offered them to Alta. "You'll strike a crossroads store about half a day east. You can buy enough grub to get you the rest of the way to San Antonio."

She sternly refused the money. "Keep it. I've done nothin' to earn it. If anything, I owe you for puttin' Farlow away. And I ain't left anything in San Antonio that I want to go back for. I'm headin' west."

Joey was pleased, but Beau protested, "You ain't goin' with us!"

"I can travel by myself, in front of you or behind you, whichever way you want it. But I'm goin' west."

Dawson shrugged. "You-all work that out to suit your-selves. I'm headin' on."

Joey pleaded, "I do wish you'd go with us, Mr. Dawson."

"Can't. There's a little bank down south that's gotten a-way too fat on high interest."

"What about Oregon?"

"It'll still be there when I get done. Anyway, I'll prob-ably catch up with you-all long before you get to Califor-nia." He clamped a firm hand on Joey's shoulder. "You take good care of yourself, young'un. You remind me an awful lot of . . ." He broke off in midsentence and turned away. Joey watched him so long as he was in sight and kept watching a while after Dawson disappeared beyond a green clump of live-oak trees.

Beau and Alta argued over the division of the food Daw-son had left them. Each wanted the other to take more.

Joey said, "If you-all would halfway try to get along, we could all ride together."

Alta said to Beau, "He makes sense. I'm surprised he's kin to you."

"Second cousin, is all."

Joey decided the two would not stop arguing, so he picked up the sack, hung it from his own saddle horn, and turned Taw west. Presently he heard the horses lop-ing up behind him, but he made it a point not to turn and look back. He had heard all the foolishness he wanted to listen to.

Neither Beau nor Alta had anything to say. Their silence was as loud as an angry shout. Beau pulled up beside Joey and gave him a look of recrimination. Joey turned his face away and ignored him. Alta tagged along several paces be-hind, in no better humor than Beau.

The road meandered, seeking the levelest course among

the hills, for heavily laden wagons would have been hard put to climb most of them. It crossed a couple of creeks where Joey would have liked to stop to rest a while, but he figured Beau and Alta would launch another argument if he did. So long as they kept riding, they stayed apart.

For the life of him, he couldn't see what they had against one another. Beau had his faults, but he was not bad company when he stayed sober. Joey didn't know much about Alta except that she was looking better to him all the time. He gathered that her life in San Antonio would not have pleased Preacher Johnson. Dawson had called her a sporting woman, and Joey had a good notion what he meant. But as far as he knew she hadn't killed anybody. That put her a notch or two above him and Beau, so he didn't see any reason for Beau to look down on her.

It was Beau who finally called on Joey to halt. "We rode all night, and we've rode all day. Unless we can ride dead horses all the way to California, we'd better quit a while."

The sun was still an hour or so above the western horizon, but Joey could see another nice creek crossing ahead, with shade and plenty of grass for the mounts. "That place up yonder looks pretty good."

Beau did not offer to help Alta down from her horse. Joey thought about it but feared he might embarrass himself by letting her fall. She dismounted easily enough without help and stood a minute holding onto the saddle, her legs weak from the long ride.

Beau ordered, "Build us a fire, Joey, so she can fix us somethin' to eat."

Joey retorted with sarcasm, "You're back to givin' orders, are you?"

"I'm the only man here."

Alta demanded, "Where is the law written that there always has to be a man in charge?"

"I think it's in the Bible someplace."

Joey doubted that Beau had ever read the Bible past Genesis, if that far. He saw that the situation was about to deteriorate into argument. "All right, I'll build the fire. No use in havin' a fight."

He saw plenty of dry timber lying about, dead limbs broken off by the wind. As he picked it up, a distant movement caught his eye. He discerned a white-tailed doe inching out into the open from a live-oak motte, taking a step and cautiously looking around before she took another. Near where Beau was unsaddling the horses, Joey dropped the wood he had gathered.

"Let me have Tolley's rifle," he said. "I'll get us somethin' fresher than salt pork for supper."

"Boy, you'll just shoot your own toe off or hit one of us."

"I'll bet I'm a better shot than you are. Give me the rifle."

Reluctantly Beau complied. "Be careful where you point that thing. You could kill somebody."

"I don't aim at anything I don't intend to hit."

Beau snorted. "Anything you hit, I'll carry back to camp in one hand."

Joey had never had reason to tell Beau that Pa had taught him how to use a rifle when he was seven, figuring that the earlier a boy learned, the less likely he was to be careless later in life.

He slowly picked his way through a protective thicket, watching his footing so he would not step on a dead limb and break it, startling the doe. He could not see her, but that meant she could not see him either. When the timber began to thin in front of him, he stopped and held still while he located her. She stood just a few yards out into an opening, browsing on a low-growing shrub. She would take a bite, then jerk her head up, wary eyes seeking any excuse to set her bounding back into the wood. Joey measured his steps, moving only when she dropped her head for a bite, stopping as soon as she looked up. She seemed to sense danger, for she turned as if to run. But she stopped to look again.

Joey braced the rifle against a tree. He could only hope its aim was true; he had not had a chance to sight it in. He squeezed the trigger. The doe made a high leap, then was back in the timber.

Beau had sneaked up behind while Joey was intent on the doe. "Told you you couldn't hit anything."

At another time Joey would have been irked at Beau because he had risked frightening away the deer, but now he was too chagrined over the thought of having missed. "I had my sights set dead on. Ain't no reason not to've hit her. This rifle must be off."

Beau gave him no quarter. "Someday you'll learn not to make a brag you can't back up."

Joey stubbornly refused to concede. He walked to the place where the doe had grazed. Seeing a large blood spot in the grass, he ventured into the motte. There she lay, her open eyes glazing in death.

Joey returned to the edge of the timber, put his fingers in his mouth, and whistled for Beau. Pointing to the carcass, he threw his chest out a little. "Which hand you goin' to carry her in?"

"Lucky shot. Don't let it go to your head."

Joey stood back and let Beau do the bloody work of gutting her. Beau cut into the paunch. It emitted an unpleasant smell.

Joey demanded, "What did you do that for?"

Beau was a little testy over having been proven wrong about Joey's marksmanship. "Wouldn't want to pass up a chance to find a hair ball. The right kind makes a good madstone."

Joey had never seen a madstone, but he had heard of its use to draw out the poison after a bite by a rabid animal. He did not know if there was anything to it or if this was another notion like turning a dead snake onto its back to bring rain. Reuben had always disclaimed superstition, but any time he had killed a snake around the barn or in the field, he had left it belly up. "A farmer grabs ahold of any chance he can get," he had said.

Beau hoisted the doe up onto his shoulder. Joey considered another jibe about his not carrying it in one hand, but the humor would be wasted on Beau. He might throw down the carcass and let Joey carry it.

Movement at the edge of the thicket drew Joey's gaze to two gray doglike animals, watching warily.

"Lobo wolves," Beau said.

Joey felt a tug of fear. He had never seen a wolf before, but he had heard and read many scary stories. "Reckon they're dangerous?"

Beau showed no concern. "They would be if we was sheep."

Alta had started a fire. She made a tentative smile at the sight of Beau carrying the deer. It was the first time Joey had seen any real light in her eyes except for anger. Her voice mocked Beau a bit. "Joey's a better shot than you reckoned him for."

"Just lucky. Probably couldn't do it again if we gave him a week." Beau got a rope and suspended the carcass from an outstretched live-oak limb, just high enough that he could reach it handily. He skinned it partway and cut out the back strap. To Alta he said, "I remember you was cookin' for Farlow, along with whatever else you was doin' for him. Reckon you can do somethin' with this?"

The warmth vanished from Alta's eyes. "I can, but I don't know if you can eat it with your throat cut."

"You've sure got a sour disposition."

"It's the company I've been keepin'." She glanced at Joey. "I didn't mean you. You're a good boy."

Joey was torn between gratification over the compliment and the fact that she called him *boy*. He wondered how long it would be before people stopped doing that.

Beau said, "This'll be enough for supper. I better hoist that carcass up higher. Them wolves might take a notion to come into camp in the night and help theirselves to it." He turned back to Alta, a touch of sarcasm in his voice. "You're not afraid of lobo wolves, are you?"

"Up against some of the men I've known, a wolf is as harmless as a collie pup."

Beau untied the half hitch which had secured the rope and raised the carcass high enough that the hind legs touched the tree limb. Holding the rope taut, he walked to the base of the live oak to secure it.

Joey heard a buzzing sound and saw a flash of movement. Beau cried out and let go the rope. The deer fell, landing with a thump. Beau hopped backward on one leg.

"Rattlesnake!" he shouted.

Joey froze in place. His mind flashed back to his own bedroom encounter with a rattler. He wanted to rush to help Beau, but he could not force his legs to move. For a panicked moment he feared that the snake was coming for him too. A wild notion flashed through his mind that this was the same one, trying to finish a job at which it had failed the first time.

Beau's excited voice broke Joey's trance. Beau sat on the ground, holding his left ankle and shouting, "Kill it! Kill it quick!"

Joey wanted to comply, but his legs felt as if he were bogged to his knees in mud. A movement in the grass drew his attention to a long grayish shape slithering away. He threw a large stone and missed. He followed, picking up the same stone for another try, but the snake vanished down a hole at the base of a rat's nest.

He turned back to see about Beau. Alta was already there, fingers racing to unlace Beau's shoe. In a rushed voice she said, "We've got to get it off before the swellin' starts, or you'll have to cut it loose."

Beau was cursing, partly under his breath, partly aloud. He sucked a sharp breath between his teeth as the venom's fire began taking hold. He demanded of Joey, "Did you get him?"

"He went down a hole."

"Damn it, you've got to kill the snake that bites you or you'll die from the poison."

Alta was examining the bite. Joey could see two tiny blood drops where the fangs had sunk in. "Superstition," she snapped. "Joey, fetch me his skinnin' knife."

Beau gasped in pain. "What you goin' to do?"

"Cut that wound open and let the blood bring out as much of the poison as it will."

She held the blade over the fire, then made a deep slit across the two fang marks. Beau jerked so hard he almost knocked the knife out of her hands. She grabbed his leg.

"Damn you, hold still. If you'd been payin' attention you'd have seen that snake in time to step back. You ought to know this is rattlesnake country." She cut two more slits at right angles to the first. The blood flowed freely at first, then slowed.

"The poison's not all out," she said. She considered the wound as if it were some ugly, crawling thing. "You owe me maybe a hundred dollars for this." She leaned down and pressed her lips over the wound, sucking blood and venom, spitting it out and doing it again. Her face twisted in rebuke. "Don't you ever wash your feet?"

Beau was beginning to break out in cold sweat. "If I only had some whiskey . . ."

"Drinkin' whiskey's the worst thing you could do. Snakebite is just an excuse men use for soakin' their guts in alcohol, like they needed an excuse in the first place."

Despite her efforts, Joey could see that Beau's leg was swelling. Alta's eyes reflected concern. "Joey, run back to where you gutted the deer. Bring me the liver."

"What for?"

"They say raw liver helps draw the poison out. Hurry."

Raw liver . . . madstones . . . probably more superstition, he thought, but this was no time to question anything that might help. He imagined he was running through a gauntlet of snakes, that they lurked beneath every shrub, every weed, striking at him as he passed. His heart felt as if it were swelling to burst. But he forced himself onward to the thicket where the doe had fallen. There the liver should be lying amid the offal.

The two wolves had found it first. They were feeding on the leavings when Joey suddenly burst upon them. They looked up in surprise, then retreated a few steps and faced around, growling protectively over their meal. The nearest had the liver in its mouth, fresh blood dripping from its teeth.

Joey picked up a rock and hurled it, hoping the wolf might drop the liver in its flight. It turned and ran but did not let go of its prize. The two animals disappeared in the timber. Joey ran a few steps after them before stopping in helpless disappointment. He turned and examined the intestines that remained, hoping some of the liver might still be there.

It was gone, all of it.

He trotted back to camp, mindful of the possibility of snakes, and told Alta what had happened.

She said, "Well, then, I reckon we've done all we can."

Beau's face was ashen, something like Pa's and Tolley's had been. It glistened with cold sweat.

Joey shivered. "You think he's goin' to die?"

Alta shrugged. "Snakebite ain't to laugh about, but it doesn't kill as often as folks make out. Your cousin's ornery enough to pull through just to spite the snake. If I was the snake, I'd worry that Beau had poisoned *me*."

Joey pulled a piece of burning wood out of the campfire and carried it to the rat's nest beneath which the snake had disappeared. He poked it into the tangle of dead wood and shoved a rock into the mouth of the hole. He backed away as flames began to lick and crackle through the tinder-dry nest. Two rats skittered away in panic.

Alta asked no questions, but Joey volunteered, "Beau said if we killed the snake the bite wouldn't hurt as bad. So I'm cookin' it."

"It's probably too deep in the hole to feel the heat. Anyway, you can't blame the snake much. It was just doin' what comes to it by nature, like a lot of men swill whiskey and fight and misuse their women."

"Is it nature that makes you and Beau hate each other so much? I keep feelin' like you're about to go to war."

Alta studied Beau's face. His eyes were half open but glazing. In mind and spirit he appeared to have drifted somewhere a long way off. "I don't hate him. It's his high-nosed attitude that makes me so damned mad. But I guess he's not much different from most of the men I've come up against. They think all a woman is good for is to cook and sew and go to bed with them." She studied Joey, her eyes softening. "You're too young to know about that sort of thing."

"I know more than you think." Joey's eyes burned as he considered the possibility that Beau might not live. "He's hard to get along with sometimes . . . drinks too much when he gets the chance. He's talked about leavin' me behind, and I've felt like leavin' him more than once. But he's all the kin I've got."

"He won't be runnin' off and leavin' you now, not with that leg angried up so. If the poison doesn't kill him he'll be hobblin' around lame for a while."

"I don't want him to die. I guess I need him more than I thought I would."

"I think he needs you more than you need him. In some ways you're more grown up than he is. At least you don't condemn a woman without knowin' her side of the story." She touched Joey's hand. "Nobody's said, exactly, but it's plain that you two are runnin' from somethin'."

Joey decided it wouldn't hurt to tell her. He saw no reason she would go blabbing to the law about it, any more than Miller Dawson would have. He explained about Pa and Reuben, about Dulcie and Mr. Meacham. He told how he and Beau had killed Mr. Meacham in self-defense, but the Bastrop sheriff's prejudice against Beau would keep him from believing the way it really happened.

A tear glistened in the corner of Alta's eye, and she wiped it away. "I was an orphan too, time I was seven. A fever epidemic down in Galveston took my mama and daddy. I was passed around by aunts and uncles that didn't want the burden or couldn't afford it, so I ran off when I wasn't much older than you are. It can be a hard, cruel life when you're all alone."

"I'm not plumb alone. I've got Beau."

"That's not much better than bein' by yourself. There's no tellin' what's liable to become of you."

"Me and Beau, we'll do all right when we get to California . . . if he lives through this."

She shook her head. "You're totin' around a lot of trouble for a boy your age."

"I reckon I'm big enough to carry it."

She squeezed his hand, and he warmed in a way that he was not used to. She said, "I believe you are."

{ THIRTEEN }

Joey watched Beau go into a fever and begin talking in a way that might as well have been German for all the sense he could make of it. He lost interest in supper, but Alta fried a piece of venison and made him eat it.

She said, "If you don't put somethin' in your stomach, you'll wind up as sick as he is."

"Beau needs a doctor."

"It's probably two, three days to where one lives. By the time you could get there and back, he'd either be dead or gettin' better anyway." She patted Joey's hand, trying to calm his fear. "Don't fret so. I'm not goin' to let him die."

Lacking anything more effective, she gathered several juicy prickly-pear pads. She split one and bound it over the wound, sticker side up. "I've heard of people usin' them on gunshot wounds. Can't do any harm on a snakebite, and it might even do him some good. Wish we had that doe's liver."

Joey took the rifle and went out hunting for another deer. All he saw were a few elusive wild turkeys and the two wolves, which kept their distance as if they knew he had the gun. He stayed out until dark, then used the flickering campfire to guide him back, empty-handed and discouraged.

Alta hugged him in an attempt to lighten his burden. "You did the best you could."

The hug was not much comfort. "My best wasn't enough."

"Nobody could ask for more. But of course, sometimes they do. They forget we're only human. We can't always live up to other people's notions." She tried a reassuring smile but couldn't bring it off. "I'm talkin' about me, not you."

"Anything you ever did, I know you had a reason for it."

"You ever been hungry, Joey? I mean hungry for days and days, 'til you hurt all over and couldn't walk straight and your gut was tied in a knot?"

Joey had missed some meals since running away from home, but he knew she was talking about something far more extreme. "I guess I ain't."

"There comes a time when you've got no will of your own anymore. You'll do anything they tell you to, just to stop the hunger. And you'll keep on doin' it so the hunger won't come back."

"I understand."

"I doubt that you do, but you're nearer to it than Beau and most of the other men I've come across." She reached out to touch his cheek. "Don't you grow up to be like them. Hang onto your understandin' ways."

"I think Beau would understand if you told him how it was."

"He'd have to hold still and listen. Right now he's holdin' still, but I'm afraid he wouldn't hear anything I told him." She leaned over Beau and felt his face. From her expression Joey knew she did not like what she found.

"This cloth I put over his head has dried out," she said. "Run down to the creek and wet it again, would you?"

Joey brought back the cloth, dripping water. She washed sweat from Beau's face and neck, then folded the cloth and laid it across his forehead. She unwrapped the pear pad and found it almost dry. Beau's fever had drawn the moisture from it. She applied the other half of the pad.

Alta said, "You'd just as well go to sleep. I'll keep a watch on Beau."

Joey tried. He wrapped himself in his blanket, then turned one way and the other, trying to find comfort. He could hear Beau mumbling at times. The faint light from the dwindling fire fell upon Alta, sitting at Beau's side, turning the cloth that covered his forehead. After a long while Joey fell into a fitful slumber and aroused a frightening dream of a snake on his bed, striking at him, sinking its fangs into his flesh. He shouted in imagined pain. He felt something shaking him and thought it was the snake.

Alta's voice was soft. "Joey! You're hollerin' in your sleep."

Joey was suddenly wide awake and trembling, his face covered with cold sweat. "A snake had hold of me," he said, ashamed for his involuntary outburst. He cast the blanket aside and raised up to look toward his cousin. "How is he?"

"No worse that I can see, but no better either."

"I'm awake now. I can watch after him a while." He knew it had been two nights since Alta had slept.

"No, I'm not sleepy. I've got to keep that cloth wet 'til his fever breaks." She remained at Beau's side, fighting the sleep that tugged at her eyelids.

Joey fed the fire to prevent its going out. Beau had assured him the wolves presented no danger, but it didn't hurt to be on the safe side. He made sure the rifle lay within arm's length. Alta had removed Beau's trousers. Joey wondered about the propriety but decided proprieties didn't count for much in an emergency. Alta had split Beau's long underwear from the ankle to the thigh. His left leg had swollen far beyond its normal size.

Joey remembered the times he had considered riding away and leaving Beau to fend for himself. He whispered, "Beau, don't you go off now and leave me."

In spite of his best intentions, Joey dozed just as the black sky began to pale in the east. He awoke with a start as a voice growled, "Where the hell are my pants?"

The voice was Beau's. He found Beau staring at him with wide-open eyes. Joey felt a stinging of tears as he realized his cousin was not only alive but in a quarrelsome mood. That was a good omen for recovery.

Alta had remained at Beau's side, though Joey suspected she had dozed just as he had. Sleepy-eyed, she retorted, "What do you care? You're not goin' out in company."

Beau turned his attention to her. "It's just you after all."

"Who did you think it was?"

"I halfway woke up a couple of times. Thought I saw an angel sittin' where you're at. She looked a little like you, but you haven't got any wings. Guess I was dreamin'."

"I guess you were. Nobody's called me an angel since I was three years old."

Joey said, "She watched over you all night to make sure you didn't die. An angel couldn't have done any better."

"I'm obliged to you," Beau told her, "but I didn't have any intention of dyin'. I've got my cousin to look out for." He raised up to a sitting position and gingerly lifted the blanket from his leg. It remained badly swollen. He removed the prickly-pear poultice, wincing as some of the tiny needle-sharp spines punched into the tips of his fingers. The entry point of the fangs was angry looking and darkly discolored.

He reverted to complaint. "Look where you cut me with that knife. Probably gave me blood poisonin'."

Alta responded in the same kind of voice. "Your blood's been poisoned since you were old enough to crawl. Keep your dirty fingers away from that cut or you'll probably lose your leg." She split another pear pad and applied its wet side to the still weeping wound. She bound it in place with the same strip of cloth she had used before.

Beau's voice softened with worry. "It don't look any too good, does it?"

"Better than I thought it might. Appears to me the swellin' hasn't got any worse the last few hours. But you won't be walkin' on that leg for a while, or ridin' a horse."

Beau gave the spartan camp a critical look. "We can't just stay here."

"Why not? There's water in the creek. That doe will last us a couple of days, and Joey's a good shot. We oughtn't to lack for meat. This road looks like it's still used once in a while. Somebody might come along."

"That's what I'm afraid of."

"You've already proved you can lie to the law and make them believe it. Just tell them we're a family down on our luck. They might even leave us some provisions." She added, "We're a long ways from Bastrop."

Beau turned his gaze to Joey. "You told her?"

"I didn't see no harm in it. I thought she ought to know who she's travelin' with and have a chance to leave if she didn't like it . . . like you wanted to leave Mr. Dawson."

"If you'll remember, Dawson wouldn't let us."

"But we wouldn't stop Alta if she wanted to go, would we?"

Beau gave her a concerned study. "We've got no hold on her. She's free to do whatever she wants to."

Alta nodded. "Just remember you said that, because if you give me any more fuss I'm liable to leave you sittin' here. And I might take Joey with me."

Joey knew he wouldn't go, but he wouldn't say so. Maybe if Beau had to worry about it he would improve his behavior.

Beau attempted to arise but quickly gave up, sweat breaking out on his face again. It was evident he wasn't going anywhere. "Lady, you never saw a man more meek and mild."

Their departure from the outlaw camp had been too sudden to allow much preparation. Supplies were scant beyond blankets and the food Dawson had given them. Tolley had farsightedly put a hatchet in his war bag along with a coffeepot and a skillet, which Beau had found after Tolley's death. Joey used the hatchet to cut firewood. He smoothed out a spot beneath the heavy shade of a live-oak motte.

Alta told Beau, "Joey and me are goin' to carry you over there where you'll be sheltered from the sun. It's liable to be a rough ride, but at least it'll be a short one."

"I'm too heavy for you-all. You're liable to hurt yourselves. I'll make it by myself if I have to walk on all fours."

It was the first time Joey could remember Beau showing real concern for Alta.

She said, "And maybe cripple yourself for life? You just lie there and be still."

Alta gripped the blankets above Beau's head and Joey those by his feet. Joey strained hard to lift the weight, but his back and arms were strong. Farm work had accomplished that. He and Alta had to set Beau down once to rest a moment. Alta let her end of the blankets slip enough that Beau dropped the last foot or so to the ground.

"Sorry," she apologized.

"Didn't hurt a bit," Beau said, though Joey knew from his expression that it had.

He wished they had a tent to keep Beau out of the rain, but this did not look like a country where it rained often. With a little luck perhaps they would dodge that problem. By the way the smaller trees leaned, Joey judged that the prevailing winds came from the south. He dug a new fire pit just east of the motte so the smoke would not likely bother Beau. Joey puzzled as he watched Alta stretch one of Tolley's blankets between two trees, forming a screen of sorts. She spread her own blankets just beyond.

"There's times a woman needs privacy," she explained.

Back home, Joey had always thought it would be fun to go camping, though Pa never seemed to have the time. The nearest Joey had come to it had been to spend the day down on the creek, fishing. Now he had the real thing. All in all, he thought, this was shaping up to be as comfortable a camp as anybody could ask for under the circumstances. It would be disloyal to feel glad Beau had gotten himself snakebitten, but inasmuch as it had happened anyway, Joey intended to make the most of it.

Other people had camped here over the decades since the military had seen fit to lay out the road. Joey found charred remnants of old campfires along the creek, as well as rusty cans, some pieces of broken harness, and a blackened pocketknife with both blades broken off. Walking

along the bank, he came upon a long, thin tree limb leaning against a heavy live oak. It showed signs of having
been trimmed neatly. On closer inspection he found a
length of rotten string tied to the end of it and a fish hook
at the end of the string. Up from the hook was a piece of
cork that had been a floater. He could only surmise that
someone had been fishing here and had left it, intending
to come back.

The string was so weathered that it broke apart in his
hands. The pole was dried out and too brittle for use. But
at least he could salvage the hook and the cork. It would
be easy enough to whittle a new pole. The problem would
be to find something to serve as a string.

He took his discoveries back to camp and showed them
to Alta and Beau. "I'll bet I could catch all the fish we
would want to eat if I just had a string."

Alta considered it but came up with no answer. Beau,
face still flushed with fever, seemed to have trouble con-
centrating. "The horses," he said finally.

Joey blinked, thinking Beau might have drifted off
into delirium again. "Horses?"

"You ever made a horsehair rope?"

"No."

"I've seen people usin' a rig to twist with, but you can
do it by hand. There's four horses yonder, and they can all
spare some hair out of their tails. Won't take near as much
to make a string as to make a rope."

"You mean I'm supposed to cut part of their tails off?"

"Not all from one place. A little here and a little there.
And be careful they don't kick the whey out of you."

Joey thought it wise to begin with Taw because his horse
would stand still for almost anything short of a dynamite
blast. Like the others, Taw was staked on a long rope. Joey

walked up to him, talking softly, patting him on the neck, then along the withers, gradually working around to the rump. He opened his pocketknife and ran his fingers carefully through Taw's tail to gauge the horse's reaction. There was none. Joey crimped a small sampling of tail hair between the fingers of his left hand, then cut them with the blade. The horse turned his head to look back at him but otherwise made no move.

Joey repeated the action several times until he had a sizeable wad of hair lying on the ground. He stepped back to see if the results of his work were visible. Unfortunately they were. Joey remembered once when he had had his hair cut in town by a barber who had been drinking all day.

"Sorry, Taw, but they'll grow back."

He repeated the operation on Git Out, who was a little more skittish about it than Taw. Joey was careful to do most of the cutting from underneath where it would not show quite so much. He had about the same results from Alta's mount. He tried with Tolley's, but that horse tried to kick him. Joey decided he had hair enough to make a line that would hold any fish he might catch in this stream.

With shaky hands Beau showed him how to twist and plat so that the strength of the individual strands was multiplied by the combination of many. It was slow work and clumsy at first, though gradually Joey got the hang of it. The line became increasingly neat as it lengthened. Joey considered doing the first couple of feet over, but what would a fish know about neatness?

Alta came at times to watch Joey's work and to feel Beau's forehead, to remove the poultice and examine the wound.

"I believe a little of the color is startin' to go out of it," she said.

"Still throbs and burns like old Billy Hell. But it'd be a lot worse if you hadn't sucked so much of that poison out. I know it couldn't have tasted very good."

"Between the venom and the blood and your dirty leg . . . no, it didn't."

"Could be you saved my leg. Maybe even my life. I don't know how I could ever pay you anything, but I owe you."

"I'll settle for a little kindness."

"I ain't run onto any excess of kindness in my life, so I don't know much about givin' it."

"Watch Joey. You could learn a lot from him."

It took Joey most of the day to complete what he thought was enough string. It was prickly to the touch, for the ends of each hair were like tiny needles, but it felt strong enough to hold a fish. He found a branch about the right length and thickness, hacked it off with Tolley's hatchet, then trimmed it up with his pocketknife. He attached the string, the cork, and the hook.

"Some little pieces of this raw bacon ought to be all right for bait," Alta suggested, holding up a slab from the sack Dawson had given them. She sliced off a portion.

Joey gave Beau and Alta a moment's study before he started down the creek. "Don't you-all be fightin' while I'm gone."

Alta smiled. "It wouldn't be any fun, whippin' a cripple."

"I won't be a cripple for long," Beau said. "Soon as this swellin' goes down . . ."

Joey had a notion that the fight had gone out of Beau. Perhaps that snakebite had done him some good.

*   *   *

The fish were slow to hit the hook, but Reuben had always said making a catch wasn't the most important element in fishing. The main thing was to get away from the demands of the busy world and hold a long, quiet conversation with one's self and the Lord. Joey was not sure the Lord was answering back, but it was soothing to the soul to sit still and contemplate the pleasant countenance of this land, the long hills, the grass-carpeted valley divided by the clear, cool waters of the narrow creek.

He knew it was not so peaceful as it might appear. A hawk circled overhead, watching for some smaller bird or animal to grab in its sharp talons. He glimpsed the two wolves prowling at the base of a distant hill, trying to scare up a rabbit or a fawn or whatever else they might turn into an evening meal. He saw a fish dart to the top and swallow a surface-running bug that had the poor judgment to put itself at risk. Joey's own fishing venture, however much it might calm the trouble in his soul, meant the end for whatever unfortunate swimmer that happened to impale itself upon his hook. Almost everything preyed upon something else that it might live. Each creature followed its own nature.

Viewing the world in that light, he could almost understand what had motivated Dulcie and Mr. Meacham, even if he could not bring himself to forgiveness. He supposed a tendency toward greed was part of human nature, just as the hunt was nature to all the predatory creatures. Most people managed to keep it bottled up, but there would always be a few who let it take control of them. It was those who caused most of the trouble in the world, outside of natural disasters such as flood and fire.

Watching the water course southward, foaming as it broke around large stones near the bank, he again imagined he could see Mr. Meacham floating along with the current of the Colorado, bobbing as the cork bobbed on Joey's improvised fishing line. He shivered and forced his mind to other matters. He tried to imagine what California must be like. Folks said the sun shone there all the time. It seemed to shine most of the time in this part of Texas, too. He wondered if he and Beau could find work there. Surely there must be farms in California.

But would they be like the farm back home? It hurt, remembering how things used to be. He wished none of this had ever happened, that he could turn around and go back.

Time would cure Beau's snakebite. But Joey wondered if it would ever cure his own homesickness.

He wondered then about Alta. Chances were that she would not go with them all the way. The law was not hunting for her. She might stop when they got to Fort Stockton or Fort Davis or El Paso. He could already feel the hurt of saying goodbye to her.

His luck as an angler was not so good as he had hoped, but he carried three catfish back to camp, one apiece for their supper. He doubted that Beau would have much appetite.

Alta knelt beside Beau, wiping his face with a wet cloth. Joey feared that Beau's fever had worsened, but the calm expression in Alta's face reassured him.

"He's improvin'," she said. "The fever's down a lot."

He noticed that she was holding Beau's hand. Probably just trying to make him feel better, he thought. At least it did not appear that they had fought while he was gone. That was a welcome change.

Beau sat up to eat his supper. He even tried to push to his feet, but he quickly surrendered to the pain. Joey thought the leg's swelling might be starting to lessen a little. In any case, though, Beau wouldn't be walking or riding horseback for a while yet. That did not trouble Joey nearly so much as he thought it should. There were still a lot of fish in the creek that had not sampled his bait. Tomorrow he would take the rifle and see if he might stalk another deer.

He was in no hurry to put home even farther behind him. Let California wait. It wasn't going anywhere.

When he returned to camp before sundown the next day, he found Beau standing, leaning on a makeshift crutch hacked and whittled from a forked live oak. He was wearing his trousers, which told Joey that the swelling had receded considerably. Joey was torn between pleasure that his cousin was recovering and anxiety that Beau would be raring to leave this good camp.

"That leg's still too sore for you to get on your horse, ain't it?" he asked hopefully. The bite was in the left leg. The left foot went into the stirrup first and had to support the body's full weight as a rider mounted.

"I tried to walk up to Git Out on this crutch, but he snorted and ran to the end of the rope. He doesn't know what to make of a three-legged man."

Joey hoped Beau could not see how relieved he felt that recovery was not *too* swift.

Beau said, "I suppose he was afraid I was goin' to hit him with this stick. I've never beaten a horse in my life. Or a woman either." He turned back toward Alta. "No matter how bad she might've needed it."

She grinned, then Beau did. Joey said, "I'm glad you-all have decided to get along."

Beau said, "I have to. She's the cook."

Alta fried the fish. Beau's appetite was better than Joey had expected, for he ate all of his. Beau said, "We've been here too long. No tellin' when some lawman may happen along with our descriptions in his pocket."

Alta touched Beau's good leg. "Don't be in a rush. We can't leave 'til you can ride."

Joey put in hastily, "Don't that fish taste fine? West of here we may not find any fit for eatin'."

Beau gave in reluctantly. "We won't be stayin' any longer than we have to."

The distant sound was slow to penetrate Joey's consciousness and even slower to identify itself. He had hooked his second fish when he became fully aware of animal bleating which rose and fell with the breeze. He turned his ear toward it.

Sheep. He had not seen a domesticated animal except the horses and the outlaw-camp dogs since they had put the German communities behind them. But incongruous as it might seem so far from any settlement, this sound was coming from sheep.

Pa had never kept any on the farm. He always said they were more trouble than they were worth for the small amount of wool he might shear and the mutton the older animals might provide when age diminished their fleeces. A couple of the neighbors had owned small flocks, however, and had fought to keep the lambs alive against the variety of predators attracted to them: foxes, coyotes, stray dogs. Sheep seemed prey also to every ill known to man or animal.

Even so, and despite Pa's low opinion of them, Joey had always wished they had a few around the place. He liked to watch neighbors' young lambs run and jump and play.

He carried his fish and the pole back to camp. Beau was

standing, leaning on his crutch, eyes squinched as they searched eastward for the source of the sound. Joey's vision was sharper. He picked out the vanguard of the flock. "Yonder they come. There's an awful big bunch of them."

Alta walked up and stood beside Beau. "I see a dog out to one side, and a wagon bringin' up the rear."

Beau grimaced, then accepted the inevitable. "It's too late to break camp, even if I could ride. It don't seem likely that a lawman would be travelin' with a sheep outfit."

Joey said, "Unless it's to guard against outlaws."

"Who'd want to steal a sheep?"

The sheep kept coming, breaking around the camp, some to one side and some to the other, lining up along the bank of the creek. Ewes bleated for lambs that trailed behind them. They all sounded the same to Joey, but evidently the lambs could sort out their mothers' calls, for they were quick to pair up after they stopped at the edge of the water. Lambs eagerly sought the ewes' udders, dropping to their knees to reach the milk. Most of the ewes shunned the faster current, seeking calmer water where it backed up into the flatter portions of the bank. They lowered their heads and drank.

The dog was a collie, its red and white coat rough and unbrushed, leaves and dry grass clinging to the belly hair. Clearly, this was a working dog, not a pet. As Joey walked toward it, it barked a protective challenge and placed itself between him and the nearest sheep.

Joey tried to speak in a reassuring tone. "I'm not fixin' to hurt them. Come here, boy."

The dog approached him cautiously. Joey extended his hand and held still, letting the animal take its time in appraising him. The collie sniffed tentatively at Joey's fingers and found no threat. It began to wag its tail. Then it looked back toward the wagon as if afraid its master might disapprove.

The driver cut through the flock and came directly toward the camp. The wagon was equipped with hoops so it could be covered in the event of wet weather, but the tarp hung loosely over the rear bow and down over the bed. Two mules pulled the wagon. A saddled horse walked along behind, bridle reins tied to the steel rod that held the end gate.

Joey could see that the man was not young, for his short beard was gray. So was the thatch of hair that bushed out beneath the brim of a grimy old felt hat that had the lumpy shape of a half-empty feed sack. He drew up on the lines and shouted at the mules. He took a black pipe from his mouth and studied Joey a moment before he shouted, "I say, my lad, you're not fixing to bite my dog, are you?"

"No sir, I wouldn't do nothin' like that," Joey responded before he realized the sheepman was joking.

The man pulled the brake, then climbed down and tied the reins to the rim of a wheel. The mules did not look as if they had enough ambition to run away.

Joey exclaimed, "I never saw so many sheep in one bunch before. Must be ten thousand of them."

The man's words were crisp and clear but spoken with a bit of an accent that Joey found unfamiliar. "Not quite so many, a couple of thousand not including the lambs. I do not count the lambs until they are raised and ready for market. What the four-legged varmints do not kill, the two-legged ones try to steal."

"I been seein' a couple of wolves around here."

"Well, then, I am afraid Old Rustler may not get much sleep tonight. It is his responsibility to herd the band and protect it." The man shoved his hand forward. It was big and rough, a couple of fingers misshapen from old breaks or perhaps arthritis. Joey's hand disappeared within the enveloping grip. "My name is Alister McIntosh."

"Joey Shipman." Joey heard Beau slowly working his way up from behind, awkward on the crutch. "That's my cousin Beau." Too late he realized he had forgotten their agreed-upon story that their name was Smith and that Beau was his father.

"Beau *Smith*," Beau said, giving Joey a look of silent reproach. He offered McIntosh his hand with poorly disguised reluctance. Joey knew he was uneasy about meeting strangers, at least until they got to California. Beau motioned toward Alta, who was walking out from camp. "That's my wife. Name's Alta. Alta Smith."

McIntosh tipped his hat, giving Alta a moment's special attention. He seemed to accept them all at face value. "You folks appear to have a comfortable camp. I shall move my sheep downstream before dark so they will not be a bother."

Alta said, "I don't see anybody with you. Are you movin' these sheep all by yourself?"

"I had a swamper to drive my wagon and do the cooking. Unfortunately he became ill and had to turn back to Kerrville. I've had no chance to hire anyone else." McIntosh looked at Beau's crutch and the foot held up clear of the ground. Beau still wore only a sock because the swelling had not gone down enough for him to put on his shoe. "Did you break a limb?"

"Rattlesnake. Got me between my ankle and my knee."

McIntosh took a long drag on his pipe. "That is one reason most men wear high-topped boots in this country. The first chance you have, you should buy a pair." He surveyed the camp again. "Are you on the move, or are you settling here?"

Beau said, "We'd be a long ways further west if it hadn't been for that snake. I can't ride a horse yet."

Alta gave the wagon a thoughtful study. "Mr. McIntosh, when you get your sheep settled for the night, why don't you come and eat supper with us? For a change, you won't have to do your own cookin'."

Beau's eyes narrowed with objection, but he did not express it aloud.

"That is most kind of you, young lady. I have subsisted mostly on coffee and smoking tobacco since my swamper turned back. I never quite mastered the art of cooking. Do you have meat in camp?"

The venison was about gone, and Joey had been unable to bag another deer. He said, "We got two fish and some turkey."

"I shall butcher a goat. I always keep a few with the sheep to provide fresh meat." McIntosh turned toward the dog and made a circling motion with his arm, then pointed at the sheep that had moved upstream. "Rustler, round them up."

The dog bounded away, going around until he had passed the last sheep, then moving back, barking. The sheep flushed ahead of him like quail. They skirted past the camp, avoiding the people.

McIntosh said to Alta, "You do not appear to have much in the way of cooking vessels. You will find a keg of sourdough and a couple of Dutch ovens in the wagon, along with flour, coffee, whatever you may need. Please feel free to use all you want, because I have gone hungry for three weeks." He untied the horse from behind the wagon and set off behind the dog and the sheep.

Alta said, "Seems like a nice old man."

"Smart one, too," Beau responded without enthusiasm. "Anybody asks about us later on, he'll remember."

In a while McIntosh returned carrying the freshly skinned and dressed carcass of a goat across his saddle. He hung it from the tree limb beside the remnant of the doe.

Joey had reservations. "I don't think I ever ate a goat."

"Always keep an open mind, my lad, and you will be amazed at the wonders the world can provide." McIntosh rode off cheerfully in the direction of the sheep.

Joey said, "I think I'll go see if he needs any help." He did not wait for permission or denial but set off in a trot.

McIntosh did not herd the sheep together as Joey expected. He allowed them to spread out and nibble at the vegetation. Seeing Joey watching, he rode over to him, removed his black pipe, and pointed the stem of it. He anticipated Joey's question. "It is in the sheep's nature to group together, so they will not stray far. Rustler will bring back any that may display undue independence."

"I don't see how you can handle a big bunch like this, just you and the dog."

"I let the sheep proceed at their own pace and graze as they walk. Rustler and I have only to keep them pointed in the proper direction. Most of the time I follow in the wagon. When necessary, I stop the wagon and use the horse."

"Where are you goin' with this bunch?"

"I have a ranch southwest of Fort Stockton, where mountains and brushy draws provide winter protection. It has been rested all spring and summer. I am in no hurry to reach it so long as I find feed enough along the trail."

"This land don't belong to anybody, so the grass don't cost you nothin'."

McIntosh smiled. "You are a sharp lad. You have already grasped an essential element of the range livestock industry. Never use your own grass until you must, and never buy a new nail if you can straighten a bent one."

The sheep browsed a while, then began lying down. Those on the outer fringe moved in closer to the main body. Joey wondered if they could smell the wolves. Rustler must have, for he paused periodically to look southward as he patroled the flock's perimeter, bringing back a few of adventuresome spirit. The goats remained to themselves but within the larger group of sheep. Joey wondered if they took any notice of the fact that their number had been reduced by one.

McIntosh said, "All appears to be well. Shall we go back to camp and see what your cousin's wife has prepared for supper?"

Joey was taken aback by reference to Alta as his cousin's wife, though he realized that was a natural consequence of Beau's lie about their identity. He was not sure what a sporting woman was supposed to look like, but evidently Alta did not fit the pattern, judging by McIntosh's easy acceptance of the story.

McIntosh said, "Your cousin indicated you are on your way west. Have you a definite destination, or are you simply prospecting?"

Joey thought it best to be noncommittal. "We don't have our minds set, exactly."

McIntosh puffed thoughtfully on his pipe but said nothing more until they were in camp. Alta had a coffeepot suspended from a steel bar set between two upright rods that had holding rings on their upper ends. Two Dutch ovens sat on a bed of hot coals. She said, "Tonight, Mr. McIntosh, I'll cook you a pot of beans that you can carry with you tomorrow when you leave."

McIntosh took a pot hook from its resting place beside a pile of dry wood and lifted the lid from one of the ovens. Sourdough biscuits were browning inside. He lifted the other lid and found goat meat roasting. His eyes lighted with pleasure. "Excellent, young lady, excellent. I have not had a proper meal since my swamper left, and even he was barely adequate."

Alta was unaccustomed to compliments and seemed a little flustered. "If you-all would like to go wash in the creek, supper's about ready."

Joey guessed later that McIntosh ate nearly half of the supper by himself. When everyone finished, little remained except some coffee. McIntosh rubbed his stomach, which did not seem large enough to have accommodated as much as he ate. "I am sure kings have fared less well than I did tonight. You are a most lucky man, Mr. Smith, to have such a wife as this."

Beau seemed startled. He was not accustomed to the fiction of Alta being married to him though he had made up the story himself. "Even a blind hog finds an acorn now and then."

McIntosh concentrated on the fire and puffed his pipe. "I understand, Mr. Smith, that you are eager to be on the move but cannot ride a horse until your leg improves. Could you ride in a wagon?"

Beau considered. "Climbin' up might be tough, but once I'm there I ought to be all right."

"Then allow me to offer you a proposition. You and your lady could drive the wagon. The lad and I could handle the sheep. I would pay your lady to cook for us and allow a stipend to the lad for his help as well."

Beau hedged. "I don't know . . ."

"Mind you, it would be slow. A band of sheep takes its own good time about grazing its way along. But I am bound for Fort Stockton, which is on your way west. You will lose a great deal of time in any case, so why not lose it riding in a wagon instead of waiting here until you are able to ride a horse?"

Beau was slow to answer, but Joey was not. He exclaimed, "Sounds like a good idea to me."

Alta said, "We'll do it."

McIntosh smiled. "Done!"

Beau finally spoke. "I didn't say we would." He saw he was out-voted. "But I reckon we will."

{ FOURTEEN }

McIntosh was out of his blankets before daybreak, so the rest of the camp was awakened by his stirring around. With daylight the sheep began to stand up and start moving, grazing hungrily after a night's rest. McIntosh had breakfast, allowing them ample time to take their fill of water from the creek. When he saw that no more were drinking, he spoke quietly to the dog. "Rustler, get them started."

The collie trotted along the edge of the band, barking, feinting at them. The ewes and lambs moved away from him.

Joey marveled. "Does he understand everything you tell him?"

"He knows the routine of the trail, and a dog learns to understand many words if you speak them to him often enough. He never questions an order, and he never complains. I find the company of a good dog preferable to that of many people."

"My stepmother wouldn't let me have a dog, said they were useless. But I never saw a dog help like Rustler."

"I take it you have never herded sheep, lad?"

"No sir. I don't know the first thing about them."

"No matter. The principal requirement is to be smarter than the sheep. And the village idiot is smarter than a sheep."

Alta supported Beau while he carefully and painfully climbed up the wagon wheel and onto the seat. Then Beau reached down for her. It seemed to Joey that Beau held her longer than was necessary to get her safely into place on the wagon seat. She gave Beau a smile that seemed almost as bright as the sunrise.

Joey had not seen her smile much until now.

On horseback, and with the dog's help, McIntosh and Joey put the band across the narrow creek, starting them in a westerly direction. Joey looked back to be sure the wagon was following. Beau and Alta sat close together, Beau holding the lines. The wagon adhered to the trail, but the sheep spread out south of it, browsing on the vegetation as they moved leisurely along.

Joey asked, "How far will we go today?"

"Perhaps three or four miles, sometimes as much as five. I let the sheep set their own pace. Ewes with lambs are not to be rushed."

"What if you don't find water?"

"Sheep can subsist a long time on moisture from the morning dew and from the plants they eat. Their needs in that respect are less than for cattle. On the other hand they require more protection and care. Cattle can endure in the wild. If domestic sheep were deserted and left on their own, in time they would perish."

"Herdin' sheep looks like an important job, then."

"Yes, to any man who understands the business. Many cattlemen hold a much lower opinion, however. If we should encounter any of those gentlemen along the way, you will find that they do not rate us very highly."

Joey felt uneasy. "You mean we might have trouble?"

"If I expected physical harm I would not let you go with me. But I hope you have a high tolerance for insult."

"My stepmother talked awful hard to me sometimes."

"These gentlemen have expressions your stepmother never heard of. Just remember that dollar for dollar invested, these sheep will probably return twice as much revenue as their cattle. Have pity for the poor and misguided."

Joey decided after a time that there was no great challenge in trailing sheep beyond the simple tiresomeness of it. McIntosh allowed them a high degree of freedom in setting their own course, riding around the far edges and turning those that might drift too far north or south. Most of the time he and Joey stayed behind the band, prompting any that might fall back too far. The dog worked much harder than McIntosh or Joey, patroling one outer perimeter, then the other. Now and then a ewe would defy him, standing to face him and stamping a forefoot. She would turn and retreat when he pressed her. Joey thought Rustler seemed to be having a great time, for after each small victory he wagged his tail vigorously and turned toward McIntosh as if asking for praise. Usually, he got it.

McIntosh explained, "Sheep have an instinctive fear of the wolf, and to them the dog represents a wolf. That is why a dog can control a flock better than a man. The old highlanders depended heavily upon their dogs."

"Highlanders? What's that?"

"My father came from the highlands of Scotland to this country when he was not much older than you. My family has been with the sheep for more generations than I know."

"My teacher talked a lot about England, but she didn't say much about Scotland."

"A beautiful country, my father said. But it had many troubles, and hunger among the common people. The old country was like a mother to him, and a man never forgets his mother, but he found this land to be like a good wife. It was a happy marriage."

"You got a wife of your own?"

"I did. She rests in a churchyard back in Kendall County."

"I oughtn't to've asked you."

"The time for mourning is long since past. The memories give me comfort on a dark night, and I take pleasure in watching other couples like your cousin and his wife. I hope they have a strong marriage."

Joey was careful in his answer. "They've had their differences."

"I noticed last night that they did not share their blankets. I trust that any problem they have will be temporary."

Joey suspected that Alta would go her own way when they reached Fort Stockton. "I imagine it will."

Toward midday the flock stopped moving. McIntosh said, "They are used to a noontime rest through the worst of the day's heat." Many of the sheep found shade beneath the scattered trees. The rest formed small circles and hid their heads in the shadows of each other's bodies.

Sitting so close to one another on the wagon seat must have had a healing effect upon the relationship between Beau and Alta. Joey noticed when they stopped to make evening camp that Alta was very solicitous of Beau as he climbed down the wagon wheel, leaning over and maintaining a strong grip on his left arm to keep him steady until he was on the ground and had the crutch tucked snugly beneath his arm. Beau reciprocated by holding her tightly as she followed him. Beau hobbled to a shallow blackened pit where someone had had a campfire in the not-too-distant past.

"I'll dig this out a little deeper for you," he told her.

Alta gently vetoed his offer. "How could you use a shovel when you can't put but one foot on the ground? You'd just aggravate that leg and be longer in gettin' well." She brought a three-legged stool from the wagon and set it down. "Now, you sit there and be still. Won't take me any time to set up camp."

She could have spoken harshly and made it an order, but her voice was soft, so that it sounded like a polite request.

Joey fetched her several armloads of dry wood, enough to cook both supper and breakfast. He lifted down the Dutch ovens and the steel rods from which she would suspend the coffeepot. Then he stood beside Beau, watching as Alta built a fire in the shallow pit. "You're treatin' her better. Maybe you've decided she couldn't help what she did in San Antonio."

"I reckon her reasons were better than mine were for spendin' half my life drunk."

"You've been sober for a long time now."

"I ain't had any choice. I was afraid if I got drunk in that outlaw camp I might not live long enough to sober up again. Since then, I ain't even seen a bottle." He held out his hand to see if it might shake. It did not. "There was a time I thought it'd kill me to go a week without a drink, but I ain't died yet."

"Not even a rattlesnake was able to kill you."

"Sheriff Gardner could still do it, him and his rope. I just wish these sheep would move along faster."

"I like it here with Mr. McIntosh and his dog and the sheep. Reminds me of the good days back home with Pa and Reuben."

"By the time we get to Fort Stockton my leg ought to be well enough to where I can ride again. Then we'll go our own way."

"What if Alta don't go with us?"

Sadness came into Beau's eyes as he studied the woman kneading dough to make bread. "I couldn't wait to get shed of her at first. Now I've got used to her bein' around."

"Then ask her to stay with us."

"And be on the run like we are? That wouldn't be fair to her. Wouldn't be fair to any woman."

"In a way she's on the run herself from all the bad stuff that's behind her."

Beau had no reply. He kept staring at Alta.

McIntosh came to camp after seeing that the band was scattered enough to graze but not enough for any of the sheep to become lost. He filled and lighted his pipe, then glanced around with contentment. "There is a lot to be said for the tranquility of the solitary life, but it is a blessing at times to have company to share the road. Are you enjoying the trip, lad?"

"Yes sir." It felt good to be doing something constructive, something of worth.

"Do you like to read, Joey?"

"I do. Ain't had any chance lately, though."

"You have a chance now. If you'll look in the wagon, up near the seat, you'll find a box of books I am carrying to the ranch. There are none that will do you harm, and they may do you some good. Reading fires the imagination and broadens the mind."

Joey climbed up and sought out the box. McIntosh said, "Have you read *Tom Sawyer*?"

"I don't think I even heard of it."

"It tells of a lad about your age, the troubles he gets

himself into and the ways he confronts them. I would not advise you to emulate him, but you could learn from his mistakes."

Joey was not sure what *emulate* meant, though he did not want to reveal his ignorance by asking. He found the book and slouched on the wagon seat, flipping through it to see how many pictures it had, then starting to read about Aunt Polly calling for Tom. He became so absorbed that Alta's first summons to supper did not penetrate his consciousness. McIntosh had to walk over and shake his leg to bring him out of the spell Tom Sawyer had cast over him.

McIntosh said, "Books nourish the soul, but you need nourishment for the body as well. One beauty about books is that when the world calls you away, everything remains suspended in place until you return. Tom will be waiting for you, right where you left him."

Joey rushed his supper so he could read more of the book before darkness forced him to quit. He remembered studying a little about the Mississippi River. From what the teacher had said, and this book, it must be at least as wide as the Llano, and maybe even the Brazos.

When Joey saw the horsemen, his first thought was of sheriffs and rangers. His heart tripped a bit faster. He looked toward the wagon on the beaten trail two or three hundred yards north of the sheep. Beau did not have time to hide, and his game leg would not allow him to run even if the brush had been dense enough to conceal him.

McIntosh had been riding south of the band, where some of the sheep were trying to drift off into a brushy draw, responding to the strong attraction of grass and

weeds made lush by runoff from some recent rain. He circled back around, his horse moving in a brisk trot. He
appeared as eager as if he had just been invited to a party.
"Let us go and meet our company, Joey. I believe I recognize a cattleman whose acquaintance I have made before."

Maybe they weren't sheriffs or rangers after all. Joey's
relief lasted only until he recalled what McIntosh had said
about cattlemen sometimes making sheepmen decidedly
unwelcome. Some party! But McIntosh showed no concern, so Joey rode alongside him, steeling himself for
whatever verbal abuse might come.

The riders, obviously cowboys, had stopped at the
wagon. Beau and Alta had halted the mules but remained
on the wagon seat, silently waiting for McIntosh.

Joey quickly picked the leader of the group, broadshoul-
dered, about McIntosh's age, heavy-browed, and wearing
a dirty-gray moustache almost as large as Miller Dawson's.
He greeted McIntosh in a deep bass voice. "Howdy,
Scotchman. I thought this looked like your outfit."

"You're an observant man, Tol Evers. It is an unusual
cattleman who can tell one sheep outfit from another."

"Your sheep smell the same as everybody else's. But I
thought I recognized that mangy dog of yours from the
last time you passed this way. I hope you're just travelin'
through, not figurin' on stoppin' a while and sheepin' off
my grass."

"I would not do such a thing to a man who has offered
me so many kindnesses in the past." McIntosh's voice carried a tinge of good-natured sarcasm.

"The kindest thing I could do for me and you both would
be to run all them sheep off of a cliff. But I ain't got a
cliff. Best I can offer is a fair-sized ditch. They'd probably
just break a leg or two. Wouldn't hardly be worth the sweat."

"Then I suppose we are each doomed to continue in our misguided ways, me with my sheep and you with your cattle."

"Looks like."

Joey sensed that beneath the bantering lay a mutual respect, even if the two men were adversaries on the subject of sheep.

McIntosh said, "You should put aside your prejudice and buy some sheep. They would fare better than cattle on this stingy type of range. You would find that they are certified mortgage lifters."

"I'm not a prideful man, but I have more pride than that." The rancher turned to one of the cowboys. "Look under that wagon bed. See if maybe he's got a broken wheel tied there amongst his trappin's."

That took McIntosh by surprise. "Now, by the eternal, why would any reasonable man be carrying a broken wheel when he has four good ones?"

"Why would any reasonable man want to saddle himself down with a bunch of stinkin' sheep?"

The cowboy reported that he found no such wheel. The rancher told McIntosh, "There was a sheepman came through here a while back and stopped at one of my best waterin's. Had a broken wheel and said he had sent to San Angelo for a new one. A week later he was still there. We found out he had a good wheel hidden under a pile of wood. He was carryin' a broken wheel to put on whenever he found a place he wanted to camp."

"An ingenious man. I must get acquainted with him sometime. Or did you kill him?"

"I don't go around killin' human bein's, or even sheepmen. We just gave him a quick escort onto the Bar Seven and warned Old Man Carrington about the feller's tricks. He hates sheep a lot worse than I do."

"I have made Mr. Carrington's acquaintance."

"He eats barbed wire for breakfast and washes it down with lye water. I'd tell you to go way around and avoid his place, but you'd stay that much longer on mine. So you'll just have to take your chances with him."

"He has no right to stop anyone from using the trail."

"Your wagon is on the trail, but your sheep ain't." The rancher began turning his horse away. "Good luck to you, Scotchman."

"I don't suppose you would know where I might find a broken wheel?"

The rancher laughed and rode away, his cowboys spread out on either side of him. McIntosh watched them, then discovered that his pipe had burned out. He refilled it and struck a match on the horn of his saddle. "Not a bad sort, that Evers, but too stubborn to recognize an opportunity that fairly pounds on his door." He drew on the pipe until the tobacco caught. "You'll see the day, lad, when there'll be sheep all over western Texas. The climate fits them well, and economics favors them too. Pride may hold the line for a while, but economics always triumphs in the end."

Joey had noticed that each day they traveled west the land took on more aspects of a desert, vegetation increasingly sparse and much of it prickly. Across the hill country, live oak had dominated for a long time, slowly giving way to smaller and shorter cedar trees, or juniper. Now cedar gave way to greasewood and occasional stands of mesquite in the draws where water collected when it rained. Joey had not known mesquite before. Most of the trees were much smaller than live oaks, though now and again he came across a huge old mesquite that had survived drought and prairie fires and had grown to be a foot or more in diameter.

"This has been a good year for the bean crop," McIntosh observed. The tree had thin, lacy leaves that yielded a spotty shade, but it bore an abundance of long bean pods that were drying and browning now in summer's heat. "I have seen lambs fatten on them in the fall. Horses like them, but they can be dangerous if they have lain on the ground and molded."

"I suppose every part of the country has somethin' good about it."

"In this western country you have to search harder to find it, but it is there. The sheep by its nature is a dry-weather animal. It fares better here than in the eastern part of the state where rainfall makes the grass grow rank and tall and where all manner of parasites thrive. Out here most parasites dry up and blow away." He looked across the flock, and alarm widened his eyes. "Except the coyote."

McIntosh drew a saddle gun from a scabbard beneath his leg. "Stay here, lad." He pulled away to the south. There, beyond the edge of the flock, Joey saw a coyote slinking along watching the sheep. Rustler was on the other side, near the wagon, or the coyote would never have been allowed so close.

McIntosh set his horse into a run, the rifle at his shoulder. He fired, and the bullet kicked up dirt two feet from the coyote. The animal bounded away, its bushy tail tucked in tightly. McIntosh pursued it relentlessly, firing repeatedly even though his chance of hitting it from a running horse was akin to his chance of being struck by lightning. He was still riding hard and firing when he vanished over the hill. Joey could hear more shots in the distance.

McIntosh returned after perhaps half an hour, his horse lathered with sweat but his face aglow with satisfaction. "Finally got the bugger. It will kill no sheep of mine."

"Is the coyote really that bad?"

"When you've found as many of your flock dead as I have, when you've seen a lamb half eaten but still alive, stepping on its own entrails as they drag along the ground, you'll have no love for the coyote."

Not only the vegetation had changed, but the face of the land as well. No longer did Joey ride among high round-top limestone hills as in the Llano River country. Now the land was flat or sloped gently westward toward the Pecos River. The hills were mostly long and gray and stony-sided with broad, flat mesa tops. Dry yucca stalks suggested Indian lances on the rough hillsides. Clumps of prickly pear protruded through the short, thin, summer-brown grass. Small cactus plants with domed tops lay in ambush, waiting for the unwary to step on them and risk crippling themselves on barbs as ungiving as steel blades. In almost every way this resembled the deserts Joey had read about in school except for the lack of sand dunes. McIntosh assured him there were plenty of those too, farther north and west.

Once when McIntosh was on the far side of the band, Joey noticed something odd about the rocks through which Taw was gingerly picking his way. Dismounting, he dislodged one from its resting place in the dried earth. Imbedded in it were what appeared to be small seashells like his teacher had brought back once from a trip to the Galveston seaside. He found snail shells as well, and an imprint of a fish skeleton. They seemed grossly out of place in this desert environment. He stuck the rock in his pocket.

In camp that evening he showed it to McIntosh. "Looks to me like there was a time when fish lived on dry land. Or else this country got covered up in Noah's flood."

Beau snorted. "At the time of Noah's flood it probably didn't rain a quarter of an inch here. Hasn't rained much since, either."

The sheepman studied the rock but a moment. "Imagine if you will, lad, the look of this region a million years ago. All this land was at the bottom of an immense sea. Gradually it was lifted up out of the water, and the sea retreated back to the Gulf of Mexico. But it left pockets that evaporated to give us salt beds and heavy deposits of gypsum. You will find the history of the earth written in these stones."

McIntosh left to take a last look at the sheep as they bedded down for the night. Beau watched McIntosh riding away. "Books are all right if you're careful which ones you read. But some of them'll fill your head with crazy notions like he's got."

The trail they had followed combined with other trails more heavily used, and the McIntosh outfit began encountering occasional travelers bound either east or west. Unable to escape, Beau would pull his hat brim down low over his eyes, and if anyone asked, Alta would say their name was Smith. Most people did not ask. Too many questions were considered impolite in this western country, and occasionally even dangerous.

They watered the sheep at a place McIntosh called China Pond. Beyond, Joey could see a broad, flat-topped mountain and what appeared to be a scallop cut out of its center.

"That," McIntosh said, "is Castle Gap. It is the gateway to the Pecos River. Gold hunters passed through it on their way to California almost forty years ago. The Butterfield stage used it, and many a westbound wagon train. Past it lies Horsehead Crossing on the Pecos."

"Is that where we take the flock over?"

"No, it is usually too deep and swift there for sheep. The weight of their wet wool would drag them under. We will follow the river up to the grand falls. There is a place where the water is usually shallow enough for sheep to wade across."

"That's a lot of extra miles, seems like."

"Time means but little to a sheep."

Next morning McIntosh and Joey rode away after breakfast to catch up to the flock, already off the bed ground at sunup and drifting westward. The stockman looked back toward the wagon, where Alta was helping Beau climb up onto the seat. "Your cousin and his wife are still not sharing blankets like most married couples."

"Beau's leg is givin' him a right smart of trouble yet." Joey felt guilty about perpetuating all this deception. The sheepman had been so generous to them that it seemed unfair. Joey had felt safe enough in telling the truth to Miller Dawson, for Dawson himself was on the dodge. McIntosh was unlikely to betray them to the authorities, but he was so scrupulously honest that he would probably experience remorse over harboring fugitives. All things considered, it was better to spare him that.

Honesty was not always the best policy.

The approach to the Pecos from Castle Gap was down a long desolate slope where grass was scarce and greasewood or tar-bush plentiful. Joey had noticed that sheep did not eat greasewood, though they browsed on other shrubs and the tough weeds that pushed up through the hard ground. The goats ate almost anything that held still long enough for them to nip at it.

McIntosh worked hard to keep the band hazed away from a scattering of alkali waterholes. Skeletons of cattle bleached in the sun, mute testimony to the deadliness of these inviting pools.

McIntosh said, "A man named Charles Goodnight brought one of the first herds of cattle through this way. He called the Pecos River the grave of a cowman's hopes."

Joey could understand why. This looked like the dreary kind of place where a sick animal might instinctively go to die.

He rode with McIntosh ahead of the flock to find a spot where the edge water was calm enough for the sheep to drink. Sight of the river reminded Joey that he was thirsty. He stepped down to allow Taw to take the water first. The horse dipped its nose three times before it reluctantly decided to drink. Joey walked a couple of paces upstream and dropped to his stomach, cupping his hand to catch the current. The first sip made him raise up, sputtering. This was the worst water he had ever sampled.

McIntosh chuckled. "Not quite like new wine, is it, lad?"

"Not like anything I ever drank before."

"It grows on you after you have lived here a while and have eaten your peck of alkali. One needs to buy but little medicine when he lives on the Pecos. It is already in the water."

The band spread out in a wide arc. One lamb ventured too far and was caught up in the current. On command from McIntosh, Rustler plunged in after it, grabbing its throat wool in his teeth and fighting his way back to the bank. The lamb scrambled out, bleating for its mother, more frightened of the dog than of the water.

Joey saw deep wagon ruts where the trail dropped down a sloping bank on the east side and others where it came out on the opposite side. He could understand how horses and cattle might swim it. The river was not particularly wide, though its current was swift. But it would be a challenge for sheep.

Once the ewes and lambs had taken their fill, McIntosh and Joey pushed them northward, moving them back away from the river far enough that its sometimes steep banks were not a hazard. Joey had considered the country they had passed in the last few days to be dry and desolate, but this along the Pecos was more so. Grass was thin compared even to the drier portions of the hill country. The sheep seemed to find enough weeds and low shrubs to feed upon, however.

To the east he could see the long blue mountain and the scallop marking the pass through which they had come. To the west, across the river, he saw open terrain that seemed almost flat at first glance, though on closer study he perceived that the land rolled gently with a gradual climb toward the west. More blue hills lay in the distance, topped by long mesas. It seemed an unlikely place for people to live. McIntosh had said thousands had passed through here on their way to somewhere else. Joey could imagine that the challenging nature of the land made most of them want to hurry.

He contrasted it to the farm he had left behind, and homesickness swept over him anew. Every day was carrying him farther away from what he had known and loved.

"I hope your ranch is better than this," he told McIntosh.

"It is. But do not judge this land too harshly. The good Lord placed it here for a purpose."

"It's hard to see what. Makes me wish I was back home, with things like they used to be."

"Perhaps one purpose is to make you re-examine the reason you left that home. I suspect you have not chosen to tell me all of it."

"I've told you that my mother died, and Pa too."

"Yes, and you have also mentioned a stepmother. I take it that you are running away from her."

"You would too, if she was yours."

"And what of Beau? Is he really your cousin?"

"Yes sir. Second cousin, anyway."

"But the young lady . . . I do not believe she is really his wife."

Joey felt warmth rising into his face. "No sir, that just seemed like the best thing to say."

McIntosh waited for more. When Joey did not volunteer it, the sheepman said, "I am not given to judging others, and I do not mean to pry into business that is none of my own. But any time you feel the need to unburden yourself, I will offer a sympathetic ear."

{ FIFTEEN }

McIntosh warned Joey not to expect the grand falls to be as grand as their name implied. "When you live in a land where water is scarce, a creek becomes a river and a small drop in the riverbed is called a fall."

Joey had been watching a dark cloud to the west and northwest, wondering if it meant rain. This thirsty land could make good use of whatever moisture it might receive. But the prospect brought no cheer to McIntosh. He said, "I would hope we could cross the river before it rains."

The precipitation, when it came, was little more than a dust-settling shower, though it was enough to make the sheep stop moving and huddle up. McIntosh said, "It looks as if rain is heavier to the north and west. Stay with the sheep while I ride ahead and survey the crossing."

Joey rode to the nearby bank and saw for himself that the river level had risen. Muddy runoff water from the rangelands had turned the Pecos brown. Dead wood, bits of old vegetation and other debris floated on top. Sheep ventured to the edge and sniffed at the moving current but refused to drink. They drank instead from rainwater collected in a hundred small potholes.

McIntosh returned disappointed. "The river is up a couple of feet at the crossing. We cannot wade the band over until the water goes down."

Joey shrugged. "We weren't in a hurry anyway, were we?"

"I encountered one of Carrington's cowboys. As soon as he recognized me he changed his course and struck a beeline for the ranch headquarters."

"I didn't think you were afraid of Carrington."

"No, but he is a most unpleasant old man. I would have liked to avoid any confrontation with him."

"That other rancher, Mr. Evers, didn't seem bad. Long as they don't do anything more than cuss you a little . . ."

"Carrington claims this side of the river as his own. I doubt that he has ever paid the state a nickel for its use, but I never enjoy arguing with an angry and unreasonable man, even when I know I am right."

The usually talkative sheepman rode along in silence, much of the time watching toward the east. Joey knew he wished to move faster, but it would be of no use if they could not cross the river right away.

They reached the place where McIntosh said the water was usually shallow enough for sheep to wade. Flotsam deposited along the bank showed that the river had dropped a foot from the highest point of its rise, but it was still too deep and too swift to risk putting the flock into it.

Joey said, "Too bad nobody's built a bridge."

"No one has seen a profit in it yet. Most of civilization's great advancements have resulted from the search for a profit. So have some of its greatest disasters."

Joey followed McIntosh to the wagon, where the sheep-

man soberly told Alta that she may as well build a fire and get the noon meal started. It would be hours—possibly even the next day—before it would be safe to put the sheep into the water. Beau climbed down from the wagon first. He moved without the crutch, though he still walked carefully and with a pronounced limp. He reached up to help Alta.

A warm smile passed between them. Joey could not shake off a nagging feeling of jealousy, though he knew Alta was too old for him. He could see that the nurse-and-patient relationship had overcome the initial antagonism between the two. She had developed a strong interest in Beau, which kept it in the family, sort of. Beau's luck seemed to be changing for the better since the snakebite, Joey thought. Perhaps Alta would not be leaving them when they reached Fort Stockton. And maybe Beau would not be getting drunk.

Joey saw the horsemen as he returned to the Dutch oven for a third sourdough biscuit to wipe up thick molasses he had poured into his tin plate. His appetite vanished, apprehension taking its place. He let the plate tip downward and the biscuit tumble over its edge onto the muddy ground as he counted the horses. "We got company comin', Mr. McIntosh."

"I see them. Just go on with your meal and try to look as innocent as a newborn. The last thing we want is to let Carrington see fear. The man's darker nature feeds on it."

Beau limped to the wagon and fetched down his rifle.

McIntosh said, "Keep it in hand, but make no threatening move with it. We will offer Carrington no excuse for violence."

Beau stepped in front of Alta, shielding her. He said, "Joey, get over here. If they start anything I want you and Alta to be back of me where I can take care of you."

Joey was surprised by Beau's protective attitude toward him. Up to now he had seen little such inclination. "They ain't goin' to hurt me."

"Damn it, do what I tell you." Beau's voice softened. "I ain't got enough cousins that I want to lose one."

Rustler trotted forward to intercept the visitors, barking a challenge and making some of their horses skittish. A cowboy spurred toward Rustler. Joey feared he might shoot the dog, but the rider tried instead to whip him with a doubled rope. Rustler retreated to one side but kept barking.

Joey had no difficulty in deciding which man was Carrington. The rancher rode a full length out in front, a tall, skinny, stoop-shouldered old man with a long white beard that would reach halfway down to his belt buckle if the strong north wind were not tugging it sideways. His bushy white eyebrows reminded Joey of piled-up snow about to slide off the edge of a roof. Beneath those brows two dark gray eyes burned as fiercely as a hawk's.

Joey counted seven cowboys, four on one side of Carrington, three on the other. Each carried a pistol, either in a holster, a belt, or the pocket in a pair of leather chaps.

"McIntosh," Carrington shouted, "what the hell are you doin' here? Didn't I give you warnin' enough the last time?"

McIntosh appeared as calm as if he were in church, though Joey suspected it took a lot of inner strength to cover up his apprehension. "You did, Mr. Carrington, and I remind you of what I told you then. I am following the river. The river belongs to everyone and to no one."

"The river, maybe, but not the land to the side of it. This land is mine."

"By what right, sir? Do you have title?"

"I got the title from the Comanches. It was theirs, and I ran them off, so now it's mine."

"The army and the rangers were the ones who subdued the Comanches. But no matter who did it, if you do not have title duly registered at the county courthouse, you have no right to prevent a traveler from using a recognized trail. Tens of thousands of cattle have been driven up this side of the river, across this very land."

"Cattle yes, but not them woolly locusts that foul everything they touch and grub my grass plumb down to the roots."

"If you will examine our back trail, sir, you will see that these sheep have grubbed up nothing. We have kept them spread out enough to avoid that. As for grass, there was precious little of it in the first place."

"And even less of it now. I doubt that my cows will go down to the river to drink because they'll smell where your damned woollies have been."

"That is an old wives' tale, long since discredited."

"My old wife still believes it, and so do I. Now, McIntosh, I've come to see that you put them sheep across the river."

"I plan to do that, but I have to wait until the water goes down. You can see for yourself that it is too high. It would drown a lot of my flock."

"And good riddance that would be. Put them across, now!"

"I cannot."

"Then we will."

"I'll sue you for every sheep that drowns."

Carrington gave him a mirthless grin. "In this county? There ain't a jury in a hundred miles that'd give you a Mexican peso for the whole damned bunch." He turned to the cowboys on his left. "You know what we came to do. Let's be movin' these sheep."

The cowboys charged in among the band, shouting, slapping coiled ropes against their legs. The nearest sheep broke away from them, pushing into the interior of the grazing flock. Some of the cowboys rode around the sides, yelling, trying to put the sheep into a run. The outer sheep ran, but not in the direction of the river. They pushed toward the center. Alarm rippled across the flock like wind rippling the surface of a lake.

Old Carrington cursed and drew his pistol. Joey gasped, thinking he was about to start shooting sheep. He turned fearfully toward McIntosh. Whatever emotions the sheepman might be feeling remained hidden from his face. He stood with arms folded defiantly, not resisting but not pleading, either.

Alta moved closer to Beau. He put a protective arm around her and motioned to Joey. "Stay back of me. They'll have to ride over me to get to you two."

Joey obeyed, but he doubted that the cowboys meant the people any harm. The animals were their target.

Carrington triggered his pistol at the sky and spurred his horse into the sheep, trying to make them run. The cowboys took his action as a cue and began firing into the air.

Joey surmised that their intention was to stampede the sheep, to run them into the river so fast that momentum and pressure from behind would push them across before they could slow down. But the swift current was sure to carry many away. Once their wool became soaked, its weight would drag them under.

Joey exclaimed, "Mr. McIntosh, they'll drown half of your flock."

McIntosh still appeared calmer than he had any right to be under the circumstances. "Perhaps, perhaps not. Cowboys know cattle. They do not know sheep."

His meaning soon became clear. The sheep did not stampede, as cattle might, and plunge headlong into whatever hazard lay in front of them. Instead, their panic carried them into a compact mass, all trying to reach the relative safety of its center. The more the cowboys shouted and fired their weapons, the tighter and more immovable the mass became.

The horsemen kept trying for what Joey thought must have been half an hour, but they made no progress. Wherever they pressed against the outer rim of the band, the sheep there simply circled, trying to move out of their way.

Carrington shouted and cursed and shook his fist, but nothing changed. The flock was wound up tighter than the spring in a clock. At length the old rancher called his men together. They sat on their horses, Carrington in the center of the gathering. He cursed and they argued. Joey saw much waving of hands and heard a lot of loud talk, most of the words undecipherable at the distance.

Carrington broke away and rode toward the wagon, his face so red that Joey half expected him to go into some kind of spasm. Beau raised the rifle, which he had held at arm's length, but the old man ignored it if he saw it at all. His wrath was focused on the unmoving McIntosh. The cowboys trailed at a respectful distance, having suffered a brutal chastisement for their ineffectiveness.

"What's the matter with these stupid sheep, McIntosh?" the old man raged. "If they had any sense they'd all be on the other side of the river by now or drowned and gone to hell, and you with them."

A slight smile lifted the gray ends of McIntosh's moustache. "You stated it correctly. They are stupid. You boogered them. When you booger a sheep it loses what little sense it ever had."

Carrington grumbled, "Only thing dumber than a sheep is the man that owns it. The minute the water goes down, you put them woollies across the river."

"That I shall."

"And I don't want to see you here ever again."

"Ah, but you will. I have not finished stocking my ranch. I intend to come this way with another band next spring."

If a stare could kill, Joey thought, McIntosh would fall dead on the spot. Carrington turned his horse and rode eastward, muttering to himself. His men followed, careful not to crowd him.

McIntosh abandoned his show of stoicism and revealed the anxiety he had kept tightly corked. "We have to go in there and scatter them or we will have a lot of smothered sheep. I am afraid we have lost some lambs already."

It took a while to break up the tightly knotted band. As McIntosh had feared, several grown ewes and twenty or so lambs lay dead, suffocated in their massing together. The rest of the sheep got over their scare and spread out looking for browse, their memories mercifully short.

McIntosh accepted his loss philosophically. "A sheep is born looking for a place to die. We would have lost far more had Carrington been able to drive them into the river."

"Looks to me like he owes you for these sheep."

"I will settle with Mr. Carrington in my own way and my own good time. Land here is cheap because no one wants it badly enough to pay for it. I intend to buy this strip from the state and make him pay me or discontinue his use of it. The law will have no choice but to support me."

Joey suspected the lease price would not be cheap.

One of the smothered ewes was fat. McIntosh said she had probably lost her lamb weeks ago, so the energy that would have been required to produce milk had gone to her own flesh instead. "She will provide meat enough to feed us the rest of the way to Fort Stockton."

That evening Joey noticed that Alta kept watching the east as if she thought Carrington and his cowboys might return. She remained close to Beau.

McIntosh sought to reassure her. "Carrington has suffered all the indignity he can tolerate for now. We'll not see him again, not this time."

Joey suspected it was not fear that made Alta stay so near to Beau. She smiled too much to be frightened. The two kept touching one another at every opportunity that arose and at some they contrived.

In the middle of the night Joey awoke to the sound of someone moving around. Beau rolled up his blankets and hobbled off to the far side of the wagon where Alta slept. He did not come back.

Joey no longer worried that she would be leaving them at Fort Stockton.

The Pecos River at that point meandered in a generally southeasterly direction. From where the sheep forded, Fort Stockton lay almost due south on a trail worn deeply by years of wagon traffic. The course crossed an irrigation canal that diverted some of the river's flow to nearby Mexican farms. McIntosh watered the flock at a large spring which poured forth what Joey considered a tremendous body of water despite the desert terrain's dry nature.

McIntosh said Fort Stockton was home to possibly a thousand people, a substantial number for a difficult land which demanded a hard and continuous struggle to produce even a modest living. The town owed its original existence to the huge Comanche Springs and the creek to which they gave birth, an oasis in a broad expanse of greasewood and mesquite and cactus, distant blue mountains and tabletop mesas edged by broken rimrock.

McIntosh explained, "Nobody knows how much water flows out of the ground, water sweet as a man ever tasted. Indians have come here since yon mountains were but anthills. All the old trails passed this way. The army built the fort to intercept the hostiles that were accustomed to using the springs.

"There are not many towns in this part of Texas, and those few exist for some good reason. The land would not support them if they had sprung up willy-nilly as in the East."

Joey was torn. On the one hand it was good to see a town again after so many weeks. On the other, he saw a strong chance someone might recognize him and Beau if word had reached this far west. He decided to avoid the settlement if possible.

McIntosh made camp on the creek east of the springs, where grass was far better than on most of the land they had traversed in the last hundred and fifty miles. Regret was in his eyes as he ate the supper Alta had prepared. "I suppose you folks will want to continue your journey."

Beau said solemnly, "We need to move on."

"I can find help here to take the sheep on down to my ranch, but I shall miss this lady's good cooking." He turned to Joey. "And I shall miss you too, lad. With your patience and your diligence you could become a real sheepman."

"I wouldn't mind that at all." Joey had taken a liking to the flock. He supposed part of the reason was their dependence. They made him feel wanted, necessary. If ever he were able to return to the farm, he would get him some sheep.

McIntosh said, "Were you to stay with me, Joey, I would give you sheep in return for your help. By the time you are grown you could have a flock of your own."

Temptation exerted a strong tug. Joey looked toward Beau and Alta. Beau shook his head, and Joey knew he was right. Though they had come far from Bastrop, it was not yet far enough. Sooner or later someone was likely to come looking for them. Huge though this Pecos River country was, the sparseness of its population meant that no one was likely to go unnoticed for long unless he hid out and became a hermit. There was no crowd in which you could lose yourself.

Joey said, "Beau's got his plans, and he's the only kin I know."

"At least I shall see that you are well provisioned. It is a long way to Fort Davis, and even farther from there to El Paso."

After supper McIntosh prepared to ride to town, saying he planned to inquire about hiring help. "Beau, if you will come to the Gray Mule after a while, I shall be glad to buy you a drink."

Joey and Alta both looked apprehensively at Beau. He caught the worry in their eyes. "Well, maybe just a beer."

A number of townspeople came out to look at the band and indulge their curiosity. Sheep had not yet become commonplace west of the Pecos. Fort Stockton was still considered cattle country.

At dusk Joey became conscious of a lone rider approaching from the direction of the fort. He assumed McIntosh was returning, until he recognized the horse.

"Beau," he said in a loud whisper, as if he feared some-body might hear him in town, "don't that look like Miller Dawson?"

"Damned if it don't. How'd he get here ahead of us?"

"These sheep don't move very fast."

Alta shrank back toward the wagon. "I hoped we'd never see him again. His kind bring nothin' but bad luck."

Dawson reined up short of camp and surveyed it cau-tiously. Remaining in the saddle, ready to spur away in an instant, the outlaw asked, "Anybody else here?"

Joey walked out to greet him. "Nobody but us. Mr. Mc-Intosh went to town."

Dawson dismounted and gripped Joey's shoulder, shak-ing it hard. "It's good to see you, young'un. I wondered what became of you-all 'til I heard talk about this bunch of sheep. By description I figured out you was with it." He shook hands with Beau and turned back to Joey. "I'm afraid you've come down in the world, playin' shepherd to woollies."

"Ain't nothin' wrong with herdin' sheep. They're kind of helpless and need takin' care of. I'm pretty good at that."

"What about your pardner, Beau? You still takin' care of him too?"

"Somebody else has been doin' that lately."

Dawson's gaze touched Alta, who remained at the wagon. He seemed surprised to see her. "The way Beau and her argued, I figured she'd gone off and left you-all long before now."

Beau said, "We got tired of fightin'. It's easier on the digestion if we get along." Beau regarded the town with some apprehension. "Ain't you afraid somebody here'll know you?"

"This desert dried me plumb out. Had to get some grub

and some whiskey. I never was in this part of the country before, so nobody recognized me. Been campin' close to the spring and waitin' for you-all to show up."

Disturbed, Alta moved out from the wagon. "Why? What do you want with us?"

"Me and Joey and Beau, we talked about goin' to California, and then on up to Oregon. I was afraid if I didn't find them here we might never get together again."

She took Beau's arm. "We'd all be better off that way."

Realization came into Dawson's eyes. "You two *did* get tired of fightin'." He seemed disappointed. "That could change the complexion of things a right smart. With a woman on your arm, you're apt to get tired of travelin', too."

"I already am," Beau replied. "But I don't see I've got any choice unless I turn back and give myself up to the law." He turned to Alta. "To tell you the truth, I been thinkin' some about that. This runnin' ain't no life for me, and it sure ain't any good for you."

Dawson's gaze shifted from Beau to Alta, then to Joey. "The law ain't much on forgivin'. Many a time I've thought what you're thinkin', but I knew what'd happen to me. Runnin' ain't a good way to live, but hangin' ain't a good way to die."

Joey could not take his eyes from Beau. This was the first indication Beau had given that he entertained some thought about going back.

Dawson asked, "What about you, Joey? You got any of the same notions?"

Joey found it difficult to answer. "Yes sir, I get to thinkin' about home, and . . . well, I been doin' a lot of thinkin' about home."

"They've probably got a hard cot waitin' for you in a reformatory."

"I know. Me and Beau have got to talk it over. Me and Beau and Alta."

Dawson squatted and poked absently at the fire, thinking. "Well, I've got no business tryin' to tell you-all what to do, but I'm goin' to Oregon, with or without you. Goin' to make me a new start and send for my son. Who knows? Might even take up preachin'."

Joey marveled. "You, preachin'?"

"Why not? I know my Maker. I've been mighty close to Him several times."

"You have enough money to buy that farm you talked about?"

"No. I got a pretty good contribution from a little bank down south after I parted company with you, but it wasn't all I hoped for. Thought I'd make a touch on a bank here in Fort Stockton, only they ain't got one yet. You'd think a town with a thousand people would have a good bank, wouldn't you?"

Joey didn't know. Banks had played no part in his life so far.

Dawson said, "There's a saloon that's got a safe, though. And I happen to know that a cattle buyer hit town this mornin' and put a sackful of money in it. So I figure to make a little withdrawal tonight after everybody's gone home."

Joey's jaw dropped. "You mean to rob the safe?"

"It ain't much of one. It'll be like openin' a can of sardines. Anyhow, let's call it a loan. Might even pay them some interest someday when I'm able."

Alta said dryly, "And you wanted us to be a party to it."

"I don't need any help for a simple job like this. But if you-all decide to make the trip to Oregon with me, cross over to the Mexican side at El Paso del Norte and look in the cantinas. I'll rest there for a week or two."

Joey said, "I wish you wouldn't do this, Mr. Dawson. There's other ways to get money."

"I'm too old to break broncs and too lazy to punch cows. I'd have a gray beard down to my knees before I'd ever earn enough. I ain't got that kind of time." He shook hands with Joey and Beau. To Joey's surprise he nodded at Alta and touched the brim of his hat, showing her a respect he had not exhibited before. "Whatever you-all decide, the best of luck to you."

As Dawson mounted his horse, Joey trotted after him. "I wish you wouldn't go."

Dawson waved his hand. "El Paso del Norte," he shouted back, and rode off into the gathering darkness.

{ SIXTEEN }

McIntosh was grim as death, riding into camp. Dismounting, he called, "Beau, we shall have to forget about that beer. There is a good chance for a shooting in town tonight."

Beau stepped away from the campfire to meet him. "I wasn't thirsty noway. But a shootin'?"

"You would never guess who I saw as I started to leave town. The outlaw Miller Dawson."

Joey swallowed hard. Beau did a good job of covering any reaction. Joey did not even look at Alta.

McIntosh said, "Evidently he has been around for two or three days. Some people in town have suspected he was up to no good, but they did not know who he was. I knew him because I saw him once in Kerrville. So I rode back and confirmed his identity to the sheriff."

Joey had trouble finding voice. "You told them who he is?"

"As citizens we all have a duty to help uphold the law. It is common knowledge that a considerable amount of money was placed in a saloon safe this morning. The supposition is that Dawson may have designs upon it. The sheriff has removed it to a locked cell in the jail, and they have set up an ambush at the saloon in the event Dawson makes a try."

An icy chill gripped Joey. "They'll kill him."

McIntosh nodded. "The choice is his own. If he leaves town peaceably the sheriff has no wish to confront him for crimes committed elsewhere. But if he tries to rob the saloon he may not see another sunrise." The sheepman mounted his horse again. "I promised the sheriff I would be back to make positive identification if need be. It is best that all of you remain here. Should there be gunfire, this camp is out of effective range."

Beau watched McIntosh fade off into the darkness. "Poor old Miller Dawson. I wish we could warn him that he's drawin' into a stacked deck." He appeared to consider going.

Alta took Beau's arm as if to hold him back. "He said he intended to reform, but he had just one more job to do. They always have one more job to do. And that one gets them killed."

Joey protested, "He saved your life, Alta. If he hadn't shot Farlow, we might all be dead."

She argued, "He didn't kill Farlow for us. He did it because Farlow was tryin' to kill *him*."

Joey fought down the urge to cry. "You heard what Mr. McIntosh said. They won't bother him if he doesn't try to rob that place. I've got to find him and tell him."

Alta reached out to Joey. "It's too dangerous to go in to town, and it'd make no difference in the long run. If we stop him here he'll just try it somewhere else . . . Fort Davis or El Paso or farther west. Luck always runs out for his kind. He'll never see Oregon."

"Maybe he can change. I've got to give him that chance." Joey grabbed his bridle and moved quickly toward the spot where Taw and Git Out were staked on grass beside the creek.

Beau hobbled awkwardly after him, grabbing his arm and stopping him. "Alta's right. If it doesn't happen here it'll happen somewhere else. We can't watch out for him forever."

Joey jerked free of Beau's grip. "I ain't fixin' to let him die without I try to help him."

"And maybe catch a stray bullet. Damn it, boy, he's of age to pick his own road, but you're not. It's goin' to be dangerous out there."

"Everything we've done since Bastrop has been dangerous." Joey slipped the bit into Taw's mouth and the headstall over his ears. Beau grabbed for him, but Joey swung Taw around to block him. He grasped Taw's mane and pulled himself up bareback.

Beau caught the bridle reins near the bit. "Joey, wait."

Joey beat his heels against Taw's ribs. The horse moved forward, jerking the reins from Beau's hand. Beau's weak leg gave way and he fell. "Damn it, Joey, you come back here. I don't want nothin' happenin' to you."

Joey put Taw into a lope. He could hear Beau hollering after him, and Alta as well, but he made it a point not to look back.

He did not know just where Dawson was camped except that it was somewhere near the springs. He could see the dim glow of lamps in town windows and lanterns hanging on open porches. Ahead and to his right lay the parade ground and the dark square walls of stone buildings on the military post.

He heard the sound of rushing water but could not see the springs. A rising moon cast a silver glow on the creek created by the artesian flow. Seeing two campfires, he rode to the first and called softly. "Mr. Dawson!"

A dark shape moved toward him, silhouetted in the fire's soft light. A voice spoke in a language he recognized as Spanish, though he did not know the words. He was disappointed to see that the camp was not Dawson's. It belonged to a Mexican family, their team of small mules tied to the wheels of their wagon, munching grain from a short wooden trough attached to the sideboard. Joey said to the man who walked out to meet him, "I'm lookin' for somebody else. Sorry I bothered you."

"No le hace."

Joey did not know what the words meant, but the shrug said enough.

He rode toward the other fire. He felt disappointment again even before he reached it, for he saw a peddler's wagon, all manner of sale goods stacked on shelves and suspended from its sides. The owner said, "I am closed for the night. Come back in the morning."

"I'm lookin' for a feller that was supposed to be camped close by. Maybe you saw him. Large man with a big black moustache. Rode a blue roan horse."

"Yes, he was over that way." The peddler pointed. "But he has broken camp. He came by here a while ago, riding toward town. He had all his belongings tied on his saddle."

Joey began to burn with anxiety. He did not know where to look. Fearing recognition, he had purposely avoided riding into town before. He had no idea how many saloons it supported or which was Dawson's target. He rode aimlessly down one street, then another, hoping chance might carry him to Dawson.

This was a quiet kind of country town where most people

believed nightfall should find them at home. Most of the store buildings were already dark. Joey saw a saloon-keeper close a front door behind him, lifting down a lantern suspended beneath the porch roof. The light shone full in the man's dark face.

Joey did not ask for advice, but he received it free of charge in an accent heavily Spanish. "*Muchacho*, is best you go home now. Is too late for a boy to be on the street. I bet your mother looks for you."

Joey wondered how much the man knew about what was planned here tonight, and could this be the saloon? He doubted it. The small adobe building had the word *Cantina* crudely painted on the plaster above the door, marking it as a Mexican saloon. He thought it was unlikely to attract many gringo customers. A cattle buyer who carried large sums of money would probably look for a larger and fancier place.

He asked, "How many more saloons has this town got?"

The Mexican shook his head disapprovingly. "Now, what business has a young boy to talk of saloons? You go home now, or I tell the *cherife*."

Joey pulled away to avoid calling more attention to himself. On another street he saw a larger structure which bore a sign reading *Liquors—Billiards—Beer*. That was another way, he guessed, of saying *Saloon*. The door was closed, the stone building dark. This, he thought, was a more likely prospect. He held Taw to the shadows and watched a few minutes but saw no sign of life. He reasoned that if they had set up an ambush here they would not be moving around and risking discovery.

He saw the dim figure of a horseman coming up the street, all but lost in the dark shadow of the buildings. He put Taw into a rough trot, which felt as if it would bounce Joey's innards up into his throat. "Mr. Dawson!" he called. "Mr. Dawson!"

The horseman rode out into the moonlit center of the street. Joey saw that he was not Miller Dawson.

Beau said, "Joey, I done everything but hold a gun on you to stop you from comin' into town." The words were of reproach, but the tone was of apprehension. "Come on, let me take you back to camp. This place is trigger-happy tonight."

Joey was amazed that Beau was sitting on Git Out, his bad leg extended awkwardly, the foot out of the stirrup. It must be causing him agony. "I didn't think you could ride yet."

"I oughtn't to be, but you didn't give me no choice. I couldn't stand by and see you get hurt, maybe killed."

Joey's throat was so tight that it pained him to speak. "I can't find Mr. Dawson. I don't know where he's at."

"I ain't seen him either, but I ran into a bunch of men with guns. They acted like they thought I was him, and I came damned near gettin' shot. Let's quit these streets before they make targets of us."

"We can't just turn our backs on him."

From a block down the street Joey saw the flash of a pistol, followed a split second later by the report. A man was running, afoot. He saw several more flashes, then heard a fusillade of shots. The man went down. The shots continued several seconds more, then stopped. The echoes reverberated against the buildings.

Joey froze, unable to breathe.

Beau's voice was strained. "Looks like we're too late."

Joey put Taw into his long, rough trot again. Beau spurred to catch up. Several men boiled out of a building, and three others emerged from around the sides. Indoors, someone lighted a lantern and brought it out. As Joey and Beau approached, the man carrying the lantern lifted it high over the body in the street.

The voice was McIntosh's. "That is your man, sheriff."

Joey was sick, bile rising in his throat. Miller Dawson lay twisted as he had fallen, a pool of blood spreading around him.

"My God," someone declared in awe, "we shot him to pieces."

"Well," said a man with a star on his shirt, "he won't be holdin' up any banks or robbin' any safes where he's gone. Like as not they'll have him shovelin' coal."

Beau rode up close beside Joey and placed his arm around Joey's shoulder. "Ain't nothin' we can do here. Come on, let's go back to camp."

Joey rode with him, his head down, his throat aching. His eyes burned, but no tears came. There had been too many tears already, and he was getting too big for them.

After a couple of hours Joey gave up trying to sleep. He laid back his blankets and went to the campfire, which had died down to a few glowing coals. He built it up with small pieces of dead mesquite. The night was not particularly chilly, but he found comfort in watching the play of the flames, listening to the crackle of burning wood. He thought about Miller Dawson and, in an effort to keep from dwelling on Dawson's violent death, forced himself to think about home. That awakened an ache of a different kind.

Long before daylight McIntosh seated himself by Joey's side. "Too much excitement," he said. "It has been a poor night for sleeping." He lighted his pipe with a blazing stick from the fire. "You're carrying the world on your shoulders, lad, and they are not broad enough to support the weight."

"Never got a wink of sleep."

"Perhaps you have never been so close to a shooting before. The man they killed was an outlaw. The world is better off without him."

Joey considered the propriety of confession and decided it was time to level with the man who had been kind to him and Beau and Alta. "I knew him. I knew Miller Dawson."

McIntosh took the pipe from his mouth and studied it as if its taste had suddenly soured. "How would a lad like you come to know such a man?"

"There's a lot we never told you about, Mr. McIntosh. Me and Beau, we're wanted back in Bastrop."

"Now, what could *you* be wanted for?"

"For murder." Joey was not surprised by the strong look of disbelief. He had seen it before. He told it all, from the deaths of Pa and Reuben to his own narrow escapes, to the fight with Mr. Meacham and the accident of fate which had thrown him and Beau into the company of Miller Dawson.

McIntosh drew thoughtfully on the pipe. "I had a feeling you were running away from something, but I assumed it was nothing more than a strict stepmother. I had no idea you had endured so much."

"I know Mr. Dawson did some bad things in his life, but he was good to me."

"Very few men are totally bad."

"Farlow was, but not Mr. Dawson. You'd have liked him."

"Perhaps. He was a predator, however, like the coyote. He took from other men the fruits of their labor instead of working for his own."

"He might've changed."

"My dog Rustler is smart, but his ways are set. It is difficult to teach him something new. Miller Dawson was too old to change. You are young and still have time to make your choices. I believe you will make the right ones. You have a good heart."

Beau and Alta arose at dawn. Beau was surprised to find McIntosh and Joey seated together near the fire. "How long you-all been up?"

McIntosh said, "Quite a long time, long enough for Joey to tell me many things."

Beau gave Joey a quizzical look. Joey said, "No use tellin' him any more lies. He knows all of it."

Joey had feared Beau would be upset, but if anything he seemed relieved. Beau told McIntosh, "You can turn me in if you want to. For all I know, there may be a reward."

"I did not turn Dawson in for a reward, nor would I do that to you. I know you are not an outlaw at heart."

"It wouldn't matter. I laid awake a long time last night, thinkin'. I've decided to go back and turn myself in. I don't want to spend the rest of my life runnin', lookin' back like Miller Dawson did, waitin' for the law to reach out and take me."

"But what of Joey?"

"I'll tell them he had nothin' to do with it. I think he'd like to stay here with you. You could teach him to be a sheepman."

Joey said, "That wouldn't be fair. I'm goin' back with you. Maybe they'll listen when I tell them how it was. Mr. Dawson did, and Mr. McIntosh too."

"Sheriff Gardner ain't like Mr. McIntosh. He'll gladly dance at my funeral." Beau jerked his head toward Alta. "I'd appreciate it if you could help her someway. Maybe you could hire her to cook for you or find her somethin' decent to do here in Fort Stockton."

Alta declared, "I'll stay with you, Beau, wherever you go."

"You can't. There's no tellin' what they may do to me."

"Whatever it is, I'll be there. I'll stay as close as the law will allow."

"You'd be lettin' yourself in for a lot of hell."

"I've already been through more hell than you can know. I'm stayin' with you. There's just one thing, Beau. I want you to marry me."

"You'd marry me, knowin' what's ahead?"

"I would, and I will."

Beau turned to McIntosh. "What can you say to a woman like that?"

McIntosh gave them a look of pride, and of sadness. "You say *yes*, and thank God you have her."

Joey and Beau and Alta attended two religious ceremonies that day, both conducted by the same minister. The first was a graveside funeral service for Miller Dawson. It drew few mourners but a large crowd of the curious to see a famous outlaw put into the ground. Joey's throat was so tight he could not speak, but he shed no tears.

The second was a wedding, performed in an almost empty church. The minister asked Beau and Alta their religious preference. Beau said, "I ain't got one, so pick any that the Lord'll approve of. About the only times I ever been in church was for somebody's funeral."

The minister smiled. "Fortunately none of them was your own. You might have been ill-prepared to pass through the Holy Gates."

"Anything you can do to get me ready would be appreciated, preacher. We never know what lies ahead."

"Marrying this young lady is a long step in the right direction. The Lord looks kindly upon the marriage sacrament. Now, who will give the bride away?"

McIntosh said, "The lady's father is no longer living, so that would be for me to do."

"And the best man?"

Beau turned his eyes to Joey. "My cousin here. He's a little short in years, but he's grown up considerable since we've been together."

We both have, Joey thought.

The only outside witnesses were the minister's pregnant young wife and a couple of neighbors who had gotten dressed up for the funeral and thought they might as well make a day of it.

The minister said, "What God has joined together, let no man put asunder."

No man except maybe Sheriff Gardner, Joey thought glumly.

Beau kissed the bride, then McIntosh did. Joey held back. The bride kissed *him*.

In gratitude for helping him with his sheep, McIntosh bought provisions for their trip eastward and provided a pack mule to carry the load. When he had said his good-byes to Beau and Alta he rested his big hands on Joey's thin shoulders.

"You'll write me a letter and let me know what's happened, won't you?"

"I sure will."

"I'll contact a good lawyer I know in Austin. I'll ask him to do whatever he can."

"The preacher said he'll pray for us."

"Sometimes a lawyer can do you more good than a minister. A minister talks to the Lord, but a lawyer can talk to the judge."

Joey said, "I wish you'd had a chance to know my pa. You-all would've liked one another."

"If the father was like the son, I am sure we would."

Beau and Alta struck out upon the trail toward Horsehead Crossing. Joey followed, leading the pack mule. He looked back once at Alister McIntosh and the collie, then turned his gaze eastward. He was going home.

Leaves were turning yellow and red and gold as they rode back through the hill country and picked up a familiar trail into Fredericksburg. Stopping there for flour and coffee, they heard about rangers finding the entrance to a hidden canyon and discovering a nearly deserted outlaw camp. The lawmen had set fire to the place and brought in six men who fitted descriptions in their "wanted" books. One was an escapee from a stone quarry near Austin.

The road led the three past the quarry, where Joey could imagine Hull back at work chiseling limestone, and into Austin, where it appeared that little progress had been made on construction of the new capitol.

"Government job," Beau said.

Joey dared not speak of it, but it pleased him that Beau passed through both Fredericksburg and Austin without mentioning need for a drink. Joey would have understood had he gotten himself staggering drunk, for the nearer they came to Bastrop the deeper was his own sense of foreboding.

They camped just outside of town the final evening, postponing the confrontation with Sheriff Gardner. Beau and Alta clung together after supper as they stared unhappily into the campfire. They went to bed early. Joey dragged his own blankets far to the other side of camp to give them privacy. They would be borrowing tonight against a long, dark, and lonely future.

He did not sleep much, and from the tired looks on Beau's and Alta's faces the next morning, he sensed they had not either. They talked little, soberly packing the mule and saddling their horses for the short ride into town. Joey's heart pounded hard as they rode up to the jail. He blinked away a burning in his eyes while Beau and Alta embraced one another before walking the final short distance.

Beau knocked. Gardner's wife came to the door and invited them inside. The sheriff sat at the kitchen table, sipping from a cup. Surprise made him arise too quickly, sloshing hot coffee on his hand.

Beau said, "I've come to give myself up."

Gardner blinked, confused and none too pleased. He wiped his hand against his shirt. "Thought you'd left the country for good." He gave Alta a long, curious study.

Beau said, "You remember my cousin Joey."

"I do. I'm surprised you ain't quit the boy someplace long before now. Or him you. Well, don't just stand there with the door open. It's drafty in here."

Gardner's wife closed the door. Beau moved farther into the room and motioned toward Alta. "This here is my wife."

"Wife? I never thought that would happen. You must've caught the poor woman on her blind side." Gardner set the cup down and came around the table toward the visitors. Joey could not take his eyes from the set of handcuffs swinging loose from the sheriff's belt. Gardner said, "The

air's startin' to get a little fall nip. You-all want some coffee to warm you up before we get down to cases?"

Beau said, "No sir, it'd only rile my stomach worse than
it already is. I just want to get this over with. I'm givin'
myself up."

"On which charge? There's so many to pick from . . ."

"For the killin' of Joey's stepdaddy, Blair Meacham."

The sheriff's mouth dropped open, but no sound came
from it. He looked at his wife as if she might know what
Beau was talking about. He demanded, "When did this
killin' take place?"

"When you sent him out to Casper Tatum's farm to fetch
Joey. He did his best to drown the boy, and he tried to pis-
tolwhip me. I stove his head in with a chunk of wood.
Last we seen of him, he was floatin' off down the river."

"And that's when you decided to quit the country?"

"Didn't seem like we had much choice. I didn't figure
you'd believe anything we told you."

"You were right. I wouldn't have, and I still don't."

"But it wasn't murder. It was self-defense."

"It wasn't murder because there wasn't nobody killed.
Meacham's head must've been harder than you thought.
He managed to crawl out of the river after you left him to
drown."

This time it was Joey's and Beau's mouths that fell open.
Joey's skin tingled with realization. "Then we've been runnin' all this time from somethin' that never happened."

Beau was stunned. "He looked awful dead."

"You rearranged his face some . . . broke his nose and
cracked his jaw. He came in here lookin' like a horse had
fallen on him. Said the boy fell in the river, and he was
tryin' to save him. Claimed you were drunk, and you were

mad because he wouldn't pay you anything for takin' Joey. Said you tried your damnedest to kill him."

Joey protested, "It wasn't that way at all. Mr. Meacham pulled me off of my horse and tried to drown me so him and Dulcie could have the farm. When Beau drug me out of the river, Mr. Meacham tried to kill him too."

Joey could not tell if he was making any impression.

Gardner frowned at Beau. "I've got a warrant for you on a charge of attempted murder."

Beau said, "And I want to file charges on Meacham for the same thing."

The sheriff grunted. "Looks to me like the two of you have canceled one another out. I don't expect Meacham will ever come back here again, and I'd be obliged if you'd do me the same favor. The county's bill for feedin' prisoners has been a lot cheaper since you've been gone."

Beau was incredulous. "You ain't puttin' me in jail?"

"And have you eat off of the county 'til God knows when? Hell no!"

Beau and Alta threw their arms around one another. Alta sobbed a little.

Gardner frowned. "You ain't figurin' on stayin' around Bastrop, are you?"

Beau held onto Alta. "I was so sure you'd throw me in jail that I hadn't made any plans."

"Your shack ain't there anymore. Couple of tramps took it over after you left. They got drunk and burned it down, so you've got no place to live." The sheriff's eyes lighted with hope. "I reckon you'll be movin' on?"

Joey felt that a hundred pounds of dead weight had been lifted from his shoulders. He wanted to jump and shout, but he kept a discreet rein on himself. "I wish you'd go home with me, Beau. I'll need you to help me with the

farm." He chose not to say so, but he also needed somebody grown to help him stand his ground against Dulcie.
Beau should be able to, and if he couldn't, Joey would bet
that Alta could.

Guardian or not, Dulcie had to leave . . . and take
Meacham with her.

Beau seemed ready to collapse. He looked at Gardner,
still not quite believing. "I'm free to go anywhere I want
to?"

"Yes. And I wish to hell you would, someplace besides
here."

Beau embraced Alta again. "Come on, Mrs. Shipman.
Joey is fixin' to make farmers out of me and you."

{ SEVENTEEN }

Joey felt a rising excitement when he reached territory he had known as far back as he could remember. Athens seemed no different from the last time he had been there. Riding by the schoolhouse, he could hear the teacher's voice and hoped she did not look out the window. She would likely come running and demand to know why he had not been there at resumption of classes in the fall. He intended to start again soon. Reading Kipling and Scott and Dickens from Mr. McIntosh's box of books had reawakened his interest in learning. But first he must get everything straightened out at home. There was a reckoning to be made with Dulcie and Mr. Meacham.

Joey said, "I'd like to talk to Sheriff Lawton before we go to the farm. He was always a good friend of Pa's. He'll know what we ought to do."

Beau was dubious. "A friendly sheriff? That's somebody I'd like to meet."

Lawton leaped from the chair in his courthouse office as Joey walked in the door. "Joey Shipman?" The sheriff's face glowed like a new lantern. Eagerly, he grabbed Joey's hand. "My God, boy, I was afraid you might be layin' dead someplace." He backed off at arm's length to give Joey's face an intense scrutiny. "You've changed. I believe you've grown a little, and you're startin' to look like a man."

Beau said, "He's seen the elephant and bucked the tiger."

Joey introduced Alta and Beau. The sheriff offered Alta a chair, then turned back to Joey. "Dulcie came and told me you'd run away. I helped her and Blair Meacham write letters to officers all over this part of the state."

"They worked," Joey told him. "The sheriff over at Bastrop made sure I stayed around 'til Mr. Meacham could come after me."

Beau said, "He came, all right. Tried to kill Joey and me both."

The sheriff frowned. "That's not exactly the way Meacham told it when he came back. I'd like to hear your version."

Joey and Beau took turns telling what had happened. Beau said, "I'm surprised he had the nerve to come back here. He ought to've known the truth would come out someday if Joey ever showed up again."

Lawton shook his head. "It would be his word against that of a boy who had already told several wild stories about his stepmother tryin' to kill him. And, bad as I hate to say this, Mr. Shipman, I gather that your reputation around Bastrop didn't shine very bright either."

Beau admitted, "No, I suppose not."

Joey feared that the prospects were dim. "So you don't believe us."

"At this point I'm not sure what to believe. I'm leanin' toward you, but Meacham sounded convincin'. Could it be that all of you misunderstood each other's intentions?"

Joey said firmly, "There wasn't any misunderstandin'. Mr. Meacham meant to drown me. Told me straight out that there wasn't no use in me fightin' him."

The sheriff walked to the window and stared out onto the street, thinking. "He would say you were in such a panic that you didn't hear him right. He told me he was tryin' to rescue you, and your cousin attacked him."

"I know what I heard, and I know what he tried to do. If it hadn't been for Beau, I'd be dead."

"I want to believe you, but I'm afraid a court might not accept your word." He reached for his hat, hanging on a peg near the door. "I'll get my horse from the wagon yard and ride out to the farm with you. I want to see if Meacham changes his story any when you're standin' there lookin' him in the face."

"If he doesn't, what can I do? I don't want Dulcie to be my guardian anymore. I don't see where I need one anyway. I can take care of myself."

"The judge won't see it that way. You're under age."

The afternoon sun was a long way down toward the horizon by the time they came in sight of the farm. Joey rode out a bit ahead of the sheriff, Beau, and Alta. He wanted to put Taw into a run, but he feared such a show of impatience would make him look like a kid.

There was no dog to bark at the new arrivals, but a peacock set up a shrill cry. So far as Joey could see, everything looked the same . . . the white frame house, the barn and windmill, the old shack where Reuben had slept. The sight of them filled him with joy, quickly dampened by an invasive sense of melancholy. They *appeared* the same, but they would never *be* the same, for Pa was no longer there, nor was Reuben.

The cotton field was white as if a winter storm had passed, leaving a spotting of snow. Joey could see that it had been picked over once already. The white bolls would yield a good second picking after frost dropped the leaves.

Only stubble remained in the field where the corn had been harvested. The milk cow grazed there, salvaging the stalks. The calf was not with her, nor did Joey see it in the milking pen. He guessed Dulcie had sold it. But the mean Jersey bull was wrapping a long tongue around dried corn leaves and pulling them into his mouth.

Me and you, we're going to have us a little head-butting, Joey thought. *You're going to learn who's in charge here.*

But the bull could wait. The first order of business would be to settle things with Dulcie and Mr. Meacham.

The peacock's cry brought Dulcie out onto the front porch. One hand gripping a post for support, the other at her throat, she fastened a dismayed gaze on Joey. He saw no welcome in her gray eyes. He saw fear.

Well, he thought, she had something to be fearful about. If he had his way, she would soon be hunting a new home. It might be that Sheriff Lawton would provide one in jail for her and Mr. Meacham. Being man and wife now, they might even share a cell.

The sheriff said, "I've brought the prodigal home."

She did not answer.

Lawton stepped down from his horse and led it to the edge of the porch. He said again, "I've brought Joey home."

She bit her thin, pinched lower lip. "So I see." To Joey she said accusingly, "I didn't know but what you were dead."

You're not that lucky, Joey thought.

The sheriff waited in vain for her to say more or to move. He said, "Aren't you even goin' to ask the boy into the house?"

Tightly she replied, "He'll do pretty much as he pleases. He always did." She turned abruptly and retreated back inside, closing the door.

Joey had half expected her to hug him as a show for the others, though he would have shrunk from her if she had tried. He thought most women under the circumstances would at least have made the pretense. He had to give her credit for being honest after her fashion.

Confounded, Lawton said, "Odd woman." He nodded toward the barn. "Joey, you'd better put our horses and the pack mule in the corral. Then we'll go in the house. It's chilly out here."

Joey thought it would be chilly in the house too, though not in the same way.

When he and Beau returned from taking care of the horses, the sheriff knocked on the door, then pushed it open. "Dulcie, we're comin' in." He paused, waiting for a reply but not receiving it. He motioned for the others to follow him. Joey held back until last, not wanting to be in the house alone with Dulcie even for a moment.

Dulcie stood near the rear door, looking out a window toward the backyard and the chicken pen.

Lawton said, "Dulcie, you and Blair put me to a lot of trouble huntin' this boy. Now you act like you don't want to see him."

Dulcie turned, her face severe. "I didn't tell him to run away, and I didn't tell him to try to kill Mr. Meacham."

Joey figured she knew it anyway, but he said, "It was Mr. Meacham that tried to kill *me*."

Lawton said, "I want to talk to Blair. Where's he at?"

She was slow and reluctant in answering. "He's gone to town."

"I didn't see him. How long's he been gone?"

"A while. I don't know when he'll be back."

He could not have been gone long, Joey thought, for he

smelled tobacco smoke. He doubted Dulcie had taken up the habit.

The sheriff tried to overlook her defensive manner. He introduced Beau and Alta. "Joey and his cousin tell things considerably different than Blair did. I'd like to hear his story again."

"He wouldn't change it none."

"I'd like to hear it anyway."

She turned hostile eyes on Joey. "You know what kind of lies Joey's told before. Why would you believe him now over the word of a grown man?"

"I'm not sayin' what I believe or disbelieve, not yet. But somebody's wrong, and I want to know the truth. So I'll wait."

"Then wait. It's liable to be a long evenin'. Sometimes Blair forgets to come home at all." Chin high, she strode into her bedroom and closed the door behind her.

Lawton gave Alta and Beau an apologetic look. "I've never seen her like this before."

Joey said, "I have. She was like this most of the time when there wasn't any company around."

The sheriff opened the back door and peered outside. Joey and Beau took chairs and sat at the kitchen table. Alta went to the stove but found the coffeepot sitting on the edge, empty and cold. "Show me where the coffee beans are, Joey."

The sheriff eyed the closed bedroom door. "It could be a long evenin', like Dulcie said. She may not know about it, but it didn't take long for her honeymoon to be over with. Blair Meacham's seein' a widow lady over in town."

Joey supposed he should feel sorry for Dulcie, but it was possible she had plotted with Mr. Meacham to get Pa and

Reuben and himself out of the way so she could have the farm. Now Mr. Meacham was playing Romeo with another Juliet. He could see a certain rude justice in that.

A new idea almost took his breath. "The only way Dulcie could own the farm would be if I was to die, ain't that right?"

The sheriff agreed. "That's the way the will was set up."

"Say somethin' did happen to me, and Dulcie got the farm. What if somethin' happened to her then? Who would get the place?"

"Meacham's her husband." The sheriff's eyes widened as he grasped what Joey was thinking.

Beau caught on too. "That widow in town . . . is she better lookin' than Dulcie?"

"Some would say so. And she inherited a fair amount of money from her husband. That helps her looks a right smart."

Beau asked, "How did her husband die?"

"An accident. A horse drug him to death." He swallowed. The look that passed between him and Beau indicated they were both thinking the same thing.

Joey was already ahead of them. He said, "I wonder if Dulcie has thought of it."

They waited in silence. Fidgety, tired of sitting around, Joey poked wood into the stove to keep the kitchen warm. Seeing that the woodbox was nearly empty, he went outside and brought in enough to fill it.

Not until daylight faded into dusk did Dulcie emerge from the bedroom, her mood subdued. "If he was comin', he'd be here by now. I'll fix you-all some supper."

The sheriff arose from the table. "I hadn't figured on spendin' the night. I'll be gettin' back home. Maybe I'll meet Blair on the road or find him in town." He beckoned for Beau to walk out onto the porch with him.

Joey became uneasy. He had counted on the sheriff's remaining until the situation was resolved. It would be awkward, he and Beau and Alta staying here with Dulcie. And what if the sheriff missed Mr. Meacham and the man showed up without the law on hand to preserve the peace? There was apt to be one hell of a fight.

After supper Dulcie sat in the chair that had once been Mama's. The creaking of the floor beneath the rocker emphasized the cold and painful silence. It was as if she had shut everyone else out, pretending to herself that she was alone.

Joey wished she were. He thought back to the pleasant nights in Alister McIntosh's sheep camp and wondered if he might have been better off staying in the Fort Stockton country. But he had made up his mind to see this thing through to a conclusion, whatever that might be.

He did not want to sleep in the house, not with Dulcie there. He chose to bunk in Reuben's shack. He told Beau and Alta they could use his old room for the night. When Dulcie left—and one way or another she was going to—they could have the room where she and Pa had slept.

Beau was concerned about Joey's leaving the house. "I'd feel better if you stayed under the same roof with us."

"That'd mean bein' under the same roof as Dulcie. I can't do that any more."

Alta seemed inclined to argue the matter further, but Beau said, "He's old enough to make up his own mind. Let him do what he wants to."

The moon was rising as Joey walked to the corral to untie his blankets from the saddle he had removed from

Taw's back and placed on a rack beneath a shed. He could see the outlines of the milk cow and the Jersey bull at the edge of the corn field. It was in his mind that he would sell the bull at his first opportunity, but not before a settlement of their differences.

The bull saw or sensed him and slung its head. It began pawing dirt and made a threatening bellow. Joey picked up a rock and sailed it, missing by a yard.

He felt a chill as he approached the shack, carrying his blanket roll. The night air carried a hint of coming frost, but his reaction was not due entirely to the cold. He felt as if Reuben might be awaiting him inside.

He pushed the door open and lighted a match so he could find the lamp. He lifted off the glass chimney and touched the flame to the wick. It caught just as the match curled black and its flame burned his fingers. He turned the wick back a little so the lamp would not smoke, then replaced the chimney. It was dusty and streaked, in need of cleaning, but it would do for now.

He shivered again and considered starting a fire in the little stove. He picked up the iron poker and stirred the old cold ashes but decided against wasting wood that he would have to replace later. He would soon be warm in the blankets anyway. He closed the stove and propped the poker against it.

He lay awake a while, stirring through old memories as he had stirred the ashes. He remembered happy times with Mama and Pa, with Reuben. He wished he had gone up to the cemetery to visit their graves, but night had overtaken him before he got to it. Tomorrow he would, he promised himself.

Sleepiness began to burn his eyes. He blew out the lamp and crawled under the blankets. They warmed quickly, and the monotonous creaking of the windmill carried him away like a lullaby.

He awakened suddenly in great fear, unable to breathe. He struggled for breath, but something pressed down against his face, closing off his nose and mouth. His hands came up fighting against the obstruction, and he realized it was a pillow. He kicked and squirmed and choked.

"Best hold still, damn you. Ain't nobody goin' to help you this time."

He knew that gruff voice. It was Meacham's.

Joey's lungs blazed like a runaway fire, begging for breath. His hands fought against the pillow that pushed upon his face. He managed to twist his neck and caught a little air before the pillow pressed down again.

Meacham's voice was angry. "How many times have I got to kill you before you stay dead?"

Joey squirmed and kicked as calves did when he tried to hold them down. He managed a kick that made Meacham curse and loosen his grip on the pillow. In an instant Joey was out from under him and on his feet.

The poker! He remembered he had propped it against the stove. He could not see it in the darkness, but he knew where it must be. He groped in desperation, his fingers closing around the cold iron handle. He swung it at the dark shape that lunged at him. From the impact he knew he had struck Meacham on the side of the head. Meacham staggered, then came at Joey again before Joey was able to raise the poker high. He swung it from just above the floor and struck the man across the shin.

Meacham screeched and hopped on one leg. Before he could recover, Joey threw himself toward the door and burst out into the nippy night air. He could hear Meacham just behind him, almost within arm's length. He stopped and swung the poker a third time. It connected with Meacham's knee. The man stumbled, then sprawled on the ground.

Joey did not wait to strike him again. He dropped the poker and ran toward the house, shouting. "Beau! It's Mr. Meacham!"

He was aware of two other figures moving in the night. Sheriff Lawton's voice commanded, "Meacham! Stop or I'll shoot!"

Meacham was limping, but he did not stop. He headed for the cotton patch. Lawton's pistol blazed. Meacham shouted, stumbled, and fell. He pushed to his feet again, turning to fire a pistol shot in the sheriff's general direction. He crawled through the wire fence and was lost in the darkness.

Beau threw his arms around Joey. "God, boy, you scared me all the way down to my toenails."

"He tried to kill me."

Sheriff Lawton cautiously advanced most of the way to the fence, then retreated. Meacham had shown himself to be armed.

"It's too dangerous to go in there after him in the dark," Lawton told Beau. "He ain't apt to travel far afoot. We'll find him at daylight." He put a hand on Joey's shoulder. "Sorry, boy. We were hid in the barn, watchin' that shack, but Meacham slipped by us someway."

"I thought you went back to town."

"That's what I wanted Meacham to think. I knew Dulcie lied about him bein' gone. He must've seen us comin' and lit out the back door, but he'd been smokin' tobacco. I smelled it when we first went into the house."

"He tried to smother me with a pillow."

The sheriff nodded, understanding. "A pillow wouldn't

leave any trace to prove that murder was done. I reckon we know now how Old Reuben died."

Joey had been too frightened to think of that for himself.

Alta and Dulcie came out onto the porch as Joey and the two men returned to the house. The sheriff faced Dulcie. "You lied to me about him goin' to town."

Dulcie offered no answer.

Lawton said, "We'll get him come daylight, and he can talk for himself. Things might go easier with you if you talk to me first."

"A woman doesn't go tellin' the law about her husband."

"She does when there's been murder, and when there might be another. Otherwise she's an accessory." He looked sternly into Dulcie's eyes. "She might even become a victim."

Dulcie trembled. "What do you mean?"

"I'll bet you've already thought about it. And I'll bet you know about that widow Blair's been seein' in Athens."

Dulcie was slow to reply. "I know about her."

"Blair tried to kill this boy with a pillow so there wouldn't be any proof of murder. What if he'd got it done, and you inherited this farm? Knowin' what you know, how long do you think he'd let *you* live?"

Dulcie hung her head. Joey thought it would not take much to make her break down and cry.

The sheriff pressed, "You ought to've known Joey would show up sooner or later and the truth would all come out."

Dulcie sobbed a moment, then regained control. "I was afraid of Blair, sore afraid. He wanted this land. I didn't know 'til afterward, but he caused John's accident, and he killed Reuben. I dreaded the day Joey might come home because Blair would try to kill him and make it look like an accident. Once I had title to the farm I was as good as dead too. All I meant to him was a way to get hold of this place."

"If you'll testify to that, I'll recommend that the judge give you probation. But there's one condition. I'll want you to leave Henderson County and never come back."

"I've got no place to go."

"You've got kinfolks, haven't you?"

"None I get along with."

"It's your problem. You'll just have to work it out the best way you can."

She will survive, Joey thought. *She still has her looks, sort of. She can find herself another lonely widower, the same way she found Pa. At least then she'll be somebody else's problem; she won't be mine.*

Sheriff Lawton stayed at the barn the rest of the night in case Meacham circled back and made a try for one of the horses. Beau wrapped himself in a blanket and took up a post on the front porch. Dulcie retreated into her bedroom and closed the door. Alta sat in the rocking chair, holding Beau's pistol in her lap. It was the one that had been Tolley's. She said, "You try to get some sleep, Joey. He ain't fixin' to hurt you anymore."

Joey said, "The only way I could sleep would be if you hit me across the head with that six-shooter."

At daylight Beau and the sheriff came in for breakfast. Dulcie never ventured out of her room. The sheriff became concerned that she might have done something to herself, so Alta went in to check on her. She came out reassured. "Dulcie's all right. Scared as she was that her husband might kill her, she's not about to do it to herself."

Alta fixed breakfast, then the two men started outside to look for Meacham. The sheriff admonished, "Joey, you stay in this house 'til he's caught. He's got nothin' to gain now by killin' you, but he might take it in his head to do it just out of spite."

"I'd like to go and help you find him."

Beau commanded, "You do what the sheriff tells you, boy. Stay in the house."

Joey's temper flared. There was Beau, ordering him around again like he was a kid. He had thought they had gotten that sort of thing all straightened out.

Dulcie did not emerge from her room until the men had gone. She looked haggard, as if she had not slept. Alta offered to fix breakfast for her, but Dulcie demurred. "All I want is some coffee. I'm cold, awful cold."

She filled her cup and walked to the door, staring out through the oval glass. "Looks like they'd've found him by now."

Joey said, "They ain't been gone that long."

"What if they don't catch him at all? There won't none of us be safe around here."

Alta sat down again, the pistol in her lap. "They'll catch him. That sheriff looks like a determined man. And so is Beau when he sets his mind to somethin'."

Joey had put aside the fleeting resentment against his cousin. "Like not drinkin' the way he used to. I reckon he found somethin' he wants more than whiskey."

Alta smiled.

Dulcie turned to Joey. "I know you've got cause enough to doubt me, but I never meant you any harm. When I married your father I intended to be a good wife to him and a real mother to you. But nothin' seemed to work out like we wanted it to. Wasn't your fault, it was mine and your father's. I suppose we were both lookin' for somethin' the other didn't have."

"After he was gone, it didn't take you long to marry Mr. Meacham."

"Another mistake. When it comes to marryin', I ain't done much good for myself."

She returned to the door and gasped. "My God! It's him!"

Joey ran to the window. He saw Meacham in the front yard, moving toward the porch. He carried a pistol.

Dulcie's face drained white. "He's come to kill us all." She retreated into the bedroom.

Alta came quickly to Joey's side, drawing back the hammer on the pistol Beau had left her. She raised the weapon, extending it in front of her, gripping it in both hands. Joey heard heavy footsteps on the porch.

Dulcie came out of the bedroom carrying a rifle that had been Pa's. "Step aside, Alta. I'm not lettin' him get me." She moved near the door and shouted, "Blair, do you hear me?"

The answer from the porch was plain. "I hear you. Send that boy outside."

"What for? You've lost any chance of takin' this farm. They're out yonder now, lookin' for you."

"That boy's goin' to get me away from here. Long as I've got him, they ain't goin' to push me. Open that door, Dulcie, and send him out or I'm comin' in."

Joey saw a dark form through the oval glass. The door burst open and Meacham stood at the threshold, pistol in his hand.

Dulcie pulled the trigger. The explosion of the rifle seemed to shake the walls. Meacham screeched and fired the pistol. Dulcie jerked as if a horse had kicked her.

Alta's six-shooter blasted, the recoil almost kicking the weapon out of her hands. Meacham screamed and staggered, dropping his pistol as he fell from the porch.

Dulcie slumped, the rifle clattering upon the floor. Joey grabbed it up and ran out onto the porch, levering a new cartridge into the chamber. He raised the rifle and aimed at Meacham, lying on the ground and gripping his bleeding leg. He bled too from a wound in his shoulder.

Meacham screamed, "No, boy, no! Don't shoot. For God's sake, don't kill me!"

Joey's blood was cold. His finger tightened on the trigger. Here was the man responsible for Pa's death, and Reuben's. Joey leveled the sights on the bridge of Meacham's broken nose.

Alta's voice was calm but firm behind him. "Ain't we seen enough of killin', Joey? Wasn't Tolley and Farlow and Miller Dawson enough? And Dulcie?"

Joey eased his grip on the rifle. "Dulcie's dead?"

"Yes."

Meacham pleaded, "Boy, don't do it. For God's sake, I'm a wounded man."

Joey lowered the rifle only a little. "Don't you move. Don't you move an inch."

Meacham's voice was shrill with pain and fear. "I think Dulcie shot my leg off. I'm bleedin' to death."

"Then lay there and bleed, but don't you move."

Blinking away a mist that clouded his eyes, Joey saw Beau and the sheriff spurring in from the pasture. He stepped down from the porch and picked up Meacham's fallen pistol. Meacham saw the two riders coming. He begged, "Please, they'll be wantin' to shoot me. Don't let them. For the love of God, I'm not ready to die."

"Neither were Pa and Reuben and Dulcie."

Joey knew Beau and the sheriff weren't going to kill Meacham. They would let him live a while. They would let him soak in cold sweat, dreading the rope that would strangle him. They would probably have to drag him kicking and screaming up those thirteen steps, but that was the way it should be.

Joey stood with Alta and Beau outside the small family cemetery, looking at the headstones. Dulcie never had put up one for Pa. Joey said, "First thing I'll do when we finish the cotton will be to get a marker carved for him." Pa wouldn't mind waiting that long. As a farmer he would have understood the necessity of finishing the harvest.

Pa was buried beside Mama, but there was a space on the other side of him, still within the stone fence. "I don't guess Mama would mind all that much. After all, Dulcie was Pa's wife too, for a little while."

Beau asked, "Are you sure you want her here? The sheriff said the county would provide a buryin' place in town."

Joey had given it a good deal of thought. "Me and her didn't get along, but I won't fight her all the way to the cemetery. We'll bury her by Pa."

Alta clasped Joey's arm. "That's a grownup way of lookin' at it. A lot of grown folks wouldn't be so forgivin'."

Beau said, "I don't know what your pa would say about me livin' in his house. Me and him didn't see eye to eye about much."

"You haven't had a drink in quite a spell now."

"Wait 'til we get the last of the cotton in."

Alta gave Beau a look that said he had better be joshing. Beau gave her a look that assured her he was. Alta was a small woman, but she was strong enough to drag Beau up against the snubbing post.

They started back down the slope toward the house. In the field the Jersey bull was feeding on stubble left from the corn crop. He and the milk cow had just about finished it.

Beau said, "We ought to turn them out into the pasture. There ain't much left for them in the corn patch."

"Good idea," Joey said.

They walked together to the gate. The bull saw Joey coming and began to paw dirt, bawling a challenge. Joey stopped. "You-all stay out here. I want to do this myself."

Beau warned, "That bull is spoilin' for a fight."

"It's time he got one." Joey looked for the iron poker he had dropped last night. He found it, entered the field, and walked around to the wire gate that opened into the pasture. He unfastened it and laid it back.

The bull pawed again, then came running, head down, its nose so near the ground that its breath raised puffs of dust. Joey stood his ground.

Reuben had always said a bull on the fight would close its eyes just before it made contact. Joey had never built the nerve to test that theory, but now he held still and waited. Just a few feet away the bull shut its eyes and came rushing with a belligerent snort.

Joey stepped to one side and swung the poker with all his strength, bringing it down across the bridge of the bull's nose.

The bull moved past him, shaking its head. An angry bellow trailed into painful protest. The Jersey pawed dirt and charged again. Once more Joey stepped aside and brought the poker down with all the force in his arms and back.

The bull kept running until it was a dozen yards away, then turned and faced around, slinging its head, trying to shake free of the hurting. Gone was the bluster, the challenge.

Joey made a run at it, waving the poker and shouting. "*Hyahh!* Git, you son of a bitch!"

The bull turned and ran, blindly bumping the gate post as it fled into the pasture.

Beau and Alta waited outside the field gate. Beau grinned. "Boy, don't you know you oughtn't to be usin' that kind of language?"

Joey closed the gate behind him and watched in satisfaction as the Jersey bull trotted farther away, slinging its head in confusion and fear and pain.

"And don't you know it's time you quit callin' me *boy?*"